Praise fo

"Reading Shannon Richard
        —Jill Shalvis, *New York Times* bestselling author, on

"Heartwarming and endearing. Richard spins a well-told story filled with love and healing."
                        —Lori Wilde, *New York Times* bestselling author,
                                                on *Dog Days Forever*

"Charming second-chance romance. . . . Richard does a fine job showing how past regrets can color a life and pushes the message that it's never too late. Caro and Max make a thoroughly believable couple and the brisk plot keeps pages turning. Small-town romance lovers should snap this up."
                        —*Publishers Weekly* on *Dog Days Forever*

"Richard . . . delivers small-town, Southern atmosphere in this story with some sexy scenes and vulnerable characters, who readers can easily champion as they grapple with larger issues such as the death of a parent."
                        —*Library Journal* on *Dog Days Forever*

"*Dog Days Forever* is a heartfelt, emotional roller coaster. Richard masterfully steers Max and Caro through ups and downs, leaving readers with tear-filled eyes and hope that endures."
                        —Jessica Lemmon, bestselling author,
                                                on *Dog Days Forever*

Puppy Love
at
MISTLETOE
JUNCTION

Also by Shannon Richard

Dog Days Forever

Puppy Love
at
MISTLETOE
JUNCTION

A Novel

SHANNON RICHARD

AVON

An Imprint of HarperCollinsPublishers

PUPPY LOVE AT MISTLETOE JUNCTION. Copyright © 2024 by Shannon Richard. All rights reserved. Printed in the United States of America. No part of this book may be used or reproduced in any manner whatsoever without written permission except in the case of brief quotations embodied in critical articles and reviews. For information, address HarperCollins Publishers, 195 Broadway, New York, NY 10007.

HarperCollins books may be purchased for educational, business, or sales promotional use. For information, please email the Special Markets Department at SPsales@harpercollins.com.

FIRST EDITION

Interior text design by Diahann Sturge-Campbell

Puppy great pyrenees clipart © Dgillustration12u/Stock.Adobe.com

Library of Congress Cataloging-in-Publication Data has been applied for.

ISBN 978-0-06-323565-6

24 25 26 27 28 LBC 5 4 3 2 1

For Teddy.
Teddsters, Tedward, Theodore, Teddy B., Teddy Bear,
Bear, Buggy Bear, Bug,
Squish, Squeaks,
Tiny Tush, Fuzzy Pants, Fuzzy Face, Grumpy Face,
My Little Love.

In a world full of best good boys, you are mine.

CHAPTER ONE
The Bet

A loud cheer filled the air of Quigley's Irish Pub as the dart hit the board, the tip embedded in the small patch of red that was the bull's-eye. Theo Taylor dropped his hand, only letting a small smile twitch at the corners of his mouth as he turned around to face his friends.

Two of the three were grinning at him . . . the third, not so much.

"Unbelievable," Gavin Quigley said as he folded his arms across his chest and glared at the dart, clearly trying to make sure it was within bounds. "That's three rounds in a row. I don't know why anyone bothers to play you."

"Hey, *you* were the one who suggested the game." Theo finished his beer before he crossed over to grab his darts. There were three boards spaced out on the wall, but only two were in use.

The group of guys on the far right were just throwing for points, but they'd been paying attention to Theo and his friends' competition. They'd also been part of the cheering when Theo had gotten that last bull's-eye.

"Yeah." Gavin shook his head. "I'm starting to wonder what possessed me to suggest it in the first place."

"That would be the whiskey. You felt confident after that first shot." Max Abbott pointed to the half-filled bottle on the table.

"Come on, GQ." Oscar Belmont clapped Gavin on the shoulder. "You know we just play for second when Theo is involved."

Gavin's nickname had been GQ ever since he was in high school, and he'd grown into his tall, lanky frame and broad shoulders. He was the perfect blend of his parents. His mother, Nari, was Korean, and she'd passed on her high cheekbones, black hair, and chocolate-brown eyes. He'd inherited his lean muscular build, square jaw, and dimples from Desmond's Irish side of the family.

The man probably could've moved to New York and been a *GQ* model. Instead, he'd stayed in Cruickshank, North Carolina, where he ran Quigley's Irish Pub with his family.

"Are we playing again?" Max asked as he tallied the totals on the bar napkin they'd been using to keep score.

"I think we need more beer first." Oscar poured the last of it into his glass and handed the empty pitcher to Gavin.

"On it." Gavin pushed his stool back and headed to the bar. He might not be working that night, but he'd been the one to refill their drinks. It gave a little relief to his family who were manning the bar.

It was a busy night too, groups of people gathered around the wooden tables or squished into booths. The bar had been built in 1904 by Charles Angus Quigley—right in the center of downtown—and was just as much of a Cruickshank staple then as it was now.

The floors were a rich mahogany, the walls mostly exposed brick with paintings of the Irish countryside scattered around. There were stuffed animal heads, stained glass pictures, and a collection of antique clocks—half of which had the wrong time. There was also a shrine of paintings and pictures depicting the Quigley family going as far back as the early 1800s. And at the very center of the room hung an impressive chandelier of Irish-whiskey bottles. The ceiling was the same dark mahogany as the floors, and exposed iron pipes stretched down with Edison light bulbs hanging from the ends.

The place was everything an old Irish pub should be, or at least it was to Theo.

It wasn't very long before Gavin was making his way back to the table with a pitcher of beer in hand, but he wasn't alone. Caroline Buchanan was next to him with a massive plate of loaded cheese fries. She was also pulling a shift behind the bar that night.

"I figured you guys were working up an appetite," she said as she set the food on the table.

Her hands were barely free before Max was grabbing her waist and pulling her toward him. "I am rather hungry." He grinned before leaning down and pressing his mouth to hers. She swayed a little in his arms, her dark brown hair brushing back and forth across her shoulders. Her left hand came up, cupping his jaw and making her engagement ring flash with the movement.

Theo wasn't one to begrudge anyone their happiness—especially these two—but their public displays of affection were a bit much. He got it, they were making up for lost time. Fourteen years of lost time.

They'd grown up together, Max spending his summers with his grandparents in Cruickshank. Their friendship had turned into something more when they were teenagers, but life had gotten in the way. When Caro's mother had died, a tragic chain of events pushed them apart. That was until Max had come to town last summer and they'd pretty much picked up where they left off.

There was no separating the duo now. That was evident by the fact that Max had given up a high-six-figure salary to move down here and buy the old Kincaid spring factory and turn it into a hotel.

Theo didn't know if there was such a thing as soulmates, people who were fated for each other over anyone else. It wasn't like he hadn't grown up seeing happy couples. After thirty-three years of marriage his parents were somehow still ridiculously in love with each other. But there was something about Caro and Max that made him buy into it a little bit more, even if he did roll his eyes at their antics. And he wasn't the only one.

"The two of you are nauseating." Oscar gestured at them with a fry before he popped it into his mouth.

"You're just jealous." Caro waggled her eyebrows at him.

"Damn straight I am. I haven't been on a date in two months. You know how hard it is to find a man in this town?"

"I do." Caro nodded. "Why do you think I was still single after all these years?"

"I don't think that had anything to do with a lack of options." Gavin shook his head as he looked over to Max. "You were just waiting for him to come back."

"You're right. I was," she said before she stretched up and pressed a kiss to Max's bearded cheek. And she did have to stretch as he was almost a foot taller than her.

"Dating was a lot easier before I moved back here. A small town in the South isn't exactly a gay man's smorgasbord." Oscar had moved away when he'd gone off to college, and as he'd become a veterinarian, he'd been gone for a good ten years before he returned.

Cruickshank had a way of keeping its residents . . . or drawing them back when they left. Max and Oscar were proof of that. Only 3.57 square miles and a population of roughly 4,300, it was a small town with a big reputation. People loved it there. Loved to live there, loved to visit there. That last part was evident by the fact that every season was tourist season.

Nestled in the Blue Ridge Mountains, Cruickshank was the perfect retreat no matter the time of year. Spring brought blooming trees and flowers; summer provided fish-filled rivers and the shimmering waters of Lake Lenox to cool off in; fall had the mountains bursting with the colors of changing leaves; and winter turned the town into its own little North Pole.

It was the second week of November, so the crisp, cold weather was here to stay. Though it wasn't cold in Quigley's that Friday night; in fact it was quite cozy. The woodburning fireplace in the corner was full of flames, the pop and crackle of the wood adding a nice little soundtrack along with the chatter of the patrons.

Home. The entire town encompassed it for Theo.

"Don't worry, Oscar." Caro lightly punched his arm. "Your Prince Charming is just around the corner."

"From your mouth to God's ears." He grinned as he *cheers*'ed his beer in her direction before taking a sip.

"So, who's winning?" Caro indicated the dartboard with her chin.

"Who do you think?" Max pointed to Theo. "The man can't be beaten."

"Yes, well, maybe he just needs stiffer competition."

"That a challenge?" Theo grinned as he held the darts in her direction.

"Oh, no." Caro shook her head. "Not me. But I do believe someone up to the task just walked into the bar." Her smile widened as she nodded toward the door.

Theo didn't need to look to know *exactly* who had just walked into Quigley's, that wicked grin on Caro's face all the evidence he needed. That, and the little prickling sensation he always got on the back of his neck whenever *she* was around.

And yet, he still found himself turning as Lucy Buchanan made her way through the pub.

There wasn't a person on this planet that drove him crazier. They'd almost always had an antagonistic relationship, even when they were children. As they had the same group of friends, they'd been forced to tolerate each other, something that had been a lot easier to do when she'd been living in Los Angeles.

She'd moved out there seven years ago to pursue her dream of music. Since then, he'd only had to see her when she'd visit a couple of times a year. Though that wasn't the case at the moment. Lucy was back . . . for now.

Something had happened in LA, something she hadn't confided in him about—not that he thought she would, they didn't have that kind of relationship—and she was here while she regrouped. He was pretty sure the Cruickshank Hold wasn't permanent when it came to her, and he wouldn't be surprised when she packed her bags again.

But until that day, he was just going to have to deal with her being around. And as she was heading right toward them, tonight was going to be one of those nights.

She was wearing a burnt-orange peacoat, jeans that he instinctively knew were molded to each and every one of her curves, and short boots that showed just a scrap of the skin at her ankles. Her soft chestnut-brown hair was down around her shoulders, a slight curl at the ends. And to top off the pretty picture, her pert nose and round cheeks were a soft pink.

"It's freezing out there." She shivered slightly as she stopped in front of them, pulling a red scarf from her neck.

The chill from outside clung to her, but it wasn't the only thing on the air. The scent of vanilla, cloves, and cinnamon filled Theo's lungs. Seeing as he was a baker, it was a scent he was more than familiar with, especially this time of year. But it had never smelled *that* good.

"Well, warm up," Max said as he filled a shot glass with whiskey and slid it across the table to her.

She didn't even hesitate as she picked it up and downed it in one. "That's better." She sighed as she set the glass on the table.

"Where's Sasha? I thought you guys were hanging out tonight," Caro asked as she moved to help her little sister out of her jacket, revealing a cream-colored sweater. Another wave of vanilla, cloves, and cinnamon filled the air and Theo found himself taking a deeper breath.

"She's over there." Lucy pointed behind her toward the door, but the crowd of people by the bar blocked the view. "Adam Dennison was on his way out when we were coming in and he wanted to talk to her about something." Lucy gave Caro a tiny little look, one that would've been missed by someone who didn't know her well.

Oscar hadn't missed it either and his eyes focused on Lucy, his mouth pulling down into a frown. "Wait. Who's my sister talking to? And what did he want?"

"Adam Dennison," she repeated. "And as I'm over *here*"—she pointed to the floor—"I don't know what he wanted."

"Didn't we meet him the other day?" Theo asked, trying to focus on the conversation and not the sweet and spicy scent that fogged his brain. "He's the new manager over at the bank."

Gavin's focus turned toward the bar, and he stretched up on his tiptoes trying to get a better view. "I don't remember him. Maybe I need to go over there and remind myself."

"Calm down, boys." Lucy patted Oscar's and Gavin's chests before she reached for a french fry. "Sasha can handle herself."

"That's for damn sure," Theo agreed. He'd gone to a kickboxing class with her once, and when they'd been partnered up, he'd found himself flat on his ass more times than anyone else in the class.

He hadn't gone back again.

Lucy inhaled dramatically, putting her hand to her chest. "Theodore Taylor! Did you just agree with me?"

"Don't call me Theodore. And don't worry, it won't happen again."

"I should hope not. It's weird when we're on the same page." She grabbed another fry before pointing to the napkin in front of Max. "Who's winning?"

"Theo," everyone said in unison.

That same wicked grin Caro had been sporting just moments before was now lifting Lucy's pouty mouth. Theo had tasted that mouth before. He tried not to think about that fact very much, but it was a lot harder when her lips were that pretty red . . . like a juicy apple.

"Want to play?" she asked him.

With her? No, no, he did not. And it wasn't because she was the only real competition. He wasn't afraid of her. He liked a challenge. It was just that playing with her always brought more complications. But he couldn't show weakness. Not when it came to her.

"Sure." He shrugged. "If you feel like losing."

"Oh, big talk. Want to put your money where your mouth is?"

"Let's play Around the Clock. Best out of three. If I win, you have to buy me a bottle of that whiskey." He pointed to the one on the table.

"Fine." She pushed up the sleeves of her sweater. "And if I win, I get a hundred dollars' worth of free stuff from Browned Butter."

The whiskey was only worth seventy-five, but as his family owned the bakery she was referring to, he had the advantage, what with markup and all.

"Deal." He stuck his hand out and Lucy didn't even hesitate before she reached out hers.

Despite her being cold when she walked in, her hands were warm. Her palm slid against his, fitting perfectly as they shook on the bet. There was a flash of something in her hazel eyes, the green becoming more pronounced.

When they let go, Theo dropped his hand, unconsciously making a fist as if he were trying to hold on to something.

On to what, he had no idea.

"What did I miss?" A new voice floated into Theo's ears, and he turned just as Sasha Belmont joined the group. Her wildly curly hair bounced around her head as she pulled off her dark purple coat and jumped up onto the barstool next to her brother.

Theo had never met a family that was more clearly related than the Belmonts. They all had freckles dusted across their brown cheeks and noses, big smiles that lit up their entire face, and golden-brown eyes.

"We could ask you the same question." Oscar looked over at her, that big smile of his nowhere in sight.

"What did Adam Dennison want to talk to you about?" Gavin asked as he folded his arms across his broad chest.

"None of your business." Sasha gave them a not-so-sweet look before she grabbed a french fry.

"Well, I don't like the guy," Gavin pushed.

Caro looked over at him with an incredulous smile. "I thought you said you didn't remember who he was."

"I don't." Gavin shook his head. "That's how I *know* I don't like him."

"Well, that's just great for you." Sasha patted him on the shoulder. "We're done talking about Adam. Now, what were you two shaking on when I got here?" She looked back to Lucy and Theo, gesturing at them.

"Lucy challenged me to a game of darts."

"Oh, well, the evening just got even more interesting. I'm going to need a drink while I watch her kick your ass."

"And I'm going to need a drink while I kick his ass." Lucy nodded to Theo.

"We'll just see about that." Theo shook his head.

"I'll get them," Gavin said. "What do you two want?"

"Whatever that is works for me." Lucy nodded to the pitcher of beer.

"Same," Sasha agreed. "But I'm going to start with one of those." She pointed to the bottle of whiskey.

"Yeah, you need to catch up." Max poured her a shot and passed it across the table. "Lucy's already one up on you."

"I've got to get back to work." Caro leaned in and pressed a kiss to Max's lips before taking a step back and looking at her sister. "If we were taking bets, my money's on Lucy."

"Hey!" Theo said in mock outrage. "See if you get any free doughnuts from me next week."

"When I win, she won't need any of your free doughnuts. She can have some of mine."

"Exactly." Caro laughed as she turned around and headed for the bar.

"Ladies first." Theo nodded to the board.

"If you insist." Lucy went over to where the darts were kept, grabbing the set with the hot-pink flags.

Theo couldn't stop his eyes from wandering down, lingering on her perfect ass as she walked. He'd been right about her jeans. The dark denim hugged her in *all* the right places.

Lucy was all curves, curves Theo had once traced with his bare hands, curves that he'd worshipped with his mouth. It was knowledge that no amount of time or distance would ever make him forget . . . even if he wanted to.

He clenched his fists at his sides before letting go, wishing the memory away for the moment. It didn't work. And he knew there was absolutely no hope for him that evening, a fact that was made evident as Lucy headed back over to him. There was a smirk pulling up the corner of her mouth that bugged him in every way imaginable.

"Ready?" She raised her eyebrows.

"Waiting for you." He waved to the board before folding his arms across his chest.

That annoying smirk of hers grew as she turned and took her place behind the marker on the floor. Theo was only a few feet behind her, and a fresh wave of vanilla, cloves, and cinnamon filled the air as she swiped her hair over her shoulders. He'd almost been close enough for the ends to hit him in the face.

Lucy lifted her arm, taking a couple of seconds to line up her shot before the dart flew through the air. It hit hard in the patch of white that was under the one. She followed up that first throw by hitting the outer rim of red of the two and the inner black patch for the three. Everyone in their group—as well as the table of guys next to them—let out an enthusiastic cheer.

Theo didn't mind the cheer but he wasn't a fan of the way two of those guys were taking an extra-long look at Lucy.

Though he really wasn't sure *why* he cared.

"Well, Theo's night just took a turn." Gavin looked delighted as he came back to the table, setting down another pitcher of beer and two glasses.

"You aren't on my side either?" Theo asked his so-called friend.

"Not even a little bit." Gavin shook his head.

"Don't worry, I'm rooting for you." Oscar clapped Theo on the back.

"Well, at least I got one."

"What about you, Max?" Sasha asked.

"You think I'm going against the family?" Max looked at her like she was crazy. "I just got back into their good graces."

"Plus, I'm your second-favorite person," Lucy added.

"That's true, kiddo." Max reached up and ruffled the top of her head.

"Hey!" Lucy stepped back to get out from under his touch, which resulted in that perfect ass of hers colliding with Theo's crotch.

A direct hit.

His hands instinctively landed on her hips, trying to stop her from pushing back farther into him. He didn't mean to do it, but his fingers pressed into her, holding on before she quickly turned around.

This time he did get a face full of her hair and was pretty much punched in the nose with the scent of vanilla, cloves, and cinnamon.

"Sorry," Lucy said as she pulled away from him.

Their eyes met and for just a second he thought he saw a flash of heat in her eyes. But she blinked, and it was gone.

"No worries." Theo shook his head in an attempt to clear it of the scent of her . . . it didn't work. She was everywhere on the air around him.

Shit. He needed something much, much stronger.

"I was just going for this." He reached for the bottle of whiskey, pouring himself a shot before he drank it in one go. The burn of the alcohol down his throat helped a little in clearing his head but it did nothing for the feel of her that still tingled along his palms.

Maybe that was the reason he missed his first shot.

. . . and the second.

. . . and the third.

CHAPTER TWO
Manic Monday

Lucy Buchanan was pretty sure she was experiencing the Mondayest Monday that ever Mondayed.

It had all started when her alarm hadn't gone off that morning. She hadn't had enough time to blow-dry her hair before work, so she had to go out into the cold November air with wet hair, which was why she was freezing for most of the day.

The thing was, she was usually cold these days as she spent most of her time in the drafty auditorium of Mount MacCallion High School. The heater only worked when it wanted to, and it wasn't every day.

It was a little bit ironic that Lucy found herself teaching at Mount MacCallion, considering that some of the worst years of her life had been when she'd gone to school there. Lucy had been a freshman when her mother was diagnosed with cancer, and a sophomore when she'd died. She'd dealt with the loss in incredibly unhealthy ways, and her life had spiraled out of control in those years.

Though there'd been a couple of bright lights, little beacons to guide her through the darkness. The biggest one had been Lucy *truly* discovering her love of music, something that her favorite teacher, Mrs. Griffith, had helped her figure out.

Janet Griffith had been the music and drama teacher at Mount MacCallion for thirty-five years. Lucy would put good money on the fact that she was the most beloved teacher who had ever worked in that building. Even kids she'd never taught adored her. Which was why it had been so heartbreaking when she'd had to take the current semester off.

Mrs. Griffith's husband, Brandon, had been in a terrible car accident before the school year had started. He'd broken both of his legs, his collarbone, and had one of his lungs punctured. He'd been lucky to survive. Even with insurance, the medical bills had been astronomical. As always, the town had rallied and raised money to help them out. But even with that, they hadn't been able to get around-the-clock medical care, so Mrs. Griffith had decided to do it herself.

It had been Mrs. Griffith's idea for Lucy to take over for the semester, and as Lucy knew her old teacher wouldn't entrust just anyone to take on the position, she'd decided to do it despite her reservations.

Besides, it was kind of perfect; the job was temporary, and so was Lucy's stay in Cruickshank. When she'd come back six months ago, she'd had no intention of it being a permanent move. It was just until she got back on her feet . . . got over the failure that had been her seven years in Los Angeles. But if she was being honest with herself, LA had never been her favorite place; she'd just picked it to put as much distance between herself and this town as she could.

It wasn't that she didn't love Cruickshank—or the people in it—she'd just known that she'd needed to get away. To move on from her past.

Though there was no moving on from her past at the moment, not when she was roaming the same hallways she had as a teenager. At least she wasn't sleeping in her old bedroom anymore. She had that going for her.

Her sister, Caro, had lived in the tiny apartment above their father's garage for fifteen years. That was, until Max had come back to Cruickshank and Caro had moved in with him. Wanting a little space to call her own, Lucy had taken over the loft. And a *little* space was exactly what it was. Not even four hundred square feet, it offered a kitchen, living/bedroom, and a bathroom.

Though that bathroom was pretty great. Caro had gotten their father and brother, Jeremy, to remodel it a few years ago and it offered a glorious tub that Lucy sank into multiple times a week . . . usually with a glass of wine and a good book.

If not for the fact that tonight was girls' night, it would've been her plan for that evening. Mainly because her feet were killing her.

In her rush to get out the door that morning, she'd grabbed the first pair of shoes she'd put her hands on and didn't even think about the fact that they were the flats she hadn't broken in yet. Not even a box of Band-Aids could save her from the blisters that had formed on the backs of her heels.

Her sore feet were yet another thing that had contributed to her Mondayest Monday that had ever Mondayed.

There was also the fact that she'd lost *all* of the grades she'd uploaded the week before. Not only that, but when she'd tried to upload them during her free period, they disappeared again. She knew she'd saved them to the system correctly, but no matter how many times she'd told that to Barty Brooks in IT, he told her she hadn't. There was nothing that could ruin her day quite like having to deal with him and his smugly superior attitude. Every time she had a problem, he always asked her if she'd restarted her computer first.

She'd finally snapped and told him she always tried *everything* before having to deal with him. He'd just given her another one of his stupid smug smiles.

Then they'd run out of chicken sandwiches at lunch and Lucy had to settle for spaghetti. It wasn't that the spaghetti wasn't good—everything was good—it was just that it wasn't what she'd wanted. Her favorite cafeteria lady was Beatrice, and she *always* saved Lucy a sandwich, but Beatrice wasn't there . . . so no sandwich for Lucy.

But the final kick in the teeth happened that afternoon. As the music and drama teacher, Lucy was in charge of the semester's musical, a musical that was about four weeks away. She'd ordered the costume for the lead two months ago, a beautiful flowing red gown. The dress that showed up today was bubblegum pink.

There wasn't enough time to send it back and get it remade, or enough money. Lucy had already pushed the budget to the limit. The only option she had was to fix the dress, but that was a conversation she was going to have with her sister that evening.

If anyone knew how to do it, it was Caro.

Lucy might not be getting that bath tonight, but a good venting session with her friends along with some wine and something sweet would do the trick. And she knew *exactly* where to go to get that last part.

She had indeed won the game of darts against Theo. They hadn't even gotten to the third round as she'd soundly beaten him in the first two. Maybe going to collect on some of her spoils would lighten up her day.

Much like many of the shops in Cruickshank, Browned Butter

was downtown. Alexander Avenue and Malcolm Lane were the two main streets, and they intersected almost right in the middle of town. From there, a handful of other streets branched off, with their picture-perfect storefronts and cobblestoned sidewalks lined with dogwoods. The leaves had all changed from green to crimson reds and deep purples, but the trees were quickly losing their color as those leaves fell.

It was just after four when Lucy parked her car in the small lot by the bakery. The shop front was made of beautiful carved wood stained a rich chocolate, the bold white letters of *Browned Butter* popping against it. One of the windows offered a view of the few tables and chairs while the other had a magnificent display of cakes.

Theo was the one who usually decorated the cakes these days, for everything from birthdays to weddings, and they were all masterpieces. He'd gone to Chicago a couple of years ago to learn from a legendary pastry chef and he'd only gotten better since. Ridiculously so.

What with the way certain social media videos were trending these days, Theo's little sister, Gia, had started an account for the bakery. One of the more popular posts was when she filmed Theo decorating. The videos hadn't gone viral or anything, but they had a pretty decent follower count.

Browned Butter had never been hurting for business, but its popularity had grown. They'd started shipping their soft and gooey cookies all over the United States a couple of years ago, and to get them now required being on a wait list to buy a box. But it wasn't cookies or cakes that Lucy was after. Well, not a whole cake. What she wanted was cupcakes, a lot of them.

When she walked inside, she was greeted with the scent of a spicy vanilla. Cinnamon, cloves, and cardamon also perfumed

the air. She looked up to the chalkboard sign to find the fancy cal-
ligraphy of Juliet Taylor—Theo's mother—announcing the flavor
of the day: Cruickshank Vanilla Chai Cupcake.

Well, she knew one thing she would be getting. Lucy *loved*
vanilla chai, so much so that it was the scent of her current bodywash and lotion.

There was a bit of a line, and Lucy could only see Gia and her
best friend, Chloe, filling the orders. The girls were freshmen in
high school. They were both in Lucy's drama class, but Chloe was
also taking choir. She had a beautiful voice but she was still too
shy to go solo.

They were a comedy act if Lucy had ever seen one. It was why
they'd been cast as the Dynamic Duo—Rosie and Gilda—in that
semester's musical. They weren't the leads, but they started and
ended every scene and would be just as memorable. There hadn't
been a single rehearsal where someone in the cast didn't crack up
while they were performing.

It wasn't until the customer who was paying shifted position
that Lucy spotted Theo working behind the register. He lifted his
gaze and when his blue eyes landed on her a frown pulled down
the corners of his mouth.

Lucy couldn't help but grin, one of the few times she'd done
it all day.

In the years since she and Theo had spent those months fooling around, she'd avoided him like the plague. As they hadn't exactly ended things on the best of terms, she'd kind of had to. But
ever since she'd been back in Cruickshank, she'd found that she
really enjoyed driving him crazy. He still had the ability to push
her buttons unlike anyone else, but that constant back-and-forth
between them was fun.

Well, for her at least.

It took a few minutes for the line to move, and when Lucy stepped up to the counter, she found that her smile had gotten even bigger. "Hello, Theodore."

His frown deepened. "How many times do I have to tell you to *not* call me that?"

"Not sure yet." She shrugged. "But I'll let you know. You're looking particularly lumberjacky today."

He had on a blue and green flannel shirt that somehow made his eyes even brighter. She didn't know how that was possible. But his eyes weren't the only thing she was paying attention to. His brown hair was longer than usual and his beard a little thicker. She'd noticed it when they'd been playing darts on Friday.

"It's lumberjack chic," Gia said as she bagged cookies for a waiting customer.

"Yeah, Ms. Buchanan, it's *totally* in this season," Chloe added.

"As much as I enjoy being the butt of your jokes, can we move this along? There are people waiting." He waved to the line behind Lucy.

"Calm down, we weren't making fun of you, Theo." Gia patted her brother on the shoulder before moving on to fill the next order.

"Yeah." Chloe grinned. "We all think you pull off the look pretty well."

"It's a lot better than your grunge year when we were in high school," Lucy said.

"Wait, what?" Gia had been popping a box open, but her hands stilled as she rounded on him. "You wore grunge in high school? How did I not know about this?"

"Because it was my freshman year when I was an obnoxious little punk. And you weren't even born," Theo said.

"Yeah, but there have to be pictures somewhere." Chloe pulled a Browned Butter sticker from the roll, sealing the box of cupcakes she'd just filled and passing it across the counter.

"Oh, there are pictures," Lucy told the girls.

"You're the worst." Theo shook his head at her.

"I know." She nodded as she pulled a napkin out of her purse and placed it down on the counter. "I'm also a winner." She put her finger on the napkin and slid it across to him. It was the same napkin they'd used to keep score the other night.

"A *sore* winner." He pulled it out from underneath her finger.

"Act like you don't rub it in my face when you win."

"Me?" He put his hand on his chest. "I'm the model of a humble winner."

Gia barked out a laugh while Chloe coughed *liar*.

"Don't ever play him in Uno," Gia whispered conspiratorially to Lucy. "He's brutal with the draw fours."

"And he's so smug about them," Chloe added.

"Enough from the two of you." He pointed to the girls.

"What?" they asked in unison. "Us?"

Theo might've let out a frustrated huff as he looked back to Lucy, but she didn't miss the twitch at the corners of his mouth. Even he couldn't resist their antics. "All right, Lucy, what are you getting?"

"Four cupcakes for girls' night. We need something to soak up our wine."

"Well, make your picks." He waved to the display before hitting a few buttons on the register. When the drawer popped open, he scrawled a number on the napkin and put it inside. "I'll make sure to deduct this from your tab."

"You do that." She gave him another smile before she moved

over to where Gia was waiting for her. "How good are the chai ones?" she asked as she leaned forward to get a better look at the few remaining cupcakes in question.

Gia made a face of pure delight, her eyes crossing for emphasis. "So good. They're topped with a vanilla and cinnamon buttercream frosting that will blow your mind. Theo was truly inspired with this one. They're amazing. They'll be gone by the end of the day."

"I don't know that there's anything Theo has ever made that wasn't delicious." Lucy looked over at him to find that he was staring at her with a puzzled look on his face. "What?" She straightened, something weird shifting in her chest.

"Nothing." He shook his head slowly, his eyes still intently focused on her. "You just paid me a compliment. I'm not used to you being nice to me."

Lucy rolled her eyes before she looked back to the display case. "I'm nice to you all the time, Theodore. You just don't listen hard enough."

"Right." He let out a huff, and even though she wasn't looking at him, she knew he was frowning at her again.

"Okay, I'll get one of the chai, a chocolate bourbon pecan, crème brûlée, and caramel apple. I think that's a good variety."

"Agreed." Gia nodded as she went to grab a box.

"Throw in the s'mores one." Theo pointed to a slightly bigger box before he gave the change back to the customer who was ordering, clearing out the end of the line.

"You're giving me a free cupcake?"

"They're all free." He shut the register.

"Yes, but this one isn't going against my tab."

He shrugged. "I guess I can be nice too."

It was then that the door to the bakery opened again, the little bell above it ringing. Lucy wouldn't have turned around except she noticed the change in Theo's face, a smile pulling up the corners of his mouth and his blue eyes lighting up.

He hadn't looked at her that way when she'd walked in.

Not that she cared *how* he looked at her . . . but then why was there a weird and uncomfortable *thing* tightening her chest? Maybe that was what had her turning around to see who he was smiling at. Maybe that was why something leaden dropped into Lucy's stomach when her eyes landed on the absolutely stunning woman coming toward them.

Her hair was a warm honey blond, not a strand out of place as it flowed down her shoulders and back. She was wearing a black-and-white houndstooth pencil skirt and a silk white blouse, her slim waist accentuated in all the right ways. The woman also had the longest legs, which ended in the tallest high heels.

They were no doubt some fancy designer label that probably cost more than Lucy's two-week paycheck.

"Hello," Theo greeted the woman as she made her way up to the counter. "Well, this is a nice surprise. I thought I wouldn't be seeing you until six."

"Yes, well, it's been a bit of a long afternoon, and I needed a little sugar rush before our date." Her pretty pink lips turned up in a flirty smile as she pointed to the display of petit fours.

"I think we can find you something."

Gia let out a very loud throat clearing, and Theo didn't look over at her as he waved a hand in her direction. "Joss, this is my little sister, Gia, and her best friend, Chloe. Gia and Chloe, this is Joss."

"Nice to meet you," Joss said to the girls.

"And you." A mischievous gleam now lit Gia's eyes. "You're going on a date with my brother tonight?"

"I am." Joss nodded.

Why did those two words have Lucy's stomach bottoming out? She didn't care who Theo dated. Never had and never would.

"You have a date and you didn't tell me?" Gia lightly punched Theo on the shoulder before turning to Joss. "How did he get you to agree to it?"

"Yeah? Did he hypnotize you?" Chloe asked. "Or a bribe?"

"No! Blackmail!" Gia snapped her fingers as if that were the answer.

Chloe leaned closer, her voice dropping to a whisper. "Blink twice and we can help you get out of it."

Joss laughed, but Theo closed his eyes, shaking his head at the pair of them. "*This* is why I don't tell you anything."

"Oh, come on." Gia grinned. "We're your favorite and you know it."

"We're *everyone's* favorite. Just ask Ms. Buchanan." Chloe nodded to Lucy.

It was true, Chloe and Gia *were* her favorite students . . . she'd never said it out loud, but facts were facts.

Chloe had recently moved to Cruickshank. Chloe's father was the new captain down at the firehouse. He'd taken the position a few months ago, moving his three daughters from Charlotte after a messy divorce. From what Lucy knew, his ex-wife had just picked up her life one day and moved to Florida with the man she'd been having an affair with for years.

It hadn't taken Lucy very long to develop a soft spot for the girl.

As for Gia, Lucy had babysat the youngest Taylor for about a decade. She was like a little sister.

"Buchanan?" Joss asked as she turned to Lucy. "Are you related to Caroline?"

Lucy straightened her shoulders, for some reason needing to fortify herself before talking to the woman. "Yes, she's my sister."

"Oh, she and Max have mentioned you. I'm working with Max on the Kincaid project." She reached her hand out to Lucy. "Jocelyn Fairbanks."

"Lucy Buchanan," she said as she grabbed the woman's hand.

Joss had a good handshake, firm but not too tight, and she looked Lucy right in the eyes with a genuine smile on her face.

"It's nice to meet you," Joss said.

"You as well," Lucy lied before she let go of the woman's hand. "I should get going." She took a few steps back toward the door, wanting desperately to get out of the bakery, but stopped when Gia called out.

"Don't forget your cupcakes!" She held the sealed box out and over the display.

"Oh, yes, the whole reason I came in here." She walked back up and grabbed the box. "See you girls tomorrow," she said to Gia and Chloe, giving Theo and Joss another nod before she high-tailed it out of there.

When she walked outside, the crisp fresh air did absolutely nothing to clear her head. What in the world had all of that been about? She didn't know, and she was pretty sure she didn't want to find out.

* * *

IT WAS FIVE THIRTY when Lucy pulled her black SUV into the driveway of the grand Victorian house that used to belong to Ava and Martin Abbott, Max's grandparents. The three-story brick building was the most beautiful house on the whole street, and in Lucy's opinion, in the whole town.

Lucy loved this house. She'd practically grown up in it, as her mother had worked for the Abbotts for thirteen years. It couldn't be more fitting that Caro and Max now called it home. Lucy hoped that when she walked through that front door, her day would take a drastic upturn.

It had been a little over an hour since she'd left Browned Butter, and Lucy's mood had plummeted even more. She'd thought cupcakes and antagonizing Theo would put her in better spirits. Turned out, not so much.

Well, the jury was still out on the cupcakes making her feel better, as she hadn't delved into them yet. Grabbing the brown box on the passenger seat, she got out of the car and headed up the path to the house. She pulled her jacket closed with her free hand.

The sun had already set below the mountains and the temperature had dropped significantly. If it was this chilly in November, she had a feeling they were in for some cold nights this winter. The front door was unlocked, and Lucy let herself in, a shiver running up her spine as she walked into the warm house.

"Hello!" she called out as she set the box on the table by the door and divested herself of her scarf, jacket, and shoes.

The sound of nails clipping against the hardwood floors filled the air a second before three dogs burst down the hallway. Leading the way was Beau, the fluffy white and brown dog that had been Ava's and now belonged to Max and Caro. In the middle was Frankie, the reddish-brown dachshund that Caro and Max had rescued and adopted a few months back. She might be longer than she was tall, but she was fast. And bringing up the rear was Cooper, a black and brown scruffy mutt, and the current foster of the house.

Caro had been volunteering for Cruickshank Cats and Dogs Rescue since she was sixteen. She'd gotten countless animals adopted in those years, but she'd only started fostering a few years ago when their beloved Sweet Pea had died. The dog had been their mother's and when she'd died, Caro hadn't been able to get another dog.

That was until Frankie had come along. Now with Beau they had two permanent four-legged companions, but Caro hadn't stopped fostering.

"Well, hello to all of you too," Lucy said as she dropped down to give everyone the pets and head scratches they deserved.

"In here, Luce," Caro said as she popped into the entryway at the end of the hall. The swinging door had been propped open and the scent of rosemary, thyme, and garlic wafted out, filling the air.

Caro was still in the middle of cooking dinner. Girls' night didn't usually start until six, but as Lucy hadn't been able to sit still in her loft any longer—and couldn't bring herself to grade another essay about the book-to-musical adaptation of *Les Misérables*—she'd texted Caro and told her she was heading over early.

"Be there in a sec." Lucy gave Beau and Cooper one last head scratch before she scooped Frankie up. She settled the dog in the crook of her arm—getting a good face lick—before she grabbed the box of cupcakes and headed down the hall, following behind the other two dogs.

The amazing scent in the hallway was nothing compared to how it smelled in the kitchen, and her stomach growled loudly when she stepped inside.

"What's for dinner?" Lucy asked as she set the box on the island.

"Slow-roasted salmon, crispy potatoes, and green beans."

"That sounds amazing. Smells amazing too. Do you need any help?"

"I got it." Caro shook her head before she nodded to the glass of red wine on the counter. "Max decanted some merlot before he left, and I poured you some. Sit down and take a load off. I've already started," she said as she picked up her own glass.

Lucy pressed a kiss to Frankie's head before she set her down. Once the dog had her feet on the tile floor, she took off for the mudroom, Beau and Cooper following behind and the doggy door flapping loudly as they all let themselves outside.

"Cheers!" Lucy grabbed her glass and clinked it against Caro's, taking a sip as she slid onto the barstool. "Where's Max off to tonight?"

"He and Dad went over to Jeremy's to help with the kids and watch the football game. What's for dessert?" Caro set her wine down, pointing to the box on the counter before she headed for the stove and pulled a boiling pot from the burner.

"Cupcakes."

"Ahh." Caro grinned as she crossed to the sink and poured the contents of the pot into a metal strainer. Steam rushed up as the potatoes and water spilled out. "Collecting on your winnings?"

"Yeah. I needed a pick-me-up, figured I'd share them tonight."

Caro turned around and leaned back against the sink, her eyes narrowed as she studied Lucy, concern filling her features. "You okay? Why'd you need a pick-me-up?"

Lucy shrugged. "Long day."

"Care to elaborate?"

"Not really."

"Okay." Caro nodded, her gaze lingering on her sister's face.

Lucy took another sip of her wine, and she'd barely swallowed it when she asked, "Who's Jocelyn Fairbanks?"

Caro straightened, her eyebrows going up in surprise. "You met Joss? She's working with Max on the Kincaid project."

"Yes, she'd mentioned as much. What's she doing for the Kincaid?"

"Joss is a lawyer out of Bergen and Hennings's New York office. She's dealing with the contracts and permits and everything."

Bergen and Hennings was the investment property firm Max had worked for before he'd moved to Cruickshank. As they were the ones who'd invested in the historic building that had once been a spring factory, he still technically worked for them, just not in the same capacity as before.

Max used to exclusively find buildings for the company or their clients to buy, but now he was the one in charge of the Kincaid remodel. And once it was finished, he would be the one running the boutique hotel.

"So, she's going to be in town for a bit?"

"In and out until the remodel is finished."

Lucy swirled her wine around in her glass. "You like her?"

"I've only talked to her twice, but yeah, I like her. Why? You don't?"

"I don't have an opinion on her. What about Max? He likes her?"

"He's worked with her before. Said she's good at her job. Smart. Nice. Excellent with people."

"Yeah." Lucy frowned. "That's what I thought."

Caro's focus sharpened on her sister. "What's going on, Luce?"

"I met her today at the bakery, when I went to get the cupcakes, and she just seems *too* perfect."

"And that's why you don't like her?"

Lucy's frown deepened. "She's going on a date with Theo, so *something* is wrong with her."

Caro's eyebrows rose high. "Theo and Joss are going on a date? Interesting." She thought for a moment before adding, "They make a cute couple."

"They do?"

"Sure. Why not?" Caro pushed off the counter and crossed over to the island, getting a closer look at her sister's face. "Luce, why does this matter to you?"

"It doesn't matter to me. He can date all of North Carolina for all I care." She waved her hand in the air as if to encompass the whole state.

"Uh huh . . ."

"He can," Lucy insisted. "I don't know, it was just . . . jarring or something."

"O-kay," Caro said slowly, dragging the two syllables out way longer than necessary.

"What?"

"It's just"—Caro tilted her head to the side, now grinning—"I thought something might be happening with the two of you. This is an interesting development."

"What's an interesting development?" A new voice filled the air and Lucy and Caro looked over as Lilah and Sasha walked through the kitchen doorway. Since the dogs were still outside, neither woman had been alerted to the new people in the house.

Well, shit. Lucy wasn't sure if she was ready to have this particular conversation to the level that was no doubt about to unfold. Caro, she could handle. Caro, Lilah, and Sasha? Not so much. The three women in that kitchen were the people who knew Lucy the best in the world . . . and she was most scared of what Lilah had the potential to figure out. The woman's chocolate-brown eyes had the ability to read anybody, especially people she knew.

Caro looked over at Lilah and Sasha and without hesitation said, "Lucy doesn't like that Theo has a date with Jocelyn Fairbanks."

"Thanks a lot." Lucy frowned at her sister.

"Um, excuse me." Caro waved a hand at Lilah. "I don't mess around with her powers."

"No one should," Sasha agreed, shaking her head. "And who is Jocelyn?"

"She works with Max at Bergen and Hennings . . ." Caro started to explain. Lucy was only partially listening, more concerned with the fact that Lilah's eyes had narrowed on her.

It had long been established by Lilah's friends and family that she had some sort of weird clairvoyant ability; she just needed to make eye contact . . . which was why Lucy wasn't quite meeting the woman's gaze.

"Do you two want some wine?" Lucy didn't even wait for an answer before she slid off the barstool and crossed over to the decanter. She knew Lilah was still staring at her, a direct beam of energy that was hitting her right between the shoulder blades.

Lucy had just begun to pour when Lilah started talking. "I like Joss. I met her last week when Theo brought her into Quigley's for a drink. She was a delight, and he seemed pretty smitten with her."

Lucy looked up so quickly that her hand jerked, wine sloshing over the side of the glass and landing on the counter. "Smitten? When has Theo ever been smitten in his life?"

The corners of Lilah's mouth turned up in a smirk. "There it is."

Dammit!

"There *nothing* is." Lucy leaned forward and snatched the towel from the counter, cleaning up her mess.

Too bad it couldn't clean up the mess that was this conversation. But mess or not, she really wanted to know about what Lilah had seen . . . luckily for Lucy, she wasn't the only one who was curious.

"So, wait"—Sasha held a hand in the air—"how long have they been dating?"

Lucy did her best to keep her mouth shut as she walked back to the island and handed Lilah and Sasha their glasses. She wasn't going to ask any more questions about Theo.

"I'm not sure." Lilah shook her head. "They've been to Quigley's a couple of times together, so my guess is maybe two weeks?"

Sasha took a sip of her wine and looked down, swirling it around in the glass. "Oh, this is some *good* stuff."

"Max bought it last week from Cheese Wheel and Wine, and I liked it so much I asked him to get some more for tonight. We have two more bottles if needed."

"Yeah, it might be needed." Lilah was peering at Lucy again.

"What?" Lucy asked, doing her best to look like she was fine. Because she was fine . . . perfectly fine. She didn't care. She was good. Completely and totally unaffected by Theo and his dating life.

She looked away from Lilah, sipping on her wine as she watched her sister grab the strainer filled with baby potatoes from the sink and bring them over to the kitchen island.

"So," Caro said as she started to place the potatoes on a sheet pan in neat little rows. "Theo's been seeing Joss for two weeks? With his track record they're practically engaged."

Lucy choked on her wine. *God*, she was a mess today.

"Okay." Lilah put her glass down before placing her palms on the counter and leaning in close to Lucy. "*What* is going on with you and Theo?"

Lucy swiped the back of her hand across her mouth. "Nothing is going on." Not currently at least. Lucy had never told anyone about those months she'd been sleeping with Theo.

Not a soul.

She was pretty sure the only reason she'd gotten away with it was because everyone had been so distracted with Lilah and Jeremy's wedding. After her brother had *finally* popped the question, it had only been four months later that the two were walking down the aisle.

Yeah, if it hadn't been for that, there wasn't a snowball's chance in hell Lucy would've been able to hide what had happened from them . . . especially Lilah. And the secret had stayed safe as she'd hightailed it out of town shortly after . . . when things had gotten out of control.

Or, out of *her* control.

And during those times she'd visited over the years, she'd done her best to stay away from Theo . . . that was, until recently . . .

"Do you want there to be something going on?" Caro asked, pulling Lucy from her thoughts.

"No," she said quickly . . . a little *too* quickly.

"Are you lying to us? Or yourself?" Sasha asked.

"What is that supposed to mean?" She rounded on her best friend.

"Come on, Luce, things have been different between the two of you since you got back." There was something knowing in Sasha's eyes . . . something Lucy didn't like . . . something she didn't want to look at too closely.

"No, they haven't."

"Sasha's right." Caro pointed a fork in Lucy's direction, her expression thoughtful. "Things have changed. You two are almost . . . flirty."

"We are *not* flirty." Even Lucy was a little taken aback by the vehemence in her words.

"The lady doth protest too much," Lilah said, that annoying grin of hers growing.

"You can say that again." Caro at least had the good grace to try and hide her smile as she looked down at the tray and started smashing the potatoes with the back of the fork.

"Look." Lucy waved her hands in the air before putting them down on the counter with a bit too much force. "All I wanted to know was who Joss was. I now know. I do *not* have feelings for Theo. Can we please drop this?"

"Sure." Sasha shrugged.

"Absolutely," Caro agreed.

"Anything you want." Lilah nodded before she looked over to Caro and Sasha. "So how long before Lucy and Theo sleep together?"

"I am *not* sleeping with Theo again!" Lucy blurted out before she could stop herself.

The entire kitchen went silent—well, except for the clatter of Caro dropping the fork on the metal baking tray—as all eyes went back to Lucy.

It was Lilah who spoke first. "Did you just say you're not sleeping with Theo *again*?"

Lucy cleared her throat, her eyes going to her glass as she ran her finger around the rim. "Yes." Her voice was barely above a whisper now.

"Ummm, when was the first time?" Caro asked.

Lucy grabbed her glass, taking a sip and swallowing before she finally answered. "After we got back from Europe."

"Seven *years* ago!" Caro shouted.

"How did I miss that?" Lilah looked like she was racking her brain, flipping through pages of the past. "I knew something was going on *now* but how did I miss it *then*?"

"How did we all miss it?" Caro asked. "And why didn't you tell us?"

"That's what I've always wondered." Sasha tilted her head to the side, her eyes not leaving Lucy as she took a very dramatic sip of wine.

"You knew!" Lucy's mouth dropped open.

"Yeah, I knew. You and Theo weren't exactly masters of mystery. I saw you making out a number of times and put two and two together that you guys were, well, putting two and two together," she finished, making a hand gesture that clearly meant sex.

"Thanks for that." Lucy frowned at Sasha. "How did you not say anything to me . . . or anyone else for that matter?"

"It wasn't my information to tell, Luce. I figured you didn't want us to know for some reason."

"And what was that *reason*?" Lilah asked, her hands on her hips.

"Well, Caro, you had just gotten back from New York and saw Max with that girl and thought that he'd moved on." She gave her sister a slightly apologetic look. "And you were devastated all over again."

A flash of pain tightened Caro's face, the one Lucy was very familiar with as she'd seen it so many times during those years Caro and Max hadn't been together.

"Sasha, you were still upset that Billy Dreskin cheated on you while we were gone and weren't exactly in a great place yourself." Lucy finally waved her hand at Lilah. "And then there was you and Jeremy. The second we got off that plane, he proposed and everything and everyone went into wedding planning mode. That time was about the two of you and I wasn't going to steal your thunder."

"Steal my thunder? When have I ever cared about anything like that?" Lilah put her hand to her chest.

"Well, considering it started *at* your engagement party, I think it would've caused a bit of a stir."

"You had sex at their engagement party?" Sasha's jaw dropped open. Apparently, she hadn't known *everything*.

"Well, not *at* but right after."

The party had been at Quigley's and Lucy and Theo had ended up taking way too many shots of whiskey as they played darts against each other. A dangerous combination, as it turned out.

It should've never happened. One minute they'd been bickering about the game, and the next they'd found themselves in a back room making out. She'd wanted him to kiss her, wanted him to kiss her for longer than she could remember.

It wasn't even an hour later that they'd ended up in the back seat of his truck, her panties on the floor and her legs wrapped around his waist as he moved inside her.

Everything about that night had been incredible, so much so that they hadn't stopped for months. And all during that time there'd never been any discussion of what *they* were because it had only been about sex . . .

Right up until it wasn't.

It was Caro's voice that pulled Lucy out of the past. "Okay, so we now know it started at the engagement party. How long did it last?"

"Ummm." Lucy dragged out the word, not because she had to think about the timeline, but because she was trying to prepare herself for their reaction. "Until I left for LA."

"You were sleeping with Theo for four months and you didn't tell us?"

"Excuse me." Sasha turned on Lilah. "Didn't you and Jeremy keep your relationship a secret for almost a year when you first got together?"

"Yes." She nodded. "But that was different."

"How?" Caro asked.

"Because . . ." Lilah trailed off, thinking for a second before finishing with "It just was."

"Great reasoning." Sasha smirked.

"Look," Lucy started, waving her hands in the air to get their attention. "It wasn't that I wanted to keep it from you guys. It was more that if I said it out loud, it would be real. And I was scared for it to be real." She hesitated for just a moment before continuing on, her voice losing some of its steam. "But then it became too real, and I bailed."

"How did it become too real?" Caro pressed.

"Theo told me he had feelings for me, and I couldn't deal, so I moved to California a week later."

For the second time that night, the kitchen went quiet. But this time it was Sasha who finally broke the silence. "Well, shit," she oh-so-eloquently said.

"Theo had feelings for you?" Caro asked but it wasn't really a question. "No wonder he gets all bent out of shape when you're around."

"Yeah, he's got his reasons. I can understand if you guys want to switch sides now."

"There are no sides." Sasha shook her head. "We're on Team Lucy *and* Theo. Team Leo!"

"O-kay, there is no *Team Leo*."

"Do you want there to be?" Lilah folded her arms across her chest, giving Lucy another one of her penetrative looks.

"It wouldn't matter if I did. I'm not staying in Cruickshank. Remember? Look, I haven't had the best day, and I *really* don't want to talk about *this* or *him* anymore. But I do need to know if you guys are mad at me for not telling you."

"No." Caro shook her head. "I understand where you were coming from."

"Well, as it was pointed out, I have no ground to stand on as I kept my relationship with your brother a secret for much, much longer," Lilah said.

"And as I always knew, I'm not mad. Besides, *we all* have our secrets, Luce."

"What secret are you keeping?" Lilah looked over so fast she had to have given herself a crick in her neck.

"That's for me to know and you to *maybe* find out." Sasha grinned over her glass before taking a sip of wine.

CHAPTER THREE

Crash into Me

*T*heo stared at the open cashbox on his desk, that damned napkin from the darts game sticking out from under the change tray. The purple of Lucy's loopy handwriting stood out against the white paper.

As he hadn't wanted to be late for his date with Joss the night before, he'd skipped this particular closing duty and put the cashbox in the safe uncounted, deciding to deal with it in the morning. Except it hadn't been the money he'd been avoiding dealing with.

And it was just too bad for Theo that locking that napkin up for the night had not pushed it from his brain like he'd wanted it to. Probably because it wasn't just the napkin he'd been trying not to think about.

Theo really liked Joss, which was why he had a nagging sense of guilt all throughout their dinner, as he'd been thinking about another woman. It was also the reason why he'd said no when she invited him in for a drink. He'd had a pretty good idea what she'd wanted, based off the kiss she'd given him. It was something he'd wanted too—very, very much so—but the last thing he was going to do was take a woman to bed when he was thinking about someone else.

He was beyond aware of the fact that he needed to end things with Joss. He knew in his gut that things weren't going to go further. It wasn't because of her—she was great—it was clearly because of him.

But ending things with Joss wasn't Theo's only problem. He needed to figure out *why* he couldn't stop thinking about Lucy.

It wasn't his fault that she'd come into the bakery yesterday before his date with Joss. It wasn't his fault that she'd been her usual antagonistic self that drove him crazy. It wasn't his fault that she was so fucking beautiful it was distracting. It wasn't his fault that he hadn't been able to get the scent of vanilla and cloves out of his head since last Friday. It wasn't his fault that he'd decided to make a cupcake that smelled like her.

He hadn't meant to do it. He'd just planned on doing a spiced vanilla . . . just a sprinkle of cinnamon. But then he'd grabbed the cloves, and the ginger, and the cardamom, and the black pepper. He'd spent a good amount of time adding this and that until it was the right flavor . . .

Until it smelled like Lucy.

Once he'd realized what he'd done, he'd been tempted to dump the whole thing in the trash. All he needed was for the entire bakery to smell like her. But he hadn't been able to do it. Not only did he hate wasting food, but there was a part of him that wanted to see how close he could get. And maybe, just maybe, he could bake whatever this was out of his system.

It was a tried-and-true technique that had worked many, many times over the years . . . but it hadn't worked yesterday. No, it had made things exponentially worse. They had indeed sold out of the cupcakes before closing, which meant he was going to have to make another batch today . . . and if those sold out, he'd be making them all week.

Whenever there was a new flavor, word of mouth traveled very quickly around town, and he had no doubt that people would be coming in to get one for themselves. It was what happened when he'd made the sticky toffee cupcakes last Christmas; he couldn't keep up with demand. Then there was the tiramisu cupcake he'd whipped up for Valentine's Day last year. He'd had to make those the entire month, three to four batches a day. The longest run had been the strawberry–pink champagne cupcake . . . it sold out every single day this past spring.

He really didn't like to disappoint his customers, which meant today was going to be another day of a Lucy-filled head.

Theo reached forward, lifting the change tray and tugging out the napkin from the till.

It had been Lucy who'd pulled the purple pen from her purse to keep score, telling Max that she liked the way it wrote better than the black ballpoint he'd gotten from behind the bar.

The paper soaks up the ink better, she'd said as she grabbed a clean napkin and wrote *Theodore* and *Lucy* across the top, underlining each name with a separate flourish.

It was such a small thing to pull up an old memory, a memory that he'd forgotten until that moment. Of her in his bed, wearing his T-shirt, the end of a pen between her lips as she looked down at a notebook, reading what she'd just written.

What is that? He'd walked across the room to her, pulling the blankets up and crawling between the sheets and settling in closer to her. It had been a chilly night in late October and his body craved her warmth.

But his body had craved her *everything*.

Working on a song. She didn't look over at him as she moved the pen from her lips, crossing out a few words with a quick flourish before writing something next to them.

Can I see? he'd asked lightly, tugging on the edge of the notebook. *I want to know more of what goes on in that pretty head of yours.*

She'd held tight to the notebook, not letting him take it as she looked over at him. The corner of her mouth had quirked up in that way that drove him out of his ever-loving mind.

Not yet. She'd shaken her head. *I haven't finished writing it. When it's done, I'll play it for you.*

Except she never had played it for him.

Theo rubbed the napkin between his fingers and was just about to toss it into the trash when his hand stopped and changed direction. He dropped it into the drawer in front of him instead, closing it with a snap before he started to count the cashbox.

He didn't know what possessed him to save it . . . and he wasn't going to look too closely at the *why* of it either.

* * *

Cardi B was blasting through the speakers at Mind & Body as Lucy's left hook connected with the punching bag in front of her. There were about twenty people in the class with her, half of them boxing while the others did Russian twists with a weighted medicine ball.

If people wanted to go to a gym, there was a twenty-four-hour fitness center about fifteen minutes outside of town; otherwise, Mind & Body was the only workout studio *in* Cruickshank. Though they didn't have treadmills, ellipticals, or weight benches, they offered a variety of classes that anyone could join no matter their age or skill level. They had yoga, HIIT, TRX training, rowing, Pilates, barre, and boxing, which was Lucy's favorite.

She worked through the combination: jab, cross, hook, hook.

With every punch, some of the tension loosened in her shoulders, a tension that had been there for the last twenty-four hours, a tension she'd been unable to get rid of no matter how much she'd tried.

She'd barely been able to focus during that afternoon's rehearsals for the musical. No doubt any and all notes she'd given to her students had been garbage.

Jab, cross, hook, hook.

Apparently, hitting things was all she'd needed to do. Better this bag than a person. Not that there was anyone in particular she wanted to punch.

Jab, cross, hook, hook.

Theo's face came into her mind . . . but she didn't want to punch him. She wasn't sure what she wanted to do with him.

Jab, cross, hook, hook.

The conversation—and revelations—from last night flitted through her brain and she started to hit the bag harder.

Jab, cross, hook, hook.

Caro, Sasha, and Lilah didn't know what they were talking about. Lucy and Theo weren't flirty. They were . . . nothing. Just like *nothing* was different between them since she'd been back in town.

Jab, cross, hook, hook.

She drove him crazy and he frowned a lot when she was around.

Jab, cross, hook, hook.

Sasha had called them Team Leo. How ridiculous was that?

Jab, cross, hook, hook.

"Look at *you* go," the instructor, Andre, said as he came up behind the bag, holding it steady as Lucy continued to punch.

Jab, cross, hook, hook.

"Add an uppercut," Andre encouraged.

Jab, cross, hook, hook, uppercut. Jab, cross, hook, hook, uppercut.

"Now add a slip."

Jab, cross, hook, hook, uppercut, slip.

Lucy kept going, all of her focus on the bag in front of her, shifting back and forth. She moved with the punches, bouncing on her feet. It wasn't until the room around her went quiet that she realized everyone else had stopped and they were all watching her.

"What?"

"I called the end of class, Lucy. What did that bag ever do to you?" Andre asked.

"Went on a date with someone else," Sasha gasped from the floor. She'd dropped the medicine ball and had flopped onto her back, her hands clutching her sides.

Andre's dark eyebrows rose high on his forehead. "Is that so?"

"No, it's *not* so." Lucy glared at Sasha, who now had a smile etched across her sweaty face.

"Remind me to never cross you." Andre shook his head. "Poor guy doesn't know what's coming."

"There isn't a guy."

"*Right.*" Now Andre was grinning at her. "Time to stretch, killer," he said as he got down on the ground, bending his left leg in as he folded his body over his right leg and grabbed his foot.

Lucy dropped down next to Sasha, both following along as Andre did a five-minute cooldown. It was another five minutes later when they were heading out the door and onto the streets of downtown Cruickshank.

Not only was it another cold fall day, but it was wet, the rain coming on and off. It was currently off, but the dark gray clouds above promised a downpour shortly. Lucy tucked her scarf into her bright yellow raincoat before she pulled up the hood, trying to protect her head from the biting wind. It didn't help that she was sweaty, the moisture on her yoga pants instantly going cold.

"Jeez." Sasha shivered next to her. "It's freaking freezing."

"All I want to do is climb into a hot bath." Not only because of the cold, but because of her already sore muscles that she knew were only going to get worse.

"Ahhh," Sasha groaned. "That sounds glorious." They walked in silence for a block before Sasha bumped her shoulder against Lucy's. "You going to tell me what that was back there?"

"Nope." Lucy shook her head. She didn't even want to discuss the comment Sasha had made. Didn't want to give any more air supply to the discussion about her and Theo.

Because there was no *her and Theo*.

"*Right*." Sasha said the word slowly. Lucy didn't need to look over at her friend to know there was a smirk on her mouth. "So, we aren't going to discuss the fact that you were hitting that bag like it pulled your pigtails?"

Lucy turned to Sasha, frown firmly in place. "Theo has never pulled my pigtails in all of the years that I've known him."

Sasha's grin grew. "You said it wasn't about Theo."

Damn it. "Because it's not. It's not about anyone. I'm fine. Perfectly fine."

"So then why are you all tense and twirly?"

"Tense and twirly?" Lucy repeated as they stopped in front of Dancing Donkey, the café that Sasha owned and ran with her mom.

"Lucy, I've never seen you so twisted into a knot. And the fact that you don't want to talk about it says way more than if you were talking about it."

"What's that supposed to mean?"

"How long have we known each other?" Sasha asked.

Lucy rolled her eyes. "Our entire lives."

"Exactly. And when you *don't* tell me things, I know it's a big deal. So, whenever you're ready to talk about this"—Sasha waved her hand in a circle as if to encompass all of Lucy—"I'll be around." She didn't even give Lucy a beat to respond before she moved on. "We still on for tomorrow?"

"Yeah." Lucy nodded slowly, a little taken aback by the change of subject. "Sushi and sake at your place."

"You bring the sake, I'll get the sushi. And you can help me pick out what I'm wearing for my date with Adam on Thursday."

"Dinner *and* a fashion show. It doesn't get any better than that."

"You know I put on a good show." Sasha wiggled her shoulders in a little dance, laughing as she opened the door to head into the warmth of the coffee shop.

"Hey, Sash." Lucy reached out, grabbing Sasha's hand.

"Yeah?"

"Thanks."

Her friend's grin transformed into a knowing warm smile. "Anytime, Luce."

Lucy squeezed Sasha's hand before she let go and headed for Fresh Harvest, the only grocery store in Cruickshank. She'd parked her car in the lot by the market as she'd needed to grab a couple of things for dinner before heading home. As she rounded the corner, her eyes automatically gravitated toward Browned Butter. The second it came into view there was that all-too-familiar feeling of something weird and uncomfortable filling her chest.

Oh, who the hell was she kidding? That feeling had been there all day, it just intensified with each and every step that she took.

Getting closer and closer to the shop. Getting closer and closer to *him*.

God, this whole thing was absolutely ridiculous. She didn't have feelings for Theo. Not like that. Not anymore.

Sure, there'd been something all those years ago . . . when the sex had morphed into something else. Something way more intense. Something that had scared her out of her mind. Something that had made her run as fast and as far as she could . . . run from *him* right across the country.

But that feeling was gone. Long gone. There was nothing with Theo. That chapter was written and closed. No more to the story. And that was very clearly the case for him as well. He was dating Joss. And Lucy? Well, she'd be going home to her cat.

Lucy rounded another corner, leaving Browned Butter and *Theo* behind her. Because that was where he needed to be. He was part of the past and she needed to think about the future. She needed to focus on this current state of limbo she was in. *What* her next step was going to be . . . *where* her next move would take her.

Because she wasn't staying in Cruickshank. Yes, she loved this town. It was home in a way that no other place could compare— *would* ever compare—but she'd been so lost here.

Though it wasn't like she'd found herself in California. No, California had been a minefield in a forest of trees so thick she'd never known which direction she was going. She'd at least learned a lot about who she was, even if she still didn't know what she wanted.

Lucy was so lost in thought that she didn't even realize she was standing in front of Fresh Harvest. Her feet had just taken her there—her brain on autopilot—and now she was staring at the display of squash in front of the store.

Maybe it was the cold dreary weather, but the idea of a warm and cozy soup sounded beyond appealing. Grabbing a cart, she loaded it up with a good variety of squash, planning to whip up a big pot of roasted butternut and acorn squash soup that weekend.

When she rolled the cart inside, she came face-to-face with the fall display and didn't make it past without stopping. She grabbed a few baby pumpkins, half a gallon of fresh apple cider, a bag of cinnamon-scented pinecones, a pumpkin-spiced coffee blend, another pack of the vanilla chai bodywash and lotion she'd become obsessed with, and two candles—one crème brûlée and the other pumpkin doughnut. She eyed the maple-flavored cookies, but there was no point in buying baked goods from anywhere besides Browned Butter. Disappointment was always at the end of such a purchase.

Besides, she still had some cupcakes left over from the night before.

Lucy pulled her cart away from the display and turned toward produce. She didn't make it very far before she was again distracted. The flower section was to the right, and she made a quick detour. She loved having fresh flowers around, no doubt something ingrained in her because of her mother and Max's grandmother Ava, the two biggest green thumbs she'd ever known.

Growing up there'd always been a bouquet of fresh flowers in the kitchen, usually cut right from the garden. Rachel had also put little vases in Lucy's and Caro's rooms. Lucy had often gone to sleep with the smell of lavender, lilies, or roses filling her head.

The roses had always been her favorite and a bouquet of vibrant orange, red, and yellow ones caught her eye. She reached out and grabbed them, pulling the bundle to her face and inhaling deeply.

Lucy stood there, journeying back to a part of her past that she never wanted to move on from. A part that she cherished beyond anything else. But all good memories of her mother were a gift, and she treasured moments like this, as if her mother were stopping in to say hello.

It couldn't have been more than a moment or two that she stood there, but as she lowered the flowers, it was to find Theo standing in front of her, a bemused expression on his face.

Because of course it was him.

She wasn't exactly sure as to the *why*—maybe she hadn't gotten all of her aggression out during her boxing class—but there was something about seeing him that irritated her.

"You know, I don't think I've ever seen someone *literally* stop to smell the roses."

"Well, now you can mark that one on your cliché bingo card," Lucy said as she put the flowers in her cart. "I've already crossed off *the apple doesn't fall far from the tree*, *like a kid in a candy store*, *a diamond in the rough*, and *cat got your tongue* on mine." Her words were a little more sarcastic than usual . . . sharper.

Well, not too much more than usual when it came to Theo. It was true that she'd been a little prickly all day, but the second he walked up she'd become a goddamn cactus. Maybe it had to do with the way his mouth quirked to the side with amusement . . . like he was laughing at her or something. Why was it that she preferred it when he was grumpy?

Because when he's grumpy you've gotten under his skin. And right now, he's under yours.

"Well, on mine I've got *there are plenty of fish in the sea*, *read between the lines*, and *all that glitters isn't gold*."

Why did all three of those things sound like a dig at her?

"I guess whoever finds *all their ducks in a row* can call bingo first."

"I guess so," he said as he glanced down at her cart. "I see you've got the basic fall girl starter kit in your cart."

She tilted her head to the side, giving him her best snarky smile. "I just need a puppy and a flannel blanket and I'll be the complete package. I like what I like, Theo; there is no shame in my game."

"There never has been any shame in your game." He reached into the cart, grabbing the package of lotion and bodywash. He turned it over in his hands before taking a moment to study the label. "You should know"—he looked back up at her before he placed the package back in the cart—"this scent works on you."

"What?"

"Have a good night, Lucy." And with that he rounded her cart with his and headed off to the opposite side of the market. Lucy stared at the back of him, her mouth hanging open in confusion.

What the hell was that?

* * *

This scent works on you?

What in God's name had possessed Theo to say that to Lucy? Had he lost his mind? Well, yes, that much had been clear when he'd come up to her.

He'd spotted her the second he walked into Fresh Harvest, like a homing beacon had been implanted in his brain and refused to turn off. Why was it that if she was anywhere in the vicinity, he always immediately found her?

She'd just been standing there, looking stupidly beautiful with her face in a bouquet of roses and wearing those damn yoga pants. But come on, she had curves in all the right places, and that stretchy material highlighted every single one. Not even her oversize yellow raincoat could hide them.

The thing about the entire situation that drove him the craziest was that his first thought was Lucy shouldn't be buying herself flowers. And yes, he understood the whole thing of women could buy themselves flowers. They could buy themselves whatever they damn well pleased. They didn't need a man. *He got it.*

But why, *why* was it that his very next thought had been that *he* wanted to be the one buying her flowers?

And then, *and then* he'd just *had* to grab that package of lotion and bodywash—the source of the scent he hadn't been able to stop thinking about—and say one of the most insane things he'd ever said to her.

Vanilla, cloves, and cinnamon; that scent was going to be the death of Theo. That smell had never been this distracting in his life, but there was something about it being on Lucy's skin that drove him crazy. But she'd been driving him crazy for weeks.

Well, if he was being honest, it had all started when she'd moved back to Cruickshank six months ago.

But that wasn't entirely true either. It had started seven years ago, that very first time he'd kissed her.

No, it was further back than that. All of this had really started in high school, it just wasn't nearly as intense as it was now.

And now he was saying ridiculous things like *this scent works on you.*

He'd had to walk away after he said it, otherwise he probably would've said something else stupid. Like that he, in fact, didn't think she was basic. Or that he found it pretty fucking cute that she liked all of that stuff that she was buying. And how much he liked that she was unapologetically herself.

Yeah, none of that was an option. Saying *any* of that out loud would be insane, mainly *because* he liked those things that drove him crazy. He didn't want to like *anything* about her. It was just too bad for him that he was too late for that.

Theo made his way through the aisles, grabbing what he needed for family dinner night at his parents'. His mom hadn't had time to get groceries and she'd gotten delayed that afternoon with her last batch of blondie brownies. They were a bonus item added to the online cookie orders that would be shipped out that week. So Theo had offered to go while she finished up with the bake and closed down Browned Butter. It was a good thing she'd written him a list, otherwise he would've forgotten half of what was needed.

This scent works on you.

Had he really told Lucy that? God, he was such an idiot. Maybe that was why they didn't always get along, because when she flustered him, he'd say the stupidest things to her. But then when he kept his mouth shut, he came off as a grumpy prick.

There really was no winning.

Theo made his way over to the next aisle but came to an abrupt stop when his cart crashed into someone else's, everything bouncing around. He looked up to find that it was Lucy's cart, because of course it was.

"I'm sorry," Theo apologized.

"No, I'm sorry. I wasn't paying attention."

Well, that made two of them. "It was clearly my fault." Theo waved a hand at their carts. "I ran into you."

"I whipped around that corner pretty fast," Lucy countered.

"Can you just let me apologize?"

"Fine. It's your fault." Lucy threw her arms in the air, very clearly exasperated with him.

"Thank you!" The words came out of his mouth with a little

too much force, and the second he said them, Lucy burst out laughing.

He liked that sound *a lot* . . . which annoyed him even more. "What's so funny?"

"Are we really arguing about who gets to apologize? We've reached a new low."

Theo couldn't help it: his own mouth cracked a smile. "It would appear so."

Lucy bit her bottom lip as she glanced at his cart. "I think you have a casualty." She pointed to the bag of chips that had been squashed by a container of sour cream. It had busted open and there were crushed blue corn chips spilling to the floor.

"Better them than the salsa."

"Not that salsa. I see you're doing Taco Tuesday," Lucy said, her eyebrows raising high. "Who's basic now?"

"Hey, it's Gia's thing. I don't argue with her." Theo grabbed the bag to stop more chips from spilling out. "And judging by the ingredients in your cart, you're doing Taco Tuesday too."

"Theo, it's always Taco Tuesday in my house. I was just stocking up on ingredients."

"Whatever . . . and what's wrong with my salsa?"

A knowing smile spread across her pretty mouth, and he hated how much he liked it. "If you aren't making it fresh, you should be buying the kind in the produce section. So. Much. Better." She reached into her own cart, showing him the container. "There's really no comparison. And I know that the pre-shredded cheese is more convenient, but if you want the best, you have to grate it yourself. But that's just a general cheese rule. For tacos, I would specifically recommend Cotija cheese; it crumbles quite nicely. Shouldn't you know this as a man of the culinary arts?"

Theo frowned at her. "I bake. If you want to discuss the uses of different flours, I'm your guy."

At his words Lucy's eyes widened, something flickering in the depths of that hazel green. But she didn't comment on it, instead looked back to Theo's cart. "Also, the premade guacamole is no good. Get some avocados, add fresh cilantro, lime juice, and some of this salsa. But make sure to drain it before you add it. Salt to taste."

"Anything else I'm doing wrong?" Theo waved his hand at his cart. "Did I grab the wrong tomatoes? Is my lettuce choice sub-par?"

Lucy shook her head. "Your tomato selection is good, but I'd go with the pre-shredded coleslaw mix. It lasts longer than the iceberg and has a better crunch. It's one of the few areas in which convenience can be to your benefit. Enjoy your tacos, Theo."

This time it was Lucy who maneuvered her cart around his and continued toward the dairy section. Theo watched her walk away until she turned a corner, somehow feeling even more off-kilter than a few minutes ago.

* * *

THEO COULD HEAR Taylor Swift playing the second he walked into his parents' house, and it got louder and louder as he made his way to the kitchen.

"Took you long enough," Gia said, dropping her pencil onto her notebook and pushing her chair back, the feet making a loud squeak on the tile floor.

"What are you talking about? It's a quarter till six." Theo's delay in getting out of Fresh Harvest was because he'd begrudgingly gone back and gotten all of Lucy's suggestions.

Fine, he wasn't a master taco maker. He never made them on

his own. Pico De Gallo had what were arguably the best tacos in North Carolina, and it was exactly five shops down from Browned Butter. If he was going to eat them, that was where he was going to go.

Theo's specialties were sandwiches, mainly because he was all about that bread. Ask him to make a grilled cheese, and he couldn't be beaten.

"Mom said you'd be here at five thirty, and I'm starving." Gia grabbed one of the bags from his hands.

"Really? We're counting fifteen minutes as late?"

"*Star-ving,*" Gia repeated with no small amount of drama as she started to pull out all of the contents. "Oh, this is the *good* salsa." She looked at the plastic container before popping the lid and pulling off the plastic seal. She then grabbed the bag of chips and ripped them open. A long, satisfied groan filled the kitchen as she crunched down on the salsa-covered chip. "My mouth is happy now," she said once she swallowed.

"You going to help me get dinner ready?" Theo asked as he grabbed a chip for himself and scooped up a generous amount of the salsa for his own taste test.

Damn it.

One bite and he knew Lucy was right: this salsa was far superior to anything he'd ever had in a shelf-stable jar. He still ate two more chips just to make sure.

"You going to cook the meat while I make the guacamole?" Theo asked.

"Sure," Gia said around another mouthful of chip and salsa. She started pulling out the other stuff from the bag, stopping to study the cheese. "This is different cheese."

"It crumbles. Apparently, it's really good on tacos."

"Fancy." She grabbed the sour cream in her other hand, taking them to the fridge. She put them away before pulling out the steak that their mother had marinated.

"Where's Dad?" Theo asked as he set up a cutting board and all of the ingredients Lucy said he needed.

"Working on his bike. Want me to get him to help?"

"Nah." Theo shook his head. "I think we can handle it. Turn Taylor up." He nodded to the little speaker in the corner.

"On it." Gia nodded and a couple of seconds later, "Anti-Hero" filled the kitchen. Theo knew this one well, and he and Gia were singing along to it together. Once the song ended, she turned the music down a little, and he looked up to see her staring at him.

"What?"

She waved the tongs at his setup. "*Fancy* cheese, the *good* salsa, a different lettuce topping altogether, and guacamole made from *scratch* . . . what's going on here?"

"Nothing." Theo shrugged before he moved his focus back down to his hands, running the knife around the outside of the last avocado. "Someone told me this was better."

"Who's *someone*?"

"None of your business." Theo carefully whacked the avocado pit with the knife before scooping out the contents into the bowl and adding them onto the mounting green pile.

"Is *someone* Joss?" Gia pressed.

"No." Theo was pretty sure Joss wouldn't be giving him any kind of cooking tips. It wasn't that things had ended badly . . . they'd just ended. He'd taken her to get a coffee that afternoon but before he could tell her how he felt, she'd been the one to call it quits.

But Theo didn't have time to dwell on what had transpired with Joss as Gia very loudly said, "Huh."

Theo looked back up at his sister. "What are you *huh*-ing?"

"Nothing." She shrugged before she looked back down to the meat she was cooking. "Just trying to figure out *why* you won't tell me who *someone* is. I mean, if it was Oscar, or Sasha, or even Jeremy, Lilah, or Caro, you'd just say it was one of them . . ."

"What are you getting at, Gia?"

"There's only one person who you wouldn't tell me gave you the suggestions."

"Is that so?"

"Yeah. The one person who gets under your skin like no other."

"Lucy doesn't get under my skin." She wasn't under anything that had to do with him.

Gia looked up, her mouth splitting into an enormous grin. "I knew it was Lucy."

"Just focus on cooking the meat." Theo pointed to the skillet in front of her with the spoon in his hand.

"*Fine.*" She emphasized the word with her own special amount of sass.

Theo just rolled his eyes, feeling his phone buzz in his pocket with a text. He pulled it out, seeing Lucy's name on the screen. That was all he needed to see before he unlocked the phone to get to his messages. She'd sent him a picture of a line of ducks walking outside Sweeny Park. The mama was followed by a dozen little babies and underneath the picture she'd typed out *bingo!*

He didn't understand the smile that pulled up the corners of his mouth . . . nor did he know what possessed him to respond with *best two out of three.*

CHAPTER FOUR
Friday Night Lights

Cruickshank was a football town when it came to Mount MacCallion High School. The stadium was always pretty full for home games, the bleachers packed with parents, teachers, alumni, and everyone else. That Friday night, it was no different. The Fighting Goats were currently undefeated and were playing the St. Sebastian Spartans in the regional finals.

The snares from both bands were playing as spectators filed into the stadium, the cheerleaders' shouts carrying across the air accompanied by the shrill whistles from the coaches as the players warmed up on the field.

"Doesn't this make you super nostalgic?" Sasha asked as they made their way through the line at the concessions stand. Neither of them had gotten dinner before the game and both were looking forward to an ice-cold soda and the chicken sandwich that Mount MacCallion was famous for. Lucy was just a little bit more excited for the sandwich than Sasha, as she hadn't gotten one on Monday.

"It does, actually." Lucy had always loved going to football games. First it had been to watch Jeremy, who was a few years older than her. Then it was to watch Oscar, Gavin, and even Theo when they'd all been in school together. The longer she worked at Mount MacCallion, the more she realized not all of high school had been so bad for her. There had been bright spots scattered in among the darkness.

When they got to the front of the line, Sasha ordered eight sandwiches, four double fries, four Cokes, and one Diet Dr Pepper for Lucy.

"Who are you getting all that food for? The football team?"

"The guys are coming. Oscar asked me to grab something for them to eat too."

"*All* of the guys?" Lucy asked before she could stop herself.

"I'm assuming Theo is coming." Sasha gave her a sly grin before grabbing a handful of napkins and shoving them in her purse.

"I didn't say anything about Theo. How many times do I have to tell you nothing is going on with him?"

"Luce, you could tell me a hundred times, or a thousand times, and I still wouldn't believe it."

Lucy just rolled her eyes as she grabbed the food and took a step back. "There are more guys than just Theo, you know."

"I do know that." Sasha nodded as she wrapped her fingers around the handles of the drink holders and followed Lucy out of the line. "But you were the one who told me Max and Jeremy weren't coming because they had a meeting for the hotel remodel with that one city council member and someone from Bergen and Hennings. And I knew you weren't asking about Gavin."

"Why wasn't Lucy asking about me?" a deep voice said from behind them.

They both turned to see Gavin and Oscar behind them.

"Oh, perfect," Sasha said as she passed her brother one of the drink holders. "We needed more hands."

Gavin took the bag of chicken sandwiches from Lucy before he repeated, "What weren't you asking about me?"

"If you were coming," Sasha answered.

"Then who *were* you asking about?" Gavin waggled his eyebrows.

"No one."

"No one being Theo?" Oscar asked.

"I was just trying to mentally prepare myself if I had to be in his presence." Not an untrue statement. She did indeed need to mentally prepare herself. She was still confused by what had happened the other day at Harvest Market . . . and how they'd weirdly fought and flirted. And then his response to her text message . . .

Not that it mattered, none of it mattered. He was dating someone else.

But *why* did she need to keep reminding herself of that fact?

"Well, then start mentally preparing yourself, sunshine." There was a knowing look in Gavin's eyes . . . one she was getting all too familiar with when it came to her friends. "He's here. He had to find Gia first. She didn't bring enough money for food so he's doing his brotherly duty."

"I'm sure he's thrilled." Sasha looked over her shoulder and flashed them a grin before she led the way up the bleachers. "Good thing he only has four more years until she goes off to college."

"You think it will end when she goes to college?" Oscar asked from behind Lucy. "The big brother responsibility never ends."

"And it isn't even *big brother* responsibility. It's just *brother* responsibility," Gavin said as they scooted into a row, Lucy and Sasha in front and Gavin and Oscar behind them.

"True," Oscar continued as they settled into their seats. "And it extends to other kinds of sisters too." He set the drink holder down before he reached over and tapped Lucy's nose. "Like ones we've personally adopted."

"Hey, I already have an overly protective big brother," she said, swatting him off. "I don't need two more."

Lucy glanced to the track to see if she spotted Theo, before her eyes moved to the field as the football players cleared off, making their way to the locker room for a pregame pep talk.

"What do you mean, two more?" Oscar asked as he grabbed his soda. "Try three more."

"Oh, I forgot about Max. Yeah, he's just as bad as Jeremy now that he's back in town."

"I wasn't talking about Max." Oscar shook his head. "I meant Theo."

Lucy let out a loud laugh. "Maybe when it comes to Sasha, but you aren't talking about Theo when it comes to me."

"What aren't they talking about when it comes to you and me?" a voice said from their right, and Lucy looked over to see Theo sidle into the row.

Gavin shifted over, giving Theo more space. "That there isn't any brotherly and sisterly love between the two of you."

Theo's blue eyes moved to Lucy's face, where they lingered for a moment too long. It was a cold night, but something warm slid along her spine at the look. "I'm going to have to agree with Lucy on that one."

"Hey! You agreed with me on something *last* week, and you promised it wasn't going to happen again."

"I'll do better."

"Hey, Luce, how's the musical going?" Oscar asked. "I haven't heard any updates in a while. Have you gotten all the music figured out?"

This year's winter musical was different from anything that

had been done before, a brainchild of Lucy's that had been approved by Mrs. Griffith. The students were the ones coming up with the story . . . and picking their own songs to sing. It had been a process, but one that Lucy had *very* much enjoyed.

"We're in the home stretch." Lucy nodded. "Costumes are all settled now that Caro is fixing my lead's dress. Though I think the real stars of the show are Gia and Chloe. Those two are scene stealers for sure."

"Really?" A smile turned up Theo's mouth.

Lucy liked it way too much. Which was probably why she couldn't help herself with the next thing she said. She grinned in that taunting way she liked to do with him, tilting her head to the side. "Speaking of Gia, I heard you took my taco suggestions, and that they were *the best ever.*"

"I knew she was going to rat me out." Theo shook his head as Gavin handed him two sandwiches.

"Yeah, your sister is good at that." Sasha ripped the top off one of the bags of fries and set it between her and Lucy before she turned her focus to Theo. "She and Chloe were at the café the other day getting some hot chocolates and they were telling me all about meeting Joss. So, what is going on with the two of you? You've been dating for a couple of weeks now."

Theo frowned at her. "What makes you think I'm going to tell you *anything* about Joss?"

"I'll tell you about my date with Adam," Sasha countered.

"That's a deal you'd need to make with one of them." Theo pointed a french fry at Gavin and Oscar. "They're the two gossips."

"Hey! We take offense to that," Oscar said.

"Take offense all you want. You two are the most meddlesome men I've ever met in my life."

"We're not meddlesome." Oscar put his hand to his chest in mock offense. "We just like to know what's going on so we can chase off any guys who aren't good enough."

"So, are we going to need to chase Adam off?" Gavin asked.

"I'm saying nothing unless Theo does." Sasha made a zipping motion over her mouth.

Lucy couldn't help but smile. Sasha was doing the Lord's work trying to get information. There might not be anything happening with Lucy and Theo, but she was still pretty curious as to what was going on with him.

"Then you're out of luck," Theo said.

But not a moment later did Oscar answer the question. "They aren't dating anymore."

Everything in Lucy stilled. Theo wasn't dating Joss anymore?

"Hey!" Theo looked at his friend. "What the hell, man?"

"You deserved it. You called us meddlesome and it isn't like they aren't going to find out anyway." Gavin gestured grandly to Lucy and Sasha. "I don't know if you've ever met my sister, but Lilah knows all and tells Caro and these two pretty much everything. Anyways"—he turned to Sasha—"spill."

"He FaceTimed his mother during dinner."

"What? You can't be serious." Oscar had been taking a sip of his Coke, but his mouth fell away from his straw.

"Yes, she was doing his laundry, which she apparently has never stopped doing even though he's thirty years old. And she needed to know if one of his shirts could go in the dryer. He also didn't tip our waitress."

"Oh, double red flag." Gavin shook his head. "What else happened?"

"He ordered chicken cordon bleu without ham and cheese."

"Isn't that just chicken?" Theo asked. Lucy couldn't help but look over at him, and she could tell he'd asked that question against his better judgment.

Their eyes caught for just a moment and so many questions ran through Lucy's mind. She wanted to know what happened with him and Joss. Wanted to know *why* they weren't dating anymore. Had Joss ended it? Or had he?

Too bad she wasn't going to ask any of those questions . . . so she focused on Sasha instead.

"Yes, it is *just* chicken, Theo. He also brought up his ex. *Seven times.*"

"You counted?" Lucy asked.

"Well, what else was I supposed to do? He didn't really stop talking long enough for me to say anything. See, Luce, you think your love life sucks. Just look at what I'm dealing with."

"I don't have a love life."

"You can't really have a love life if you aren't dating," Oscar said.

"Look. Who's. Talking." Lucy frowned at him.

"I'll have you know that I have a date tomorrow." His mouth split into a grin.

"With who?" Sasha said in mock outrage. "And how am I *just* finding out about this?"

"Because it happened about two hours ago. And it's with Edward."

There was a beat of silence in their little circle before Lucy said, "Edward Roberts? Max's assistant?"

When Max had left New York to turn the Kincaid into a hotel, Edward had come with him to help with the remodel. He still worked for Bergen and Hennings and went back and forth between Cruickshank and New York.

"Yes." Oscar shifted his shoulders in an excited little wiggle.

"Edward's gay? How did I miss that?" Sasha asked. "More importantly, how did I miss that you were into him?"

"I got a vibe last time he was at the bar. And then I ran into him at Kathleen's Corner Bookstore after work today. The vibe was still there. He was looking for a good read. I made a suggestion. He bought the book. He said we should get together to talk about it when he was finished. I said *why wait?* So, we're going out tomorrow."

"Smooth." Theo fist-bumped Oscar.

"Yes, well, it's always good to go after what we *really* want." He held Theo's gaze for a beat too long.

But this particular conversation came to an abrupt end as a loud voice boomed through the stadium: *"Hello, ladies and gentlemen, and welcome to Friday night footballlllllll!"*

Everyone's attention moved to the field, where students from both schools were lined up, creating a path for their respective teams to run through. The announcer was introducing St. Sebastian's when Lucy felt Theo's mouth at her ear.

Her skin immediately broke out into goose bumps.

"I'm calling dibs on a cliché for our bingo game." His warm breath on her skin made her own catch in her throat.

Lucy straightened, barely turning so that she could look at him. "Which one?"

"If we win, *the writing is on the wall.*" He pointed past her, and her gaze followed to the side of the school where that week's mural from the art department showed the mascot, Thaddeus the Goat, running off a group of Spartans.

Lucy looked back to him, her eyes narrowed. "Technically that's a picture and not writing, but I'll allow it."

"How magnanimous of you. You must've woken up on the *right* side of the bed this morning."

There was a glint in his eyes that made her stomach do a weird little flip. It had her picturing *him* on the right side of the bed . . . or any side of the bed, actually. But their gaze broke a second later as he pulled back and looked to the field.

"*And now for the Mount MacCallion Fighting Goats!*" The announcer's voice boomed through the stadium.

Lucy moved her own focus to the field goal, where the players clad in blue and white busted through a paper banner that read *Go Big Blue!* But as she watched them storm the field, her mind was actually flashing through moments of the past. Of *their* past. She was still thinking about beds . . . discarded clothes littering the floor, tangled sheets, and cozy blankets.

"Hey, Luce." An elbow nudged her in the side, and she looked over at Sasha, who whispered, "Be careful, your denial is showing."

* * *

WHAT IN GOD'S NAME had Theo been thinking? Why had he leaned forward and gotten that close to Lucy? Why had he let his lips touch her skin? And why, *why* had he taken a deep breath and let that spicy vanilla and clove scent fill his lungs?

Because you're clearly a masochist who really likes to suffer.

He'd known she was going to be at the game, and the second he saw her all rational sense went completely out of his brain. What was his problem?

She, *she* was his problem. She always drove him crazy, but this was reaching a new level that he didn't know how to deal with. But deal he would have to do.

The next two hours were a very specific brand of torture. Her hair was down, and whenever she moved it would brush against his legs or his hands. She had the softest hair, and he couldn't stop imagining what it would feel like to twine his fingers in the strands. It wasn't hard to imagine as he had a very clear memory of it.

But the smell of her and the memory of her hair weren't the only things driving him crazy; there was the sound of her laugh as she joked around with everyone, including him. It was sensory overload.

One of the few things he had going for him was that the game provided a little bit of distraction, especially as it was pretty tight all the way into overtime. Mount MacCallion won, thirty-eight to thirty-five, getting a field goal in the last four seconds of the game. The eruption from the crowd was deafening. Lucy and Sasha hugged as they jumped up and down. It was a moment before they let go and both turned to join in on the high fives the guys were passing out to each other.

Lucy lifted her hand in front of Theo, and he didn't even hesitate to slap his palm against hers. The gentle sting lasted for much longer than any of the others, not because it had been a harder hit, but because of the feel of her skin on his.

And he apparently wasn't done with the torture, because when Gavin suggested they go to Quigley's to celebrate, there wasn't a moment of hesitation from any of them. The thing was, they weren't the only ones who had that idea. On any given night at the bar, there tended to be a crowd; that night it was slammed.

Theo, Oscar, and Gavin got there before the girls. When they walked in, they spotted Jeremy and Max at a table by the dartboards, both of them half a beer in.

"I heard we won," Jeremy said as he pushed one of the empty seats out.

"It was a great game." Oscar sat down and started telling them all about it while Gavin and Theo headed to the bar to get a round of drinks. It was a little backed up, but there was no waiting as Gavin headed around the bar.

Theo leaned against the counter, looking out and across the room, taking everyone in. But as he scanned the bar, his focus landed on Lucy the second she and Sasha walked inside . . . and it stayed on her as she made her way to their table.

"Soooo, Theoooo," Gavin dragged out the two words, and Theo turned to find his friend behind him, his mouth split in a massive grin. "You going to tell me what's going on with you and Lucy or what?"

"Nothing," Theo said, just a little too fast. He paused for a second, pulling himself together. "Why would you think something is going on with her?"

"Because there is. You just tracked her all the way across the bar, and you've barely taken your eyes off her all night. You watched her more than you watched the game. Is that why things ended with Joss?"

"Things ended with Joss?" Caro asked as she stopped next to Gavin, pulling empty glasses off the counter and setting them in a bin.

"Yeah, because he's into Lucy," Gavin answered for Theo.

"*Ohhhhh*," Caro said excitedly.

"At least one of you has figured it out." Lilah had just sidled up to their group and passed two drinks across the counter to some patrons.

"What do you mean, one of us has figured it out?" The question was out of Theo's mouth before he could stop himself.

"Oh, I'm sorry, has he *not* figured it out yet?" Lilah turned to her brother.

"Apparently not." Gavin shook his head.

Well, if other people were noticing, he really was screwed. So totally screwed. He needed to get ahold of himself . . . get a little distance . . . but that wasn't going to be an option anytime soon.

"There's nothing to figure out." Theo frowned at all of them. "Can we just get our drinks?"

"Sure thing, sugar bean." Caro laughed as she grabbed a pitcher and started filling it up while Gavin stacked the glasses on a tray.

They were barely back to the table when Lucy turned to him, the tip of her nose still pink from sitting in the cold for hours. "Up for a rematch, Theodore?"

His eyes narrowed and his frown deepened as he set the two pitchers of beer on the table. "Are you ever going to stop calling me that?"

"Nope. It's your name, isn't it?"

"Yes, one that only my mother and grandmother call me, and just when I'm in trouble."

"You're thirty-one. Do you still get in trouble with your mom?" she asked, that grin of hers playing at her lips again.

Her smile always had the ability to distract him, probably because it hadn't been directed at him very often. And because it was so damn beautiful.

"All the time. I think she's grounded me three times today. Anyway, you know it annoys me when *you* call me that."

"Fine, if we play and you win, I won't call you that anymore. But if I win, you can't correct me anymore. Or are you scared of getting beaten again?"

"I'm not scared of anything."

"Jellyfish," Lucy countered.

"Hey, you try getting stung by a swarm of jellyfish when you're five years old and it's the first time you've ever gone to the beach. It's more rational than being scared of lizards."

A full-body shiver ran through her. "I don't like the way they move. Now, are we playing or what?"

Theo sighed as he rolled up the sleeves of his shirt. "Yes, we're playing. For the name *and* the same stakes as last time. I'm getting that bottle of whiskey."

Lucy's eyes lingered on his arms for just a second before she looked back up at him. "Fine, I'll get you your whiskey if you win, but if I win you have to make me that bourbon toffee apple cake for Thanksgiving."

Theo inwardly groaned. It was the most complicated and labor-intensive cake he'd ever made. He'd done it a few years ago, and while it had been a success, he'd vowed never to make it again. The apples had to be slowly cooked in a bourbon sauce that took hours, the spun sugar was a bitch to work with and had a tendency to dissolve if there was too much humidity in the air, and the soaked sponge had to be carefully layered with frosting.

"Deal," Theo agreed. He wasn't making that cake, so he *would* be winning this game.

Lucy dug around in her purse for a moment before she pulled out that same purple pen she'd used last time. Max passed her a napkin from the dispenser, and she wrote their names across the top. "Same rules as last time?" She looked up at him.

"Same rules as last time," he agreed.

Sasha slapped a five-dollar bill on the high-top table. "I'm putting my money on Lucy," she said.

"Me too." Max threw his money down.

"I've got to go with my man." Oscar added his wager to the growing pile.

"Well, you guys can figure that out." Lucy indicated the pile before she turned and headed toward the cabinet where the darts were kept.

Theo's eyes again followed her, just like they always did these days. He was so easily distracted by the sway of her hips. Not wanting anyone to see him watching her again, he forced himself to look away. It was just too bad for him that Jeremy had caught him in the act.

"You okay, man?" Jeremy grinned in an obnoxiously knowing way.

"I'm great. Just great."

"You sure about that?"

But Theo was saved from answering as Lucy was back in front of him.

"What are you two whispering about?" she asked, handing Theo the green set of darts he always used.

"Theo's just trying to get me to bet on him."

"Uh huh," Lucy said slowly as she looked between the two men. "Well, who are you betting on, then?"

"My money's on Theo." There was something in the way that Jeremy said it that made Theo think his friend was talking about more than the game of darts.

"Traitor." Lucy lightly punched her brother on the shoulder.

"Got to keep things interesting," Jeremy said.

"I guess so." She turned to Theo. "Ready to lose?"

"I won't be losing. You won last, so you're up first." He nodded to the board.

Lucy pulled out three hot-pink darts from her case before moving into position. A weird little sensation prickled at the back of his neck and he glanced to the group of guys playing at the board at the end. There was a tall blond who wasn't paying attention to his friends but was instead looking at Lucy.

She was too beautiful for her own good, and it felt like every time he was at this bar with her, he always caught guys looking at her.

He didn't like it.

A loud cheer pulled his focus back to his own group. Lucy had thrown all of her darts, hitting the one, two, and three.

"Your turn." She made a grand sweeping motion for him to take the spot to throw from.

Theo moved into place, quickly throwing his darts. He got the one and the two, but just missed the three, landing in the seventeen instead. He blamed it on the fact that out of the corner of his eye, he caught blondie looking at Lucy again.

Get it together, man.

But there was no *getting it together*. Theo lost the first round . . . by a lot.

* * *

THE CHILL THAT HAD SET into Lucy's bones when they'd been watching the football game was long gone. She was warm from the top of her head to the tips of her toes.

Maybe a little too warm. She was wearing a thick sweater and kept pushing the chunky sleeves up to her elbows . . . where they'd inevitably just fall back into place again. There was also the crowd around them and the crackling fire burning a few feet away. Or it could be the bourbon that was now coursing through her body.

Once the first round of beer was gone, Gavin had disappeared to the bar to grab some spiced apple bourbon drinks. The tumblers had a massive round ice cube floating around the amber liquid, and the cold drink burned in her veins.

But maybe the real cause of her warmth was Theo. She was having too much fun, the two of them trading spaces as they took their turns at the board, and trading jabs while they did it. When she ended up losing their second game of darts, she found that she didn't care.

And that was when she realized the real reason she was so warm was because she was playing with fire . . . and she wasn't the only one who knew it either.

At that moment Sasha paused her game with Gavin at the next dartboard over and held her tumbler up in the air—giving Lucy a significant look over the rim—before polishing off the last of her drink. "You guys want another round of these?"

Max, Jeremy, and Oscar were at the pool table a few feet away and they all agreed instantly.

"Perfect." Sasha looked at Gavin and Theo. "Why don't the two of you practice for a little bit while Lucy and I go get this round." And with that, she looped her arm through Lucy's and pulled her to the bar.

Lilah looked over at them from where she was pouring a scotch. "Whatcha want?"

"Another round of spiced apple bourbons and for Lucy to tell us what the hell she's doing with Theo."

"I've been wondering that myself," Caro said as she joined their group. "I can see you flirting with him all the way over here."

"We all can." Lilah nodded as she grabbed a tray and set seven tumblers down in a circle.

"Can you please just admit it?" Sasha pulled on Lucy's arm.

"Fine. There is . . . *something*. But I don't know what it is, or if it's even reciprocated."

"Oh, honey." Lilah shook her head pityingly as she gently dropped an ice ball into each glass. "It's reciprocated. I can practically smell his pheromones from over here . . . and yours."

"*Grossss*." Sasha dragged out the word and did an exaggerated body shiver.

"Shut up," Lucy told Sasha before she turned to Caro and Lilah. "What do I do?"

"Grab him and kiss him?" Caro suggested.

"Isn't that what you did with Max?" Sasha asked.

"Well, I was kind of crying *at* him first, but basically." She nodded before pulling out a clean pitcher and putting it under the tap.

"I'm not grabbing him and kissing him in here."

"Ask him to go outside for some fresh air," Lilah said as she added shots to each glass.

"Seriously? That's the best you've got? I need help here."

"Well, that's for sure," Sasha agreed.

"You know what?" Lucy turned to her friend. "You are *no* help."

"Luce, what do you *want* to do?" Caro asked.

God, she had *no* clue what she wanted. Well, when it came to Theo she didn't know. "I . . . I want another drink." *Or three*.

"Mind if I buy it for you?" a low raspy voice said from Lucy's right.

She turned to the man next to her, looking up . . . up . . . up and into his face. As she'd gone to the football game that night, she was wearing her bright blue Chuck Taylors, and there was pretty much no added height to her five-foot-three frame. As this man was a good six-foot-something, there was a definite height difference.

He was from the group of men who'd been playing darts next to them. His square jaw was clean-shaven and he had blond hair and cool blue eyes. Damn, he was handsome.

But she wasn't into him.

Probably because she liked guys with brown hair, thick beards, and deep blue eyes that made her feel like she was sinking into a warm bath.

Not guys. Just *guy*. One guy. She wanted Theo.

"Now, why would you want to buy me a drink?" Lucy asked, trying to figure out how to let the man down easy.

"Because I think you're beautiful."

A line like that should totally work for her. Lucy had confidence enough to know that there were plenty of men out there who appreciated her curves. Men who liked a woman with rounder hips and a bigger butt. And she liked it when she was appreciated.

Except he wasn't the one she wanted to be getting the appreciation from.

"That's a little forward from a man whose name she doesn't even know," Lilah said in her no-nonsense tone as she added the spiced apple mix to the tumblers.

"I guess it is. I'm Joseph." He stuck out his hand for Lucy to shake, the sheepish smile pulling up his mouth was one that made her think he was a good old southern gentleman.

"Lucy." She stuck her hand out too. His grip was firm, but not overly so.

"Well, *Joseph*," Caro emphasized his name as she leaned over the counter, "you just walked into the lioness den to hit on my sister, Lucy, so I hope you know what you're in for."

"So, what you're telling me is that it was a mistake to wait for her to get away from all of the lions over there?" He waved over her shoulder, indicating the group of guys still at the dartboard and pool table.

"They're actually much less dangerous than these three." Lucy indicated the women around her.

"So should I just hand you my number and back away slowly?" he asked, holding his hand out again, this time with a napkin sticking out between two of his fingers.

"No, you should just back away slowly," Theo said from behind Lucy.

His voice was a little gruffer than usual, and it rasped in her ears. It took everything in her to combat the shiver that ran down her spine, but she managed to keep it under control. What she couldn't control was the need to look over her shoulder and up into his blue eyes, eyes that were intently focused on her.

He wasn't even looking at Joseph. Nope, he only had eyes for her. Why did it thrill her so much?

"When did you start answering for me, Theodore?"

"I wouldn't dream of answering for you, Lucy. I was answering for me. Can I have a word with you?"

Lucy turned back to Joseph, who looked both disappointed and annoyed. "If you'll excuse me, I need to go talk to my friend. It was nice to meet you, Joseph."

"Yeah." He took a step back, before sliding the piece of paper with his phone number into his pocket. "You too, Lucy." And with that he turned around and headed back to his friends.

Lucy waited a couple of seconds before turning back to Theo— purposely not catching the eyes of any of her friends as she did so. "Where would you like to talk?"

"Outside."

"See." Lilah lightly slapped the bar with her palm. "Didn't I just suggest you two go outside to talk?"

Theo looked at Lilah, his eyebrows bunching together in confusion. "What? Who did you suggest that to?"

"No one." Lucy shook her head before making a motion toward the door. "After you."

"No, ladies first. I insist."

"Fine." Lucy reached out and grabbed Theo's hand, pulling him away from the bar. He didn't even hesitate in following behind her. In fact, the hand in hers moved, their fingers twining together as his grip tightened. Meanwhile the other moved to her hip as they made their way through the crowd.

She'd tried to take the lead by pulling him, and here he was guiding her. Yet another thing that thrilled her beyond words. Neither of them let go as they walked through the door, Lucy continuing to pull him to the other side of the building . . . and away from the windows.

The second they were in the clear, she turned to him, reluctant to let go of his hand. "Okay, Theodore, what did you want to—"

But that was all she was able to say before he had both hands on her hips and was pulling her against him, covering her lips with his.

CHAPTER FIVE
Lose Control

*W*hat with the family business and his profession, Theo felt like he was fairly knowledgeable when it came to baked goods. Cupcakes, cakes, cookies, pies, he'd had them all and tried more flavors than he could name. But in all his life nothing— *nothing*—had ever tasted sweeter than Lucy Buchanan's mouth.

That fact was true seven years ago, and it was still true now.

Bourbon, apple, cinnamon, cloves, and vanilla. It was because of those last three that he was in his current predicament. That scent had been haunting him for a week, and it filled his head as Lucy had pulled him across the bar. That alone would've been enough for him to lose his mind, but then there was the added fact that her hand had been in his. She hadn't even flinched when he'd laced their fingers together, and he didn't miss how she'd pressed herself into his hand at her hip.

It all magnified the possessive feeling in his chest, the one that had always been there like a flickering flame but was now a full-on inferno. The second he'd seen blondie start to talk to her, it was like someone had poured kerosene on him.

When he'd asked her for a word, he'd had absolutely no idea what he was going to say to her. All he knew was that he wanted to get her away from that guy . . . get her alone to tell her . . . something. *Anything.*

Maybe that she was driving him out of his ever-loving mind. That would've been a great place to start.

But then they'd gotten outside, and she'd let go of him, and the very last thing he wanted to do was talk. So, he'd just done the thing that he'd wanted to do for months now: pulled her into his chest and kissed her.

There'd been a moment, just a second of sanity after his lips touched hers when her body tensed, that he thought he'd gone a step too far. But that fear was gone when she started to kiss him back, her lips parting and letting him in as she wrapped her arms around his shoulders. Before he knew it, he had her pushed against the brick wall, one hand at the back of her head, his fingers in her hair as he deepened the kiss. The other was still at her hip, holding her against him.

They got lost in each other, neither of them coming up for a breath, neither of them letting go. It wasn't until a shrill wolf whistle split the night air that Theo reluctantly pulled his mouth from Lucy's.

"Get a room," someone called out while people laughed.

Theo had never been big on public displays of affection, but in that moment, he didn't care that someone saw them kissing. He wasn't embarrassed in the slightest that they'd both lost control for a moment. And as he looked down into Lucy's face, he was pretty sure she wasn't either. The streetlights were bright behind him, and he could clearly see the dazed look in her eyes, and the flush on her cheeks.

"You kissed me," she whispered.

"You kissed me back. Were you going to take that guy's number?" The hand on her hip instinctively tightened.

"No. I was planning on letting him down easy before you walked up. As it turns out, I'm kind of into somebody else."

"Is that so?" His hand at the back of her head moved to her face, his palm cupping her jaw.

"Yeah."

"For how long?"

"Subconsciously?" She smiled, biting at her bottom lip as she tilted her head to the side in thought. Theo couldn't help but move his thumb to her mouth, pulling that lip from her teeth. "I'm pretty sure it's been months. I just didn't realize it until you started dating someone else. What really happened with Joss?"

"She ended it before I could. As it turns out, it's really hard to date someone when you're into someone else."

"Yeah, I'd imagine it is."

"So, what do you want this time, Luce?"

"I don't know what I want beyond wanting *you* . . . but I'm not staying here, Theo. I'm not moving back to Cruickshank permanently."

"I know you aren't. So, you don't want anything complicated. Just sex?" Could he go down that path and not fall for her again? He had no idea, but the need inside of him was too much to deny any longer. He wanted her. He didn't care how much he got, or for how long, he just wanted *something*.

"Just sex." She nodded.

"Done."

"Now that we've established what we're doing, kiss me again." She moved her hand to the front of his shirt, fisting the flannel before pulling him closer to her.

It was ingrained in him to always want to do the opposite of what Lucy wanted. To needle and poke her and drive her as crazy as she drove him, but there was no denying her. In that moment there was nothing he wanted more *in the world* than to put his mouth on hers.

She opened for him immediately, their tongues twisting. Lucy's hand tightened in his shirt, the fabric pulling at his shoulders. Her other hand was at the nape of his neck, her fingers playing in his hair. It was something she'd always done before. Something that drove him out of his mind.

"Okay." He pulled away from her mouth, shaking his head as he tried to catch his breath. "We have to stop."

"Why?"

"Because at some point we have to walk back into that building where our friends—and your family—are currently located and I would prefer not to embarrass myself."

"Oh . . . yeah . . . *that*. Can't we just go? I'm one hundred percent sure it's no secret to any of them what we're doing out here."

"Of that I have no doubt. They all figured it out before we did. But your purse and our coats are inside."

"I could make it home without them," she said as a shudder ran through her body.

Theo lifted his eyebrows.

"It's not the cold making me shiver. And I have a hide-a-key. We can get into my place, no problem."

"Who said we're going to your house?" he asked as he moved both of his hands to her arms, rubbing his palms up and down in an attempt to keep her warm.

"Oh, is that how it's going to be?" Her eyes narrowed in that way he knew meant a challenge.

"Yeah, that's how it's going to be."

"Fine." Lucy pulled him close again for one last kiss before grabbing one of his hands and leading him back to the front door. "We're finishing our last round of darts and changing the bet. Loser goes home with the winner."

"Agreed." Theo again laced his fingers with Lucy's, reveling in the feel of her hand in his. He didn't let go when they got back to the table either. The need to touch her was more of a demand at this point.

"You two good now?" Sasha grinned as she looked at their joined hands.

"Work out whatever you needed to work out?" Jeremy asked.

"I don't know what you guys are talking about." Theo shook his head, squeezing Lucy's hand before reluctantly letting go. If they were going to play, they were going to need two hands.

"You know you're not fooling us. Right?" Oscar chimed in.

"Dude, Lucy's lipstick is *in* your mustache." Gavin pointed to Theo's face.

"Shit." Theo immediately reached up, wiping his palm over his mouth.

"Yeah, that's not going to help you." Max laughed as he pushed one of the apple bourbon tumblers across the table. "Take a drink, man."

Theo downed a good portion of it before he looked over at Lucy, catching her eyes, which were brighter than usual, a lightness in them that he hadn't seen in a very long time.

Lucy moved closer to him, grabbing the glass from his hand. "I believe you're up first as I lost the last round." She nodded to the board before she tilted her head back and took a long drink. When she brought the glass down, she licked her lips.

It was so fucking sexy he couldn't think straight.

"You're playing dirty," he said.

"You ain't seen nothing yet." Her lips slowly curved up into a seductive smile and it was then that he noticed her red lipstick was lightly smudged around her mouth.

Theo leaned forward, bringing his mouth to her ear. "Just so you know, I will be kissing off every last bit of that lipstick before the night is over."

She turned, her lips brushing his earlobe. "I can think of a few other uses for my lipstick."

Her words caused him to inhale quickly, which was a huge mistake since he was so close to her. His lungs and head were now filled with vanilla and cloves, not the best circumstances for him right before taking his turn.

They pulled apart when Gavin loudly cleared his throat next to them. "So, apparently this is going to be different than last time. You two aren't hiding anything this time around?" He gestured to the two of them.

"Last time?" Oscar asked. "What do you mean, last time?"

"You knew what happened seven years ago too?" Lucy turned to Gavin, her mouth open in surprise.

"*Too?*" Theo looked to Lucy. "Who else knew?"

"Sasha, but I didn't tell her. Apparently, she . . . uh . . . caught us making out."

"You weren't very stealthy." Sasha shook her head. "At least I didn't catch you in the act."

"You what?" Theo rounded on his friend.

"Wait a second." Lucy moved her hands in the air to get Sasha's attention. "You knew that Gavin knew?"

"How did any of you know and not tell me?" Oscar asked in mock outrage.

"You were off at college." Sasha waved off her brother's protests. "Gavin and I had to confide in each other. But we promised not to tell anyone else since these two clearly wanted to keep it a secret."

"Did you know?" Oscar asked Jeremy.

"I didn't find out until Lilah told me last Monday."

"Hey, that's when Caro told me." Max *cheers*'ed his glass against Jeremy's.

"Can open, worms *everywhere*." Theo grabbed the glass of bourbon back from Lucy and downed the last of it.

"Well, now that we've gotten all *that* out of the way, let's finish this game." Lucy patted Theo on the chest. "Unless you would like to discuss it further."

"Not at all." Theo shook his head, setting the empty glass on the table before grabbing his darts. He moved around Lucy, doing his best to focus as he took aim. They were going to need to wrap this game up real quick so that he could get her naked and underneath him.

Or naked and over him; he really wasn't too picky at this point.

* * *

THEO *JUST* LOST THE THIRD ROUND, only one throw behind Lucy. But as he was going home with her, he didn't really think himself much of a loser. Besides, he'd had a few beers and two of those spiced apple bourbons, so he was in no condition to drive. His house was a few miles away while hers was only a ten-minute walk . . . seven if they were quick about it.

Considering what he was dealing with, it was a miracle that he'd been so close to winning. Throughout the entire round she kept touching him, running her palms across his chest or up his arm. Though it wasn't like he was exactly keeping his hands to himself either. He grabbed her hips on more than one occasion, pulling her in close before whispering something into her ear.

"You ready to go?" he asked as his mouth moved along her jaw.

She pulled back, biting at her bottom lip again in a slightly nervous way. "Yeah."

Theo let go before he grabbed her coat, holding it open. Lucy slipped her arms into the sleeves, and once he had it settled on her shoulders, he gathered her chestnut-brown hair in his hand, pulling it free. She tilted her head to the side while he did it, and he got a glimpse of a tattoo where her neck met her shoulder. It was the black outline of a kite, the string disappearing down the back of her sweater.

Lucy had only had one tattoo seven years ago, a vine of roses on her hip and upper thigh. He'd been fascinated with it then and was more than excited to get reacquainted with it that evening.

Though now he was thinking about her new tattoo . . . where that string led down her back . . . and if there was something at the end of it. He wanted to know if there were more tattoos on her body. He wanted to know what else had changed over the years.

"You in a hurry to get out of here or something?" Gavin waggled his eyebrows.

"Yeah, you two have plans after this?" Max laughed.

"Why weren't we invited?" Sasha added.

Theo really didn't care about his friends razzing him, because he was about to go home with Lucy.

"We're just giving you guys an opportunity to talk about us once we leave." Lucy pulled the strap of her purse over her shoulder.

"Yeah, there will be some talking." Oscar frowned. "I still can't believe I was the last to know about this."

"You're going to have to get over that," Sasha told her brother.

"You two have fun!" Max said.

"But not too much fun." Jeremy shook his head.

"Okay, you all better enjoy this while you can." Theo frowned at his friends. "Because there will come a time that I'll be giving it back tenfold. Especially you two." He pointed at Sasha and Gavin.

"Hey, why are we worse than them?" Sasha asked in mock outrage.

"You just are," Theo said as he held his hand out for Lucy. "Good night." And for the first time that evening, Theo was the one who led her through the bar.

The second they were outside—and clear of the patrons coming and going from the door—Theo pulled her to him again, covering her mouth with his. It was a good couple of seconds before he finally pulled back. "I've been wanting to do that since we walked back in there."

"Well, there are a number of things that I want to do to you. Take me home, Theo."

"Let's go, then." He kissed her one last time before he pulled away and they started heading through downtown Cruickshank.

It was cold outside, but it wasn't a bad walk to Lucy's house. Just a couple of blocks down, a turn to the right, and another few blocks before they'd get to her neighborhood. The streetlights were all shining, their amber glow illuminating the sidewalks. It was just after eleven, so all of the shops and restaurants were closed. The people mingling about on the street were most likely doing a bar crawl, going among the handful of establishments open late.

"So," Theo started. "I know how Sasha knew what happened; how did Caro and Lilah find out?"

Lucy hesitated for a moment before awkwardly clearing her throat. "You might've come up in conversation at our last girls' night after I found out about Joss . . . and they might've all correctly called me out for whatever this is." She gestured between the two of them. "And in my denying it, I might've accidently let it slip that we'd slept with each other previously."

"So, I'm assuming you never mentioned anything before then."

"Nope." She shook her head. "And you didn't either."

"Nope. We'd agreed it was just sex then. There was no need to complicate it any further getting everyone else involved."

Just sex . . . exactly like it was this time too. It hadn't worked out well for him then, and he wasn't sure it would this time either. But it was what it was. He'd deal with the consequences—whatever they were—later.

"Well, I think the cat is out of the bag this time." Not wanting to stay on that particular topic of conversation, Theo moved the subject along. "Ever had that one on your cliché bingo card?"

"Well, as Estee often likes to jump into my grocery bag before I can unload it, yes, I have. She's also fond of getting into my suitcase when I pack."

Theo was well acquainted with Lucy's cat, the dark gray Scottish fold with orange eyes and a penchant for mischief. He'd seen the videos on Lucy's social media when she'd found the cat on the side of a busy road in LA three years ago. The feline was easily won over with treats and belly rubs. Though the belly rubs were always on Estee's terms.

Lucy leaned into Theo as they crossed the road from the downtown area and made their way onto Avondale Drive.

He turned his head, pressing another kiss into her hair and she shivered. "That the cold or something else?"

"Both."

"Well, you'll be warmed up in no time at all."

"Of that I have no doubt."

When they got to the house, Theo was a little relieved to see no lights flickering through the windows, meaning her dad was asleep. Not that he thought Wes was going to come out with a shotgun or something. It just had the potential to make for an awkward conversation.

They made their way through the yard and to the detached garage. There was a porch light above her door, illuminating the stairs that led to her little loft apartment. It took Lucy a moment to fumble around in her purse for the keys. All the while Theo played with the ends of her hair.

The click of the lock echoed in the cold air before Lucy pushed the door open and they were inside. They were greeted with warm air, the soft glow from a lamp in the corner, and a loud meow from Estee, who was on the squishy teal sofa.

Theo shut and locked the door behind them. Lucy flipped on the overhead light before making her way into the living room. She pulled her coat off and tossed it onto the magenta accent chair, toeing off her Converse sneakers in the process.

It wasn't the first time he'd ever been in a space that belonged to Lucy. She'd snuck him into her bedroom a number of times during those months they'd been sleeping together. Just like he'd taken her to the shabby house he'd once shared with Gavin. It had been easier to go over there as Gavin was working at Quigley's and typically didn't get home until after one in the morning. Theo had thought it was the perfect setup as Lucy was always long gone before Gavin got back . . . but as he'd learned that evening, they weren't as slick he'd thought.

He pulled off his jacket as he looked around, taking in the turquoise walls. "I haven't been up here since you unpacked. You painted. Wasn't it yellow before?"

It all contrasted well with the teal sofa, magenta accent chair, and deep purple rug that took up the majority of the living room. Her throw pillows were sapphire blue and emerald green and the floor lamp in the corner sported a burnt-orange tasseled shade. He stopped by the sofa, leaning down to scratch Estee's exposed belly. The cat's purr started to fill the room.

"Yeah. It was a girls' night with *a lot* of wine when Caro, Lilah, and Sasha helped me paint," she said before pointing toward the kitchen. "Do you, uh, want a drink or something?"

"Sure, but probably not any more alcohol." As he didn't plan on going to sleep anytime soon, he didn't want to drink anything else that would make him tired.

"I have that cider I bought the other day. Want me to heat some up?" She moved toward her tiny kitchen.

"I can help you." Theo followed.

"Well, take off your boots first." Lucy looked over her shoulder and pointed to his feet. "I do believe you're staying awhile."

"I do believe that I am." It wasn't lost on him that they'd never stayed the night with each other . . . never slept in the other's bed . . . that he'd never slept next to her. But tonight would be a different story.

Theo made quick work of his shoes, putting them by the door, before joining Lucy in the kitchen. She was messing with the burner, trying to get it to light. The white stove was on the small side . . . though most stoves seemed smaller to him, what with what he used at the bakery and the six-burner he had at his own home.

Once the flame popped up, Lucy reached for a pot that hung from a hook on the wall. There were a few open shelves on the other side with half a dozen mismatched cups, plates, and bowls stacked up.

Lucy reached for the jug she'd already gotten from the fridge, pouring its contents into the pot before setting it back on the counter. Deciding to be useful, Theo grabbed the cap, popping it back on before returning it to the fridge. It was one of those retro refrigerators—mint green and also smaller than normal. It was covered in random magnets that Theo assumed Lucy had collected over the years.

A loud meow filled the kitchen as Estee came padding in, circling their feet and rubbing her body against their legs.

"I fed her before I went to the game, but she wants a snack. Can you stir this while I get her something? She won't leave us alone until I do."

"By all means." He waved a hand at the cat before they switched places, Theo grabbing the handle of the whisk and taking up where she left off.

Lucy moved back toward the living room and the mustard-yellow cabinet that apparently held the cat's treats.

"If you've got that under control, I'm just going to . . . uh . . . freshen up," Lucy said from behind him.

Theo turned around just as she disappeared into the bathroom.

* * *

LUCY LEANED BACK AGAINST THE DOOR, taking a deep steadying breath. Her hands were shaking a little while her heart was beating out of her chest.

Theo was in here, in her home.

She didn't know why she was so nervous. She'd done this before, had done this with *him* before, and yet there she stood, with a handful of lingerie clutched in her fist. She had no clue what she'd even gotten, she'd just stuck her hand in the drawer and grabbed what she could. She set the pile on the counter, picking through it.

If someone had told her when she'd woken up that morning that this was going to be how the day ended, she would've said they were crazy, there was no way. Because if she'd been even remotely prepared, she wouldn't have been wearing the nude bra that was more for comfort than style, nor the cotton pair of pink panties that could only be described as *granny*.

She held up a red lace teddy, pretty sure it wasn't the night for that. They needed something with easy removal, not complicated snaps. A bra and panties would do the trick. Too bad nothing she'd grabbed was a matching set. In the bra department her options were leopard or black lace.

"Black lace it is." She nodded as she set it aside, now looking for a pair of panties. There was a green satin pair with black lace edges. "Perfect," she said before she opened the top drawer of the vanity and shoved everything else inside.

Lucy stripped down in record time, making quick work of her "freshening up" before slipping into the lingerie. She stuck her hand inside the cups of the bra, pulling up and giving her cleavage the best possible opportunity. The bra was definitely more for looks, the underwire digging into her skin. Good thing she wouldn't be wearing it for long.

She had a thin cotton robe on the back door, black with big flowers on it. Tying the sash in place, she gave herself one last look in the mirror before taking a deep breath and heading out of the bathroom.

Theo had done more than heat up the cider. The overhead light was off, and he'd turned on the strand of twinkle lights that hung across the beam that separated the living room from her bedroom. The electric fireplace was also on, adding an amber glow to the room along with the candles he'd lit. He'd found the toasted marshmallow one that sat on her dresser, and the spiced chai on her bookcase.

There was also music playing; she hadn't heard it in her rush to get ready but could now pick out the deep sultry voice of a man.

Theo had apparently figured out how to pair his phone to her Bluetooth speakers.

Theo was standing in front of the television, looking at the wall that she'd covered in a wide variety of art. He turned at the sound of the door opening, his eyes going wide as he pulled in a breath through his nose, his nostrils flaring. He didn't comment on her change of attire, instead just held out an orange mug with tiny white hearts patterned on it. Had he somehow known it was her favorite?

"Your cider."

She crossed over to him, taking the mug from his hands. "Thank you," she said before taking a sip. He'd gotten it to the perfect temperature, the sweet apple and cinnamon flavor filling her taste buds and making her go warm all over.

"I've just been admiring your art wall. Where'd you get that?" He pointed to a framed vintage map of the world.

"A flea market in Pasadena."

"And that?" He indicated the old guitar that had been turned into a clock.

"When I went to New York with Caro."

He took a sip from his own mug, covered in a black and white cow print. "Your record collection is pretty impressive."

They were hung up in a square, all four of them signed by the respective artists—Joni Mitchell, Dolly Parton, Stevie Nicks, and June Carter Cash.

"But I think my favorite is that one." He nodded to the framed drawing that was the main focal point. It was a charcoal sketch that Caro had done a few years ago. It was Lucy's favorite as it was a portrait of their mother.

Rachel was wearing a crown of flowers, and her dark hair was blowing behind her in the wind, the ends turning into birds that were taking flight. Her lips were parted, her head tilted back as if she were singing.

Rachel had always loved music, something she'd instilled in all three of her children, but most specifically in Lucy.

There was something about watching Theo as he took it all in, as he looked at her little home, that felt more personal than she was prepared for . . . an intimacy that she'd never experienced with him before.

A feeling that was intensified as she was standing next to him wearing next to nothing. Her eyes lingered on his beard, and she had a sudden urge to rasp her fingertips over it.

Theo's focus moved from the wall of art and back to her. "This whole place is so unmistakably you."

"I can't tell if you mean that as a compliment."

"I do. I very, very much do." He smiled before he leaned down and kissed her. She could taste the apple and cinnamon on his lips, so much stronger than the bourbon drink at the bar. He pulled back after a moment, his eyes lingering on her mouth. "You should finish your cider."

Lucy took a step back, putting a little space between them before she lifted the mug and took a good, long drink. It warmed her up way more than the bourbon had. She'd finished about half of it before setting it on the coffee table. Theo followed her lead, putting his down too. And then he moved in closer to her, his hands landing on her hips as he pulled her in, their bodies starting to sway with the music.

"Have I told you how much you drive me crazy?" he asked as one of his hands grabbed hers, weaving their fingers together. "The way you smell." He pressed his face into her throat. "I've been absolutely obsessed with vanilla, cloves, and cinnamon for a week. I haven't been able to get it out of my head. Haven't been able to get *you* out of my head. And then I walk in here and the whole place smells like you."

"Well, you're the one who lit the candles."

He pulled away enough to look into her eyes, giving her what she could only describe as a wicked grin. "You can just call me a masochist."

Lucy pulled in a shallow breath, finding it harder to breathe. "How much longer do you plan on prolonging the torture?"

"I haven't figured it out yet." He lowered his mouth to hers, this time his tongue slipping between her lips. And then his other hand was in her hair, tilting her head to the side so he could deepen the kiss. But it wasn't deep enough for Lucy; she wanted more.

Theo groaned into her mouth, his lips leaving hers only long enough to say, "The taste of you drives me even crazier than the smell of you." And then he was kissing her again, his body no longer swaying to the music but backing her toward the bed.

Both of his hands were at her waist again, and she felt his fingers at the front of her robe, untying the sash. Then he was parting the fabric, his palms sliding across the bare skin of her shoulders and pushing the robe away before it fell to the floor. He pulled back enough to look down at her, his breath ragged as his gaze traveled the length of her body.

"Holy shit, Lucy." He reached out and traced the curve of her breasts, his fingertips barely touching her, and yet they were like a brand on her skin. And then they moved to the very top of her panties, where he fingered the lace. "Is this for me?" he asked before his eyes were back on her face.

"Yes."

"And what about this?" He moved his hand down, finding the heat between her legs.

"Yes." She licked her lips as she grabbed his shoulders.

"And is this for me?" His fingers moved under the fabric before he slid them inside of her, finding her wet.

"Yes." Her nails dug into him as her head fell back and she moaned to the ceiling.

"Good." He pressed his face to her throat again, as he pumped his fingers in and out of her. "I want you so much it hurts, Lucy."

"Then have me," she told him.

His hand moved from between her legs and she immediately felt the loss of him. He stepped away and started unbuttoning his clothes. He tugged the flannel shirt from his arms before reaching behind his head and pulling his T-shirt off in one swift move.

She didn't think she'd seen anything sexier in her life.

He'd barely dropped it to the floor before she was moving toward him, starting to work on his belt, then the button on his jeans, and finally pulling down the zipper. Theo kicked his pants off and then his hands were on her again, his mouth covering hers. Lucy took the opportunity to slide her hand underneath the band of his boxer briefs, her fingers wrapping around his hard cock.

Now he was the one groaning.

"Is this for me?" she asked, biting at his lower lip.

"Yes," he growled before tumbling them down onto the bed.

Theo wasted absolutely no time to settle himself between her legs, her thighs parting with ease. And his hands were everywhere, moving over every inch of skin he could touch. His mouth left hers to join the mission, trailing down her throat and over her breasts.

"Front clasp or back?" he asked.

"Front."

It was barely a flick of his fingers before the bra popped open and Theo's head was down again, his mouth covering one of her nipples. Lucy's back arched off the bed as she cried out, her hands in his hair as she held him to her.

Theo moved to her other breast, showing it the same amount of appreciation, his tongue flicking and causing her body to shake underneath him. And then that mouth of his started to move down her body, his beard rasping across her skin in the process. He sat up, his fingers moving to the sides of her panties.

"So, can I cross off getting *your* panties in a twist from my cliché bingo card?" he asked as he started to twist those fingers in the lace.

"Theo, if it means getting your cock inside me, you can mark whatever you want off your bingo card."

"Good to know, but we haven't quite gotten to that part of the evening, Lucy. Didn't I tell you that the taste of you was driving me crazy? Well, I have yet to sample every part of you." He pulled at the sides of her panties, and she lifted her hips from the bed, helping him. He tossed them to the floor before settling his shoulders between her thighs.

And then his mouth was on her, doing that thing only *he* could do so well. It would've been enough with just the rasp of his beard on the sensitive skin of her inner thighs. That alone could've set her off . . . but he was doing *so much more* than that. He parted her with his fingers before his tongue started to move over her, move in her. But then he found her clit and it took him absolutely no time at all to make her come apart, the orgasm ripping through her.

Theo didn't stop, pushing her higher and higher, the waves of pleasure almost more than she could handle. God, no one could destroy her like this man.

And she was pretty sure no other man would *ever* compare.

CHAPTER SIX
Caught Up in the Moment

There was no greater sound in the world than Lucy screaming Theo's name, nor was there a better image than her naked body stretched out in front of him. Theo looked up the length of her, still marveling at the fact that she was underneath him.

He started to kiss his way up her body, over her belly, and across her chest. He lingered at her breasts, running his tongue over her nipples. She squirmed underneath him, letting out another gasp.

"Theo." She moaned his name as her hands moved to his head, her fingers delving into his hair as she tugged. "Come here."

Trailing his mouth up her neck, he nipped at her skin until finally landing on her mouth. She parted her lips, letting him in with no hesitation, her tongue twisting with his. Her hands were still in his hair, and she raked her nails across his scalp, making him groan.

"I need you inside of me," she told him as she began to move her hips, rocking them into him. Thank god he was still wearing his boxer briefs and there was a thin layer of cotton between them.

It took a force of will stronger than he knew he possessed to pull back from her. "I think you're forgetting something. Let me grab a condom from my wallet." Theo wasn't typically the kind of guy who had one-night stands, but he was always prepared.

He was an Eagle Scout, after all.

"No need." Lucy shook her head. "I have a box in my nightstand."

Theo's only comment was to raise his eyebrows in question. Apparently, he wasn't the only one who liked to be prepared . . . he just wanted to know *who* she'd been preparing for.

"They're unopened. I just bought them."

That answer could've been satisfactory enough . . . but he wanted more. "For me?"

"Don't get too cocky." Lucy reached for him, tracing his erection with her fingertips. That challenge in her eyes only intensified when she moved down to his balls.

Theo grabbed her hand, his nostrils flaring as he pulled in another unsteady breath. He was pretty sure he hadn't taken a normal breath all night . . . ever since he'd leaned closer to her at the game to whisper in her ear.

Twining their fingers together, he stretched her hand above her head, pinning her to the bed. "Did you buy them for me?" he repeated, wanting to hear her say it.

"Tell me why you want to know." She clearly wasn't going to let him win so easily. But she never did.

"Because"—he started to move his hips, pressing his erection into her—"I want to know that it's my cock you've been thinking about. And *only* my cock."

"Yes." Lucy closed her eyes, her body arching under his. The movement caused her neck to stretch, and Theo took full advantage of the perfect access, burying his face in the spot and placing open-mouthed kisses across her throat. "Theo, please," she begged. "I need to feel you inside of me."

Yes, well, he needed to be inside of her, so there really was no need to prolong the torture any longer. Letting go of her, Theo sat up, reaching over to the nightstand. He pulled at the top drawer a little too exuberantly, causing the entire thing to shake. Her journal and pen, Chapstick, and alarm clock all flew off the top and clattered to the floor. He was only able to grab the lamp in time to save it from falling.

"Shit." He slid off the bed, bending over to pick everything up.

"Just leave it." She laughed, grabbing on to his boxers, her fingers twisting in the fabric as she pulled down.

"No problem." Theo nodded, pushing his boxers the rest of the way off and kicking them to the side. He then reached for the box at the back of the drawer, pulling at the cardboard flap and ripping it in the process. Once he tore a condom open and rolled it down his cock, he tossed everything back into the open drawer.

Moving back to the bed, he knelt on the mattress, his hands going to her knees to push them farther apart. But the second he touched her again, something in him stilled. There was a need to pause for a moment to take everything in. To take *her* in.

Her hair was spread out across the pillow, the satiny chestnut brown somehow even more beautiful against the white. Her skin was glowing in the amber light, her perfect breasts moving as she breathed. And then he let his gaze move down to the thatch of curls between her legs. Fuck, she was perfect.

He wasn't the only one looking their fill either. Lucy's eyes moved down his body, lingering on his erection, before slowly coming back up to his face. "What are you waiting for?"

"I just . . . I need a second." It had been seven years, *seven years* that he'd been waiting to be in this exact same position again. It felt like a lifetime; he had to take a couple moments to appreciate what was happening.

"Come here." She held her hand up in the air, and when he leaned forward her palm landed on his chest. As he moved over her it slid up and to his shoulder.

"Hi," he said as he settled over her.

"Hey, you." She bit her bottom lip, her top teeth sinking into the plump flesh.

It didn't take much for him to get distracted by her mouth, and he noticed that he had indeed kissed off every last bit of her lipstick. Well, except for the little bit on the left corner. He dipped his head, pressing his mouth to hers, kissing her slowly as he notched his cock to her entrance. She tilted her hips up and he slid inside of her.

Theo was immediately lost, consumed with everything that was Lucy Buchanan. He was wrapped up in her in every possible way. Her arms were around his shoulders, her thighs bracketed his waist, their mouths consuming each other, all while he sunk inside of her sweet body. It took only a few thrusts of his hips before they found their rhythm, Lucy matching him move for move.

But she'd always matched him . . . been the only one who could *ever* match him in this way. Time ceased to exist, *everything* ceased to exist except for her and him. He felt his own release building, but he wanted to feel her come around him. Wanted her to come apart in his arms just like this.

He slowed his thrusts, hooking one of her legs in the crook of his arm and spreading her wider as he began to grind against her.

"Oh, god. Yes, just like that, Theo. Just. Like. That."

Theo pressed his face to Lucy's throat—his current favorite place in the world to be—and just focused on pleasing her. Focused on the feel of her, the taste of her, the scent of her skin, the moans and gasps that kept escaping her sweet mouth, the sight of her beautiful face in total bliss.

It was a complete sensory experience, and he was in control right up until Lucy sunk her teeth into the skin at his shoulder, her body tightening around him as an orgasm rolled through her. And just that quickly, Theo was gone, all of his self-control disappearing in a snap as he started to pump his hips again, his own release coursing through him.

It took everything in him not to collapse on top of her, and he tried to brace himself, but Lucy tightened her grip on him, giving him permission. "Let me feel you," she whispered into his ear before she nipped at his earlobe.

The last bit of strength left his body, but he rolled just slightly to the side, continuing to hold her close and enjoying the feel of her pressed against him. Lucy's hands moved up and down his back while they each caught their breath, him more than her.

"I'll be right back," he said before he kissed her, their mouths lingering for a good long moment. The last thing in the world he wanted to do was let go, but he forced himself to pull away, and out of her body.

Snatching his boxers from the floor, he headed for the bathroom. It took him just a minute or two to get situated, and as he washed his hands in the sink, he spotted something bright blue and satiny sticking out from the top drawer of the vanity. Pulling it open, he discovered a wide variety of lingerie shoved into the drawer.

He was pretty sure she didn't usually keep this stuff stored next to her hair dryer and brush and had the distinct feeling she'd shoved it in there when she'd gone to the bathroom earlier. It was then that he spotted something red and lacy among the pile. He looped his finger in the strap, holding it up in the air.

A grin split his mouth, and he stepped outside of the bath-room, continuing to display the lingerie prominently in front of him. "My vote is for you to wear *this* next time."

Lucy sat up, clutching the sheet to her chest. "Who said there's going to be a next time?"

Theo leaned against the doorjamb, the red teddy continuing to swing in the air. "Are you telling me you don't want to do that again?"

Lucy's eyes narrowed. "No, I'm not saying that."

"So, we *are* going to do that again." The grin continued to spread across his mouth.

"You tell me." She leaned back against the pillows, letting the sheet fall to her waist and exposing her breasts.

Theo's mouth started to water; he needed her nipples in his mouth again. He tossed the teddy onto her dresser before crossing to the bed. His knees sunk into the mattress as he knelt down, placing his fists on either side of Lucy as he crawled up to her. He hovered over her, his mouth barely an inch above hers.

"If I have any say in the situation, we *will* be doing that again. Tonight, as a matter of fact. Many, *many* times." He barely brushed his lips over hers before he dipped his head, his mouth landing on her breast.

This round Theo took his time getting her to fall apart under-neath him.

* * *

A MUFFLED BEEPING pulled Lucy from sleep, but it took her brain a good couple of seconds to catch up with consciousness. She was so comfortable, her body sinking into the soft mattress . . . and something less soft and very warm.

Theo.

He had his arm under her pillow, cradling her head close to his chest. His other arm was wrapped around her, his hand slipped under the fabric of her shirt and resting on her lower back.

Lucy blinked her eyes open, the soft morning glow helping the room slowly come into focus. She tilted her head and could just make out his throat and chin. Her fingertips itched to touch him and she reached up, tracing his beard.

"Hmmm," Theo hummed as he rolled closer to her, his hand sliding up her back and pressing her to him. "What's that noise?" he murmured.

"The alarm clock."

"How do we make it stop?"

Lucy laughed as she made to pull away but didn't get very far as Theo's arm tightened around her, holding her close.

"I can't make it stop unless you let go."

"Then we have a problem." He pressed his face to her neck and started kissing her, his beard rasping against her skin and tickling her.

"Theo." She laughed again, managing to pull herself away as she rolled over to the nightstand and found it empty. It took a second for her to realize the alarm clock was still on the floor. She slid out of bed, and Theo groaned as his hands left her body.

"Hey, it's not my fault. You're the one who knocked this over last night."

"Sorry, I forgot to clean up my mess." He sat up slightly, leaning against his elbows as he watched her. "We literally made time fly, though."

They both paused for a second, looking at each other before she called out "It's mine!" and he yelled "Dibs!"

"I think we both get that one," Lucy said as she grabbed the alarm clock, the beep becoming increasingly louder as it was no longer muffled against the rug. She silenced it before setting it down and finding the other things that had fallen.

Theo stared at the clock for a second before looking back up at her in confusion. "Why is your alarm set for seven? Isn't that a little late for you to get up when you use it on a school day?" He pulled the covers back—careful not to disturb Estee, who was curled up at the foot of the bed—holding them in the air as she slid back in and settled into his chest again.

"I usually use my phone for an alarm. I've experienced too many power surges to take a chance on it not going off in the morning. The alarm on the clock must've gotten set when it fell on the floor. Probably for the best as I need to be at a yoga class in an hour and then I'm helping with the hot drinks stand for the school's drama department fundraiser. Are you working at the bakery today?"

"Yeah, I'm supposed to be there at nine." His hand moved under the hem of her shirt before it started to trail up, his fingers moving over her spine. "Though I'd much rather linger here with you."

Lucy shivered into him, burrowing closer. "I think we can plan a date for lingering. Maybe tonight or tomorrow . . ."

"I'll have to look at my schedule, but I'm pretty sure I can fit you in."

Lucy pulled back, her eyebrows raised as she looked up at him. "I think if *anyone* would be seeing if they could *fit* the other in, it would be me with you."

"You had no issues last night." He grinned.

Lucy shook her head, trying so hard not to smile back at him. She knew he was clearly joking, but two could play at this game.

"Yes, well, I think there might not be enough space now with that big head of yours. Nor is there enough space in my shower."

Theo's grin slipped. "What do you mean?"

"I was going to ask if you wanted to shower here, but since you're so busy, I guess you don't have time." She patted his chest before slipping out of bed.

"Hey"—he sat up, that grin now completely gone—"I was just kidding!"

"Well, if you want an invitation to be there again"—she pointed to her bed—"or here again"—she waved a hand in front of the apex of her thighs—"you're going to have to earn it."

"How?"

"I guess you'll figure it out." Lucy took a few steps back, her hands going to the hem of her shirt before she turned around, pulling it off in one fluid motion. She started walking toward the bathroom, hearing him groan over the sound of the door shutting behind her.

* * *

THEO STARED AT THE SHUT DOOR, unable to figure out if he was amused or pissed. Well, that was par for the course when it came to Lucy. Apparently, she'd decided to up the game of their taunting each other, and now that sex was involved, the stakes were higher.

Much, *much* higher.

Theo got out of bed as he heard the shower turn on, inwardly cursing himself. He'd been playing checkers that morning when Lucy was clearly playing chess. He was just going to have to figure out how to get her back. Luckily for him he had some time.

His clothes were scattered all over the floor, and he snatched them up, pulling them on one piece at a time. Sparing one more glance at the bathroom, he shook his head before crossing her apartment and opening the front door. He was about halfway down the stairs when he heard someone say his name.

"Well, I'll be damned. Theo Taylor."

Theo looked over to the house to find Lucy's father walking down the path. His feet faltered, his eyes going wide in horror. "Mr. Buchanan."

"Now, how many times do I have to tell you to call me Wes? Whatcha doing here, son?" he asked, clearly amused.

"I . . . um . . . I was just . . . um . . ." The very last thing he wanted to do was lie to the man. But he couldn't exactly tell him the truth. "We were at Quigley's last night and I walked Lucy home."

"And stayed the night, I see."

Theo reached up, rubbing his hand across the back of his neck. It couldn't be more than thirty degrees outside and he was *sweating*.

"Don't worry." Wes laughed. "My shotgun is in the house, so you're perfectly safe."

"Promise?"

"Cross my heart." He made the motion over his chest. "Where's your truck?"

"At the bakery. I parked it there after the game last night."

"I'm heading that way. Want a ride?"

"So you can torture me a little bit more?"

Wes smiled behind his bushy beard, his hazel eyes crinkling. "You ain't seen nothing yet."

"That's what I was afraid of." Theo rounded to the passenger side of Wes's red truck. Yup, this was what he got for messing with Lucy that morning, no sex and an awkward car ride with her father.

When Wes started the engine, the stereo flared to life and "Fortunate Son" by Creedence Clearwater Revival filled the cab. Well, that was fitting.

Wes put the truck in reverse and the locks all clicked into place ominously. He backed out of the drive, getting to the end of the block and rolling to a stop at the sign before saying anything. "So," he started as he turned left. "What are your intentions with my daughter?"

"Um . . . I . . . it's not . . ."

Wes started to laugh again. "Relax. I'm not as naive as you may think. I've noticed you and Lucy dancing around each other for months."

Theo let out a breath, his shoulders sagging in relief.

"However, if you hurt her, you can go back to calling me Mr. Buchanan."

"You're having too much fun with this." Theo shook his head.

"It's my right as her father. Don't act like you haven't messed with the guys your sisters have dated."

It was true; before his little sister Naomi had gone off to college a couple of years ago, he'd been pretty ruthless with the unfortunate souls she'd brought home. She'd yet to bring any of her college boyfriends home for a weekend visit.

"Well, Naomi has terrible taste in guys, so it's justified. And thank god Gia hasn't started dating yet."

"You sure about that?"

Theo looked over at Wes. "What do you know?"

"Nothing." He laughed. "I've just raised three kids, and they know how to sneak around. Well"—he glanced over at Theo, his mouth twitching—"apparently not as well these days. Or in yours and Lucy's case, not seven years ago either."

"You knew?"

"Yeah, I knew." Wes laughed again.

"Great, so how long can I expect the hazing to last?" Theo asked.

"From me? A while. But you know it isn't just me you have to contend with. There's Jeremy, Lilah, Caro, Max, Sasha"—he made another turn as he continued to list off the names—"Oscar, Gavin, your mom, your dad, your sisters, your brother, your grandparents. Pretty much anyone who knows you and Lucy. I could keep going if I need to."

"No." Theo shook his head. "I think I'm good. And I already got a taste of that last night at Quigley's."

"Good, so you know what to expect." The buildings of downtown came into view and Wes slowed the truck as they drove along the cobblestoned streets. "I have one piece of advice for you, Theo. Well, one piece of advice for you this morning."

"And what's that?"

"All of those people I just mentioned? They've got nothing on what Lucy is going to throw at you."

"Of that I am beyond aware." This morning was proof of that.

Wes pulled to a stop in front of the bakery. "Good," he said as he clapped Theo on the shoulder, squeezing affectionately before letting go. "Then you'll do just fine. I guess I'll be seeing you around my backyard."

Theo coughed uncomfortably before nodding. "Thanks for the ride, Mr. Bu—"

Wes's bushy eyebrows rose high.

"Wes," Theo corrected.

"You're welcome, Theo."

Theo jumped out of the truck, hesitating for just a moment before opening the door to the bakery. *Shit.* He hadn't thought this through, his pre-coffee brain not firing on all cylinders. The last thing he needed was for someone in his family to see him getting dropped off by Wes Buchanan.

It wasn't like he was trying to keep what had happened with Lucy a secret. It was just that he didn't really want to explain that it was just sex.

Luckily for him, there was a pretty long line at the registers, people grabbing their morning pastries before heading over to the Cruickshank Saturday Market. It usually ended in early fall, but with the demand it had begun to garner, it was extended until Christmas this year. Vendors set up their booths and tables all around Sweeny Park. They sold their art, crafts, wares, and locally grown produce.

As it was close to seven thirty—and the market opened at nine—the people at the bakery were mostly the vendors, wanting to get something good to eat before the busy day. There was enough of them to mostly block him from view as he sidestepped the line and headed for the hallway at the back. The bathrooms were to the left, while a door locked with a keypad was to the right. Theo punched in the code and slipped inside, heading up the stairs.

Way back when his great-grandparents—Cornelius and Betty— had started the bakery, they'd used the second and third floors as their home. It was where they'd raised their family and where they'd continued to live long after everyone had moved out. It was where they'd lived until the end of their lives.

It had been his great-grandparents who'd instilled that love of baking in Theo's bones. Some of his fondest memories growing up had been coming to Browned Butter after school and baking cookies and cakes. He'd gotten a good twelve years with them before they'd passed away. But they'd never be totally gone, not when their little bakery had become an institution in Cruick-shank.

Browned Butter was an entire-family affair these days. His grandparents were usually there to start things up at five o'clock in the morning, still the same early birds that they'd always been. Marjorie and Albert Taylor were in their early seventies and were still going strong. Their idea of retiring had been going from work-ing ten-hour days six days a week, to six-hour days five days a week.

Theo's parents, Isaac and Juliet, were part of the second shift, one of them coming in to open up at seven, while the other got there after getting Gia off to school. Theo was more of the nine-to-five shift, coming in after the crazy rush in the morning and when the kitchens were slightly less chaotic, and staying until closing.

He was the only one of his siblings who'd joined the family business, and odds were he'd be the only one.

His younger brother, Declan, had joined the air force and was currently stationed over in Germany with his wife, Natalie. His sister Naomi was a junior at UNC-Chapel Hill, getting a com-puter science degree. And then there was Gia, who might work at the bakery after school and on weekends but had found her real love acting stuff out onstage or being behind the camera.

Baking wasn't everyone's passion, but for Theo, it was part of him.

These days, the floors above the bakery were no longer used as a place of residence, though a lot of his great-grandparents' belongings still occupied the space. The desk in the second-floor office had been built by his great-grandfather's own hands, and there were a number of framed cross-stitches on the wall from his great-grandmother.

Theo rounded the banister as he made his way up to the third floor. It was still set up as a little apartment, a cozy little kitchen in one corner with yellow and blue tiles, and an old leather sofa in the other with a TV mounted to the wall. Down the hall there was a bedroom and a bathroom. When family from out of town would visit, they'd usually stay up there for the weekend, enjoying their mornings woken up by the smell of freshly baked bread.

But Theo probably used the area more than anyone else. He sometimes needed his own space to work on his cakes that was away from the chaos. The kitchen in the bakery was always crazy, everyone coming and going as they made their specialties throughout the day.

It took Theo a good fifteen minutes to get showered and changed—he always kept clothes there in case of a powdered sugar or flour explosion. As he got ready, his mind was still replaying the night before and how everything had happened. A perfect chain of events. Well, it had been perfect up until that morning.

He grinned, shaking his head as he looked at himself in the mirror, combing his wet hair back. Lucy didn't make things easy, but she never had. And as much as he'd wanted to get another round in with her before work—and he'd *really* wanted to—he enjoyed this game with her. He just needed to figure out how to win the next round.

Pulling on a brown, white, and black flannel shirt, he worked on the buttons as he made his way back downstairs. When he pushed the door open, it was to see that the line had doubled. He rounded the counter to where his mother and father were filling orders while Kylie—one of their part-timers—manned the register.

"Morning." He grabbed an apron, tying the strings around his back.

"You're here early." His mother stretched up and pressed a kiss to his cheek, before pulling back and looking into his face.

"What?"

"Nothing." She shook her head, her eyes narrowing.

But she didn't get to study too much longer as Theo turned to his father, reaching for one of the boxes in his hand.

"Order forty-two is cookies. Half a dozen chocolate chip, the other half butterscotch." Isaac pointed to the little screen where they tracked orders before moving on to the Danishes. "I saw your truck around back this morning and figured you'd stayed at the apartment. Late night at Quigley's?" There was something leading in his tone . . . like he was going somewhere with the question.

Theo took a moment before answering, hesitating as he pulled on a pair of gloves. He was trying to figure out how to answer his father and not lie. "Yeah, decided not to drive home last night."

A true statement. Theo had indeed decided not to drive home last night, and it had partly been because of the bourbon. As for the assumption that Theo had stayed at the bakery apartment, he chose not to correct it. At least not for the moment . . . and not when there were about twenty people within earshot.

When Theo stood from the cookie display and turned, he found his father studying him.

"What?" he asked for the second time.

"Nothing." A small smirk played at Isaac's mouth that clearly said there was *something*.

"Well, I'm glad you're here early," his mother told him as she grabbed a chocolate croissant and a cinnamon-raisin bagel. "It's been a busy morning. Your grandparents are manning the kitchen by themselves at the moment."

"Where are Daisy and Blake?" Theo asked of two of their other part-time employees.

"Daisy got sick, and Blake had a flat tire. He said he'd be in as soon as he got it changed. And Gia and Chloe are volunteering at the hot drinks stand to raise money for the drama department."

"Lucy's working that booth this morning too," Theo said before he could stop himself.

Both of his parents looked over at him, his father's knowing smirk getting bigger while his mother gave him that *look* that said she clearly knew he was hiding something. "You want to tell us what's going on?"

"What do you mean?"

"You never offer up information about Lucy. Not freely."

Shit.

"Sure, I do."

"*No*, you don't." His mother shook her head.

"Could that name drop have anything to do with the fact that your mother and I saw Wes drive you to work this morning?" Isaac asked.

Double shit.

"You aren't as sneaky as you think you are, son." Juliet patted Theo's chest. "You work out here with your father while I finish the cookies that I promised to make for the hot drinks stand. You can bring them down there when I'm finished."

"Yes, Mom."

"Good boy." She grinned before heading to the kitchen.

Well, that took absolutely no time at all for them to figure out. And how was it that he'd gotten busted by both Lucy's father *and* his parents? Just another thing he was going to have to get Lucy back for. She was no doubt having a much easier morning than him.

CHAPTER SEVEN
Rescue Mission

The Saturday yoga class had a tendency to draw a large crowd, sometimes thirty to forty participants on busier weekends. When the weather was nice, it was down in Sweeny Park. Everyone would spread their mats out down by the trees and in view of the lake. When it was cold or rainy, it was taught at the Duncan-Finley barn, which was where Lucy headed that cold November morning.

Lucy had two minutes to spare when she pushed through the doors and was greeted with a comfortable amount of warmth from a few space heaters set up around the room. It was just enough to combat the chill, but not turn the session into hot yoga. Twinkle lights were always strung up among the rafters and up the pillars, and they'd been turned on, giving the room a lovely glow. Soft meditation music was playing in the background, providing the whole setup a perfect vibe.

She didn't need to scan the room to find Sasha, Caro, and Li-lah. They were already sitting down, claiming their usual spot at the front left corner.

People were still coming in and setting up their space, but most of the participants were lying down on their mats, starting to get into a good headspace. Talk started to dwindle down about five minutes before class, which was why Lucy had waited to come in. She could postpone her interrogation for another hour.

As she sat down on the empty mat next to them, they all gave her the most obvious self-satisfied grins she'd ever seen in her life, but they didn't say anything as they all settled in for the class, lying down on their backs. This was supposed to be the time when everyone cleared their minds, but there was no clearing hers that morning.

All she could think about was Theo's hands on her . . . and his mouth. There was an ache between her thighs that she knew could've been satisfied that morning. Maybe she'd made a mistake leaving him in her bed. At the time, that look of longing on his face as she'd backed away had been totally worth it. Now she wasn't so sure.

She'd just have to see how it all played out, *play* being the operative word. They were having fun . . . *just sex.*

Taking a deep breath, Lucy let it out, trying to focus on her body. It wasn't too long before the instructor started to speak, walking them through their positions. As she moved, she realized she'd used muscles last night that hadn't been used in a while. A *long* while. No better way to work through the soreness than with a little bit of yoga.

As the class continued, it became pretty clear that it was a lost cause to clear her mind of Theo, so she stopped trying. Instead, she let everything that had happened replay itself, and thought about what she wanted to happen next.

That was easy; she wanted to have sex with him again. Wanted to enjoy whatever this was for as long as possible. It was going to be a lot easier than last time as they weren't keeping it a secret.

No, he'd put an end to that possibility when he'd pulled her outside. Well, *she'd* actually been the one to pull *him* outside.

But the fact that it wasn't a secret was so much better . . . even if she did have to deal with all the questions from her friends.

"I don't think I've ever seen someone grin that much in a yoga class."

Lucy moved her focus from her folded hands and over to her sister. Everyone in class was sitting up with their legs crossed in front of them. Some lingering *namaste*s were still being whispered around the room.

"Well, you know how long a postorgasmic glow lasts," Lilah said to Caro. "Hell, you've got one yourself."

"So do you." Sasha waved her hand at all three of them. "I'm the only one here who isn't glowing."

"Well, I know what we should all chip in to give Sasha for Christmas."

Sasha just rolled her eyes before focusing on Lucy. "So, was it as good as you remembered?"

Lucy bit at her bottom lip, trying—and failing—to hide her grin. "It was better, actually."

"Did he stay the night?" Caro asked.

"Yes."

"And *when* will he be staying the night again?" Lilah raised her eyebrows.

"Not sure yet. He has to earn it."

All three women paused as they rolled up their mats, but it was Sasha who asked, "What do you mean, he has to earn it?"

"Can we not have this conversation here?" Lucy looked around. Nobody was really paying attention to them, but she didn't particularly want to be overheard. She was fine talking to them about Theo, but she didn't want strangers to know.

Once they got outside, Lucy launched into the story of the night before . . . and that morning. When she got to the part where she'd left him in her bed, Sasha burst out laughing.

"Oh, god, I bet he was so mad."

"You just can't help yourself when it comes to taunting him, can you?" Caro shook her head.

"I bet you anything he's plotting his revenge," Lilah said as she pulled her scarf tighter around her neck.

It was nine o'clock and still pretty cold outside. The skies were dotted with clouds and the sun was having a little trouble getting things warmed up. It didn't help that there was also a biting wind blowing, cutting right through Lucy's fleece-lined yoga pants. She was very much looking forward to a hot cup of coffee.

"Well," Caro started as they made their way through the crowd, "it sounds like you had a good night. That's for sure . . ."

"Why do I sense that there's a *but* at the end of that sentence?"

"Because there is one," Lilah said.

Lucy looked over at her sister, waiting for the follow-up. "*But* where is this going to go?" Caro asked.

"I was wondering that too." Sasha looped her arm through Lucy's, pulling her toward Sweeny Park. "You've said since you came back that you have no intention of staying in Cruickshank permanently. Has that changed?"

"No, my plan hasn't changed." Lucy shook her head. "I'm not moving back. Theo and I are just having fun."

"Fun," Lilah repeated. "Isn't that what you and Max were having before he decided to stay?" She turned to Caro.

"That's *exactly* what we were having."

"And look how that turned out." Lilah reached forward, lifting Caro's left hand in the air and showing off the diamond ring.

"Theo and I are *not* getting married. I promise you. Look, a lot of stuff has happened in the last"—Lucy looked at her watch before glancing back up—"ten-ish or so hours. Can I have coffee before dissecting this more?"

"Sure, you can." Sasha patted Lucy's arm as they got to the pavilion, where three of the four of them were volunteering that morning.

Caro and Sasha were manning—or womaning—the booth for the Cruickshank Cats and Dogs Rescue. And right next door to the rescue booth was where Sasha's mother, Lorraine, was helping Lucy at the hot drinks stand. It made sense as Dancing Donkey was providing the coffee, hot chocolate, and spiced cider.

Both booths were pretty much set up, and Max and Wes were taking care of the rescues—something they did almost every Saturday. Meanwhile, Lorraine had got the school's hot drinks stand ready with Principal Patel, Gia, Chloe, and Harrison Savage, Chloe's father.

The new fire captain was that week's parental volunteer, and Lucy had a feeling they'd be making a lot of money with the ladies swarming their booth. The man was beyond handsome, and single. Somewhere in his early forties and sporting a full head of salt-and-pepper hair—more salt than pepper—and a matching beard. To top it all off he had eyes that were a striking sea green.

Though Lucy was clearly partial to a certain shade of blue.

As they got closer, Lucy focused on her boss, Fatima Patel. That morning she'd swapped out her usual well-tailored suit and pointy flats for jeans, a Nirvana T-shirt over a bright purple turtleneck, a fuzzy black jacket, and cheetah-print sneakers. Her black hair was pulled up into a ponytail, which bounced around her shoulders as she stacked the cups with the girls.

Thirteen years ago, Principal Patel had just been Mrs. Patel, Lucy's honors English teacher in eleventh and twelfth grade.

When it came to favorites, Mrs. Griffith had always been Lucy's number one, but Principal Patel was easily in second place.

"Hello, my dearies." Lorraine looked up from where she was filling the half-and-half. "You hanging out around here today?" she asked Lilah.

"No, just going to get a drink before meeting my mom at Quigley's. We're making japchae and kimchi fried rice for tonight's special and she needs some help."

There was always the usual pub fare at the bar: fish and chips, pot pies, burgers, etc. But when Nari had joined the family, they'd broadened their menu to include a variety of Korean dishes. They were probably more popular than the rest of the menu.

"Oh my gosh." Lucy groaned in delight. Japchae was one of her favorite Korean dishes . . . really, one of her favorite meals ever. Sweet potato noodles, tons of vegetables, and Nari's magically marinated beef. It was the perfect blend of sweet and umami. No one could make it like Nari Quigley.

"I think she's trying to make all of your favorite meals so you don't move out of Cruickshank again."

"Can you tell her that I approve of that plan?" Wes called out as he and Max strung up the rescues banner in front of their table.

Lucy knew just how much her father wanted her to stay . . . how much they *all* wanted her to stay. None of them were quiet about it. They all made comments here or there about her moving back permanently.

"I think we *all* approve of whatever plan it takes to keep Lucy around," Lorraine agreed.

Lucy rolled her eyes. "Wow, I think this is a record. It's barely nine o'clock and that's Sasha, Caro, Lilah, Dad, and Lorraine"— she held her hand in the air as she ticked off all the names— "who've all made a comment about me staying in Cruickshank.

Can we at least stagger this throughout the day? This is a lot to take first thing in the morning."

"Those aren't the only people who don't want you to leave." Max shook his head. "You can add me to that list."

"Us too!" Gia and Chloe called out. "We don't want you to leave either."

"I agree with all of them." Fatima indicated everyone around her.

"As well as your brother, niece, and nephews." Lilah held her own hand in the air, ticking them off.

"And Oscar, Gavin, and *Theo*," Sasha added, a grin turning up her mouth as she said the last name.

"Hey, unless they're here to add to this conversation, their vote doesn't count." Lucy frowned.

"What is it that I'm voting on?" someone asked from behind Lucy.

She didn't need to look to know who was standing behind her; his voice alone had caused that familiar warmth to creep up the back of her neck. But she turned around anyway—obviously— her eyes landing on his face before traveling down to see a giant bag from Browned Butter in each hand.

"Theo." Her eyes went wide as heat filled her cheeks. "Hey, you."

"Hey. I brought cookies"—he lifted one bag in the air—"and breakfast," he said as he lifted the other.

"I can take that." Fatima grabbed the bags. "Thanks for bringing all of this, Theo, and tell your mother thank you for making the cookies."

"You're welcome and will do." Theo nodded. "So, what is it that I'm voting on?"

"Whether Lucy should stay in Cruickshank permanently. I'm sure you have an opinion on that as well, Theo." Wes folded his arms across his chest as he leaned against one of the pavilion pillars, a knowing expression on his face.

Oh, god. Did he know about what had happened with Theo too? Lucy wondered.

"Ahh, yes, I know that's been a topic of conversation for months." Theo looked back to Lucy, and though he was smiling at her, there was something guarded in his expression. "I think that Lucy should do whatever makes her happy."

"I think she *finally* is doing just that." Sasha lightly punched Theo on the shoulder.

"I guess we'll just have to see how that turns out, then." His eyes lingered on Lucy's before dipping to her mouth.

"I guess we will," she agreed.

"Do you have a second?" he asked, taking a step back from everyone, who were all watching them like hawks.

Well, almost everyone. Gia and Chloe were currently opening the breakfast boxes and figuring out what they wanted to eat.

"Sure." Lucy nodded, following him to the side of the pavilion. At least the distance would make their conversation private.

"So," he started as he turned back to her. "I've had a very interesting morning."

"How so?"

"First, your father caught me coming out of your apartment."

"No!" Lucy covered her mouth in horror. She'd been right, Wes apparently *did* know something.

"Yes, and Gavin and Sasha weren't the only ones who knew about us seven years ago."

"*What?!*" It just kept getting worse.

"Yeah. But my morning didn't stop there. Because then your father dropped me off at the bakery, where not one but both of my parents saw."

Lucy dropped her hand from her mouth. "So, you were caught by my father, and your parents, doing the walk of shame?"

"Hmm." He shook his head as he reached out, his hands landing on Lucy's arms as he pulled her in close, his mouth hovering over hers. "There was absolutely *no* shame in what happened between us last night." And then he pulled her against his body and kissed her.

What was it with this man grabbing her and kissing her? This was two days in a row now. Her arms wrapped around his shoulders, holding him to her as he deepened the kiss. It was a good few seconds before he ended it, grinning as he pulled away.

"Have fun explaining that." He nodded over her shoulder.

And just that quickly all of the warmth that had been coursing through Lucy was gone. She might as well have been doused with a bucket of cold water.

"You jerk." She spared a glance behind her to find that everyone was staring at them. They were all sporting massive grins; well, everyone except for Gia and Chloe, whose mouths had fallen open in shock. Captain Savage and Principal Patel at least had the good grace to look away as they put the cookies out.

"I've got to get back to the bakery, we're slammed this morning. See you later." He took another step away from her, giving her a little wave before he turned around.

She couldn't believe him. Well, yes, she could, actually. She'd done the exact same thing to him about two hours ago. She just hadn't done it with an audience.

All eyes were still on her when she got back to the booths, but it was Gia who spoke first. "You and my brother? *You* and *Theo*? How? When? You two drive each other crazy."

"Gia, as you get older, you'll learn that's part of the fun of it." Sasha grinned, her voice low so as not to be overheard by anyone around their group. "As to the *when*, last night. But I don't think you're old enough to know the *how*."

"Eww." Gia's shocked expression turned to disgust. "I don't want to know about *that*!"

"Thanks a lot, Sash." Lucy frowned at her friend.

"Anytime."

"I guess he got you back for this morning," Lilah said through a laugh.

"You can say that again."

"At least he softened the blow." Caro shoved a box across the table.

Lucy grabbed it, catching her name written across the top before she popped it open and looked inside. It was filled with everything fall. A crème brûlée doughnut, a cinnamon-apple muffin, a pumpkin-spiced bagel, and a vanilla chai cupcake.

"It's like he knows you or something." Sasha looked over her shoulder. "Those are all your favorites."

Lucy looked up in the direction Theo had just gone. She could still make out his hunter-green jacket as he made his way through the crowd. How had he both won the first round of this little challenge she'd set up *and* won himself back into her good graces?

She'd met her match . . . something she'd been aware of well before that moment.

* * *

THE CRUICKSHANK SATURDAY MARKET usually ended at two, but that afternoon the crowd started to thin out a little before one. The cold breeze had blown in some rain clouds, the sun now completely covered up. There were scattered raindrops falling, nothing consistent yet, just a few here or there.

As their group was under the pavilion, they were covered, but it did make for a rather gloomy day. People were heading into the downtown shops for lunch or to continue their shopping at the stores, which provided more shelter from the cold.

When it had really died down, Fatima let Chloe and Gia go.

"My parents will be very grateful. Apparently, it's still slammed at the bakery," Gia said before they headed off, pulling the hoods of their jackets up and over their heads.

"I think we might as well call it too." Fatima looked around at the vendors, who were starting to pack up. "This weather isn't going to get any better."

"Luckily we were busy at the beginning." Lucy nodded.

"That's an understatement," Lorraine said as she started to stack the cups.

For the first three hours, they'd had a consistent line, everyone heading over to them to get a hot cup of something to warm up with. Lucy had welcomed the rush. They were so busy that there wasn't a lot of opportunity for chatting. She did, however, have to contend with all of the knowing looks coming from her family and friends.

And there were a lot of them.

Not surprisingly, Sasha was the worst. She looked so smugly satisfied by the entire situation. It was more amusing than annoying, though. Everyone else was less obvious, just giving Lucy sideways smirks or making little comments here and there.

But the person who Lucy really noticed a change in was her father. Wes looked happier than usual, which was interesting considering his morning had started with him catching Theo sneaking out of her apartment. She knew she wasn't going to live that one down for a *long* time.

But as Lucy watched her father and Lorraine boxing up the last of the drink dispensers, she realized it wasn't just today that he'd looked happier than usual. He'd been that way for a few weeks now.

He laughed, leaning closer to Lorraine as he whispered something in her ear. Lorraine smiled, her hand grabbing his forearm and giving a gentle squeeze.

That's new.

Lucy wondered if Sasha had seen it, but as she looked around for her friend, she found Fatima stepping into her line of sight. "I can't thank you enough for filling in today. I know it was a little last minute when I asked yesterday." She'd stopped by in the morning with the request, needing someone to fill in for the English teacher, Mrs. Michaels, who'd gotten the flu.

"It's no problem." Lucy waved her off.

"Well, you're appreciated. And I know you felt like it was a lot, with everyone telling you they want you to stay in Cruickshank this morning, but I really do think that there are a lot of people who are glad you're back in town. Me being one of them. You've become an integral part of my staff this year. I can't tell you how many of your students have told me how excited they are for the winter musical. They're loving that class."

Lucy smiled but couldn't hide the twinge of sadness in her eyes. "I appreciate that. But I know it's not permanent. Mrs. Griffith will be back next semester."

"Actually, she won't be. Her husband still needs her to be home with him and she's asked to take next semester off as well."

"Oh, no. I knew Mr. Griffith was healing a little slower than they'd initially thought, but I didn't know it was enough to delay her another semester."

"I don't think Jan did either. She just told me yesterday." Fatima shook her head. "The position would be yours for the rest of the year if you want it. You don't need to give me an answer today,

I just wanted to let you know and give you some time to think. Though judging by the way Theo Taylor kissed you a little bit ago, I'm guessing you might not mind staying in Cruickshank a little longer."

"Um, well, yes, there is *that*." Heat filled Lucy's cheeks. It was one thing to have her family and friends say something, but it was totally another to have her boss say it. Not that it was inappropriate or anything; Fatima had become more like a mentor in the last few months. A confidant in a lot of ways. There were a number of afternoons that they'd eaten their lunches together in the break room, or when the weather was nice at one of the tables outside.

"I always liked him," Fatima continued. "He was a good student. Always polite and respectful. It's also an added bonus that he makes the best cupcakes in all of the Carolinas."

"That, he does."

"Anyways." Fatima took a step back. "Thanks again for your help and let me know what you decide. I don't need an answer until finals week."

"Okay." Lucy nodded before turning around and heading for the rescue booth, where Sasha and Caro were packing up.

"Everything okay?" Sasha asked. "That looked a little serious."

"Not serious. She was just thanking me for helping last minute."

There was a small pang of guilt in not telling Sasha and Caro about the offer to work next semester, but she needed a little time to think about it . . . to think about *everything*. She already knew what her family wanted; if she told them this, they'd be relentless.

For months she'd reminded herself that coming back to Cruickshank wasn't going to be permanent. Sure, the last semester had been great; she'd really enjoyed teaching. But this wasn't what she wanted to do.

Was it?

No. No, her dream was to sing, was to get up on a stage and share her music with people. She couldn't do that here, at least not how she'd always wanted. It was why she'd left seven years ago. Well, not all of the reason. She'd been running from something too. From *someone*.

How was it that not even twenty-four hours since she'd fallen into bed with Theo, she was offered the opportunity to stay here longer? A little bit of security in her professional life while her romantic life revisited the road not taken.

No, it was just sex. It didn't need to be more than that.

"Hey, you okay?" Caro asked as she reached out and touched Lucy's forearm.

"Yeah." Lucy nodded, coming back to the moment. "Just thinking about the rest of the day. I need to run some errands. What are you guys getting into after this?"

"Mom and I need to head back to the café. Oscar is there with the morning shift, and I know he'd actually like to enjoy his day off." Oscar might be a full-time vet, but he still helped out here and there at the café.

"I think he will. He's got his date tonight with Edward," Caro said excitedly.

"Oh, yeah." Lucy grinned. "I can't wait to hear how that goes."

"Speaking of which, you going to tell us how *your* evening goes?" Sasha asked.

"Who says it's going anywhere?"

"Oh, please." Caro pointed in the direction that Theo had pulled Lucy a few hours ago. "If you and Theo don't end up spending the rest of the weekend together, I'll eat my shoe."

"You think he's going to spend tonight and Sunday with me?"

"The bakery is closed, it's supposed to rain today and all day tomorrow"—Caro waved her hand at the sky—"and he can't get enough of you. If that man lets you put clothes on, I'll be shocked."

Someone uncomfortably cleared their throat behind them, and they all turned to see Wes standing there. "Maybe I don't need to be here for this particular conversation."

That now familiar heat crept up Lucy's cheeks again.

"Sorry, Dad." Caro fought to keep a straight face while Sasha burst into laughter.

"Well, if you're going to be busy *all day* tomorrow, maybe we should solidify our plans for Monday." His beard twitched, his own smile playing on his mouth.

Lucy rolled her eyes. "I'm not going to be busy *all day* tomorrow. But we can still make our plans for Monday now."

"So, it's a two-hour drive to Freddie's Farm, and they open at nine. I'd like to be on the road no later than seven. We've got four hams and seven turkeys ordered and you know there's always a line."

"Eight," Lorraine called out.

"Sorry, eight turkeys," Wes corrected himself.

Freddie's Farm was just outside of Knoxville, Tennessee, and they had the best turkeys around. Eight might seem excessive for most Thanksgiving dinners, but their annual Thanksgiving at Quigley's wasn't a small event, never had been.

For as long as Lucy could remember, her family had always celebrated the holiday with their friends' families at the Irish pub. Among the families—local and extended—of the Quigleys', Taylors', Belmonts', and Buchanans', the guest count was already up into the sixties.

But the attendees didn't end there. There were a number of people in town who didn't have the resources or the ability to celebrate the holiday to the fullest, and others who didn't have families to spend it with. An invite was offered to all of them. There was always an open door.

A typical Quigley's Thanksgiving had more than a hundred people, everyone contributing as they could with side dishes. It was a whole thing, and the preparation started days in advance. Since they were out for the week at school, Lucy had told her dad she'd go with him to get the turkeys.

"I'll be ready to go by six thirty; that way we can get some coffee and breakfast before getting on the road."

"That's a must," Wes agreed. "See you later." He leaned in and pressed a kiss to Lucy's cheek before heading off to help Lorraine load everything into the back of her SUV.

Lucy turned to her friends. "I'm going to head out now that this is all cleared up." She waved a hand at the now empty spot they'd occupied under the pavilion. "See you guys Monday night at the latest."

"We'll be there." Sasha rubbed her hands together as another gust of wind blew around them.

Lucy pulled the hood of her jacket up before heading for downtown. She wanted to get some of her Christmas shopping out of the way, knowing that things were going to get crazy next week, and only get crazier from there.

First there was Thanksgiving, then the musical would be coming up, and then finals week right before the end of the semester. She'd been dreading the end of the school year, not wanting it to be over . . . but now she had the opportunity to teach for a few more months.

It should be good news, really, but she felt the longer she did this, the more attached she was going to get to something that wasn't hers. It was one of the reasons she'd never been able to foster pets. She didn't know how her sister, Sasha, and Lorraine did it.

There was just too much to think about when it came to the future, so instead, she let herself get distracted with a little retail therapy.

First up was the music store. She found some old records for Max, flicked through the sheet music to see if anything would be good for her classes, and got some replacement guitar strings. One had broken the other day, and she hadn't had any to restring the guitar.

At the hobby store, she got a 3-D puzzle of the *Millennium Falcon* for her dad, and one of those night-lights that turned the ceiling into the solar system for her nephew Matthew. She spent a lot more time at Kathleen's Corner Bookstore, browsing the aisles before ordering a beautifully illustrated book all about dinosaurs for her other nephew, Christopher, and a wide variety of coloring books for her niece, Emilia.

She stopped by the pet store to get some toys and treats for Estee and the numerous dogs owned by everyone in her family. It was nice that there were so many to love on since Lucy didn't have one. She'd long wanted to adopt one, but it hadn't really been feasible when she'd been in LA, both from a money and time standpoint. Estee had already been an unexpected expense, but once she'd rescued the kitten, Lucy hadn't been willing to give her up.

Cats were a lot less maintenance. They didn't need walks, or regular baths, or to be let outside to go to the bathroom. They were independent creatures who, besides needing food and water, had the ability to pretty much take care of themselves.

Though Lucy knew that Estee loved to be around other animals, especially dogs. As much as she'd like to get Estee a dog for Christmas, her life was just too much up in the air to make that kind of commitment.

It was a little before four when Lucy headed to her last stop of the afternoon.

She'd been trying to figure out how to get Theo back for his little stunt that morning, and as she made her way to the bakery, she still wasn't sure how she was going to do that. Maybe she'd figure it out when she saw him.

There weren't a lot of people out, almost everyone heading home before the rain really started. The gray clouds were now swirling, and the wind was only getting more biting.

Lucy pulled her scarf tighter around her neck, the chill creeping down her back. It was at that moment her phone buzzed in her pocket. There was a small—or not so small—hope that it was Theo.

But as she looked at the screen, she saw a name she hadn't seen in months: Stephanie Jenkins. Stephanie was one of her old friends from college. She'd been out in LA for a few years with Lucy before she'd packed up and moved to New York.

"Hey, Steph," Lucy said as she picked up the phone.

"Hey, lady, long time no speak."

"How you doing?"

"Good, I heard you left LaLa Land like me."

"Yeah." Lucy stepped into the little inlet of the post office, taking shelter from the wind. As it was closed, she wasn't in anyone's way. "It wasn't for me, as it turns out."

"Maybe because you need something edgier. Something like New York."

"You think so?"

"One of my roommates is moving out, and as soon as she told me I was thinking about who I should ask to take the room. And your name came to mind."

"New York . . ." Lucy let the city's name roll around on her tongue, getting a taste for it. She did love that city, there was no doubt.

"Think about it. She's moving out in February."

"I will . . ." Lucy nodded, her thoughts racing as Stephanie continued to talk.

It was a few minutes before Lucy hung up, her mind reeling even more than before. She hadn't thought it possible, and yet here she was. How was it that within less than twenty-four hours she was having *just sex* with Theo again, she'd been offered another semester of teaching at a job she was enjoying more and more every day, and she now had the possibility of a fresh start in a new city?

Lucy wasn't sure if she could take another complication. And yet, the universe seemed to have other plans. As she passed the alleyway that led behind the bakery, her feet faltered. Out of the corner of her eye she saw something move.

What with it being a little dark and gloomy outside—and the fact that the creature was down at the far end of the alley—Lucy's first thought was a bear. But it only took a second for her brain to register that it was just a *very* large, and rather dirty, dog. It was massive, definitely more than a hundred pounds and with huge paws. Its fur was matted and wet with mud and it was shivering as it sniffed around the dumpster.

Lucy didn't even realize she'd made a step toward the animal when it looked up at her, its sad expression so clear that her heart broke to pieces in an instant.

"Hello," she said softly as she took another step toward it. "It looks like you need a little help. Maybe a little food and water."

As she talked, the dog tilted its head to the side, watching her.

"It's awfully cold and wet out here. A warm and dry place to sleep would probably be nice too."

The dog continued to watch, its tail coming up and wagging slightly.

"Yeah, don't those things sound good?"

Its tail wagged more.

Lucy looked around, trying to figure out what to do to accomplish those things. The alleyway ended in a brick wall, so it couldn't run away, but she didn't want to corner it before earning its trust. It wasn't showing aggression, but she knew from experience how quickly that could change.

What she needed was help.

Setting her shopping bags on the ground, she pulled her phone out of her pocket and called the man who'd been on her mind all day.

"Hey, Luce," he said after exactly two rings.

"I need you."

"Is that so?" The smile in his voice was clear even through the phone.

"Yeah, I'm out back. There's a large dog sniffing around your trash cans and I want to help it."

"I'll be right there," he said without hesitation before hanging up.

* * *

THE AFTERNOON CROWD had settled down around two, Theo's grandparents leaving for the day, while he worked in the kitchen with his parents. Gia, Chloe, and Blake—who'd gotten his tire fixed—were up front manning the counter and restocking.

Theo had just pulled his cakes from the oven when his phone rang, Lucy's name lighting up the screen. He wasn't used to her calling him, and he found himself hoping that her name appeared on his screen way more frequently from here on out.

He also found himself hoping that she said *I need you* a lot more too.

His mother looked up from where she was slicing apples, her eyebrows raised high at her son's change in tone. "Everything okay?"

"Lucy's in the alley," Theo said as he started to untie his apron. "She said there's a dog back there and she needs help."

"Do you want me to help?" his father asked.

"I don't know yet. If it's a stray, too many people might spook it. Do we still have spare leashes upstairs?" Theo asked, as he grabbed his jacket and pulled it on.

"Probably. Let me go look." His mom dried her hands on a towel before pushing through the swinging door and into the front of the bakery.

Theo followed behind her, heading for the front door while his mother went for the stairs.

"Where are you going?" Gia called out behind him.

"None of your business," Theo said as he stepped outside into the cold.

It would've been quicker to go out the back door and into the alley, but as he didn't know exactly where the dog was, he didn't want to scare it. As he rounded the side of the building, he spotted Lucy standing in the mouth of the alley. She turned toward him, a smile lifting her lips as he got closer.

God, he could stare at her mouth for hours if given the chance. Though this clearly wasn't the time.

"Bear is down there." Lucy pointed as he got closer.

"Bear?"

"Yeah, it's what I thought it was at first."

He stopped when he got to her side, looking to where she indicated. The creature at the end of the alley was indeed large, though at first it looked more like a massive gray wolf to him. But he could understand why Lucy had thought it was a bear. It didn't happen all too often, but bears had been known to wander out of the woods and come into town to scavenge. What with it being so gloomy outside, the dog was a little hard to make out all the way at the end of the alley.

"We've got a bit of a standoff thing going on." Lucy frowned at him. "Its tail wags when I talk to it. But it won't come closer."

"Well, the tail wagging is a good sign."

"Agreed. Any ideas on how to get closer?"

"Food." He pulled out his phone, hitting a few buttons before holding it to his ear.

"Hey, Dad. Can you bring out some bread and ham?" There was a pause on the other end as Isaac said something. "Yeah, that too. The dog is by the dumpsters so you can use the back door, just open it slowly." Another pause. "Okay, perfect. Thanks."

He hung up and slid the phone into his pocket before looking back to the dog. "My mom found a leash upstairs, and they're going to send out some food and water. We'll just go from there." He tilted his head to the side, and if he didn't know any better, he thought that the dog mimicked the move from the other end of the alley.

"Did it just . . . ?" Lucy trailed off.

Theo leaned his head to the other side, and the dog followed the movement.

"I think it did *just*."

They stood there for a few moments, the dog watching them while they watched the dog. And then the door slowly opened next to them, and Gia and Chloe popped their heads out. Even with the small amount of movement Bear tensed, taking a step back.

"So, this is the *none of my business*?" Gia whispered but she didn't hide her exasperation as she looked over to them. "Hey, Luce."

"Hi, Ms. Buchanan!" Chloe's voice was soft, but she didn't hide her delight. It didn't matter that they'd *just* spent hours working at the drinks stand together. Lucy was their favorite teacher, a fact that Theo knew all too well as both Chloe and Gia never stopped talking about Lucy, or their drama class, or the play that they were in.

If there was a Lucy fan club, these two would be the presidents. Though Theo was a card-carrying member too.

The girls stepped outside, both sporting jackets. Chloe was holding a bowl of water and the leash, while Gia lifted her phone up and pressed *record*.

Theo shook his head at his sister as he took the water from Chloe. "Must you document everything?"

"Oh, come on, these videos always go viral."

"Yeah." Chloe nodded. "Everyone loves a good rescue mission."

"Fine, but stay back until we see how the dog reacts."

"Mom and Dad already made us promise." Gia looked up long enough to roll her eyes at her brother before focusing back down to the screen as she slowly circled behind him and Lucy. "They're working on getting the food."

"Good." Theo moved closer to Bear, setting the bowl of water down before stepping away.

Bear didn't move any closer. The dog did, however, take a few more steps back when the door opened again, Theo's dad on the other side. "How's it going?" he asked as he handed Lucy the bowl of food.

"No real progress yet. But I think it's warming up to us," she told him.

"Let us know if you need any help," Isaac said before he slowly closed the door again.

Lucy took the leash from Chloe—looping it around her neck like a scarf—before she moved to where Theo stood. "Okay, let me try. You need to go back there and try and look small and less intimidating." She pointed behind them.

"How do I do that?"

"Sit." She nodded to a crate that was leaning up against the side of the building, one of the few things that was dry as it was under the overhang.

He did as he was told, slowly flipping it before sitting down. Lucy moved closer to Bear, and the dog watched, waiting until she was about six feet away before taking another step back.

"Okay, so we've found our threshold." Lucy squatted down, making herself smaller as she set the bowl of food down.

Theo couldn't stop his eyes from lingering on Lucy's perfectly round ass as it stretched the back of her yoga pants.

Jesus Christ, man, get it the fuck together.

He shook his head, trying to clear it as Lucy grabbed a piece of ham, wrapping it in bread before tossing it in the space between her and the dog.

Bear didn't move.

"If you don't eat it, you're really going to be missing out." Lucy threw another piece of ham wrapped in bread closer to the dog. It took the few steps to get to it, gobbling it down before moving for the other piece. "This sourdough is what Browned Butter is known for. The starter is like seventy years old."

"Eighty," Theo couldn't stop himself from correcting.

Lucy glanced over her shoulder, rolling her eyes.

"What? It was my great-grandmother's recipe."

"Excuse me." She turned back to the dog. "The starter is *eighty* years old. Anyways, the bread is even better when you toast it. The best way is with butter in a cast-iron skillet, but a toaster will do."

She tossed another piece of bread and Bear moved in closer.

"It's great for grilled cheese," Lucy continued, her voice soft. "Now, the key is using a variety of cheese. You start with sharp cheddar, get some mozzarella, and then add a little Gruyère. It all melts together and it's pretty much perfection."

She continued to talk, Bear moving in closer and closer. Judging by the slightly wagging tail, Theo was pretty sure the dog liked the sound of Lucy's voice. Well, that or the bread, but Theo would put his money on Lucy.

"Now, the best thing to pair with the grilled cheese is tomato soup, but not from a can. You have to roast the tomatoes in the oven with some onions, a little garlic, and olive oil. And once they start to blister and the onions are soft, that's when you blend everything together with a little cream. And you top it all off by sprinkling fresh basil on top."

Bear was about four feet away from Lucy, and Theo could clearly see how thick the layer of mud was that had caked onto the dog's matted fur. Lucy threw another piece of bread toward the dog. It hesitated, unsure. It wasn't until a second piece flew through the air that the dog moved even closer, now just two feet away.

"You know Bear, this weather is only going to get worse tonight. If you let us, we can get you cleaned up. Get you dry and warm. Make you a soft bed with blankets and some toys. Let's get you safe."

This time Lucy held her hand out, a large piece of bread on her palm.

"Come on," Theo found himself whispering.

Bear took a tentative step forward, and then another, before stopping in front of Lucy. The dog stretched its big head forward, sniffing at the air before gently taking the piece of bread from Lucy's hand.

Everyone involved felt a sense of triumph as Lucy continued to feed the dog piece after piece until the bread and ham were gone. It was then that Lucy slowly reached her hand out, letting Bear sniff the back of it. In only a heartbeat, Bear licked Lucy's knuckles.

"That's it, sweet baby," Lucy purred before she moved her hand to Bear's head.

The dog closed its eyes, finding pleasure in the gentle touch. Lucy moved her hands to Bear's back, continuing her ministrations until Bear's head lowered to the water bowl and started drinking. And that was when Lucy very carefully pulled the lead from around her own neck and slipped it around Bear's.

CHAPTER EIGHT

Mama Bear

Lucy let out a sigh of relief the second she had the lead in place. At the sound, Bear looked up, giving Lucy another big lick on the hand, this time with her mouth dripping with water. Lucy had gotten a quick look to confirm that the dog was indeed a girl.

"Thanks for that," Lucy said as she gave Bear another good pet on the shoulders. Her hands were dirty from all of the mud that was caked onto the dog's fur. "Let's get you cleaned up, sweet girl. Doesn't that sound nice?"

Bear looked at her and it was then that Lucy noticed her eyes were light brown. And in those eyes there was a sadness and exhaustion that Lucy knew all too well.

"I promise I'll take care of you," Lucy whispered before she could stop herself. She meant it too, even if Bear didn't understand her.

Except the dog moved forward, bowing her wet, muddy head and rubbing it against Lucy's chest. And right then and there, something in Lucy's heart cracked open. There was suddenly a burning sensation at the tip of her nose—the telltale sign that tears were gathering at the corners of her eyes—but she shook it off.

Lucy wasn't really a crier, and this was no time to get emotional.

"All right." Her voice broke a little bit, betraying her. "Let's go, Bear." She wrapped the leash in her hand as she slowly stood and turned.

Her eyes landed on Theo first. He was still sitting on the crate, something like shock and awe etched on his face. "That was impressive." There was an earnestness in his voice that did not help the already growing fissure in her chest.

Nor did it help when she looked to Chloe, who was wiping tears from her eyes, or Gia, who was still filming as she beamed at her like she was a superhero.

But she wasn't a hero. She'd just been able to get the dog. It wasn't that big of a deal.

Lucy cleared her throat, trying to get rid of the lingering emotion. It didn't help that at that moment Bear pressed her body against the side of Lucy's leg. "Okay, should we take her home?" she asked, her voice just a tad bit shaky.

Theo shook his head, holding his phone in the air. "I texted Oscar. He's going to meet us at his office. He'll probably get there before we do."

That was probably accurate. Mountain View Veterinary Clinic was a few blocks away, and Lucy had no idea how Bear was going to be on a leash.

"Okay, let's go." Theo slowly stood, clearly trying not to spook Bear.

"Us too!" Chloe whisper-shouted.

"Yeah! We're going too!" Gia pressed the screen of her phone as she stopped recording.

Theo frowned as he moved back to the door, knocking lightly. A moment later it opened, this time with Theo's mother on the other side. "Did you get the dog?"

"We got it."

Isaac's head popped up over Juliet's shoulder. There was a pause as they both looked around, their eyes going wide. "Holy cow."

"It's massive," Juliet finished. "Boy or girl?"

"A girl. Oscar is meeting us at the vet, and Gia and Chloe want to go. Can you guys handle things here?"

"We got it covered." Juliet nodded. "I'll put your cakes in the freezer once they cool. Keep us posted, though I don't think things will be too tough with that dog. Looks like Lucy has a new fan."

Lucy followed Juliet's gaze to find that Bear had sat down next to her and was looking up adoringly. "You're going to be okay, pretty girl." Bear nuzzled her head against Lucy's leg, leaving another smudge of dirt behind. "Thanks." Lucy reached down, petting that spot between her ears, causing those sweet eyes to close in pleasure.

"That dog already trusts you."

Lucy looked up to find Theo watching her . . . they were all watching her, actually, but it was Theo's face that she couldn't look away from. "Well, let's get her taken care of, then."

"Let's." He nodded.

"I'm going to record you guys as we walk." Gia already had her phone out again as she and Chloe moved to the mouth of the alley.

"How are you planning to do that without falling over?" Isaac asked.

"Easy." Chloe—who was facing forward—looped her arm through Gia's free one. "I'll guide her."

It continued to amaze Lucy that these two girls had only known each other since the beginning of the school year and not their entire lives, and apparently, she wasn't the only one who thought it.

"I swear you two have been friends longer than four months." Juliet shook her head as she and Isaac made to disappear back inside.

"Hey, wait up," Theo called out, stopping them. "Can you take these?" He grabbed the handles of Lucy's bags before giving them to his father.

Isaac winked at Theo before stepping back and letting the door shut.

"All right, let's go," Theo said as he took up the spot on the far right of the sidewalk, acting as a barrier between the street and Lucy and Bear.

Out of the corner of her eye, Lucy could see that Theo's focus was on the dog. Bear was sticking to Lucy's left side, as far away from everyone else as possible. She was walking along easily enough, but her tail was tucked between her legs again and she kept looking up at Lucy nervously.

"You know," Theo said as they rounded a corner, "I've been a part of many a dog rescue with Sasha and Lorraine and even Oscar lately, and I don't think I've ever seen one that went as smoothly. I didn't realize you were a dog whisperer."

"I'm not." Lucy laughed as she looked over at him.

He smiled in that way that was just for her. "Could've fooled me."

"Oh my gosh, could you two *be* any more into each other? It's so gross."

"Thanks, Gia." Theo frowned at his sister, who was still being guided down the sidewalk by Chloe.

"So, are you guys like boyfriend and girlfriend or what?"

"Do you remember when we talked about things not being any of your business? This is one of those times."

"Yes, but you've never dated someone that I know personally. So, I'm making it my business. What's going on with the two of you?"

"Do you honestly think I'm going to answer that question while you're filming?"

"Oh, don't worry." Gia looked up. "I'll be cutting out all of your chatter and putting in a dramatic music montage. So, what's the deal?"

"I'm not telling you."

"So grouchy." Gia grinned before looking back down at her phone. "Will you answer the question, Lucy?"

Lucy paused for a moment, a smile playing at her mouth. "Sorry, kiddo, I agree with Theo." She looked over at him, his blue eyes brighter.

"What is that? Three times that we've agreed with each other, and now it's documented."

Lucy leaned toward him, her mouth close enough to his ear so only he could hear. "I think there was *a lot* of agreeing last night."

When she pulled away, he was smiling at her again. "That's a true statement."

"Fine." Gia sounded exasperated as they turned a corner. "If you won't tell me about *this* relationship, tell me about the last one. Why did it end with that guy in California?" she asked Lucy. "The one you told me you were dating when you visited last Christmas."

"Gia, stop it." Theo shook his head.

"No. It's fine," Lucy told him before she focused on the girls.

"To say that things didn't end well would be the understatement of the year. He wanted to change me, to make me into something *he* wanted. I figured it out too late . . ." She trailed off.

Beyond her sister and friends, Lucy hadn't really talked a lot about what had happened at the end of that relationship. But in that moment, she didn't care if Theo and the girls knew. She'd made mistakes, and she'd learned from them. She wasn't embarrassed about what had happened. She was stronger because of it. And if there was anything that she could tell Gia and Chloe to help them avoid being in a similar situation, she wasn't going to keep it to herself.

"When it started, it was just small things, and I ignored the warning signs." She looked directly at Gia and Chloe. "*Never* ignore the warning signs, girls. *Always* trust your gut."

Gia looked up from the camera again, a question in her eyes, but it was Chloe who spoke first. "What was it that you ignored?"

Lucy simply said, "That if someone doesn't like you exactly as you are, if someone tries to change you to fit their standards, they aren't for you. The problem was, he didn't try to start changing me until I was in too deep."

Her ex had thoroughly messed with her head. A master manipulator in every way.

"What do you mean?" Gia asked, stopping when they were in front of the veterinary clinic. "Like you were in love with him?"

Lucy wasn't looking at Theo, and wasn't close enough to feel him, but she *knew* he tensed next to her.

"No." Lucy shook her head. "It was never love." She'd never let herself get to that point with any man. The closest she'd ever come was Theo, and that was the reason she'd left Cruickshank seven years ago . . . because it had scared her so much.

"Then what was it?" Chloe asked.

"An infatuation, I guess. I couldn't believe he was into me and I . . . I opened myself up to him before really learning who *he* was. In the end, he took all of the vulnerable parts of me and turned them against me. It was a toxic relationship, one I couldn't be happier to be out of. It's just sometimes hard to see when you're *in* it."

Gia nodded her head slowly as if she didn't quite understand. Chloe gave a small nod and looked through the window of Mountain View Veterinary Clinic. "We heading in? Oscar's here."

"Yeah," Theo said. His arm brushed against Lucy as he moved for the door. Even through all those layers of clothes, Lucy's skin still broke out into goose bumps. She was pretty sure she'd never get over the way he touched her.

Lucy waited for the girls before leading Bear through the door that Theo held open. As she passed him, she couldn't stop herself from looking up into his face. Those blue eyes of his were focused intently on her, his mouth turned down into a frown.

"What?"

He shook his head slowly, like he didn't understand. "It's just that you drive me crazy in absolutely every way imaginable, and I wouldn't change *anything* about you."

Lucy's mouth fell open on an inhale. It took her a second to remember how to speak. "I think that might be the nicest thing you've ever said to me."

"You sure? I thought I said some nice things last night." He grinned.

Lucy's head fell back as she laughed.

"Are you two coming or what?" Gia's voice cut through the air, but it didn't break the moment.

Something had changed between them since last night. Something she had no clue if she was ready for. At least she knew she wasn't ready for it to end.

* * *

It took the combined effort of Theo and Oscar to get Bear into the elevated tub. The second they had the dog lowered in, she moved to the corner, tail tucked between her legs. Bear looked at them with those sorrowful eyes she'd been giving them for the last half hour.

Theo wondered what it would take to get that sorrow out of the dog's eyes.

"It's okay, sweet girl," Lucy soothed, her voice soft and calm as she moved forward and petted the dog under her chin.

Bear's tail slowly rose, wagging just slightly.

How had she already earned the dog's trust? It would astound Theo if he didn't know the woman so well.

Too well.

She was infuriating, and stubborn, and competitive—qualities that would have the tendency to drive a person crazy, especially when they had the exact same ones themselves—but she was also loyal and passionate and brave and so beautiful it was insane.

Why would anyone try to change her?

An elbow into his side had Theo coming back from his thoughts and he turned to see Oscar staring at him. "Go help her wash the dog while I finish up in the exam room." He handed a bottle of shampoo over before heading out the door.

Lucy was messing with the water, turning it on and adjusting the knobs to get a good temperature.

"How do you want to do this?" Theo asked as he set the bottle on the tub's ledge.

"We'll rinse Bear off first. You're in charge of water," she said as she handed the sprayer to Chloe. She then turned to Theo and looked up at him. "You don't mind getting your hands dirty, do you?"

God, he was so close to her. Close enough to smell that spicy vanilla on her skin again. Close enough to feel the heat of her body. Close enough to see the specks of gold in her hazel-green eyes. This wasn't the dirty he'd *like* to be getting with her.

"Nope." He shook his head—trying to clear it—as he rolled up the sleeves of his shirt.

Lucy's gaze followed the movement, going from his hands to his now bared forearms. She gave a funny little nod before she turned away and looked back to Bear. "Good."

Well, apparently he wasn't the only one affected by the other . . . though there would be no acting on it anytime soon. They had other fish to fry . . . or other dogs to bathe, in this case.

It didn't take long for them to discover that Bear apparently enjoyed baths. Getting the dog into the tub was as far as their trouble went, because when the warm water hit Bear's back, her whole demeanor changed. She looked like she was in heaven.

Chloe moved around, gently spraying the water while Lucy and Theo scratched and rubbed at the dog's fur, loosening the dirt and grime. Bear sat down, her head falling back with her eyes closed. Her tail started to pick up speed as it wagged back and forth.

Meanwhile, Gia continued with her filming, getting every adorable moment. It took a good five minutes of scrubbing before the water started to lighten up. As the dirt and grime disappeared, the dog's coloring became more apparent. She was mostly white but had larger spots of buff and a few areas where she was a darker brown.

Lucy squeezed a generous amount of shampoo onto the dog's back. It was when Theo started to lather up the soap on Bear's chest that her back paw began to thump loudly against the white porcelain. "I've never seen a dog love a bath more in my life."

"Wouldn't you enjoy one if you were that covered in mud?" Chloe moved around to rinse another spot.

"I'm sure it feels good. Doesn't it, Bear?" Theo asked.

The dog's answer was to stretch down and lick his arm.

"Look at that." Gia moved up closer, getting a new angle. "It didn't take too long for you to win her over too."

"Yeah, she's not untrusting, just scared," Theo said. "It makes me wonder if she belongs to someone." Theo started to work the soap into Bear's side and the dog's back leg began to hit the tub with more force, the echo in the room louder.

"Maybe." Lucy nodded. "We're going to have to get a picture of her loaded into the lost pet database. Though maybe the person who lost her already has one up."

It had been Caro who'd created the database. A website for rescues, shelters, and vets within a couple of counties to access for cases just like this. They'd been able to reunite many owners with their pets over the years. The site was also connected to the Cruickshank Cats and Dogs Rescue and had the added benefit of helping lost and unclaimed animals get adopted sooner.

"Well, you'll be safe tonight. *That*, I can promise," Lucy said as she lathered the fur around the dog's neck. "You're so pretty, and sweet."

Bear's eyes opened at the praise, as if she understood what Lucy was saying. She moved her head down, nuzzling Lucy's hand.

"How's it going in here?" Oscar asked as he walked back into the room.

"Mostly clean," Chloe answered. "She needs rinsing and conditioning, though."

"Yeah," Lucy agreed. "That might help with some of the more

matted areas of fur, but we're probably going to have to shave under her arms where it's really bad."

"Let me see," Oscar said as he took up the space toward the middle of the tub. His hands moved over Bear's back and sides before moving to her belly. He felt around for a second before saying, "I think she might be pregnant."

"What?" Lucy looked over in shock.

"Once she's dry, we can do an ultrasound and find out for sure."

It was another ten minutes before Bear was done with her bath. They all tried to towel her off as much as possible in the tub before carefully lifting her out again. Once she had all four paws on the ground, she took over the task of getting dry. Bear was all over the pile of towels, rolling around on her back, rubbing each side of her head, and scooting along her side.

"Come here," Lucy said as she grabbed a dry towel from the counter and held it open wide. Bear came to her immediately, letting Lucy rub it all over as she spun around in circles.

Theo moved to the side of the room, giving the dog space to move and roll around. But it wasn't long before Bear was crossing over to him. At first, he thought it was because she wanted to be petted, but as it turned out, she was heading for the bowl of water at his feet. She took a good *long* drink, and when she finally lifted her head, she moved to him and rubbed her sopping-wet mouth across his jeans.

"Thanks," he said as he bent down and scratched her neck, but he couldn't stop the little smile that tugged at the corner of his mouth.

Bear closed her eyes, her head falling back like it had in the tub, her leg starting to thump against the floor.

"See, she really does like you." Lucy patted him on the shoulder. "No need to have your feelings hurt anymore."

He looked up at her. "My feelings weren't hurt."

"Yeah, they were." Lucy smiled as she slipped a new lead over Bear's head, guiding her to the door. "Come on, Bear. Let's get you to the exam room."

Bear didn't need more than a gentle tug to follow behind Lucy, but she hesitated in the threshold, looking back at Theo. If he didn't know any better, the dog's expression seemed to say, *Are you coming?*

* * *

It took about forty minutes for Oscar to get Bear all checked out. She had an ear infection as well as hot spots where her fur had been matted and was now shaved away. She had *not* been a fan and cried and flinched through most of the process.

Lucy did her best to try to calm Bear down, talking to the dog while rubbing her back and attempting to soothe her. Bear stared up at Lucy, and the more Lucy looked into those soft brown eyes, the more she was a goner. There was something about this dog . . . something that pulled at her heart more than usual.

It was pretty clear that she'd be breaking her no-fostering rule.

As Oscar continued on with the exam, he found good news—Bear was heartworm negative—but was concerned with her weight. She was too lean for his liking, especially because she was pregnant. With the help of the ultrasound, he guessed there were about eight puppies.

"Eight?" Chloe's eyes went wide. "Isn't that a lot?"

"It is, but it could be more." He moved the wand around Bear's stomach. "She's a big dog, which means she could have a very large litter. On average dogs are usually pregnant for about nine weeks and I think she's about four. We're going to have to watch her closely."

"Yeah, we are," Chloe agreed.

"Oh, are you helping?" Theo asked, his eyebrows raising high.

"Yes. This is now a group effort." Gia waved her hand around at everyone in the room.

"How do you know she doesn't have an owner?" Oscar looked to the girls.

"If she does, they clearly aren't looking very hard, and they don't deserve her." Lucy's words came out a lot harsher than usual . . . but she meant them, nonetheless. She'd taken a second during the exam to pull up the lost-pets website, and Bear was not on it. She also didn't have a microchip.

"Well, that might be the case," Oscar agreed. "But we'll deal with that at a later time. As for now, who's taking her?"

"I am," Lucy said before anyone else could answer. "I'll get her settled in tonight."

"Can we come over too?" Gia asked Lucy.

"I can't go." Chloe shook her head. "It's family dinner night and I have *got* to get my homework done." She gave a sheepish look at Lucy. "I still haven't started my history paper for Mr. Damon's class. And it's due Monday by five o'clock."

"But you guys are off for the week." Lucy looked at them in confusion.

"They were due on Friday, but he gave us an extension because of the football game. He said he didn't want to stress any of the players out so we could email it to him."

"Well, that was nice of him." Theo turned to his sister. "Have you finished yours?"

"*Noooo.*" Gia dragged out the word as she shifted on her feet. "But I need more footage."

"We'll film some stuff tonight and send it to you," Lucy promised.

"*We* will?" Theo looked over at her, his eyes alight. "Is that an invitation?"

Dammit. She'd walked right into that one. "Do you want it to be?"

"Do you want me to want it to be?" Theo countered.

"Wow is it weird when you two are openly flirting." Gia's expression turned pained.

"They've always been openly flirting," Oscar said. "There just isn't all of that hostility behind it. Now they're being nice to each other."

"Yes, well, it's weird."

"Fine." Lucy frowned at Gia. "I don't like his shirt. Does that make you feel better?"

"Yes, that does make me feel better."

"What's wrong with my shirt?" Theo was clearly affronted as he looked down at what he was wearing.

"It's mostly brown." Lucy shrugged. "Blue and green always make your eyes pop."

"And now you've ruined it again." Gia waved her hand in the air as if to erase Lucy's words.

Theo was full-on grinning now. "So, is it an invitation or not? Because if you take Bear home with you, you're going to have to introduce her to Estee, and you might need help."

If Lucy was being totally honest, she hadn't even thought about how her cat was going to react, mainly because she hadn't thought beyond the fact that Bear wouldn't be going home with anyone *but* her. Her cat had always been good with dogs . . . but that didn't mean Bear was good with cats.

If they didn't get along, she'd have to reevaluate the situation. Count on Theo to be prepared three steps in advance. He always had been a Boy Scout.

"Fine. It's an invitation."

His mouth twitched behind his beard. "Good."

Lucy moved her focus from Theo back to Gia. "We will send you videos as we record them. And you guys can come over after you turn in your paper. Deal?"

"Deal," Gia agreed begrudgingly.

"Well, now that that's all sorted"—Oscar rubbed his hands together—"let's finish up so we can get everyone on their way. You two aren't the only ones who have a date." He nodded at Lucy and Theo.

"Who said it's a date?" Lucy asked.

"Is there going to be dinner involved?"

Before she could answer, Lucy's stomach let out a very audible growl. She'd been hungry when she'd headed for the bakery more than an hour ago. Now she was starving.

"It's a date." Oscar grinned.

"How much longer do you need?" Theo turned to Oscar.

"Probably thirty minutes."

"Okay, we're going to go back to the bakery," he said, indicating Gia and Chloe. "I'll get them home before it starts really raining, and then come pick you and Bear up. That sound good?" he asked Lucy.

"Yeah. That sounds good." She nodded.

"Okay. See you in thirty," he said before he ushered the girls out the door.

Lucy watched them go, her eyes lingering on Theo's broad shoulders and up to the back of his neck. His hair was getting long, and as he disappeared down the hall, she couldn't help but think about how soft it had been under her fingertips.

"You going to be okay?"

Her friend's words pulled her out of her slight daze, and she shook her head as she looked over at Oscar. "I'm fine. What are you talking about?"

An amused smile was turning up the corners of Oscar's mouth. "The two of you have got it so bad for each other. I always thought there was *something* going on, but I didn't realize it was *this*. I'm ashamed that I missed how intense it was."

Heat filled Lucy's cheeks. "It isn't intense." A lie. *Such* a big lie.

"Sure, it isn't." He gently patted her on the shoulder. "I'm surprised you didn't rip that shirt off him that you hate so much."

Lucy's eyes narrowed. "Remember when we talked about payback last night? You're now on the list with Sasha and Gavin. I'm going to be unbearable when it comes to you and Edward."

"Okay, okay." He held his hands up in surrender, but that smile of his was still firmly in place.

"Speaking of you and Edward . . . where are you going tonight?"

Oscar's grin was now one of excitement. "I made reservations at Bernardine's."

The little French bistro had absolutely amazing food. "Ohhh, fancy. What are you wearing?"

"Well, since you have such strong opinions about fashion, any ideas?"

"Your brown leather jacket. You always look sexy as hell when you wear it."

"Oh, I do, do I? Do I need to tell Theo he has competition?"

Lucy rolled her eyes. "You know I stopped having a crush on you when you figured out you were gay. I'm still slightly devastated about it, but here we are."

"Here we are," Oscar agreed. "Let's finish up with Bear so we can *both* get on with our evenings." He dropped his hands and his focus back to the dog.

* * *

THEO WAS PULLING UP IN FRONT of Mountain View Veterinary Clinic with three minutes to spare. Considering he'd added an extra stop on the way back, he thought that was pretty damn impressive.

The rain had finally started in earnest—a cold steady drizzle—so he grabbed the large umbrella from his back seat before heading inside. Everyone was in the reception area, Lucy and Bear standing in front of the desk while Oscar sat behind the computer on the other side. As there was no one there to run the office on the weekend, he had to do it.

"How about we schedule Bear's next appointment for the Wednesday after Thanksgiving?"

"That works." Lucy nodded. "And I'll keep you posted if we find her owner."

"Same here." Oscar typed a few keys before clicking the mouse and standing up. "Here you go," he said as he handed Theo a bag of medicine before rounding the counter and walking them to the door. "Let me know if you need anything with her."

"Will do."

Oscar locked the door and gave them a little wave before he disappeared back into the office.

"Ready?" Theo asked as he popped the umbrella over Lucy and Bear, huddling in closer. He got a hit of the vanilla chai scent and it made his head swim a little.

"Yup." She glanced up at him, and he couldn't help but pick out those gold flecks in her hazel-green eyes again.

Why did he have the sudden urge to count them? There were far too many; he'd have to stare into her eyes for ages . . .

"Then let's go." Theo nodded, forcing himself to turn away before he did something embarrassing, like say what he'd been thinking out loud. They rounded to the passenger side of his truck, and he opened the back door before handing the umbrella to Lucy. "I'll get her up." His truck was a bit high off the ground, and he knew the dog would have a tough time getting in. He slowly bent down, wrapping his arms around Bear and lifting her up in one easy move.

"I'll sit back here with her," Lucy said as she handed the umbrella back to Theo. She made to reach up for the truck's interior grab handle; instinctively his free hand was at her waist, guiding her into the back seat. She looked at him as she settled in the seat, her cheeks pink. She let out an awkward little throat clear before saying, "Thank you."

Theo nodded as he shut the door, fisting his hand around the feel of her that still lingered on his palm.

He took a deep breath of the cold, crisp air, trying his best to clear his head as he rounded the truck. It worked for about a second, and then he was climbing inside and closing the door behind him. He'd never thought that his truck was small until that moment. His only saving grace was that the cab didn't smell like her.

"Oh my gosh. Did you pick up food from Quigley's? It smells like Nari's kimchi fried rice."

"That's because it *is* Nari's kimchi fried rice. Gavin told me his mom was making it today, and since it's my favorite, I went and got us some." He glanced up at the rearview mirror, catching her gaze. "And since I know that you love her japchae, I got an order of that too."

"How do you know that's my favorite?"

"Because you always order it when it's available." He started the engine, music filling the cab. He was only just able to hear her say "thank you" again over the sound of the guitar.

CHAPTER NINE
Right into Place

*I*t wasn't even a three-minute drive to get to Lucy's, but by the time Theo pulled in behind her father's truck, the skies had opened up.

"What's the plan?" he asked as he turned around, palming the back of the passenger seat headrest. Her eyes lingered on his hand, remembering for just a second how it had felt on her waist earlier . . . and the rest of her body the night before.

She pulled her gaze away and looked out the window and up the narrow stairs that led to the little loft above her father's garage.

"I say we just make a run for it. We can dry her off again when we get inside."

"What about Estee?"

"She's at my dad's. I usually take her over when I'm not going to be home so she can hang out with Leia." Leia was her father's German shepherd, who got along with almost all creatures, four-legged and two-legged alike. "What with the storm, I'm thinking it actually might be best if we introduce Bear to both of them tomorrow. I'll text him when we get inside and let him know."

"Works for me." Theo nodded. "So, you get Bear, while I'll get our dinner."

Our dinner. Oscar's words from earlier flitted through her head . . . did dinner make this a date? First sex. Now dating. It was a little backward.

"I'll go first," Lucy said as she fished her keys out of the pocket of her rain jacket. "See you up there." She pulled up her hood before opening the door and hopping out. It was a little awkward helping Bear down, but they managed before making a mad dash for the door. Bear was just as eager to get out of the rain and she didn't require too much coaxing up the stairs.

The little overhang provided some shelter and Bear did a full body shake, the water that clung to her fur soaking into Lucy's already wet yoga pants.

"Good girl," Lucy said as she fit the key in the lock and turned it. "Better to get it off out here than inside."

She left the door open behind her, quickly pulling off her raincoat before leading Bear to the mustard-yellow dresser in the corner that served as her makeshift linen closet. Grabbing a towel from the top drawer she threw it over Bear, running the hot-pink terry cloth up and down the dog's back.

Out of the corner of her eye, she saw Theo walk through the door, heading for the little lime-green table and chairs at the end of the kitchen. He set the food and her shopping bags down before slipping off his shoes, putting them on the mat by the door. It was exactly where he'd left them the night before. When he straightened, he pulled his rain jacket off, hanging it up on the hook next to hers. His coat was a hunter green, way more subtle than her yellow.

She couldn't help but like the contrast of him in her apartment. He was flannel and scruff and leather work boots, while she was bright colors and moody jewel tones, squishy pillows and mismatched furniture. They were so different in some ways, and yet . . .

It worked. *They* worked.

He looked up at her, catching her watching him. "What?"

"Nothing." She stopped drying Bear, standing up as she leaned back against the wall. The dog took a few steps away before slowly moving around and starting to check everything out. They watched for a moment before Theo turned back to Lucy.

"So, what's next?" he asked, moving toward her.

"Get her settled? And then get us settled?"

"Okay." He reached out, his hands landing on her hips. "I just need to do something first." He leaned in close, his lips brushing hers.

"And what's that?" Lucy asked, feeling just a bit breathless.

"This." His mouth covered hers, his hands tightening on her hips as he pulled her closer. He tilted his head to the side, deepening the kiss. It was a good minute before he pulled back, looking down at her. "Your mouth has been driving me crazy for the last hour."

"Doesn't my mouth usually drive you crazy?"

"Well, yes, but today it was for different reasons. All I've wanted to do was kiss you."

"Well, do it again." Lucy laughed as she stretched up and pressed another kiss to his lips . . . and another one after that . . . and another one after that.

* * *

THEO RECORDED BEAR as she did another perimeter check around the apartment, sniffing all the things and smelling all the smells. She was no doubt looking for Estee. Once she settled down a little—and the rain had lightened up—Theo took her for a little walk around the backyard so she could use the bathroom.

Again, it was another round of sniffing all the things and smelling all the smells. As there was another dog who lived there, and a number of others who visited, there was a lot to check out . . . and scents to try and cover up.

When Theo and Bear got back inside, the next priority was food. Well, food for Bear, more accurately. Theo and Lucy's dinner sat untouched in the bag on the table, but luckily for them, the longer it sat the better it tasted. Besides, they could wait.

Given Bear's pregnancy, and how underweight she was, Oscar had given them special food to get her calorie intake up. So, Theo stood in the kitchen, again filming while Bear ate. Meanwhile, Lucy was in the living room, getting a little bed together with old pillows and blankets.

It wasn't as slow of a process to get her to eat as it had been in the alley. The dog was warming up to them more and more as the time passed, feeling safe for the first time in Lord only knew how long. She was still a little skittish, but he was pretty sure it had more to do with the wind now whipping around the house than it had to do with him or Lucy.

Bear had just finished the food in her bowl when a loud bang echoed from outside. She moved closer to Theo, pressing her side into his leg.

"No need to be so scared." He reached down, petting the dog's head. "You're okay now."

Bear cautiously looked up at him, her sad eyes assessing.

"No one is going to hurt you." He moved his hand down the side of her face, scratching under her ear and down her neck.

One of her back legs started to move a little.

"See, she *really* likes you."

Theo looked up to see Lucy watching him from the living room. She'd turned on the electric fireplace and plugged in her twinkle lights. He'd done the same thing the night before. Then it had been about *setting the mood*, but tonight with the rain, it just seemed cozy.

"I just found her spot."

"Well, you're good at that." Lucy grinned.

Theo laughed, shaking his head as he looked back to Bear. The dog rubbed her head against his leg, clearly wanting more attention. Moving slowly, Theo carefully sat down next to her, getting in a better position to give her more pets and neck scratches. She closed her eyes, her head falling back.

"You're a good girl, aren't you, Bear?" He ran his fingers through the soft—and now clean—fur on her back. It was so thick, a good thing considering how cold it had been. "How long were you out there?" he whispered, still trying to film.

She obviously couldn't answer him in words, but those sad tired eyes were on him again and she seemed to say *long enough*.

"I wish she could tell us what happened," Lucy said as she walked into the kitchen, taking the phone from Theo so she could film, and he had the use of both hands to pet the dog.

"Tell us if someone hurt her." Theo nodded. "But it's okay that she can't; no one will hurt her again."

At his words, Bear dropped her head, pressing it right over his heart. Something inside of Theo's chest shifted.

"She trusts you." Lucy's voice was so soft. Theo looked up at her, finding that same softness in her expression.

As if to prove the point, Bear flopped down into Theo's lap— all eighty-seven pounds of her—giving him better access. Theo returned his focus to the dog, scratching the side of her belly. Her leg really started to move in a powerful kick that he'd hate to be on the other end of.

Theo continued to give Bear attention for a couple of minutes before he looked back up at Lucy. "Well, I think she's settled. Wasn't the next part of the plan getting *us* settled?"

Lucy tapped the screen of her phone before lowering it. "Yes. I feel like a shower is in order. Bear might be clean, but we are not."

"Will this shower be separate or together?" Theo raised his eyebrows.

Lucy looked him over. "You think she'll be okay if we're . . . *occupied* for a bit?"

"Only one way to find out." Theo glanced down at the dog, who was still luxuriating under his ministrations. "You think you can handle twenty minutes on your own? There's a soft bed in the living room. It even has a few toys. Let's go check them out."

Bear nudged his hand, licking his knuckles before she rolled over and got to her feet.

"Did she just understand me?" He looked up at Lucy.

Lucy laughed, shaking her head. "Probably not all of those words, but I'm guessing she understands *let's go*."

At those two words Bear began to excitedly wiggle her butt.

"See." Lucy scratched Bear on the head. "Such a smart girl. And a pretty girl. Come here." She patted her thigh as she headed for the living room, and Bear trotted along behind her.

And for the second time, the dog looked back at Theo as if to ask *are you coming?*

* * *

THE BATHROOM STEAMED around them as they divested themselves—and each other—of their clothes. Lucy worked on the front of Theo's pants while he pulled his shirt over his head. The second she got the button undone and the zipper down, she slid her hand under the elastic of his boxer briefs, palming his cock.

He groaned and she laughed, but a second later he covered her mouth with his.

It took them a little bit to get completely naked, but they eventually made their way into the shower.

Lucy had always thought that the bathroom was a decent size for one person—especially when taking into consideration the size of the rest of the apartment—but with her and Theo sharing the space, it was rather small . . . and awkward.

But they figured out a way to make it work.

When they got out, it was to find Bear in exactly the same spot they'd left her. Nice and cozy, curled up on the bed in front of the electric fireplace.

"She must be exhausted," Theo said as he crossed the room with only a towel wrapped around his waist. He reached behind Lucy's shopping bags on the table, pulling out a small gym bag.

"What's that?" Lucy asked, running a towel through her wet hair.

"When I went to the bakery, I grabbed some clothes. Figured I'd need something to change into."

Lucy shook her head, grinning. "You're always one step ahead, aren't you?"

"With you I have to be."

They both pulled on some cozy clothes, Lucy another pair of yoga pants and a hot-pink sweatshirt with a cat wearing sunglasses, and Theo a long-sleeved Carolina Panthers T-shirt and a pair of gray sweatpants.

"You just had to wear those, didn't you?" Lucy waved her fork at him before she scraped the fried rice into a pan on the stove.

"What's wrong with these?"

"Act like you don't know."

"I have no idea what you're talking about."

"Gray sweatpants are like the unofficial symbol of cold weather horniness."

Theo laughed. "Excuse me?"

"It's a whole thing. You should google it."

Theo came up behind her, wrapping his arms around her waist as he kissed her neck. "There are much better things I'd like to do with my time than that."

Lucy tilted her head to the side, giving him better access. "Is that so?"

"Mmm hmm."

"Well, if we're going to be doing *that* again, we need to eat first."

"Very true. How can I help?"

"Want to get us something to drink?" Lucy asked as she moved her attention from the fried rice to the pan of japchae, stirring the noodles around. "I've got wine, beer, and sparkling water."

"We could do a bottle of wine." Theo pressed another kiss to her neck before letting go and moving off to the fridge.

Lucy couldn't stop herself from getting a glance of those sweatpants from behind. But that glance turned into something much longer as he bent over, the soft gray fabric going tight over his ass.

And man, did Theo have a nice ass.

God, this whole thing was crazy. Him being in her apartment. The two of them eating at her tiny kitchen table. Them spending the evening curled up on her sofa, snuggled together under one of her fuzzy blankets while they watched *Friends*. Lucy had wanted to put something on that she didn't have to focus too intently on. Mainly because they kept talking . . . and kissing.

They were a few episodes in when the storm picked up outside. It started to thunder and lightning, and Bear got up from her bed of blankets and pillows, making her way over to them. There was just enough room for her to get up on the sofa, and she curled up on Theo's other side, resting her big fluffy head on his lap.

"I think she's comfortable," Theo said as he gently scratched the back of her neck. The dog closed her eyes in pleasure, letting him pet her to sleep.

It was a few hours later when Lucy was the one being lulled to sleep by Theo's touch. She lay in his arms, her back to his front, his hand on her hip as he traced slow lazy circles. After their last round she could barely move, her body sinking into the mattress.

Her body sinking into *him*.

"Lucy," he whispered as he kissed her shoulder, his lips moving across her skin until he paused at the spot beneath her neck.

"Hmm," she hummed, stretching her head to the side to give him better access.

"When did you get this?" This time when he kissed her, his mouth was open, his tongue flicking out.

She shivered in his arms, her mind going a little fuzzy. She couldn't think straight when he put his mouth on her. "Get what?"

"This kite tattoo. You didn't have it before."

"I got it a few months ago . . . after I moved back . . ."

His hand left her thigh, moving up and brushing her hair away from her back. She sucked in a breath as his fingers traced over the string that trailed down her back. At the end of that string was a little girl in a dress, her head tilted up to the sky.

Theo's fingertips outlined the little girl, but a moment later his touch was replaced with his mouth. This kiss wasn't sexual, but sweet. It had been so long since someone had been gentle with Lucy and it affected her more than she was prepared for, knocking the breath from her lungs.

"What does it mean?" His words were soft, just like his touch.

"I asked Caro to draw it for me. I wanted something hopeful and when you're flying a kite, you have to have your head up to look at it. I needed a reminder after everything that's happened. I mean, I've always needed a reminder of that since my mom died, but I needed it after this year too."

"Luce . . ." He trailed off, pausing for a second before continuing. Like he was trying to figure out if he should. "What . . . what happened in California?"

Now Lucy was the one hesitating, pulling in an unsteady breath at his question. Sure, she'd opened up a little that afternoon when Gia and Chloe had asked, but this was different. Theo wanted to know *more*, and Lucy hadn't really gotten into the *more* with a lot of people. Caro, Sasha, and Lilah knew the most, but she hadn't even told them everything.

"You don't have to tell me if you don't want to." Theo moved his hand down and to her side, sliding it back into place at her hip. His fingers were stretched out, spanning as much of her skin as possible.

"I wasn't . . . enough," Lucy whispered. "I wasn't thin enough. Or pretty enough. Or musically talented enough. My ex—"

Theo tensed behind her when she brought him up.

"H-he pointed out every flaw, every imperfection, but he did it in this way where it came off as helpful advice at first, and then it slowly morphed into something else. I think it was all a big game to him. One that he's played many times before. And when he wins, he moves on to hurt someone else."

"How did he play the game?"

"He'd comment on what I ate or didn't eat. He had an opinion about everything that had to do with my appearance, especially my body. At first it was all positive. He'd tell me I was beautiful, and how he liked things . . . but it slowly changed to him *picking* at things. Picking at *me* . . . pulling me apart. It was like he read my mind and found everything I was self-conscious about. And then he'd bring it out into the light. He'd tell me I needed to fix myself, pinch the underside of my arms and say I needed to do more to tone them. Or he'd grab my thighs and say that they were too big. He wanted me to be different."

"It sounds like he *fucking* sucks."

"That's an understatement." Lucy laughed humorlessly.

Theo's hand flexed on her hip before sliding down. "I like your thighs, Lucy. I especially like when they're wrapped around my waist." He nuzzled his face into her neck before kissing her shoulder again. "I meant what I said earlier: I wouldn't change anything about you."

"Theo, I . . . I don't think you understand how much that means to me. I haven't always had a healthy self-image. In high school, I battled with bulimia for years."

That fact was something she'd only told four people in her life: Caro, Sasha, Lilah, and her therapist. And in that moment, she wanted to share it with Theo.

He tensed behind her again. "Oh, Luce," he whispered her name as he held her tighter.

His touch emboldened her, made her want to share more with him. "It was when my mom got sick . . . and for some time after she died. I used it to control everything that I couldn't control . . . and then everything got out of control." Lucy rolled over in his arms, her hand going to his jaw as she looked up into his face. "Being with my ex, it brought all of that self-doubt back to the surface, stuff I hadn't felt in years. I started to feel out of control again and I knew I had to get out. *That's* the real reason I left."

"Are . . . are you okay now?" There was so much concern etched across his face. He was worried about her.

"I'm okay now," she reassured him. "I started seeing my old therapist when I came back, and I still see her every month. I never want to get back to that place again."

"I can't imagine how hard that was for you then, or how hard it was for you to share it with me now."

Lucy gave him a small smile. "It was easier than I thought. I trust you."

Something flickered in his blue eyes, his features softening. "That means a lot to me. I'm glad I can be a safe place for you . . . that you let me be one. I don't know all the right things to say or do, but if you tell me what you want or need, I'll do it."

"I'm really glad you're here, Theo."

"There's nowhere else I'd rather be than here with you, *exactly* as you are." He leaned forward and kissed her. It was Lucy who pulled him over her, her body sinking into the mattress as he sunk into her.

* * *

Sunday dawned cold and wet, the skies still covered with clouds as the rain continued to come down. It was a bit of a struggle to get Bear to go potty outside, but Lucy stayed nice and warm in bed while Theo dealt with that. She didn't fight too hard when he offered to go out in the rain, but she did reward him when he crawled back in bed with her.

They had a lazy morning, languishing in the cozy bed for a while before finally getting up for breakfast. Lucy cooked the bacon while Theo worked his magic with the pancake batter.

She couldn't help but grab her phone and start recording. She wasn't sure who she was focusing on more, Theo or Bear. But having the phone in her hand gave her an excuse to watch him—to *really* watch him—as he moved around her kitchen.

It wasn't very often that Lucy got to watch him bake or cook. Sure, there were gatherings that included her family, and his, but there were usually twenty-plus people running around and in charge of their own specific tasks.

It was always chaos, chaos that Lucy loved, but chaos nonetheless.

Lucy never really had time to watch Theo do what he was good at. He was a professional baker, but it turned out, he was also a damn good chef, something he proved when he helped make her squash medley soup and whipped up a batch of focaccia bread. The man made bread like it was an art, his hands working the dough. She knew what it was like to have those hands move over her too.

She couldn't help but marvel at how easily he navigated her kitchen. Like he'd cooked in it a thousand times before. Maybe that was just part of his talent. He could turn any kitchen into his own.

But there was something about him making *her* space his own that made her feel some type of way. What that way was, she didn't quite know.

Theo grabbed a few sprigs of rosemary from one of her herb pots on the windowsill, pulling off the leaves in a practiced slide before running a knife over them in a quick and precise chop. He sprinkled the rosemary and a good amount of salt over the top of the bread before sliding it into her oven.

"Maybe I'll whip up some eggs for Bear for dinner and add some of that rosemary to them."

"Ohh, fresh herbs and eggs. She'll be getting a fancy dinner too." She looked down at the dog, who was sitting next to Theo's feet.

"The rosemary should help with her digestion. I'm sure her stomach isn't feeling good with all the medicine she's gotten and who knows what she was eating before we got her."

The rain let up later that afternoon, and that was when they decided to introduce Bear to Leia and Estee. Her dad brought Leia outside, not missing an opportunity to razz Theo.

"That's two days in a row, Theo. This going to become a habit for you?" Wes asked as they all watched the two dogs run around the backyard, tails wagging as they sniffed each other.

"Well, as Lucy and I have joint custody, I think I'm going to be around a good bit."

"So, it's just for the dog?" Wes's bushy eyebrows rose high.

"No." Theo shook his head.

"That's what I thought." Wes clapped Theo on the back before he turned to his daughter.

Lucy's eyes lingered on Theo. She'd opened up to him last night in ways she'd opened up to no man before. It should've scared the shit out of her . . . but it didn't. How was it that he'd fit right into place? Like he'd always been a part of her life.

Because he has always been a part of your life.

At least she knew he'd be a part of her life until she left again . . . *if* she left.

No, *when* she left. Where had that *if* come from? She didn't know and she wasn't going to think about it too much. Instead, Lucy focused on the next hurdle that she knew she had to deal with: introducing Bear to Estee.

Bear wasn't aggressive toward the cat at all. More curious in a somewhat exuberant way. While Lucy, Theo, and Wes all had soup and bread for a late lunch, Estee stayed in her safe place in the laundry room, moving from the shelves to the top of the washer and dryer. Bear whined as she watched, but patiently waited until Estee finally came down to the ground.

One boop later—Estee's little gray paw on Bear's black nose—and the two were friends.

CHAPTER TEN
Attached

*I*t was 6:32 in the morning when Lucy unlocked the front door of Dancing Donkey and led Bear inside, her father right behind them. They'd decided to bring the dog with them, not wanting to leave her alone all day. She'd been well behaved so far, but who knew what would happen if they left her unattended for hours.

It had finally stopped raining, but it was still wet, windy, and dreary. The sun hadn't yet risen, but there were wispy clouds swirling, just visible in the bluish light of the dawn sky.

The little café didn't open until seven, but Lucy had had a key to the place ever since she'd worked there in high school. Lorraine had refused to take it back, saying she'd need it in the future. Turned out she did, as she stopped by the café just about every morning before heading to the high school.

The scent of freshly roasted coffee enveloped her, the warmth of it sinking through the cold morning air that clung to her burnt-orange peacoat. It was a cozy space, the twinkle lights strung up around the room giving off a warm amber glow, lighting up the mint-green walls. Taylor Swift was playing over the speakers, one of her more haunting songs that always made Lucy think of fall.

The whole café was pretty much one of those ambiance videos on YouTube.

There were two massive windows at the front, outside them a great view of downtown Cruickshank. Right now, the lampposts were shining, lighting up the wet cobblestoned street. But looking in there was a display of coffee and merchandise on one side. The current theme was fall, with everything pumpkin spice, harvest blend coffees, and cozy knit caps and sweaters with the Dancing Donkey logo.

The other window always had a number of adoptable canines behind a sturdy wooden pen. Above their sweet little heads was a sign that read *Adopt Me*. Two were in there currently: Carl the hound dog, and an Australian shepherd mix named Bingley. Both perked their heads up as Lucy and Bear walked in. Bingley let out a small yip while Carl leaned his head back and howled his hello.

Bear squirmed a little next to Lucy, releasing a low whine. It sounded like an *I want to go over there and play* sound, but she was going to have to wait for a proper introduction.

The curtain behind the counter fluttered, moving aside and revealing a doorway in the exposed brick wall that led to the back. Lorraine walked out, wearing a flowy skirt covered in fall flowers and leaves and a T-shirt that read *Drink Coffee. Rescue Dogs. Sleep. Repeat.* Her long braids were wrapped up in a bun on her head, held back with a purple scarf headband.

"Ahh, two of my favorite Buchanans." Lorraine smiled widely, her honey-brown eyes moving from Lucy to Wes—where they lingered for a beat longer and went just a little warmer—before moving down. "And this must be the ever-popular Bear," she said as she rounded the counter.

"She is indeed."

Lorraine took absolutely no time at all to win the dog over. Bear was wagging her tail and dancing as she got all the pets. "Oscar told me about her yesterday. Said that you and Theo rescued her."

"I want to meet her!" another all-too-familiar voice said as Sasha pushed through the curtain, rounding the counter and joining the group.

Bear was the center of attention for a good couple of minutes, her butt wiggling like mad as she moved from Lorraine, to Lucy, to Sasha, back to Lucy, then to Wes, before repeating the whole cycle.

"She sure does like to check in with you," Lorraine said.

"She's like that with Theo too."

Sasha's eyes narrowed on Lucy, and there was a smirky little lilt pulling up the corner of her mouth.

"Soooo." Sasha dragged out the word. "Theo stayed all weekend?"

"Yes."

"Is that all I'm going to get out of you?" Sasha frowned, putting her hands on her hips. "You know you'll only get the caffeine if I get the details."

"Fine, you'll get all the details tonight with everyone else. And I'll take a chocolate chai tea latte, *please*."

"That's what I thought." Sasha nodded before looking over Lucy's shoulder. "Wes, what can I get you?"

"Are you brewing the Cinnamon Toasted Marshmallow today?"

"Yes, sir. That one won't be leaving the menu until after Christmas."

"Perfect. Thanks, Sasha."

"Make sure to get his thermos filled too," Lorraine told Sasha.

"Oh, I didn't bring one."

Lorraine frowned at him. "Then I guess you're just going to

have to borrow one of ours. It's freezing out there and you two have a long drive. You need to stay warm and caffeinated."

"There's a heater in my truck, you know."

"Are you arguing with me about free coffee?" Lorraine asked.

"No. I would never. You must've misheard me."

Lorraine's eyes narrowed. "You're the one with hearing aids, old man."

"Who are you calling old?" Wes laughed. "I'm only sixty-two. Last I checked I was two years younger than you." There was a twinkle in his eye as he said it.

"Oh, you hush." Lorraine's frown turned into a scowl as she put her hands on her hips. It was a clear sign with the Belmont women that they were gearing up for an argument. "You're as young as you feel, Wesley. So, I'm still somewhere in my forties."

"Well, by that logic so am I, Lorraine."

It was very clear that there was a teasing banter going on between Wes and Lorraine. There always had been . . . but it seemed like something *more* in that moment. Lucy followed their conversation like she was watching a tennis match. Back and forth, and back and forth again.

Okay . . . something was *definitely* going on here.

After Lucy's mother had died, Lorraine and Juliet had taken it upon themselves to look after the Buchanan family. As Rachel's best friends, they wouldn't have had it any other way.

But this felt different from Lorraine . . . and her father.

Not wanting to be too obvious, Lucy focused on Lorraine. "I think Bear would like to meet Carl and Bingley before we leave. I want to make sure she's used to being around other dogs, especially as she might need to spend some time here next week if she isn't . . . well . . . you know."

"Claimed?" Lorraine finished. "Are you hoping she isn't?"

"I didn't say that."

"Are you already getting attached?"

"Getting?" Wes asked. "She's already there."

Her father wasn't wrong. Bear had fit into place faster than Lucy could've imagined.

For most of Sunday, the dog had usually been a few steps behind her and Theo or watching them from her bed, or the sofa. She'd been in the kitchen with them for most of the afternoon, sitting next to Theo and pressing her body against his leg while he'd made the bread. And it had been Theo who'd made room for her on the bed both nights, helping her snuggle into a spot on the other side of his feet. She'd also crawled up between them when they'd gotten up in the morning, looking for pets and kisses.

She hadn't been denied, just like she wasn't being denied now. Lucy looked over at the dog, who was currently getting a whole lot of attention from Lorraine, her tongue lolling, tail wagging.

"Fine." Lucy threw her hands in the air. "I'm attached." Beyond attached. It had taken no time at all.

"Admitting it is the first step." Sasha patted Lucy on the shoulder before she moved behind the counter. "Now, let me go get your coffees. I'm doctoring it up the usual way, Wes? A little coffee with your cream and sugar?"

"Yes, please."

While Sasha got their drinks, Lorraine did her magic in introducing all the dogs. Bear was twice the size of Bingley, and three times bigger than Carl, but she was beyond gentle with both of them. It took almost no time at all for the three of them to start playing.

"Well, looks like Bear gets along with the other dogs," Sasha said as she slid their drinks across the counter. "Here is your caffeine. You going to get something to eat next?"

"Yes, Theo said he'd have our food ready to go, but I suspect we will be delayed as his parents and grandparents all want to meet Bear."

"Theo's already there? That's a little *early* for him to go to work, isn't it?"

Lucy glared at her friend. "He got up with me this morning . . . and left before we did."

"But not before I caught him sneaking out of her apartment again."

"He wasn't sneaking. There is no sneaking around this time."

"This time?" Lorraine sounded scandalized, her golden-brown eyes going big. "When was there a time before?"

"Seven years ago," Wes answered before Lucy had a chance.

"Thanks, Dad." Lucy looked up at the ceiling, letting out a breath of frustration. She hadn't mentioned that little detail, mainly because she hadn't had a chance to discuss it with her father herself.

"You knew too?" Sasha asked Wes. "Oh, this is so good. We're going to have to compare notes with Gavin."

"Can. We. Not?" Lucy emphasized every word.

"We can do it at Thanksgiving. Turn it into a drinking game," Wes suggested.

"We're leaving now. *Bye.*" Lucy grabbed the thermos and shoved it in her father's direction before handing him his coffee. Then she turned to Lorraine, holding out an open palm.

Lorraine handed over the leash, giving Lucy a stern look. "We aren't done with all this Theo stuff. You've got some explaining to do, young lady." That stern look of hers stayed firmly in place as she turned to Wes. "And *you* better drive safely today."

"I will." He grinned at her. "I've made it this far in life, I think I'll be okay."

Lorraine made a harrumphing noise that clearly said *that remains to be seen*. Wes just leaned in and pressed a quick kiss to Lorraine's cheek. "Thanks for taking care of us," he said so low that Lucy wondered if he'd only meant for Lorraine to hear it.

He pulled away and headed for the door, and Lucy didn't miss it as Lorraine slowly unfolded her arms, reaching up and gently touching her cheek as she watched Wes.

Lucy grabbed her own coffee, sparing a quick glance at Sasha. It was clear from her best friend's expression that she had questions too.

* * *

THE DRIVE TO FREDDIE'S FARM was two hours, just to the other side of Knoxville. Lucy played DJ—going through a rotation of Creedence Clearwater Revival, Fleetwood Mac, Bruce Springsteen, and Tom Petty—while her father drove. They both munched on a variety of baked goods from Browned Butter. Theo had put together a box with Lucy's favorites, and another with all of her father's. He'd even thrown in a bag of treats for Bear.

Because of course he had.

As it turned out, Bear seemed to love car rides. She sat up in the back seat for the first hour, staring out the window in fascination. For the second hour she lay down in the pile of blankets and took a nap.

"She seems comfortable," Wes said as he looked over his shoulder to check his blind spot, getting a glance of Bear while he did it.

Lucy looked back to the dog too, taking in her sweet sleeping face. "Yeah. She just needed a safe place to land for a little bit."

"She ain't the only one." He looked over, giving Lucy a significant glance. "You seem like you've gotten *comfortable* too."

"Maybe a little bit." Lucy gave a small shrug of her shoulder, unable to stop the smile that turned up her mouth. She traced over the Browned Butter emblem on the box in her lap.

"Oh, I think more than a little bit. And I'm not just talking about whatever is going on with you and Theo. I mean the last couple of months. You've looked almost *happy*."

"When did I not look happy?"

Her father looked over at her, giving her that look that clearly said *come on*. "Only every time I've seen you in the last few years. You always looked lost . . . like you were looking for something that you couldn't find."

"And what, now you think it's found me?"

"Maybe. You sure seem to have found your place at the school, teaching those kids, working on the winter musical that is now weeks away."

"I have, but that's not a permanent position." Lucy waved her hand in the air. "Mrs. Griffith will be back next school year, and I'll have to figure out what I'm going to do next."

"What do you mean, next school year?" Wes quickly glanced over at her again before turning back to the road. "I thought it was just a semester."

Crap. That had been a slip. Lucy still hadn't told anyone that she'd been offered the position for the next semester, mainly because she still hadn't decided if she was taking it.

"*Yeahhhhh.*" Lucy dragged out the word. "About that. Principal Patel, I mean Fatima, she said that Mrs. Griffith needed another semester off to take care of Mr. Griffith. So, she asked if I'd finish out the year."

Wes's hands tightened on the steering wheel. "What did you tell her?"

"Nothing yet. She said I had until finals week to make a decision."

"Is there a reason why you *wouldn't* take it? I thought you enjoyed it."

"I do." Teaching hadn't exactly been her dream career—she'd kind of just been thrown into the position—but she'd found something there that she hadn't found anywhere else. "I didn't know what I was doing in the beginning, but day by day I figured it out, and . . . and I really enjoy it. I enjoy the students. It's been so nice being a part of something bigger than me. And now that I've found a place where I feel like I fit, I know I'm going to have to say goodbye to it. I'm going to have to let go. So, I guess the reason I wouldn't take it is because I'm scared of falling in love with something that I'm just going to lose in the end."

"Are we still talking about the job?"

"What else would we be talking about?"

"Oh, I don't know, maybe the dog in the back seat, or a certain young man who you've been spending a lot of time with."

Lucy let out a bit of a hysterical laugh. "I'm not in love with Theo!" No, no, no, no, no. It was too soon for anything like that. They were just having sex. Good sex. *Really* good sex.

Not that she needed to be thinking about *that* right now. God, why was it suddenly very hot in the cab of the truck? She reached forward and started fussing with the vents.

"Theo and I are just . . ."

"*Yes?*" Wes pressed.

"I don't know what we are. We haven't put a label on it beyond . . ." She trailed off again, her cheeks suddenly even hotter. "Can we not have this conversation?"

"Fine, let's go back to you teaching. So, let's say you finish the school year out and Mrs. Griffith comes back; why can't you get a job at another school? There are other places you could teach. They might not be in Cruickshank, but you'd be able to find something closer than across the country."

"I'm not moving back to California, Dad. You don't need to worry about that."

"Then where are you thinking about moving?"

Lucy hesitated again, biting her lip before letting it go. "Nashville or New York. They both have good music scenes. And . . . and one of my old friends from college, Stephanie Jenkins, she's in New York and one of her roommates is moving out in February. I'd have a place to live if I went there."

Another thing she hadn't discussed with anyone.

Even from the side, Lucy could tell her father's mouth had pulled down into a frown. "Is that what you want?"

"I don't know yet. I don't know what I want," Lucy said softly.

"Luce." Wes reached out and touched her arm, squeezing gently before letting go. "I'm not going to lie to you. I'm sure you are fully aware that the last thing I want is for you to leave Cruickshank again."

"Of that I'm more than aware."

He spared a quick glance at her, grinning. "But what I want more than anything in this world is for you to be happy. So, whatever your choice is, I support you. And I will *always* support you."

"Thanks, Dad."

He paused for just a moment before he asked, "Can I offer just one piece of advice?"

"You can always offer me advice, and as many pieces as you want."

"I wouldn't wait too long to tell Theo what you're thinking about. I know you don't know what this is with Theo, but that boy doesn't look at you like you're just a passing thought. He never has."

There was a part of Lucy that wanted to press her father to elaborate . . . and there was another part of her that knew she wasn't ready to hear the answer.

The latter part won out.

"I . . . I won't . . ." Lucy shook her head, her voice trailing off as she looked out the window. The song changed and "Landslide" by Fleetwood Mac started playing. Her father reached over and turned it up. He loved this song, no doubt because her mother had loved it too.

Lucy let herself sink into the song as they drove. The blue sky was crystal clear now, all of the clouds gone and the sun shining bright and warm. She looked to the almost bare trees, focusing on the last few leaves that stubbornly clung to the branches. She missed the vibrant yellows, oranges, and reds that had painted the mountains just weeks ago.

As much as she loved fall—which was a lot—she knew there was something even greater on the horizon. Christmas had *always* been Lucy's favorite time of year, not surprising as it had been her mother's favorite time too.

Rachel had gone all out at Christmas. Multiple trees, holiday music playing at all hours, the house smelling like a different baked good every single day. Her mother had *loved* to bake, and while Lucy wasn't bad at it, she'd never quite been able to hold up to her mother's talent. It was one of the many reasons she loved Browned Butter so much; the Taylors' goods had come the closest to what Rachel had baked.

God, she missed her mother. It was a permanent ache right over her heart. One that hadn't lessened with time; she'd just learned to deal with the pain. To cope with it. She felt like that was the case for a lot of things in her life, learning to cope with loss and disappointment. Part of her felt like she'd been in limbo for years. She knew she wasn't the only one. Caro had been like that in those years after she and Max broke up. And then there was her father . . .

"Dad?" She looked over at her father. "Can I ask you a question?"

"Always." He turned the music down a little bit.

"Have you . . . have you ever thought about being with someone again . . . since Mom, I mean?" She'd been wondering it for days now, and as they seemed to be having a fairly serious conversation about *her* life, it was only fair to ask about *his*.

Wes's hands moved on the steering wheel before he awkwardly cleared his throat, shifting in his seat.

"Your mother was the love of my life. *Is* the love of my life. Losing her was an indescribable pain, and for a long time I told myself I didn't want to do it again. That I *couldn't* do it again. Now, that's not to say I regretted anything about being with her. I wouldn't trade those years for anything in the world. It gave me my three beautiful children." He glanced over at Lucy.

"Do you *still* feel like you can't do it again?"

"Lately, I— I have thought that it would be nice to come home to a house that isn't empty. To share my life with someone."

"Anyone in particular?" Lucy pressed, trying to sound innocent.

Wes looked over at her again, a little smile playing at his mouth. "Have I been that obvious?"

"You've just seemed to be awfully close with Lorraine lately."

"We have been spending a lot more time together. I mean, she's always been my friend, but when Rachel died, and Robert left her, we leaned on each other a bit more than anyone else. Both of us were dealing with being single parents. It bonded us in a different way."

"And now?"

"I don't know . . . it's Lorraine. Would that be weird? Me dating your mother's best friend?"

"I think that Mom would want you to be happy."

"You kids wouldn't think it was weird?"

"I think Caro and Jeremy also want you to be happy. And Sasha would *officially* be my sister."

"*Okay*, you can just slow your roll with that. I haven't even asked Lorraine if she feels the same way."

"I'm pretty sure she does. I can ask her for you."

This time when her father looked over at her, his expression had gone stern. "Luciana Evelyn Buchanan, you will do no such thing."

"Oh, dear." Lucy laughed. "Not only did I get middle named, I got *full* named."

"I don't need any of your interference."

"You're a fine one to talk!"

"It's different. I'm your father. It's my job to interfere."

At that moment, Lucy's phone started to ring. "Well, speak of the devil. Want me to ask Lorraine how she feels right now?"

Her father glared at her.

"Calm down, I'm not going to say anything." Lucy stuck her tongue out at him before putting the call on speaker. "Hey, Lorraine, what's up?"

"So, I got some news about Bear—"

Lucy's stomach immediately bottomed out. Her father reached over and squeezed her leg reassuringly.

"Dr. Sumpter is a vet over in Weaverville, and he was checking the lost animal website when he came across Bear, who he knew as Betty. She belonged to a farmer over there who had died a couple of weeks ago. His kids inherited everything. When Dr. Sumpter called them to let them know Betty was down in Cruickshank, whoever answered the phone said they didn't care and hung up the phone."

Lucy leaned forward in her seat, suddenly furious. "Seriously?"

"Yeah. Real pieces of work." The anger in Lorraine's voice was apparent as well. "Dr. Sumpter suspects they dropped her off so she couldn't get home."

Lucy looked back at Bear, who was still sound asleep, lying in the patch of sun shining through the window.

"What a bunch of assholes," Wes said. "Well, she's safe now."

"That, she is. I just thought you'd want to know that she isn't going anywhere." The anger had lessened in Lorraine's voice. "So, get as attached as you want."

"Thanks, Lorraine." Lucy sat back in her seat, letting out a little sigh of relief.

"Is your father driving safely? Both hands on the wheel?"

"Ten and two," Wes called out.

"Good, see the three of you later," Lorraine said before she hung up.

"Well, would you look how that worked out." Wes shifted in his seat. "Though now that you're keeping Bear, that's going to affect where you might move, right? I don't know how she'd do in a New York City apartment."

"Who said I'm keeping Bear?"

"Aren't you?"

Lucy looked back at the dog again. She was no longer sleeping, her sweet brown eyes open and focused on Lucy.

Yeah . . . she was keeping the dog.

CHAPTER ELEVEN
Mistletoe Junction

*T*heo was beyond busy at the bakery all day. Once he finished with his three custom cakes, he helped his dad with the pumpkin pie orders. Usually by the time Thanksgiving rolled around, he was pumpkin-pied out after making them, and never got around to eating any.

This year, his opinion was different. Maybe it had to do with how all those spices now very much reminded him of a certain curvy brunette with a penchant for all things fall. Since the crust on one of the pies got messed up in the oven, Theo brought it home to his parents for dinner.

Family dinner night was usually on Tuesdays, but it had gotten bumped up a night as his sister Naomi was in town for the Thanksgiving break from college. She'd had to work the weekend and Monday morning, so she hadn't been able to drive back until this evening.

When he walked into his parents' house, he heard the usual commotion of music, laughing, and clanking dishes coming from the kitchen. The closer he got, the stronger the garlic scent became. It was something his father never skimped on. As they were having spaghetti and meatballs—Naomi's favorite—he was pretty sure that garlic scent was coming from the Italian bread baking in the oven.

Theo set the pie down on the counter, and the second he had his hands free, Naomi was coming in for a hug.

"Aren't you a sight for sore eyes," he told her.

Of the four Taylor children, she was the only one who'd gotten their mother's blond hair and their father's green eyes. Everyone else had gotten Isaac's dark brown hair and Juliet's blue eyes. But Naomi always did like to be different.

Speaking of which.

"What is this?" Theo asked as he tapped her nose, just to the side of where a little sparkling diamond stud sat. "You got your nose pierced?!"

Naomi pushed him off. "Mom thinks it's cute. Leave me alone."

"What does Dad think?" Theo looked over at Isaac.

He was cooking the meatballs, but he turned long enough to clap the pair of tongs in his hand toward his daughter. "I offered to pull it out with a pair of pliers."

"Like Operation?" Theo's eyes went wide with excitement. "That would be a fun after-dinner game."

"We'd need tweezers for that," Gia said as she walked into the kitchen. "Where's Bear?"

"With Lucy."

"Ugh! Why didn't you bring her?" Gia asked as she dramatically sat down on one of the barstools.

"Because Lucy took Bear to her girls' night. She wanted Caro and Lilah to meet her."

"Who's Bear?" Naomi asked as she took the seat next to Gia.

"The dog Theo and Lucy rescued. Want to see the video I've

edited together?" Gia grabbed her laptop. "I should have it finished tonight to post. I've been working on it all day."

"Hopefully after you turned in your history paper?"

"I turned it in this morning." Gia rolled her eyes. "Jeez, I already have Mom and Dad hounding me about homework, do I really need to deal with you too? It's bad enough you're now dating one of my teachers."

"Hold up." Naomi waved her hands in the air. "*Who* are you dating?"

"*Lucy.*" Gia said the name with a little too much glee.

"Noooo." Naomi looked from her sister to her brother before punching him in the shoulder. "How did you not tell me this?!"

"Ow." Theo rubbed the spot. "It just happened like three days ago and we aren't dating. We're just . . . seeing each other regularly."

"Isn't that dating?" Juliet asked as she put the noodles into the boiling water.

"No, Mom, it's code for they're just having sex," Naomi answered.

"Naomi Danielle!" Juliet all but shouted her daughter's name.

Theo glared at his sister. "I'm going to go find those pliers for Dad."

"I'll stop, I'll stop." Naomi held her hands in the air in surrender.

"I'm surprised Gia didn't tell Naomi the second she walked in the door," Isaac said.

"I wanted to see her expression when she found out." Gia grinned. "And I wanted Theo to be here for it. This is so much more fun."

"I'm going to remember this next time you ask me for a favor."

Gia was unfazed by the threat, making a kissy face at him

before she started to click buttons on her computer. "Do you guys want to see the video too?" she asked her parents.

"Yes," they said in unison. Juliet pushed the last of the pasta under the boiling water while Isaac turned off the burner and moved the pan of browned meatballs toward the back of the stove.

Gia paused the music playing in the kitchen before she turned the screen toward them and pressed *play*. Slow keys of a piano started to play, and while Theo didn't immediately know the song, he knew he'd heard it before. And then he heard Lucy's voice starting to sing.

His skin immediately broke out into goose bumps. Something that always happened when he heard her sing.

On the screen, Lucy lured in a scared and dirty Bear in the bakery's alleyway; he could just hear her talking about the ins and outs of sourdough bread and grilled cheese over the sound of the music. The camera panned to Theo every once in a while as he interjected his own comments. He was sitting on the crate and watching intently, a worried expression on his face.

The video cut to Bear moving in closer and Lucy getting the leash on her, and then cut again as they made their way through downtown Cruickshank toward the vet clinic. Gia had a montage of moments from the bath, Bear looking transformed as they washed the mud off her. There was that moment when Bear had closed her eyes, her head tilted back as they scrubbed her chest. She had indeed looked like she was in heaven, her tail moving rapidly through the water.

But Bear wasn't the only interesting part of the video; there were so many moments in which Gia had caught Theo looking at Lucy . . . and Lucy looking at Theo. There was something in the way that they watched each other that caught him entirely off guard.

Was it something that was only apparent to him?

The video continued with more of the footage that Lucy and Theo had recorded before sending it along to Gia, and it finally ended with a clip of Bear curled up and sleeping. She looked all warm and snuggly at the end of Lucy's bed.

When the screen went black, everyone turned to Theo—all of them looking a bit speculative—but it was Naomi who said, "You two are cute together."

"*Pliers*," he repeated to her.

"What? You *are*!"

"Stop harassing your brother and set the table." Juliet looked at all of her children.

"Thanks, Mom." He kissed her on the cheek before she moved back to the stove.

"Fine." Naomi crossed to the cabinet and pulled out some plates. "I'll stop with Lucy. Tell me more about Bear."

"Well, she's pregnant." Theo pulled open the silverware drawer. "And Oscar thinks she's going to have eight or more puppies."

Naomi let out a long whistle. "That's a lot of dogs. What are you going to do if she isn't claimed?"

"She won't be claimed." Theo launched into the story that Lucy had told him earlier. She'd called him as soon as she'd gotten off the phone with Lorraine.

"What assholes," Gia all but shouted when Theo finished.

"Gianna Jacqueline! Language!" Juliet waved the wooden spatula at Gia before she turned back to Theo. "Though she's not wrong. Those people are assholes."

"They are that," Theo agreed. "So, Lucy decided to keep her."

"Oh, she did, did she?" Isaac's eyebrows rose high.

"*Yessss!*" Gia made a fist, pulling her arm in close to her side. She then immediately turned to her parents. "Can we get one of the puppies? *Please?*"

Juliet and Isaac looked at each other. They'd recently lost their dog Bailey, a Lab mix that they'd brought home as a puppy fifteen years ago. They'd had to put her to sleep last spring, and Gia had been begging them to get another dog for a couple of months now.

"We'll think about it?" Isaac asked his wife. Juliet nodded.

"That's better than no," Gia said happily.

"So, if Lucy is keeping Bear, does that mean she's staying in Cruickshank?" Naomi asked. "Last I talked to her, this was only temporary."

"I don't know . . ." Theo trailed off. He had no idea what Lucy's plans for the future were. She'd told him she had no plans of staying that first night they'd had sex. He didn't think her decision to keep Bear was going to change those plans.

"Well, I've certainly come home to some very interesting developments," Naomi said.

"You can say that again." Gia grinned. "Wait until you see the clips Lucy sent me from yesterday. Bear meeting Lucy's cat, Estee, is gold, but there's a whole scene with Theo making Bear eggs that is—" She made the chef's kiss motion. "Who knew our brother was such a teddy bear?"

"I am *not* a teddy bear."

"Sure, you aren't." Naomi patted her brother on the shoulder. "Whatever makes you feel better."

* * *

THE NEXT COUPLE OF DAYS went by in a whirlwind for Theo. Usually he liked to be busy, liked the frenzy and fast-paced days at the bakery, especially during the holidays. But due to recent developments, he wanted more quiet time with Lucy. He looked forward to the evenings the most, when'd they curl up on her sofa and watch something . . . or make out. He especially loved the part when they'd end up in bed and he'd get to explore her body.

The mornings always came too quick, and way too early.

Theo spent the days at the bakery, where it was all hands on deck. His grandparents, parents, Naomi, and he were in the kitchen, while Gia, Chloe, and their part-timers were up front. There wasn't a point in the day when they didn't have a line.

Lucy might've had the week off from school, but she wasn't getting any sort of vacation. When he went to Browned Butter, she headed for Caro and Max's, where Thanksgiving prep had already started. As the kitchen in the old Victorian was the largest of all the families', it made the most sense to do it there. Anyone who had free time was over there helping, coming and going all day long.

But that wasn't the only chaos Theo and Lucy were contending with. Nope, their phones were blowing up with so many notifications they'd had to silence the app where Gia had posted the rescue video. She'd done it on Monday evening, and by Tuesday morning it had more than ten thousand views. By Tuesday evening, it had tripled. And the numbers just kept climbing, especially as Gia had posted two more videos.

The second one had been of Bear meeting and playing with Estee, and how their friendship had progressed over those first few days. The third was of the car ride back from Tennessee. By the time they got back to Cruickshank, it had warmed up a little bit. Lucy and Wes had rolled down the windows and Bear had happily just sat in the back seat, almost smiling as the wind blew her white and brown fur back like she was in a shampoo commercial or something.

In the original video, "The Chain" by Fleetwood Mac was playing in the background, so Gia redid it so the song was a lot clearer—not to mention the lyrics were perfectly synced with the wind—and there was no other sound interference.

Bear had her own account, and with just those three videos, she had close to twenty thousand followers. Apparently, people were invested in the dog's story, and what with the coming puppies, that follower count was sure to grow.

But it wasn't just Bear who had a growing follower count.

Gia had tagged Lucy as the singer in that first video, which had prompted a number of people to click over to her page and follow. The last video she'd posted of herself singing had been back in March, and the likes and comments had exploded with the new post.

Browned Butter had also been tagged, people jumping over to that page to check out the videos of Theo decorating cakes. Those videos usually saw upward of a few thousand views. Now they were over ten thousand.

"They keep calling you 'the hot baker.'" Gia grinned as she showed him the screen on Thursday afternoon. "Do you think we should change the handle on the bakery's page?"

"Ha. Ha," Theo deadpanned.

"Let me see." Naomi held out her hand for the phone. Gia passed it over, giving Theo a massive smirk while she did it.

"I want to see too." Harlow Belmont moved in behind Naomi, looking over her shoulder. Oscar and Sasha's baby sister had come back from Charlotte for the holiday, getting a break from cosmetology school. As she was best friends with Naomi, they'd been pretty much joined at the hip all day.

"Yes, please, let's show everyone." Theo shook his head before taking a sip of his beer and looking around for Lucy.

As it was Thanksgiving Day, he was currently at Quigley's, the crowd around him increasing as everyone was trickling in for the celebration. Irish pub music was playing, the fiddle clear among the chatter. It was another chilly day, below thirty even with the sun shining. The fire was going strong, Desmond making sure to add logs as needed. Christmas decorations had been put up: garland and lights strung across the mantels, mistletoe hung from a number of places around the room, and a tree was glowing in the corner, covered in decorations.

Theo and Lucy had gotten there about an hour ago, stopping by the bakery first to get all of the desserts. She was now helping Lorraine and his mother organize the dishes that everyone had brought in to contribute to the feast. They'd lined up tables on the back wall, allowing for people to move down either side when the time came to eat.

Lucy was wearing a crimson sweater, and a long plaid skirt with a pattern of golds, reds, and browns. Her hair was down and around her shoulders, curled at the ends. As she brushed her hair back, he spotted the little gold earrings he'd watched her put in that morning. He'd never known he could be so fascinated with the simplest of things, but there'd been something about the way she'd tilted her head to the side, and how it exposed the slope of her neck.

And he couldn't help but be distracted by Lucy now. Every time she laughed he'd look her way. Every time she smiled his gaze would get caught on her mouth. A second later Lucy looked up—as if she'd sensed he was looking at her—and he watched as her mouth curved to the side in that smile he'd wanted to see. The secret one he was coming to know more and more. The one he was pretty sure she only shared with him.

She was starting to share a lot of things with him. It had

started that second night they'd spent together, when she'd told him about what had happened in California . . . and before. He hated that she'd battled with bulimia, and he'd done his best to show her how much he enjoyed her body since then . . . every part of it. To him, she was perfect, the most beautiful woman he'd ever seen in his life.

But it wasn't just her beauty that he enjoyed. It was her mind, her heart, her presence. It was absolutely everything about her.

Something filled Theo's chest . . . a feeling he was becoming more acquainted with. Something that felt a lot like a certain four-letter word. A *dangerous* four-letter word. The only time he'd ever thought about that word had been with Lucy . . . but that had been years ago. He wasn't anywhere close to where he'd been then . . .

Was he?

No, no, he was fine . . . he wasn't in danger.

* * *

DINNER TOOK HOURS, people taking their time between courses. They spent their breaks between eating by watching the football games on the TVs behind the bar, playing a round of pool or darts, and even getting involved in a pretty intense game of dominos.

Lucy was off in a corner with Caro, Lilah, Sasha, Harlow, and Naomi playing rummy and working through glasses of apple and cranberry sangria.

"So," Lilah started as she grabbed the four of clubs that Naomi had just discarded. "Are we going to discuss the elephant in the room?"

"If it's about me and Theo, I think we've about discussed it to death." Lucy shook her head.

"That wasn't who I was referring to." Lilah grinned, throwing the queen of hearts down. "I was talking about Wes and Lorraine." She nodded to a spot across the room where the two were playing checkers. They were both leaning in close, smiling like idiots.

"Yeah." Sasha nodded, grabbing the queen. "Lucy and I noticed something the other day at the café. They were almost *flirting* with each other. And he's been coming into the café *every day* for coffee too."

"Seriously?" Harlow lightly slapped her sister's shoulder with the back of her hand. "How did you not tell me?"

"I didn't know if it was anything, and I *just* noticed the flirting."

"You know, it wouldn't surprise me," Caro said. "Dad has been helping the animal rescue at the Cruickshank Saturday Market every week for the last two months. He's been there every once in a while in the past, but not this often."

"You're awfully quiet over there." Naomi pointed in Lucy's direction. "I thought Sasha said you guys both noticed something."

"We, uh, did," Lucy mumbled as she reached for her wineglass and took a sip of sangria.

"What else do you know?" Lilah's eyes narrowed on Lucy.

"I mean . . . it . . . kind of got brought up on the car ride to Tennessee."

"And you didn't tell us?" Sasha asked, scandalized.

"Dad told me not to interfere. Those were his *exact* words. And I didn't want to say or do anything that would scare him off. So, I just told him that all we'd want"—she indicated herself and Caro before pointing to Jeremy, who was playing pool with the guys—"is for him to be happy."

"That's accurate." Caro nodded before leaning in closer and whispering to the group, "But he confirmed he has feelings for Lorraine?"

"Yes."

"Does she have feelings back?" Naomi asked.

"He said that they haven't talked about it." Lucy shook her head. "I think he's nervous."

"Hmmm." Lilah looked over her shoulder to where Wes and Lorraine were now laughing, Lorraine's hand on his forearm.

"Oh, no, you don't." Lucy pointed at Lilah. "We are not getting involved in that. We can't spook them."

"They need something to get going. I bet we can figure it out," Harlow said conspiratorially.

"Just think, Lucy, if they get married, we'd be sisters."

"Hey, that's what I told Dad too!" Lucy laughed.

"Now, this is becoming ridiculous." Naomi shook her head. "You guys are connected by marriage"—she indicated Lucy, Caro, and Lilah—"and if your parents get married, then you guys would be connected." She pointed to Lucy, Caro, Sasha, and Harlow. "At least when Lucy and Theo get married, I'll be connected to the Buchanans."

Lucy choked on her wine. "Excuse me? I am not marrying Theo. I'm not even staying in Cruickshank."

"Oh, right, it's just sex, or *whatever*"—Naomi very dramatically made air quotes—"until you leave."

"Well, I think the next step is for Sasha and Gavin to get together," Lilah said.

Now it was Sasha choking on her drink. "What?"

"Oh, come on, my brother's a catch. He's handsome, has a job, doesn't have his mother do his laundry. You two would be great."

"Gavin and I are *just* friends. Nothing is going to happen."

Lilah's expression became stern. "What's wrong with my brother?"

"Nothing! I love Gavin."

"See, you two are perfect."

"I love him, I'm not *in* love with him. There's a difference."

"We'll see." Lilah shrugged.

"We will *not* see."

"Well," Naomi interrupted the back-and-forth between Lilah and Sasha, "that just leaves the two of us with no possibilities for a marriage connection." She looked to Harlow. "Unless your brother starts playing for the other team."

They all looked over to where Oscar and Edward were talking by the bar. Edward pointed up and Oscar followed the gesture, spotting the sprig of mistletoe above them. Oscar didn't even hesitate before he leaned in and pressed a kiss to Edward's mouth.

"Yeah, I think it's safe to say *that* isn't going to happen." Harlow shook her head.

"Hey." Lilah put her cards face down, lightly slapping the table as she leaned in. "I have an idea on how to help Wes and Lorraine."

"What part of *he doesn't want us to interfere* did you miss?" Lucy asked.

Caro turned and looked at her sister. "Are you helping or not?"

Lucy sighed, knowing she had no choice. "Helping."

* * *

IT WAS A LITTLE AFTER SIX when all of the food was packed up—everyone getting their own set of to-go boxes—and dessert was brought out. Theo was in charge of unboxing and organizing the table, but he'd enlisted the help of Gia and Chloe. Though Chloe's father and uncles were more than happy to help.

Theo liked the Savage brothers. There was Harrison—or Captain Savage—Cameron, and Weston. Weston and Cameron were the younger of the trio. The pair had moved to Cruickshank from

Charlotte a few years ago, opening Hamish's Fine Furnishings—a shop named after their grandfather—which was located just a street over from the pub. They specialized in handmade furniture and wood features.

After Harrison's divorce, he moved from Charlotte too, joining his brothers in Cruickshank for a fresh start. Plus, he needed help with his daughters. The brothers didn't live together, but they had a bit of a *Full House* situation going on.

"Where does this one go?" Chloe's uncle Weston asked as he pulled the lid off a cake box.

Theo looked inside to see the bourbon toffee apple cake he'd made for Lucy. "Oh, could you go and put that one on the table over there?" he asked as he pointed to where Lucy was sitting with all the girls.

They'd been playing rummy earlier, but all of their cards were now face down on the table and they were leaning in close like they were conspiring about something.

Weston nodded, not asking any questions as he walked over. The women all looked up as he set the cake in the middle of the table. Lucy immediately looked over at Theo, her mouth dropping open in shock.

She then pushed her chair back from the table before crossing over to him. "I thought we scratched the previous bets when we changed the terms the first night."

"We did. But I made it for you anyway."

"Thank you." She leaned in, pressing a kiss to his cheek. Why did those two words do such funny things to his chest?

Shit. He *really* needed to get a grip.

"What are you guys talking about over there? It looks like you're plotting something." He reached up, brushing the hair back from the side of her face and pushing it behind her ear.

"Oh, we are, and you're going to be a part of it."

"I am?"

"Yeah." She patted him on the chest.

"What is it that I'll need to be doing?"

"Dancing with me. You up for it?" She looked up at him, her long eyelashes fluttering. Just another thing for him to get distracted by.

"I think I am." He nodded. "Am I allowed to know what we're doing?"

"Nope. Plausible deniability is going to be your best bet."

"Nobody is getting murdered, are they? Sasha is part of the plan, and you never know when it comes to her."

"This is true, but no one is dying. I promise." She stretched up, this time pressing a kiss to his mouth. "I'm going to go get some of my cake now."

"Save me a piece."

"Will do." She grinned before she turned and headed back to the table. And for what felt like the hundredth time, Theo again got distracted, this time by the way her skirt was draped over her ass.

* * *

As was Thanksgiving tradition, after everyone had their dessert, the tables were all pushed to the sides of the room, making way for the floor to be clear enough for people to dance. Desmond and his father, Finn, moved to the little area in the corner where a piano and microphone sat. Desmond pulled out his fiddle, while Finn grabbed his accordion.

Finn Quigley might not work behind the bar of the pub anymore, but he did often come and play when they had parties like this. Nari took her usual place at the piano while the pub's two cooks manned the drums and guitar.

Theo found Lucy, his hands landing on her waist as he pulled her out onto the dance floor. She laughed as they started to move, their feet picking up pace with the music. They weren't the only ones spinning around either. The couples were keeping up with the beat as the people on the sides of the room clapped their hands, adding their own contribution to the song.

One of Lucy's hands was on Theo's waist, and her fingers tightened in his shirt, holding on. He held her other hand in his, and he moved their fingers so that they were twined together. She looked up at him, that secret smile of hers turning up her mouth.

"What?" he asked as he pulled her in closer.

"Nothing. Just don't let go, okay?"

"I won't." Theo shook his head. The second he said the words, he knew he meant more than just this dance.

She opened her mouth to say something else but was cut off as Lilah and Jeremy danced up to them. "You ready?" Lilah asked.

"Yes."

The song came to an end and Desmond held his fiddle to the side as he leaned into the mic. "This next is a Christmas tradition, and we're going to get the season started, so don't get caught when the music stops." He paused for a second as he looked around. "Unless you want to." He grinned as he pulled the mic around so that his back was to the crowd.

No one needed to hear the first chords of music to know what song was next. "Mistletoe Junction" wasn't a famous Irish jig by any means. In fact, Theo was pretty sure that Charles Angus Quigley—the man who'd built the pub with his own two hands more than a hundred years ago—was the one who'd come up with the tune in the first place.

It was kind of like musical chairs: everyone would dance around in a circle while one couple would move to the center, right under one of the sprigs of mistletoe that had been hung. They'd dance for ten seconds or so, and then move off for the next couple to take their turn. But if the music stopped and they were in the middle, they had to share a kiss while everyone chanted, *"Kiss under the mistletoe!"* It was supposed to be random, which was why the person leading the song turned their back to the audience.

"What are you guys up to?" Theo asked Lucy and Lilah.

"Oh, you'll see." Lilah winked.

"Should I be scared?" He leaned closer into Lucy as they started to dance.

"No." She shook her head but stopped after a second. "Well, Lilah's involved . . . so maybe."

"Great."

The beat of the music moved faster and faster until it came to a stop for the first time. Caro and Max were in the middle, and they didn't even hesitate to kiss as everyone chanted, *"Kiss under the mistletoe!"*

Once the music started again, they moved out of the middle, as Lilah and Jeremy took their place, and so on, and so on. The next couple in the center when the music stopped was Oscar and Naomi. Naomi turned her head and Oscar gave her a quick peck on the cheek. The music picked up again, but it didn't go for too much longer until it stopped; this time the people at the center were Sasha and Gavin.

Sasha shot an accusatory look at Lilah before she grabbed Gavin's face and kissed him squarely on the mouth. Theo was pretty sure he wasn't the only one who saw Gavin lean into the kiss . . . nor was it possible to miss the slightly stunned expression on Gavin's face as Sasha pulled him back to the outer circle.

There were a few more music stops—and the subsequent cheers as the couples kissed in the center—before it was Wes and Lorraine's turn to make their way to the middle. And that was when Theo saw it: one of Nari's hands left the keys of the piano and she tugged on her ear. Not three seconds later, the music stopped.

The crowd went silent as they watched the two in the center, and as Wes made to kiss Lorraine on the cheek, she turned at the last second and kissed him on the mouth. He didn't pull away; in fact, he reached up and cupped the side of her face. The cheer that went up around the room was deafening.

"So that's what you were plotting?" Theo asked as the music picked up again.

"I don't know what you're talking about."

"Plausible deniability?"

"Exactly." Lucy nodded.

"I think that's the excuse that Lilah is going to make. Because I'm going to put good money on the fact that the music is going to stop when we're out there. Watch Nari; if she pulls on her ear it was planned."

"I'll pay attention."

It was a few more spins around the room when Lucy and Theo made their way into the center, and as he predicted, Nari tugged her ear, and the music stopped.

Lucy looked right at him and said, "Give them a show."

So, Theo did just that, dipping her back and kissing her deeply. He was pretty sure they got the loudest cheer of all. When he pulled Lucy back up straight, their mouths were still locked together. A few wolf whistles split the air, and they finally broke the kiss, both smiling.

"Like that?" he asked.

"Not bad."

The music didn't pick up afterward, the song now over. Desmond was facing the crowd again as he spoke into the mic. "I think maybe it's time for a slower song, and I was hoping we could have a special guest come up and sing it. Lucy." He nodded to her. "Would you do us the honor?"

"Yeah." She turned to Theo, pressing another kiss to his mouth. "Be right back," she said before she let go and made her way over to the band, taking up the spot behind the mic.

"I think you might know this one," Desmond said as Nari started to play familiar chords on the piano, the haunting notes of "River" by Joni Mitchell echoing in the room. Theo took a step back and off the floor, wanting to watch Lucy instead of dance. Besides, his partner had just left, and there was no one else he wanted to dance with.

Just like it always did, the second Lucy started to sing, his skin broke out into goose bumps. He remembered the first time it had happened, all the way back when they were in high school.

There was a year and a half difference in their age, but they'd only been a grade apart in school. It had been during his junior year that being around her had started to feel like something *different* for him.

Theo had never been involved in the theater or music program, and he'd never had any interest in going to the plays or musicals. But that year he'd gone to the winter musical to see Angie—his then-girlfriend—perform. He'd started to feel bored and antsy halfway through; that auditorium was the very last place he wanted to be.

It was the first performance after intermission, and when the curtains had parted, there was absolutely no light to be able to tell who or what was onstage. The only sound was the slow plucking and strumming on a guitar before someone started to sing.

In all of the years he'd known Lucy, Theo had never heard her sing before. But the instant her voice cut through the darkness he'd known it was her. That was when the goose bumps had broken out across his skin and his entire body had shifted forward in the seat, like he just wanted to be closer. And then the subtle sounds of the orchestra started, her voice and guitar now accompanied by violins, flutes, and a piano.

A small light at the front of the stage had turned on, and as the music built up and up and up, it slowly got brighter, illuminating her.

She was wearing a green velvet dress and bright red Converse sneakers. He remembered her hair had been down, curled at the ends, and held back with a gold headband. Every time she moved it sparkled in the lights.

His first thought had been that she looked like Christmas. The second was how beautiful she was.

It wasn't that Theo hadn't known Lucy was pretty. He hadn't been blind then just like he wasn't now. The thing was, he hadn't ever thought of her as beautiful . . . hadn't ever literally had the air knocked out of his lungs. She was the first to do it.

She was the *only* one to do it.

Sure, he'd been attracted to other women, but not like how he was to Lucy. She was . . . different. A different he'd never found anywhere else. *Lucy* was another dangerous four-letter word. One that he'd done his best to avoid for years, but without success.

Well, there was no avoiding her now. That was for damn sure . . . because he was in love with Lucy. *Had* been in love with her. He couldn't deny it any longer.

CHAPTER TWELVE
Just a Little Bit

Lucy stayed at the mic for a couple of songs, singing as everyone danced around the room. It had been a while since she'd sung like this, and it made her feel something deep in her soul that she'd been missing. Sure, she'd rattle off a verse or two when she was teaching, but she hadn't made her way through an entire song in months.

There was a part of her that had lost that joy . . . but here it was again.

Gia and Chloe joined her to sing "White Winter Hymnal," their sweet voices blending with hers to become the echoing chorus that the song required.

The room around them broke out into applause as they finished, the three of them linking arms and all taking a bow. But it was Theo's eyes that Lucy found in the crowd. She made her way across the room, and he held his hand out to her as Desmond started to sing "The Blower's Daughter" by Damien Rice.

"Will you dance with me again?" Theo asked.

"Yes." She put her hand in his and let him pull her into his body. His other hand landed on her hip, before sliding around to her back.

"So, I was wondering something," he whispered in her ear as he slowly spun them around.

"What's that?"

"If you'd come home with me."

Lucy pulled back so that she could see Theo's face. There was a hope there in his blue eyes, one that she wouldn't have been able to deny under normal circumstances, but definitely not in that moment.

"Yeah." She nodded. "I'll come home with you."

It was at that moment that Caro and Max danced up to them, Caro pointing to the ceiling above. "I do believe you two are under the mistletoe again."

They glanced up in unison, and as their eyes came back down, they looked at each other, both of them grinning.

"I do believe we are." Theo nodded as he let go of her hand, cradling the side of her face as he opened his mouth over hers.

The second their lips touched, Lucy knew there was something different in the kiss. Something *more*. She didn't know what it was, couldn't figure it out, probably because her head was spinning, and her heart was beating out of her chest.

Lucy had no clue what was happening with Theo. The more she was with him, the more it felt like it wasn't *just sex*. What could this be if they let it? If *she* let it. The question was equal parts thrilling and terrifying . . . and she wasn't sure which part was going to win in the end.

* * *

IT WAS AFTER NINE when Lucy and Theo left Quigley's and headed for her loft. She needed to grab a few things since she was staying the night, and they also needed to get Bear to bring with them.

The dog hadn't been by herself all day. They'd taken turns

checking on her in two-hour intervals, making sure she was okay the first time she'd been left on her own.

"Dad's going to have to bring her out," Lucy told Theo as she shoved some clothes into a bag. "Estee will get mad if she sees me and we don't bring her. She's probably already going to be upset that we're taking Bear, but she'll at least have Leia to distract her."

Lucy tried not to fidget in the passenger seat of Theo's car as he drove them back through town and to his house, which was on the opposite side of Cruickshank. He owned a cabin in a neighborhood on the east side of Lake Lenox, just a few blocks from the high school. Mount MacCallion's crew team used the lake for their practices. So did the swim team when it was warm enough.

The three-bedroom cabin had been a little run-down when Theo had bought it a few years ago, most of the interior outdated from when it had been built in the seventies. He was fixing it up room by room, doing what work he could, and paying Jeremy for the stuff that he couldn't.

Lucy had seen the living room after the old shag green carpet had been pulled up and the original hardwood floors had been refurbished. But she hadn't seen any of the other changes. She and Theo hadn't exactly *hung out* over the years.

Well, at least not until recently.

Her eyes landed on the stone fireplace—how could they not, as it was the focal point of the room?—and the beautiful mahogany mantel above it.

"That's new," Lucy said as she moved across to get a closer look. The piece of wood was massive, thick and stretching across the six-foot space.

"I got Chloe's uncles to do that for me," Theo said as he poured them each a glass of bourbon at the bar in the corner.

Lucy's gaze moved up to the framed artwork. It was of Lake Lenox and the forest beyond, the mountains climbing in the distance. Lucy focused on the little signature in the corner.

"This is one of Ava's." She smiled, thinking of Max's grandmother. She'd been a beyond-talented painter.

"She gave it to me a couple of years ago," Theo said as he came up behind her and handed her the shot glass. "She was very generous."

"That, she was." Lucy nodded before she clinked her glass to Theo's. "Cheers." She didn't wait for him to say anything as she downed half of the amber liquid.

She'd needed something to warm her up, a chill having settled into her skin that she couldn't quite shake. She was nervous for some reason that she didn't understand. It wasn't like she was uncomfortable being in Theo's space or anything, it just felt different since that second kiss under the mistletoe at Quigley's. Since that moment she felt things between them could be something more.

"You okay?" Theo asked before he took a sip of his own drink.

"Yeah." She nodded. "Just, you know, taking it all in." She gestured around the room with her free hand.

When he'd been at her apartment, he'd told her that the whole place was unmistakably hers. The same could be said about his house. There was a giant sofa in front of the fireplace, the leather worn in and buttery soft. Bear had already taken up residence on it.

She apparently had no issues adjusting to being in the space.

There was a matching chair and ottoman on either side of the sofa, both big enough for two people to snuggle up on. The coffee table in the center matched the mantel, no doubt another piece purchased from Hamish's Fine Furnishings and designed by the Savage brothers. Lucy moved away from the mantel, her stocking-clad feet going from the hardwood to the plushy red-and-brown-patterned rug that covered much of the floor.

"You've done a lot of work on this place."

"Wait till you see the kitchen."

"We can do a tour later, I want to see your bedroom," Lucy said before she could stop herself.

Something darkened in Theo's eyes, and he nodded to the glass in her hand. "Finish your drink."

Lucy didn't even hesitate. She knocked the rest of it back in one go, as he did the same with his. And then he was crossing over to her, pulling the glass from her hand before setting both on the coffee table. He laced their fingers together and pulled her across the room in an instant.

Not one to be left alone, Bear jumped down from the sofa, following behind them.

"I think we're going to have an audience."

"Don't worry. I'll make her a bed in there."

The second they crossed the threshold, Theo flipped the light switch, and a soft glow illuminated an absolutely gorgeous bedroom. It wasn't the light above that he'd turned on, but two that were recessed on either side of the wall of windows. As it was so dark outside, Lucy couldn't see out of them, but she was pretty sure they provided a view to the lake during the day. The king-size bed was covered in sage-green linens and held up with a rustic wooden headboard and frame.

There was a leather love seat on the opposite wall, from the same set that was in the living room. Theo grabbed the fuzzy blue blanket from the end of his bed, making a little nest on the love seat, which Bear immediately curled up on.

"I think she'll be okay for a bit," Theo said before he crossed over to Lucy, one of his hands moving to the back of her head as he brought his mouth down to hers.

Lucy started to undo the buttons on the front of his shirt while he worked on the clasp and zipper at the back of her skirt. They stumbled backward and Lucy laughed.

"God, I love that sound," Theo groaned against her mouth.

Lucy pulled her mouth from his, biting at her bottom lip. "What?"

She let her lip fall from her teeth as she shook her head. "Nothing, I just . . . I'm really glad you asked me to come here."

"I'm really glad you said yes."

Lucy stretched up again, pressing her lips to his. They didn't say much else as they undressed, each of them removing a piece of the other's clothing until they were naked. Theo pulled the covers back before laying Lucy down on his bed. She shivered against him, the sheets cold on her skin.

"Don't worry, you'll be warm in a second." He kissed the side of her neck before dragging his mouth to her throat and then to her breasts. He moved down her body, leaving a trail of heat across her skin until his head was between her thighs.

"Theo." Lucy gasped his name as he parted her with his tongue. She got lost in the feel of him, the way he touched her, his hands gripping her hips, his beard rasping over her skin. The orgasm that ripped through her was not a gentle one, and she couldn't catch her breath as he kissed his way back up her body.

"Why isn't it ever enough?" he asked as he pushed inside of her body, filling her in one easy thrust. "How come I can't get enough of you?"

Lucy's back arched off the bed, her nails clawing at his shoulders.

"I've never wanted someone this way. You consume me, Lucy," he whispered into her neck between kisses.

"I'm yours, Theo." The words fell from her lips of their own volition, but the second she said them, she knew they were true.

Theo's hips slowed, his head coming up so he could look down into her face. "What did you just say?"

"I'm yours." She repeated the words.

That hunger on Theo's face multiplied tenfold, his mouth was on hers again, the kiss more of a claiming than anything she'd ever experienced in her life. His hips started to move faster again, harder. The pleasure inside of her built, and built, and built until she was right there on the edge.

"Say it again," Theo demanded.

"I'm yours, Theo," Lucy gasped.

The orgasm that crashed through her was more intense than anything she'd ever experienced in her life. She clung to him, needing something to hold on to for fear that she'd float away into nothing.

But Theo kept her tethered to the earth, and he didn't let go of her for the rest of the night.

* * *

THE NEXT THREE DAYS went by in a blur for Lucy. The following morning was another early one, Theo having to be at the bakery by seven. As Lucy didn't have any plans, and she knew they needed the help, she joined him in the kitchen at Browned Butter. People needed their carbs and sugar to fuel them for their holiday shopping, and since Lucy's was mostly done, she had no desire to join those crowds.

She helped Juliet with the cookie baking, becoming the official dolloper of the batter on the baking sheets. By Saturday, they had a system going.

They finished up a little early that afternoon and Theo took her to the Christmas tree farm, where she helped him pick out a mighty fine Fraser fir. It was late by the time they got back to his house, so they didn't decorate it until Sunday. As Theo had a number of Christmas decorations to put up, they spent most of the day doing just that.

The very last thing that Lucy wanted to do on Monday was go back to work, but she managed to pull herself out of bed when the alarm went off at five. It helped a little when Theo started kissing her neck.

That night she found herself at Sasha's with Caro and Lilah, all of them grateful that Sasha had ordered in hamburgers and fries. They were all a little tired of the Thanksgiving leftovers. Topic one for girls' night was *the kiss* between Wes and Lorraine during that year's inaugural rendition of "Mistletoe Junction." Sasha had tried to press her mother on the issue, but she hadn't really gotten anywhere.

"I think we pulled off our mission successfully, though," Caro said.

"Yeah, except *someone* apparently had some other *hidden* agendas." Sasha glared at Lilah before she started piling pickles onto her burger.

"I don't know what you're talking about." Lilah shook her head.

Sasha grabbed a french fry, waving it in Lilah's face. "Admit that you told your mom to have Gavin and me kiss or I'm going to shove this fry up your nose."

"Fine! I did. But it didn't look like you put up much of a fight."

Sasha shrugged as she popped the fry into her mouth. "I never back down from a challenge. It's not like it's the first time we've kissed."

"Excuse me?" Caro leaned forward.

"How many times did we play spin the bottle in middle school? I will say, he's a much better kisser these days than he was at fourteen. Softer lips." She waggled her eyebrows.

"Gross." Lilah threw one of her own french fries at Sasha.

"Well, you weren't Lilah's only target," Lucy told Sasha. "Theo spotted Nari pulling at her ear, and he saw her do it again when we were in the middle of the dance floor."

"Yes, well, I figured the two of you needed a hard launch."

"A what?" Lucy laughed.

"A hard launch to your relationship. We got the soft launch when he kissed you at the park. This was the hard launch."

"*O-kay*, there isn't anything *hard* happening with Theo."

"Oh god, I hope that isn't the case." Sasha's eyes went wide in mock horror.

"In that department, things are perfectly fine."

"What about in other departments?" Lilah pressed. "You can't tell me it isn't getting serious. Have you spent a single night by yourself since the two of you started having sex?"

"Well . . . no."

"Lilah's right. Is it getting serious?" Caro asked.

"I don't know what it's getting." Lucy shook her head, but the second she said the words, she knew they weren't exactly true. Things had sure felt serious when he'd brought her back to his house after Thanksgiving dinner . . . when she'd told him she was his.

The words had tumbled out of her mouth, and she hadn't been able to stop them. She hadn't *wanted* to stop them. She also hadn't been able to get the expression on Theo's face out of her head. Or how things had shifted between them. The sex had definitely become more intense the last few days, that was for damn sure. She'd tried not to focus on it too much; it was one of the reasons she'd made an effort to stay too busy to think.

She was thinking now.

"Where are you staying tonight?" Caro asked.

"He's coming over to my apartment. Dad's been watching Estee since Thursday, and I'm starting to feel like an irresponsible cat owner. Plus, I know Bear has been looking for her."

"So, that's how many nights that you've spent together?" Lilah grabbed her wineglass and took a sip.

Lucy cleared her throat uncomfortably. "Ten. Tonight will be eleven."

All three women gave her their own variation of *the look*.

"Fine. Something is happening. I don't know what it is, and I don't know where he stands."

"Maybe you should bring it up," Sasha suggested. "Asking him would probably be a good idea."

"Like I just said, it's been ten days." Ten. Days. Could things have really gone from *just sex* to something else entirely in ten days? "That might be a little too soon for that talk. Can you guys just give me a break? Please."

"Okay, we'll back off." Caro held her hands up in surrender.

"For now," Lilah said, her eyes not leaving Lucy's.

* * *

LUCY'S BRAIN WAS BEYOND PREOCCUPIED when she came into work on Tuesday morning, her friends' words from the night before replaying over and over again. It didn't help that Theo had noticed, asking her if she was okay more than once when they'd gotten back to her place.

But she was okay . . . mostly. Just because she was a little confused about life didn't mean that she wasn't perfectly fine.

Fine. Fine. Fine.

She hated that word. Especially as after third period, she was anything *but* fine.

Lucy stood in the auditorium, the scene in front of her making her sick . . . well, that along with the acrid scent of burnt wood and plastic that lingered in the air.

The fire had been started by three boys who'd snuck in during their free period to smoke a joint. One of them had been playing around with their lighter, not noticing that it had started to leak. When the sleeve of his shirt caught on fire, he'd thrown the lighter at the musical's main backdrop, which was covered in layers of paint as it had been changed over the years. It hadn't taken much for the rest of the set pieces to light up like kindling.

Once the sprinklers had turned on, everything was ruined.

"Hey, Ms. Buchanan." A hand gently grasped her shoulder, tightening for a moment before letting go.

Lucy turned, looking up into the face of Captain Savage, Chloe's father.

"How many times do I have to tell you to call me Lucy?"

"Sorry, habit. Chloe talks about you all the time, so I'm used to hearing all about Ms. Buchanan at least ten times a day."

"Well, it's nice to have a fan." A small smile lifted her lips, a miracle considering the situation. "It's as bad as it looks, isn't it?"

"Actually, it's considerably better. The stage should be fine once it's dried up. There are a few boards that will need to be replaced, but nothing significant. The sprinkler system did its job. Luckily, the seats are mostly vinyl, and they should dry in no time, especially if you get some boxed fans in here. The carpet is probably going to have to go, though."

"Well, that's one upside. This carpet is older than me."

"It's older than me too," a voice said from behind them.

Lucy turned as Fatima walked up to them.

"I just finished up with our culprits and their parents in my office. Marcus Reynolds has some first-degree burns on his hand, but the paramedics got him cleaned up. He won't need to go to the hospital."

"That's a relief."

"What's the prognoses, Captain?"

"I was just telling Lucy that it isn't as bad as it looks. It's mainly just the set pieces that were destroyed."

Lucy looked back to the charred and waterlogged mess that had once been her perfectly painted set pieces.

"Yeah." Her voice cracked on the word, and she took a shallow breath, desperately trying to keep it together. She really didn't want to lose it in front of Harrison or the other half a dozen firefighters that were walking around the stage.

"Hey." Fatima reached out and gently squeezed Lucy's shoulder. "I already have three teenage boys who will be volunteering for the job." She grinned. "And I'd bet good money we will be able to rally the troops. Right, Captain Savage?"

"I might be an amateur carpenter, but my brothers are what you call experts. We'll help where we can. This program is the best thing that has happened to Chloe in the last couple of years."

"See, now we have six volunteers. The numbers will keep climbing. I know it's going to be a lot of work, but we have ten days before the musical. That's plenty of time to get this fixed."

Ten days. There was that number again.

Well, it had certainly been enough time for Lucy to get thoroughly tangled up in whatever was going on with Theo. Maybe it was enough time to fix the musical too.

* * *

THE USUAL AFTERNOON RUSH was in full swing at Browned Butter, the line consistently a good four or five people deep. Isaac was in the back working on the dough for tomorrow's focaccia bread while his mother had gone to grab another tray of the Cruickshank Vanilla Chai Cupcakes from the back cooler.

They hadn't stopped selling out of them since Theo had put them on the menu two weeks ago. He'd even tripled the recipe that morning, and it looked like they were going to be selling out again.

It was one of his better creations, but he'd had a pretty good muse.

Theo was in the middle of ringing up a loaf of sourdough and two of those vanilla chai cupcakes for Lilah when the bell above the front door rang. He glanced up and was surprised to see Gia and Chloe walk inside. They were supposed to have an extended rehearsal that afternoon—one with the entire cast and crew—and should've been at the school until five. It wasn't even two thirty yet.

"What are you guys doing here?" he asked as he set Lilah's box of cupcakes on the counter.

It was when he turned back to Gia that he saw the sheer dejection on her face. Chloe looked worse.

"What happened?" Theo was around the counter in an instant, the line of customers forgotten. All he cared about was what had upset his sister . . . and either fixing the situation or dealing with the person who'd upset her.

"The set for the musical burned down."

"There was a fire in the auditorium this afternoon. Some stupid boys who wanted to get high."

"Is anybody hurt?" Lilah asked.

"No." Chloe shook her head. "Well, one of them got burned, but he's going to be fine. No one else was in there besides the three of them."

"What about Lucy? Is she okay?" Theo was obviously concerned about Gia and Chloe—how could he not be?—but throwing Lucy into the mix escalated things even more.

As it tended to do these days.

There was no doubt in Theo's mind that he was in love with Lucy; it was clearer now than it had ever been. What wasn't clear was how Lucy felt. He'd replayed her saying *I'm yours* more times than he could count. Neither of them had addressed it after, and Theo was hesitant to go down that road.

Last time he had, she'd moved across the country.

"She looked defeated by the whole thing," Gia told him.

"She was trying to be optimistic," Chloe added. "But it was pretty clear that she was struggling by the end of the day."

Theo started to untie his apron before handing it over to Gia. "You two help Mom and Dad."

"And where are you going?" Lilah asked him, something like a knowing little smile turning up her lips.

"I'm going to fix it." He nodded before he grabbed the box of cupcakes from the counter. "Get Lilah another box of these, and throw an extra one in on the house," he said as he headed for the office to grab his jacket and the keys to his truck.

* * *

IT HAD BEEN more than thirteen years since Theo graduated from high school, and he remembered how to navigate the hallways of Mount MacCallion as if it had been yesterday.

Theo didn't have the mentality that high school had been the "glory days" for him, but he did have a certain nostalgia for that time in his life. He'd been on the football team along with Oscar and Gavin, and he'd been the starting wide receiver, and caught a number of game-winning throws.

There were blue and white banners up in the hallway, cheering on the team for that Friday's state finals game. The mascot, Thaddeus the Goat, was painted on most of them, his black and white face looking out, his eyes seeming to follow Theo. He was actually Thaddeus IV, from the same bloodline as the first mascot when the school was built in 1974. The goat was getting up there in age, having taken over the position Theo's senior year when they let Thaddeus III retire.

Making a left at the language arts hallway, Theo headed down to the end where the music and art classrooms were. The auditorium was at the very end, the four double doors on either side wide open, a whirring sound echoing into the hallway. It was only a few seconds later that the acrid burnt scent hit him, getting stronger as he got closer.

He stepped inside, the temperature dropping a good ten degrees. All of the windows had been propped open, and ten or so boxed fans were set up around the room and blowing on the seats. He saw the destruction on the stage, but after a quick look around, he realized the room was empty.

Theo headed back out and it was then that the sound of piano keys floated along the hallway from a classroom a couple doors down. It was half a dozen steps to that open door, but he stopped in his tracks when he heard her voice, goose bumps breaking out across his skin.

Lucy was singing.

Her voice was low and melodic, perfectly accompanied by the haunting chords she played on the piano. It wasn't a song he'd heard before . . .

"Before I know it, I'm at your door. I know I broke us once before. You're all I've wanted all these years. Please don't make me leave in tears."

Why did those words make his chest ache?

It was only a few more seconds before the music stopped. Theo shook his head, but there was nothing he could do to get the sound of her voice and the melancholy chords from the piano out of his mind. He took the last few steps to the door, knocking lightly on the frame before walking inside.

Lucy was sitting at the old baby grand piano, crossing something out in the notebook that was propped on the music stand. She looked up, a small smile pulling up the right side of her mouth, but it did nothing to hide the lingering sadness on her face. "Hey, you."

"Hey, you. I heard about the fire. You okay?"

"I've been better."

"I brought cupcakes."

"Well, you should've led with that." She stood up, running her hands down her sides, smoothing out the dark green sweater dress that clung to her hips.

Theo set the box down before opening his arms wide. Lucy walked right into them, pressing her face into his chest as he hugged her tight.

"This really sucks," she mumbled into his shirt.

"I know. We'll fix it."

Lucy pulled back enough to look up into his face. "We?"

"I'm here. That's why I brought the cupcakes; we might need a little energy for our planning session."

Now she looked bemused. "What planning session?"

"Operation Fix the Auditorium. Or maybe, Operation Musical Still a Go? Operation No More Sad Teenagers? I don't know, we can work on the name. That can be the first part of the planning session."

She laughed and Theo took the opportunity to press his mouth to hers.

* * *

LUCY STARED AT THE MAN sitting across from her, more than a little amused, which considering her day was no small miracle. He had his head bent over the yellow legal pad she'd found for him, and at the top of the paper he wrote out *Operation High School Musical* in his tidy scrawl. He was using her purple pen and there was something about that one little detail that pushed this entire situation into *hilarious.*

Theo was sitting in her classroom—surrounded by the cheesiest of motivational posters—in all of his scruffy flannel-wearing glory. Today's shirt was red and black and he looked even more like a lumberjack than usual.

Hey, that rhymes. Lumberjack, red and black.

It was taking everything in her not to burst out laughing. It didn't help that she felt jittery, probably a high from the sugar rush of the cupcakes. She hadn't eaten anything since breakfast, her overnight oats turning into cement in her stomach after she found out what had happened to the auditorium. She'd had no appetite for lunch and had been mainlining Diet Dr Pepper to get through the day.

But then Theo had opened that box of cupcakes and she'd found that she was suddenly starving. Even with the sugar rush, she felt better with a little sustenance in her stomach. Or maybe it had to do with the man sitting across from her.

"I went and saw Bear at Dancing Donkey during my lunch to-day," he told her as he looked up from the paper. "She got a snack, and we took a walk around the park."

Even though Bear had been good the few times she'd been left on her own, they'd decided to have her stay at the café during the day.

"How'd she do?"

"She got distracted by a few squirrels, but that was pretty much it."

"Did you film it for Gia?"

"I already sent it to her," Theo assured her. "The way she keeps uploading videos, I know we have to keep her supplied in content."

"Have you seen how many people are following the page now? It's over fifty thousand. That's insane." Lucy shook her head.

"I'm aware of my sister's ridiculous social media skills. It's not even December and the cookie preorders for the bakery are filled through January. They've never filled up that fast."

"Well, you aren't the only one who's gotten the Gia Golden Bump. She filmed me singing at the pub on Thursday."

"Did you post it to your page?" Theo asked.

"Yeah. The response has been pretty positive."

Theo's eyes narrowed on her. "What do you mean, *pretty* positive?"

"Well"—Lucy shrugged—"there will always be haters."

"What are the haters saying?"

"The usual." Lucy waved a hand in the air like it didn't matter. "That I have a pretty face but need to lose a few pounds. That they've heard better. That I shouldn't quit my day job."

"Well, fuck those guys. They wouldn't know talent if it hit them in the face. Though they probably need to be hit in the face with something."

"Are you going to go beat up all of my bullies?"

"I wouldn't even hesitate."

"I—" Lucy started, but words failed her. It wasn't that she was surprised by what Theo had said . . . it was just . . . God, she didn't even know how that made her feel. "Thank you," she managed to say a bit lamely. She reached across the table and grabbed his hand. "I'm okay, though. It's taken me some time, but I don't focus on that noise too much. Some days are better than others. Though today isn't one of the better ones."

"Well, let's fix that. What's first?" Theo asked, his blue eyes filled with a determination she was well aware of.

She'd never known him to not accomplish *exactly* what he set out to do. Something she couldn't say about herself. Lucy cleared her throat, sitting up straighter in her seat. "Well, first up will be clearing out the auditorium of all the debris and getting the carpet ripped up."

"Okay." Theo nodded before writing it down, not looking back up at her as he added number two and three. "After that would be supplies. What will we need?"

"More wood and paint . . . which involves money."

"How much is in the budget?"

"What budget?" Lucy pressed her finger to the few cupcake crumbs on her desk, getting them to stick before rubbing them off on the empty wrapper. "Fatima is working on money, but I don't know how we're going to get enough on such short notice."

"Hey." He pointed the purple pen at her. "One step at a time. We're just making the list right now. Stop being a Negative Nelly."

The laugh that burst from Lucy was unstoppable. "Did you call me a Negative Nelly?"

A slight blush colored his cheeks. "Yes, I did. Because that's what you're being." He pointed to the motivational poster behind her, the one of a mountain range. *"Focus on the next step. If you only think about the distance to the summit, you'll never get there."*

Lucy glared. "I hate those things. I want to replace them with *demotivational* quotes."

"What would that one be?" He pointed to the mountain quote again.

"The path up Mount Everest is paved with corpses that were once highly motivated."

This time it was Theo letting out a loud laugh. "What about that one?" He looked to the one above the window with a flying bald eagle, which had a quote about being unique.

"Be yourself. No one wants to be you anyway."

"And that one?" His smile got bigger as he nodded to the cat hanging from a tree limb.

"Trying: Sometimes you shouldn't." She turned and looked to the one that was of a lake, the shore made up of tiny pebbles. *"Remember, you're just an annoying pebble in the shoe of the universe."*

"Wow. Whose idea was it for you to teach children again?"

"Hey, my students love me, something that I was only able to accomplish with my sparkling sense of humor and sarcastic wit."

"Don't forget your humble nature."

"Oh, I could never forget how humble I am." Lucy put her hand over her heart in a demure gesture. "But for real, I had to work to win them over. It was hard in the beginning. They were pretty disappointed Mrs. Griffith wasn't going to be here for the semester."

"I never would've known. I'm pretty sure Gia and Chloe are about to start the Ms. Buchanan fan club."

"Chloe never knew Mrs. Griffith, so she was easier to lure to the dark side. As for your sister, I've been her favorite since I used to babysit for her."

"So, what you're telling me is she's biased?"

"Yes."

"You should give yourself more credit, Luce." Theo shook his head. "I know from personal experience how easily you can win people over."

"Have I won you over?" Lucy asked before she could stop herself.

"Yes," Theo said without hesitation. "Why do you think I'm here? If you haven't figured it out yet, Lucy, I like you."

"Just a little bit?" she asked, holding her hand in the air, her finger hovering above her thumb.

"Yeah." But this time Theo did hesitate before he repeated, "Just a little bit."

CHAPTER THIRTEEN
Harder and Harder to Leave

*T*hat evening, Theo found himself sitting at his parents' dining room table with Lucy across from him. They were making their way through the call list they'd brainstormed earlier at the school. Once they'd come up with what they needed, they'd figured out who'd be able to help them get those things. They'd gone over everything with Fatima, and she'd even taken a portion of the list home with her.

As they made phone calls, his parents whipped up some French onion soup and chicken Caesar salad for dinner, while Gia played with Bear and recorded more videos.

It wasn't like it was the first time Lucy had been at his parents' house, or even sat at their table. But it was the first time she'd been there because of him. Sure, Theo had introduced women he'd dated to his family, but he'd never brought anyone to family dinner night. Having Lucy there was new, but familiar at the same time. She fit right in . . . like she was always supposed to be there.

Theo wasn't going to draw too much attention to the situation . . . or any attention, really. It hadn't been the plan for Lucy to come over that evening, not that he hadn't wanted to ask her. It was more that he was being very cautious about asking for too much too soon.

He watched her from across the table, not missing a word of what Captain Savage was telling him over the phone. She looked less tense than when they'd first sat down, maybe because once they'd started making phone calls, it was clear that people were more than willing to help. Or maybe it was because of the wine that his mother kept pouring into her glass.

Lucy got off the phone a few seconds after Theo, and she danced in her chair for a second. "Jeremy said that Barrett approved for us to use some dumpsters to clean out the auditorium. He'll haul them off too. They'll be delivered to the school on Thursday. *And*," she emphasized as she reached for her wineglass, "he's going to donate some lumber and other material that we need."

"I always liked Jeremy's boss," Theo said as he grabbed his pen and checked off *dumpsters* from the list. "Well, Barrett isn't the only one who's offered to help with supplies. Cameron and Weston Savage will donate what they can, *and* they've volunteered to be in charge of the set rebuild. They'll be at the school on Saturday and Sunday once we confirm everything. Harrison also said some of the firefighters have offered to help. So, we can check those things off as well." Theo made little ticks next to *supplies* and *volunteers*.

"What else do you guys need to get taken care of?" Juliet asked, looking up from where she was cutting lettuce.

"Well, we've got meals covered for everyone on Saturday and Sunday." Theo glanced down at the list. "Dancing Donkey has got drinks, Browned Butter will be covering breakfast, and Quigley's is taking care of lunch. Desmond also said that whoever volunteers can get a drink on the house and a bowl of their Irish stew, so I'm sure plenty of people are going to take him up on that."

"No doubt," Isaac agreed as he slid another beer down in front of Theo. "Are you feeling better about everything now, Lucy?"

"For the most part." Lucy nodded. "It looks like paint and lights are the only other things left on our list."

"What kind of lights do you need?" Juliet asked.

"Christmas lights. We had them strung up on the trees. Luckily that was the only electrical thing that we lost. Unluckily, it's Christmas season. I was told the ones we had were purchased last year when they were like seventy-five percent off . . . so I don't know if we'll get enough money to replace them."

"We'll cross that bridge when we get to it. Let's see how much money Fatima can get us. But until then, what have I told you about being a Negative Nelly?" Theo pointed the pen at her.

"I believe, *Theodore*"—she emphasized his name with her usual sass—"that you told me to stop being one."

"I thought you weren't allowed to call him that?" Gia asked as she walked into the kitchen, Bear following at her side.

"I've gotten used to it." Theo shrugged. "Lucy's going to have to figure out another way to get under my skin."

"I'll work on that." The little smirk at the side of her mouth should cause him concern, but he had a feeling whatever she came up with would probably be more fun for him in the end.

Gia did a full body shake like she was creeped out by something. "It's still so *weird* when you two are nice to each other. I'm not used to you being a *couple* yet."

Well, shit. Thanks, Gia. That was the first time that word had been used.

"Leave your brother and Lucy alone," Juliet scolded Gia before she gave Bear a piece of chicken. "She's so gentle," she marveled, waiting a beat before giving the dog another piece. "I can see why you aren't giving her up."

Theo noticed how his mother had quickly changed the subject . . . and how Lucy went along with it.

"She's fit right in," Lucy replied, shifting in her chair.

"The people who abandoned her are monsters." Juliet petted Bear's head, scratching between her ears.

"Karma will get them."

"Keep doing that and you'll win her over," Theo told his mom. "You thought any more about keeping a puppy?"

Juliet made a furtive glance toward her husband. "It's been discussed."

Gia had been focusing on her phone, and she looked up so fast she had to have given herself whiplash. "It has been?"

"It has been." Isaac was grating cheese, and he set the parmesan down as he focused on his daughter. "If we say yes, you understand that it's going to be your responsibility to walk and feed the dog before school?"

"Yes, absolutely." Gia nodded.

"And you're going to be in charge of pooper-scooper duty," Juliet added.

"I'll do that, no problem."

Isaac leaned back against the counter, folding his arms across his chest. "And potty training is nonnegotiable."

"I'll write up a contract and sign it right now." Gia pointed to her computer on the counter.

"I think we'll discuss more of the specifics later, but the answer is yes. We can keep one of the puppies."

"Really?" Gia jumped up and down for a moment before she ran at her parents, pulling them both into a hug.

"Merry Christmas," Juliet said as she kissed the top of Gia's head.

It was a couple of moments before Gia pulled away, wiping beneath her eyes. The excitement on her face was almost enough to get Theo choked up.

"Can I be there when the puppies are born? It should be during Christmas break, so there won't be any school to worry about. Can I get first pick?"

Theo looked to Lucy, who was smiling. "You can have first pick. But let's just hope she doesn't go into labor in the middle of the night." She held her crossed fingers up in the air.

"You've just jinxed us." Theo shook his head.

"So, question," Juliet said, and Theo knew whatever was about to follow would be prying. Those were the two words his mother always started with when she was about to ask something that she probably shouldn't. "If you're keeping Bear, and the puppies will need to be with Bear for . . . what . . . a couple of months?"

"They'll need to be with her for eight or nine weeks." Lucy nodded.

"So that means you'll be in Cruickshank for at least that long."

Theo froze for a second. He still had no idea what Lucy's plans were. She hadn't mentioned leaving after the semester . . . but she also hadn't said she was staying.

"I don't have any plans to leave at the moment."

"Good to know." Juliet grinned.

That was an understatement. Theo purposely didn't look over at Lucy, and instead made eye contact with his father, who got the message.

"Is there anyone else who's shown interest in keeping any of the puppies?" Isaac asked, changing the subject.

"Gavin said he wants one. And Jeremy has been hinting to

Lilah that he'd like to get another dog. So that's three homes . . .
only like five more to go. Hopefully we'll get a better puppy count
tomorrow at Bear's vet appointment."

"Yeah, Theo told us it was going to be a good-size litter." Isaac
bent down and started to pet Bear, who'd begun circling around
his feet, no doubt because he had cheese. "Are you two planning on keeping Bear at Lucy's apartment when the puppies are
born?"

"I don't know what we're going to do yet, but I think my apartment is out of the question. Luckily, there is some time for us to
figure that out. Though with all of this"—Lucy gestured at the
table—"I feel like I just lost a week. And I still need to figure out
where we're going to do rehearsals because we can't lose any more
practice."

"What about the gym at the school?" Juliet suggested.

"We can't." Lucy shook her head. "Basketball season has
started, and they already have a hard enough time getting the
boys' and girls' teams scheduled in there. And the library is out
because it's the science fair this week."

"What about the cafeteria?" Isaac asked.

"They're using it for ACT prep," Gia answered.

The four of them continued to brainstorm spots while Theo
kept quiet. It wasn't lost on him how quickly Lucy had changed
the subject of where *they* would be keeping Bear and her puppies.
Though Lucy had continued to say *we*. Lucy might be the one
who was officially adopting the dog, but they had been making
decisions together ever since they'd rescued Bear from the back
alley of Browned Butter.

They hadn't discussed what they'd be doing when it got closer
to the puppies being born, though. Theo had thought about it
himself . . . especially as Bear was getting bigger and bigger. She

wasn't having issues with the flight of stairs up to Lucy's apartment, but he figured it was just a matter of time before she started to struggle. They were more than a little steep.

It wasn't like he didn't like Lucy's place—because he did—it was just that it was a little cramped, especially at night in her queen-size bed. Besides, he'd really liked having her at his place, liked her in *his* bed regularly.

He'd enjoyed the weekend they'd spent together, though it was pretty clear that a certain cat's presence was missed, by both Lucy and Bear . . . and by Theo, if he was being totally honest. He'd come to really like Estee. Getting the cat to his house was the first obstacle he needed to tackle, because once she was there, Lucy would have less of a reason to not stay over.

He made a surreptitious glance in Lucy's direction, wondering how to broach this particular topic. He was already treading so lightly with her.

Don't go too fast too soon, he reminded himself. Just one step at a time.

* * *

LUCY STARED AT THE SCREEN of the ultrasound through her phone, recording as Oscar pressed the wand to Bear's belly. He started counting as he moved it around. One, two, three, four . . .

It wasn't until he got to double digits that Lucy started to panic a little.

"Eleven?" Her eyes went wide as she looked over to Theo. "Holy crap."

"That's a lot of puppies, Mama Bear." He petted the dog's head reassuringly. She licked his hand.

"There could be one or two hiding," Oscar said as he continued to move the wand, searching.

"Stop looking for more!" Lucy all but shouted. "We don't need any more. Eleven is enough," she looked down and told the dog.

"I don't think she has any control in the matter." Theo laughed as he shook his head.

"No, I don't suppose she does." Lucy pressed the button on her phone and stopped recording. She tapped a few more buttons, forwarding the video to Gia before dropping the phone in her purse.

"Well, no matter what, you're going to need to get her a good-size whelping box," Oscar told them as he turned the machine off and pushed it away. "I know we've got a few weeks until her due date, but I'd get her one sooner rather than later. Sometimes they start to nest early, so it's a good idea to get her comfortable with the box. Make sure she has blankets, her favorite toys, that sort of thing," he finished as he wiped the ultrasound gel off Bear's belly.

"Well, she is quite partial to her Beyoncé sloth."

Oscar looked over at Theo, his eyebrows bunched together in confusion. "How is it a Beyoncé sloth?"

"It's wearing a shirt that says *I Woke Up Like This*." Theo made a gesture over his chest as if to indicate where the words were. "It was either that or the Taylor Swift cat. That shirt said *Karma Is My Boyfriend*, but I didn't think Estee would approve of Bear chewing on something that looked like her."

"Definitely not," Lucy agreed.

"So, sloth it was."

"Clearly." Oscar laughed again as he looked at Theo.

"What?" Theo asked.

"Nothing." Oscar shook his head. "It's just . . . I don't know." He waved his hand in the air, gesturing at Theo. "The way you are with Bear is kind of . . . adorable. I'm not used to you being adorable. It's new. Endearing almost."

Lucy looked over at Theo, her head tilted to the side as her eyes moved up and down, studying him. After a moment she shrugged. "I don't know if I'd go with *adorable*. He's okay."

"*Okay?*" Theo repeated. "Wow, what high praise."

"You're welcome." She grinned at him before turning to Oscar. "Speaking of adorable people, how are things going with you and Edward these days?"

Oscar's face went a little dopey. "He's in New York at the moment, but he'll be back on Friday. He volunteered to help at the school on Saturday. He might be the business suit type, but apparently he's no novice when it comes to swinging a hammer."

"Are we still talking about construction? Or . . ." Lucy trailed off, waggling her eyebrows.

"Well, in that department I can *confirm* he's no novice."

"So, things are going *very* well." Lucy grinned.

"Well, I'm glad it's not just *okay*." Theo narrowed his eyes on Lucy.

"Oh, Theodore." She patted his chest. "You know how to swing your hammer too."

Oscar laughed but turned it into a cough, taking a moment to control himself.

"Seriously, Lucy?" Theo asked. She could tell that his skin had gone a little pink under his beard.

"You're the one who started it." Lucy bit back her own grin.

"And now I'm regretting it. Can we please move back to Bear?"

"Yes." Oscar let out another awkward cough. "We're around week six now, so she's going to need more food and more rest. But you'll need to make sure she doesn't overeat. I'll get you an updated calorie intake."

"What about walks?"

"Exercise is good, but I'd start to limit her being around other dogs. This is both for health reasons, and because she might start to become territorial. So, I'd be careful there. I'd say in another week or two, you need to make sure she isn't around any other dogs."

"What about Estee?" Theo asked. "They've been getting along."

"Just watch for signs. If it's clear Bear doesn't like the cat around her, you might need to reevaluate. This is where your whelping box will help. If she has her own space, she'll feel more comfortable."

"Okay."

"Besides that, she seems to be doing well and the puppies looked good on the ultrasound. I think we've got a healthy pregnancy on our hands. You guys found her in the nick of time."

"Yeah, we did." Theo petted Bear's head again, rubbing his palm between her ears. She looked up at him adoringly.

"We can schedule her next appointment for two weeks from now, but I'd just monitor her behavior and if she starts to act weird or you aren't sure about something, you know how to reach me."

"I think we do." Lucy nodded.

"In the meantime, have fun swinging your hammer." Oscar clapped Theo on the back.

"*Jesus Christ.*" Theo dropped his gaze to the floor, rubbing his forehead. He didn't look at either Lucy or Oscar as he helped Bear off the exam room table.

* * *

REHEARSALS FOR THE MUSICAL had found a new place in the chorus room. It was a little cramped—even after they moved all of the chairs and stands out of the way—but they made it work. They'd be back in the auditorium by Monday anyway.

Thursday's rehearsal was done at five, but Lucy had to stay a little longer, needing to be there when the dumpsters were dropped. She wasn't too late for her family's dinner night and was able to enjoy a glass of wine with Lilah, Caro, and Sasha before Wes finished cooking the chicken marsala.

Sasha wasn't the only one who'd joined; Lorraine and Theo were there as well. The Belmonts were regular guests at the Buchanan family dinner, but there were a few more raised eyebrows with Lorraine that night. While no one was addressing the elephant in the room, it was clear everyone was wondering about that Thanksgiving kiss between Wes and Lorraine . . . and what had happened since.

On the other hand, it *was* Theo's first time coming to dinner. Lucy had asked him if he'd join after she'd gone to his parents' on Tuesday. She hadn't done it because she'd felt obligated; she'd wanted him to come. There was something about him standing outside with Jeremy and Max. All three of them had a beer in their hands as they watched the kids riding their bikes up and down the driveway, the dogs all running around.

Bear was walking with Emilia, the little girl leaning into the dog's side. Jeremy and Lilah's schnauzer, Angus, was circling around them protectively. The little dog had been around Bear a number of times in the last couple of weeks, and he was very clearly smitten with her. It didn't matter that Bear was roughly seventy pounds heavier than him, and twice as tall. Apparently, there were short kings in the canine world too.

It was very clear that Bear had gotten bigger in the weeks since they'd rescued her. Not only had she put on some weight, but her belly had grown with her eleven puppies.

Eleven puppies . . . if not more.

"Hey, Lilah," Lucy called out as she turned to her sister-in-law. "Have you and Jeremy talked any more about keeping a puppy?"

Lilah moved closer to Lucy, looking out the window and to the backyard. "Yeah, we've talked about it. I think it would be good for Angus. He loves being around the other dogs. I was concerned about how big Bear was when it comes to Emilia, but she's so gentle with her."

They all watched as Bear slowly moved with Emilia, not leaving the little girl's side as she stopped to pick up the ball that Leia had just dropped at her feet. Emilia made a pathetic little throw, the ball not going very far in the air before rolling into the grass. All of the dogs took off except for Bear.

It was then that Emilia stumbled, but Bear moved her body, preventing the little girl from falling to the ground.

"You think her babies will be like that?" Lilah asked.

"Yes," Lucy said without hesitation.

Lilah laughed. "I'm pretty sure we're going to keep one. I'll confirm with Jeremy tonight and let you know."

"You going to try and get all of those puppies adopted before they're even born?" Lorraine asked.

"That's my current plan." Lucy nodded. She'd been a little anxious since the vet appointment the day before.

Lucy had known Bear was pregnant almost from the moment they'd rescued her, but there'd been something about seeing those babies that had made it feel more real than before . . . if that made any sense. Maybe it was because it had been confirmed that there were so many of them now.

Bear had already been abandoned, and Lucy didn't want that to happen to any of her babies. Gia had told her that there were messages flooding in about people wanting to adopt the puppies. Maybe it was unrealistic, but Lucy wanted them to go to people she knew, not strangers. If they were with families in Cruickshank, she'd get to see them grow up, and so would Bear.

Well, that was if Lucy stayed in Cruickshank.

New York was still on the line; the apartment offer from Stephanie hadn't gone anywhere. Then there was the job offer

from Fatima for the following semester. Lucy hadn't made a decision about either of them. But what with the puppies, there was
no chance she was leaving until they were all adopted, and that
wouldn't be until mid to late February.

But Bear wasn't the only reason she was dragging her feet . . .

Lucy glanced back out the window, looking to where Theo was
now squatting next to Emilia, helping her throw the ball for the
dogs.

She'd be lying if she said she wasn't falling deeper and deeper
into whatever this was with Theo. Every day it was something
new, and it fucking terrified her.

But it went further than whatever things were with Theo. She
knew they were at a point where she was going to have to address
something she'd been avoiding for weeks: what to do with Bear.

The fact that the dog couldn't continue to stay in that little loft
apartment through the rest of the pregnancy was not lost on Lucy.
She'd been thinking about it for a while now and had come to the
conclusion that she had two options.

Option one: She could stay at her dad's. The last thing she
wanted to do was start sleeping in her childhood bed again,
mainly because Theo wouldn't be in it with her. Going that route
would significantly slow things down with him.

Which led to the other option: she could stay at Theo's . . .
which would significantly speed things up with him.

They hadn't spent a night apart from each other since everything had started, and sure, some of those nights had been at his
place. But once Bear was settled, once she had the puppies, there
would be no moving her, or at least not without some difficulties.
The last thing that Lucy wanted was to create any complications
or stress for the dog.

Where Bear went was where Lucy would be. So, she just

needed to figure out which path she was choosing. And what with the ticking clock that was Bear's due date, she'd never felt more unsure about anything in her life.

* * *

THE LUMBER AND SUPPLIES were delivered to the school on Friday afternoon. Lucy was grateful that it wasn't a late delivery as they had the high school championship football game to watch. The game was a couple of hours away, and while some people were making the drive, Lucy was not one of them. She had to be at the high school at eight o'clock in the morning, so she wasn't going.

It was a sacrifice, but the musical was her top priority.

Instead, she and Theo went to Quigley's to watch the game. They were broadcasting it locally and it was way more fun to watch with a crowd than at home alone, especially as it was another close game. The Fighting Goats didn't pull out the win until the very end.

Both Lucy and Theo were so hyped up after the game that neither was ready to leave. So, darts it was. As Theo wrote their names on the top of a napkin, Lucy leaned over and whispered in his ear.

"Winner gets to pick who's on top."

His head had come up so fast he nearly collided with her. "Why do I have the feeling we're both going to have the same answer no matter who wins?"

Lucy just grinned at him before she turned to go get their darts.

And as it turned out, Theo was right. He might've won the game, but it was Lucy who found herself riding him when they got back to her place. One of his hands gripped her thigh as they moved together, while the other was between their bodies, his fingers playing with her clit.

He paid attention to her body in ways that no man had before.

He knew exactly how and where to touch her, knew what she needed to come. He knew *her*.

Lucy screamed his name to the ceiling as the orgasm rolled through her. She collapsed onto his chest, trying to catch her breath, and Theo's hands moved up and down her back, his fingers tracing her spine. It was a couple of moments before she realized he was still hard inside of her.

"Theo?" she whispered his name.

"Now it's my turn." He rolled until she was underneath him, his arms moving under her legs until the backs of her knees were looped on the insides of his elbows. "I want another one," he said as he started to move in and out of her.

"A . . . a little greedy, are we?" she managed to ask before another moan filled the room, her back arching off the bed.

"With you? Always. It's never enough, Lucy." He kissed her neck, his teeth nipping at her skin. "It's *never* enough." He emphasized the words as he continued to thrust his hips.

Every move he made had the pleasure climbing higher and higher inside of her. The buildup consumed her, took over every part of her. *He* had taken over every part of her. Her hands were in his hair, her fingers twisting in the strands and holding on for dear life as another orgasm ripped through her.

How was it more intense than the first?

Theo let go of his own release, groaning Lucy's name into her throat as his hips slowed. He didn't let go of her as he rolled to the side, pulling her with him as he caught his own breath. Lucy held on to him too, unable to let go.

* * *

THE ALARM WENT OFF at six thirty the following morning. Considering the fact that Lucy was usually up at five, she counted it as sleeping in. Theo left before her, needing to go to Browned Butter to get breakfast for everyone who was coming to help with the auditorium while Lucy got Bear fed, watered, and walked.

It just so happened that the walk took them to Jeremy and Lilah's place, just around the corner from her dad's house. Lucy and Theo were going to be at the school for most of the day and they didn't want Bear to be alone. As Lilah would be home with the kids, she'd offered to keep an eye on the dog. Plus, Bear would get to hang out with her new boyfriend, Angus.

It was cold that morning, but at least there were no clouds covering the clear blue sky or the sun. Lucy took the long way to Lilah and Jeremy's house, going around the bigger part of the loop. Bear needed to stretch her legs a little and moseyed along like she usually did, sniffing all the sniffs and taking her time to empty her bladder. The dog sure did like to mark her territory.

It was just before seven thirty when Lucy walked inside of the house, Angus making a beeline for them the second they stepped through the door.

But the little dog wasn't the only one to greet them. Emilia set her milk down before she sleepily stumbled over to Lucy, her arms wide open. Her hair was a halo of messy curls and she was wearing thermal pajamas patterned with reindeer and green fuzzy socks with the Grinch.

Lucy put her purse down on the coffee table before scooping up the four-year-old and pressing a kiss to her cheek. "How's my favorite niece?"

"Good," Emilia huffed out as she pressed her tiny face into Lucy's neck. One of Lucy's absolute favorite things in the world was when Emilia was snuggly. Her nephews used to be this way too, but not so much anymore.

"You going to keep an eye on Bear for me today?" Lucy asked as she played with Emilia's little foot.

Emilia lifted her head so she could look at her aunt. Her blue eyes were the exact color that Rachel's had been. Sometimes Lucy thought she was seeing her mother again when she looked at Emilia. So many similarities, even the freckles on her little nose. "I will." She nodded exuberantly before she resumed snuggling.

Lilah came into the living room, her hands wrapped around a coffee mug with a gingerbread man missing his leg and the words *Bite Me* printed underneath. She looked quite cozy with her own candy cane–striped socks—also fuzzy—and all bundled up in a thick white robe.

"Morning, sunshine," Lilah said. "You ready for today?"

"I will be after another cup of coffee. One wasn't enough."

"It never is." Lilah shook her head. "You guys going to come to the pub tonight? Mom's making japchae again. Didn't think you'd want to miss it."

"Is this still part of her plan to get me to not move out of Cruickshank?"

Emilia pulled away from Lucy's neck again, a startled and scared expression on her face. "You're moving?!"

"No, bug," Lucy soothed the child. "I'm not moving."

"Not any time soon, at least," Lilah said.

"I want you *hereeee*." Emilia's voice went up many octaves, usually the telltale sign she was about to start crying. Well, that and her now trembling bottom lip.

"Emilia, I was just joking, and so was your mom."

"I d-d-don't want you to go," she all but wailed before she started to cry, her arms tightening around Lucy's shoulders as she buried her now very wet face into Lucy's neck.

Lucy looked up to Lilah for help and found that her friend had a funny little smile pulling up her lips. "This isn't funny."

"What isn't funny?" Jeremy asked as he walked into the room. "And why is Emilia crying?"

"B-be-because Aunt Lucy is leaving," Emilia hiccuped as she turned to look at her father, tears streaming down her face.

"Just for the day, bug." He reached up, gently running his fingers across his daughter's cheeks. "We'll be back tonight."

"N-n-no. She's moving."

"What?" Jeremy's somewhat severe gaze moved up to his sister's face, alarm in his eyes.

"I'm not going anywhere." Lucy shook her head. "Look what you started." She turned to Lilah. "You've got everyone upset."

"I didn't start anything." Lilah bit her bottom lip, trying not to laugh.

"Oh, really." Lucy indicated Emilia, who was still crying.

Lilah waved it off like it was no big deal. "If Emilia doesn't start the morning having some sort of emotional breakdown, it's just not a normal morning in this house. Yesterday it was because she couldn't find her penguin pants."

"Well, that would upset me too." Lucy nodded before moving her focus back to her niece. "Listen, bug, I have no plans on going anywhere anytime soon. I might even be teaching for another semester."

"What?" Lilah and Jeremy said in unison.

Lucy looked up at them. The only person she'd told about the offer was her dad. She wasn't exactly sure *why* she hadn't told anyone . . . especially why she hadn't told Theo.

Maybe because things already felt too intense with him . . . and she wasn't ready for another step. But there was always another step no matter if she was ready or not. Things kept moving even though it all seemed too fast already.

Way too fast.

"I haven't decided yet," she told them. "Mrs. Griffith isn't ready to come back. And there's Bear and the puppies and—"

"Theo?" Lilah finished.

"Yes, and Theo."

"What's going on with him—" Jeremy started to ask, but Lilah cleared her throat loudly, shaking her head at him. "Never mind, I'm just glad to know you could be here through the spring."

Lucy looked over at Lilah. She knew her sister-in-law was dying to know the answer to Jeremy's unanswered question too. As promised, Lilah had taken a step back from her usual meddling the last few days. Lucy wondered how long that was going to last.

"Just until spring?" Emilia started to wail again. Lucy knew the child had no concept of time. She was just crying to cry at this point.

It was then that Lilah finally took pity on Lucy. She set her coffee cup down on the dining room table before crossing over to them. "It's going to be fine, Emilia. Aunt Lucy is here now, and that's what we need to focus on. Okay?"

"O-kay." Emilia's arms tightened around Lucy again, like she was never going to let go.

"Now give her a kiss, and give one to your daddy, and then we can go make waffles."

"Gingerbread waffles?" Emilia asked, the tears very quickly stopping.

"Whatever you want."

"Okay." She sniffled before pressing a very wet kiss to Lucy's cheek. And then she unlatched her arms, holding them out to her father. He scooped her up, snuggling her a little as he whispered something in her ear for only her to hear. "Promise?"

"Cross my heart." He made the motion over his chest before

moving his mouth to her throat and giving her a raspberry. A high-pitched squeal filled the room as she started to laugh. He then set her on the floor, where she ran over to her mother.

"Waffles," she said as she grabbed Lilah's hand and started to tug her in the direction of the kitchen.

"Hold on, little miss." Lilah shook her head before she looked up at her husband. "I'll see you later."

"See you later, my love." He nodded as he pressed a kiss to Lilah's lips.

They didn't get to linger too long, as Emilia started pulling on Lilah's hand again. "Let's go, Mommy."

"Okay, okay." Lilah turned, letting herself get dragged away to the kitchen. Jeremy just stood there for a moment, watching with that dopey lovestruck expression that he always had on his face when it came to Lilah.

It was only after his wife and daughter disappeared through the door that he turned to his sister, catching her staring at him. "What?"

"It's just that . . ." She shrugged. "You're adorable."

"I'm what?" He looped his arm around her neck, gently pulling her close as he gave her a noogie.

"Hey, don't do that!" Lucy tried to pull away.

"Don't call me adorable." He let go of her and she pushed at his side.

Yet another reason it was getting harder and harder for Lucy to think about leaving again: she'd miss out on all of this. Miss out on Emilia and the boys growing up, on being around her friends and family.

Maybe staying was more of an option than she'd realized.

CHAPTER FOURTEEN

Lights

*T*heo was pleased to see the number of volunteers they got that morning, and even more so that everyone who showed up was ready to work.

There were four crews for the day. First were those running the food and drinks station in Lucy's classroom. Sasha was in charge there and was working with a majority of the students, most of them looking bleary-eyed from the game the night before. At least it was a safer job than the repair work—even with the hot liquids and sharp knives—but not any less busy. The coffee was constantly being brewed and they were making a massive batch of freshly squeezed lemonade.

The next crew was taking down the old set pieces and hauling them off to the dumpster. Captain Savage was leading that area and had most of the firefighters helping him.

The third group was dealing with carpet removal out on the auditorium floor. Jeremy and Wes were team leaders there, the father-and-son duo used to working with each other at construction sites. Wes was usually doing all things electrical, but he could use a crowbar just fine.

And last was set construction, which was happening in the cafeteria. It was warmer in there than the metal building out back and they wouldn't have to haul the set pieces too far. Weston and Cameron Savage were running that group alongside Mr. Wallace, who'd been teaching shop class since Theo had gone to school.

Theo and Lucy were the ones in charge of the clipboard, directing the volunteers to their assigned areas and making sure that everything was running smoothly. And smoothly it did run.

Before long, the sounds of hammers and saws filled the air as everyone got to work. By lunch, half of the carpet had been ripped up and hauled out. The stage was cleared of debris, and the black soot and burnt mess that was underneath cleaned up. Luckily the janitors had worked on what they could during the week, mopping up the water and cleaning to preserve the parts of the stage that were okay. There were more than a few boards that needed to be replaced, and the guys had that finished by the time five o'clock rolled around.

The whole stage would need to be stripped and restained, but that was a job that could wait until the next semester, when there was more time and money. That was also when the now-uncarpeted floors would be dealt with; for now, they were just going to make do with the bare concrete.

Theo and Lucy were the last to leave that evening, and as he looked at the cleared-out space, he had more hope for the next day. Even Lucy seemed wholly optimistic about everything.

They didn't spend too much time at Quigley's, just enough for dinner, two drinks, and a quick round of darts. The winner got to again pick that evening's position, which was why Theo found himself kneeling on Lucy's bed, her perfect ass in the air as he took her from behind.

The very last thing he wanted to do when the alarm went off

the next morning was to let go of Lucy and get out of bed, but after a few stolen kisses, he made himself. They split up like they had the day before, Theo heading to the bakery to get the pastries that had been packed the night before, and Lucy taking care of Bear and dropping her off at Jeremy and Lilah's.

There weren't that many vehicles in the parking lot of Mount MacCallion when Theo pulled in before eight. He immediately spotted Jeremy's truck, but the one he was actually looking for belonged to Weston Savage. He and Cameron were at the tailgate, grabbing their tools.

"Just who I needed to talk to," Theo said as he rounded his own truck. "I wanted to ask you guys a favor."

"We're kind of in the middle of the last favor you asked for." Weston looked at the school.

"Yeah, but this one I was actually going to pay you for."

Cameron grinned. "We're all ears."

"Excellent." Theo grabbed one of their bags, walking with them up to the school as he explained what he wanted.

* * *

FOR THE SECOND NIGHT IN A ROW, Lucy found herself alone in the auditorium with Theo. They were sitting in the fourth row, passing a flask of whiskey back and forth. He'd thought they needed to have a little toast to their success. So toast they did as they stared at the stage, all of the set pieces complete.

In the very back were a dozen trees, intricately cut with wispy branches and the wood stained to look like bark. They were so much more beautiful than the ones they'd had before. There was a staircase on wheels, and each step had been painted a different shade, transitioning from reds, to oranges, to yellows. They looked like a sunset.

The set piece that represented the house was now a door, with two framed windows on either side. Dark teal curtains were hung and there were little vases of flowers on the windowsills. The new park bench had been built from scratch and was solid and sturdy. The one they'd had before was missing a few boards from the back and had a wobbly arm that would never tighten.

But Lucy couldn't take her eyes off the piece that Caro had worked on. Her sister had spent most of her time painting the massive full moon that was hung in the corner. It had been paper before but was now made of wood and looked like it was glowing with the spotlight shining on it.

"Look, you can even see the man in the moon," Theo said as he pointed to it.

"It's my favorite part." Lucy's voice cracked, a wave of emotion she hadn't been ready for crashing into her. She couldn't have fought the tears in that moment even if she'd wanted to.

"Luce?" Theo's voice was soft as he touched her hand.

She looked at him, the tears slowly falling from her eyes. "Thank you, Theo. Thank you for doing this with me . . . for doing this *for* me."

"Haven't you figured it out yet, Lucy? I'd do anything for you." He reached forward, gently wiping the tears away before his fingers trailed down to her chin. Then he leaned down and kissed her. His mouth tasted like whiskey and felt like sin as it moved against hers. But it always felt like sin.

And just like that, Lucy was lost in the moment, unable to think about anything but him. How was it that he could always make her feel this way? Warm and comforted and content . . . happy.

Theo pulled back, looking down into her face with an expression that was just a little bit sad. "I wish you got to enjoy all of this for more than just the winter musical."

Maybe it was the high of the moment or the whiskey—or both—but in that moment, Lucy *finally* made her decision. "I'm going to get to, actually."

Theo pulled back even more, his eyes searching her face. "What do you mean?"

"I'm going to be teaching next semester. Mrs. Griffith isn't ready to come back, so Fatima asked if I would stick around in the spring."

"So, you're staying?"

"I'm staying." Lucy nodded.

"Thank god." The wave of relief that washed through his blue eyes was unmistakable and it did something funny to her chest. She grabbed on to the front of his shirt, pulling him toward her. He didn't resist, pressing his mouth to hers again. This kiss continued to build and build and build until Lucy started to lose her breath.

"We should go," she said against his lips. "So I can thank you properly." She wanted to be lost in more than just the moment; she wanted to be lost in *him*.

"You don't have to tell me twice," Theo said as he got to his feet, holding his hand out to her. Lucy put her palm in his, letting him pull her to her feet, and out of the auditorium.

* * *

REHEARSALS ON MONDAY went off without a hitch, all the kids loving the new set. The transitions between scenes were seamless, none of the cast having to struggle with a broken wheel or a wonky leg of a set piece. The Savage brothers and Mr. Wallace couldn't have done a better job.

It was perfect.

Well, almost perfect. The only thing that wasn't going to get fixed was the Christmas lights. As Lucy had predicted, there wasn't enough money to buy them at their current price. But it was okay, they'd make do with what they had. She was planning on scrounging around in her father's attic to look for a few strands and she'd sent some texts out to her friends asking them to do the same.

But Lucy would deal with that later. She'd felt like she'd been going nonstop since the fire and she was looking forward to a relaxing girls' night at Lilah and Jeremy's house. Lilah had sent them a text that Jeremy was working late that night, and since she didn't have any help in the kitchen or with the kids, they were having pizza for dinner.

"Yummm," Lucy hummed as she opened one of the boxes from La Bella's, revealing a margherita pizza. She found the box with plain cheese, getting the kids each a slice.

"Thanks, Aunt Lucy!" they all chorused as they headed to the living room, Angus and Bear following behind them. The kids were setting up camp in front of the TV, and that night's feature film was *The Grinch*.

Lucy and Lilah brought them their apple juice and a stack of napkins, and as Lucy helped Emilia get seated at the coffee table, she pointed to Bear. "Don't give her *any* pizza, okay? Even if she gives you *those* eyes. She's on a special diet because of her pregnancy and we don't want her to get sick."

"Okay." Emilia nodded.

Bear had already had her dinner anyway, Sasha feeding her before Lucy had even gotten to Lilah and Jeremy's house. The dog had spent the day at Dancing Donkey, coming over with Sasha when they closed. It had been a great help since Lucy had a late rehearsal and Theo was helping Oscar with some project before going to Quigley's for dinner and a drink.

Once the kids were settled, the four ladies got their own pizza and wine before heading to the small sitting room. When Lilah hosted girls' night, they usually spent it on the back porch, but it was way too cold that evening.

The sitting room was supposed to be a formal dining room, but as Lilah liked to say, there was nothing formal about their family. They'd instead turned it into a library/office with a large desk on one end and built-in bookshelves around an electric fireplace on the other. A large squishy leather sofa and two cozy sapphire-blue armchairs were placed in the middle. Lucy grabbed one of the armchairs, settling in before taking a bite of her pizza.

"So why did Jeremy have to work late tonight?" Lucy asked as she reached for her glass of wine.

Lilah hesitated for a second. "It was, uh, something about a light order that he had to help Max with."

"Are they already ordering lights for the hotel?" Lucy asked Caro. "Isn't it kind of early?"

"Yeah, a little early." Caro nodded, clearing her throat. "But they have to get a lot and the company Max wants to order from is having some delays. He wanted to make sure to get everything picked out now so they don't have any problems in the future."

"Gotcha." Lucy nodded.

"So," Sasha said a bit too loudly, the subject change pretty clear. "Are you ready for the musical?"

"I think so," Lucy said slowly, getting the sense that the three of them were acting a little bit weird. "There are a few costumes I need to do some hemming on. Luckily Caro fixed my dress fiasco, so my lead, Hannah Gregory, will be wearing red like the Christmas heroine she's supposed to be, and not bubblegum pink like the tooth fairy."

"Well, no one wanted that." Caro shook her head. "So, nothing else is going on? Work-wise or . . . or otherwise?"

"What are you getting at?" Lucy asked, narrowing her eyes at Lilah. "Did you tell them about next semester?"

"I, uh, might've mentioned that you could possibly, maybe, be teaching longer."

"No secret is safe with you."

"Hey!" Lilah protested. "You didn't mention it was a secret."

"Fair point," Lucy conceded. "Well, just so you know, I *am* going to be teaching next semester."

"Does Theo know?" Sasha asked.

"I told him last night."

"What did he say?"

Lucy hesitated for just a moment before saying, "I believe his exact words were *thank god*. And we didn't really do a lot of talking afterward."

"So, what you're telling us is that you're having more sex than talking?" Caro grinned.

"Basically."

"Oh, brother." Sasha sighed, rolling her eyes.

"I can't tell." Lilah turned to her. "Was that exasperation or jealousy?"

"Both," Sasha answered and they all laughed.

* * *

THEO STOOD IN THE AUDITORIUM, right in front of the seats where he'd sat with Lucy the night before. He was partial to that spot as it was the exact same place he'd sat all of those years ago the first time he'd watched her sing.

But this time, he was marveling at something else.

It had taken *hours* to unbox and hang the hundreds of lights they'd gotten. They were now strung among the branches of the trees. And there'd been a number of helpers doing it too. Theo had managed to wrangle Jeremy, Max, Gavin, Wes, Lorraine, his own father and mother, Gia, Chloe, all three of the Savage brothers, and Oscar—who'd brought Edward along.

The Christmas lights had been purchased at half price, Max working his own magic with the company that would be providing all of the lights for the hotel. Everything from lamps to chandeliers, sconces, and all things recessed. Name it and they were the ones doing it.

Theo had called Max as soon as he'd been able to last Wednesday, explaining what they needed and asking for help. Max told him he'd take care of it. Theo had offered to pay for the lights, but Max said he'd take care of that too.

"Well, would you look at that?" Jeremy said as he clapped Theo on the shoulder. "You did it, man. The final touches are done."

"Yeah." Theo nodded. "I can't wait for her to see it." He'd wanted to surprise Lucy, which was why he'd done the whole thing in secret. And everyone there that evening had helped him pull it off.

Jeremy cleared his throat as he let go of Theo's shoulder, his hand dropping to his side as he rocked on his heels. "Can I ask you a question?"

"Yes." Theo looked over at his friend.

"Are you in love with my sister?"

"Yes." There was no hesitation in the answer.

Jeremy glanced down at his feet for a second before looking back to the stage. "Have you told her that?"

"No."

"And why is that?"

"Because I'm not sure she's ready to hear it."

"So, what, instead of telling her, you're trying to show her?" Jeremy waved at the stage.

"Actions speak louder than words, right?"

"That's what they say. But according to my wife, communication works too. What if actually telling her how you felt changed her mind about leaving?" Jeremy asked.

"I've been down that road with her before, man." Theo shook his head. "I told her I wanted more and it made her run, all the way to California. She's going to have to make the decision to stay on her own. Decide if she's going to pick Cruickshank . . ."

"Pick you," Jeremy finished.

"She's got to see that this is where she wants to be."

"For what it's worth, I think you deserve her . . . and that she deserves you. You're a good guy, Theo. Not everyone would do this for somebody else." He waved his hand in front of them, indicating the stage. "I just hope she figures it out sooner rather than later."

"Thanks, man. I do too." Theo looked back to the stage. "I do too. At least I know we have more time for her to figure it out. She's teaching next semester too."

"She finally decided to take the job?"

"Yeah, when did you—" But Theo wasn't able to finish the question.

Max called out as he plugged in another strand, the last tree in the back lighting up. "Well, I think we're almost done."

Isaac was grabbing the empty boxes on the floor, throwing them into the garbage bag that Juliet was holding open. "You know, it's really a shame that Lucy's only going to get one musical with this new setup."

"That's what I said yesterday." Theo looked over at his father. "But as it turns out, she's teaching in the spring." He turned back to Jeremy. "When did Lucy tell you about the job?"

But before Jeremy could answer, more people in the auditorium were speaking up.

"She is?" Gia and Chloe asked in unison, their heads popping up from where they'd been hunched over Gia's phone, looking at something on the screen.

"She told me this morning she decided to teach next semester too." Wes flipped the clasps on his toolbox, opening the lid. "I was so relieved. She's been sitting on that offer for weeks now."

Everything in Theo stilled at those words. The question he wanted to ask was right there on the tip of his tongue, he just didn't get it out fast enough.

"Dad, what do you mean, weeks?" Jeremy asked first. "When did she tell you?"

Wes straightened, his eyes going big as he realized he'd said something he shouldn't have. "She, um . . . well . . . she told me when we went to get the turkeys and ham."

"She got the job offer two weeks ago?" Theo said softly. Why hadn't she told him? That seemed like a pretty big thing to leave out, especially as her staying in Cruickshank had been brought up on more than one occasion, typically during conversations that revolved around Bear. Hell, it had been discussed in his parents' kitchen less than a week ago.

In that moment, something clicked into place. Here he was making an idiot of himself trying to show her how much he loved her, and it didn't matter. She had no intention of staying.

"You know what, man?" Theo looked over at Jeremy. "I don't think Lucy is going to figure it out."

* * *

THE CONVERSATION AT GIRLS' NIGHT moved from Lucy staying for another few months to Sasha and her current online dating saga.

"I really need to delete the apps." She shook her head as she took another sip of her wine. "Everyone on there is the literal worst. I matched with a guy yesterday and his conversation starter was *do you have big boobs?*"

"Seriously?" Caro looked horrified.

"It was a better opener than the guy who asked if I was a good girl or a bad girl."

"That's a *low* bar." Lucy shook her head.

"See how lucky the three of you are?" Sasha waved her hand at them. "You all have great guys."

"You know who is *really* great?" Lilah asked, waggling her eyebrows.

"If you say your brother, I'm going to shove that piece of crust up your nose." Sasha pointed to her plate.

"I'd like to see you try."

It was at that moment that the front door opened and closed, a loud squeal filling the air as Emilia no doubt ran to her daddy. A moment later Max and Jeremy walked into the room, Jeremy holding Emilia in his arms as she told him all about her day.

"Me and Mommy made sprinkle cookies to take to school tomorrow, and Matty and Chris helped and it was really fun. And then I colored a picture of Santa!"

"Santa? What color was his suit? Blue?"

"No!" Emilia giggled hysterically. "It was red, Daddy. Santa always wears a red suit."

"Well, I can't wait for you to show it to me. Can you give me a second with Mommy?"

"Yes." She nodded exuberantly before he set her down. And a moment later she scampered back into the living room.

"How was your evening, honey?" Lilah smiled up at him. "Get all of the stuff done with the lights?"

Jeremy nodded slowly, the smile he'd had with Emilia now gone.

"What's wrong?" Lilah asked her husband.

"Well, after we finished with the lights, Max and I were with Theo, Oscar, and Gavin. And Dad was there."

"Uh huh?" Lilah pulled her legs out from under her, putting her feet on the floor as she sat up.

"And you came up, Lucy." Max looked over at her, and that was when Lucy realized he was looking a little uncomfortable. Something in her stomach plummeted. "And you teaching in the spring was mentioned . . . and . . . your dad kind of let it slip that you were offered the job two weeks ago."

Caro's head snapped in Lucy's direction. "Two weeks? I figured Fatima *just* asked you. Why didn't you tell us?"

"Because I wasn't sure what I was doing. I know how much you *all* want me to stay. You haven't exactly kept it a secret as you've repeatedly told me so since I moved back in May."

Caro sat back in her chair, looking a little hurt. "You think we wouldn't support you in whatever you wanted?"

"No, I didn't think that at all. I just . . . I knew you all would be disappointed when I left again."

"*When* or *if*?" Sasha narrowed her eyes.

"I don't know." Lucy shook her head. The pizza in her stomach was now churning. "It's not like I have anywhere to go at the moment. And I can't leave with Bear pregnant."

"Is that the only thing holding you back?" Jeremy asked. There was something a little hard in his question.

"You know it's not. I've missed all of you and then there's—"

"Theo?" Jeremy finished for her.

"Yes, being with Theo has complicated things."

"I'm sure he'll love to hear that he's a complication."

"That's not fair." Lucy stood up. "Everything with him has been moving fast. Too fast, and I can't keep up. I just . . . I don't know what I want."

"Well, that's apparent."

"Okay, what's going on? Why are you being a jerk?"

"I'm being a jerk? Jesus Christ, Lucy. You're the one who can't make a decision. Can you imagine how Theo felt tonight when he found out you were lying to him?"

"I didn't lie to him."

"Well, you didn't tell him the truth," Max said.

"Hey!" Lucy turned to him. "What the hell is this? A gang up?"

"An intervention," Lilah corrected.

"Well, I don't need either. I'm going to go." She stepped around her brother and Max and headed for the living room. The problem was, Lucy wasn't getting out of the line of fire. She was just trading the frying pan for the inferno.

CHAPTER FIFTEEN
Camera

Theo sat on the top step of the stairs outside Lucy's apartment, the air fogging up around him with every breath that he took. It was about thirty-nine degrees outside, but he didn't mind the cold. He needed to cool off before Lucy got there anyway.

It had been at least two weeks since she'd been offered the job, and she hadn't mentioned anything to him. Though they'd only been doing whatever they were doing for seventeen days.

God, had it only been that long? Why did it feel like it had been a lifetime with her? And yet, it hadn't been nearly long enough. He wanted more, he'd always wanted more when it came to Lucy Buchanan, and she clearly didn't feel the same way.

So, what was he doing?

Theo looked up as her black SUV rolled into the driveway, the tires crunching on the gravel. She looked at him through the windshield and even from here he could see that her shoulders were slumped.

Apparently, Jeremy and Max had said something to her. He'd told them not to bother, he'd deal with it on his own, but they clearly hadn't listened. They'd said they wouldn't reveal the surprise with the lights, but Theo wasn't sure that he even cared anymore. It was a comfort to know that they had his back though. He had a feeling he was going to need it after tonight.

"Hey, you," Lucy said as she got out of the car, shutting the door behind her.

"Hey." Theo stood up, shoving his hands in his pockets.

She gave a little nod before she turned and opened the back door. Her brown hair was down around her shoulders and it floated in the air for just a moment.

He felt like there was a clock in his head, ticking down. The sound echoed in his ears. It was all coming to an end. He couldn't do this with her anymore. He couldn't let himself get deeper into this, not when he was clearly falling on his own.

Falling? You've already fallen, man.

Lucy and Bear made their way up the stairs and Theo took a step back to let her unlock the door. The scent of vanilla and cloves filled his head as she moved in front of him, and the ticking of that clock only got louder.

When they stepped inside, Lucy turned on the lights while Theo shut the door behind them. She moved farther into her apartment, pulling off her scarf and jacket before kicking off her shoes. Bear jumped up on the sofa with Estee, making herself comfortable among the blankets and pillows.

Theo stayed by the door, not taking off his jacket or his shoes. Lucy's eyes moved, measuring the distance between them. "You're not staying?"

"I don't think so." He shook his head. "I think we should talk, and I'm pretty sure by the end of it I'm going to want to leave."

"Why?"

"Because I know what lies at the end of this conversation, which is probably why I've been avoiding it. We might've started on the same page, but tonight it became clear that we no longer are."

"Are you saying this because I didn't tell you about the job offer as soon as it happened? I didn't tell anyone about it. I didn't even mean to tell my dad."

"Is that supposed to make me feel better? Because it doesn't."

"Theo, Fatima literally asked me to teach another semester the morning after I slept with you. You and I had already said it was just sex and that we weren't going to—" She hesitated for a second as if she was trying to figure out what word to use. But then she shook her head and continued. "We weren't going to *complicate* things and then almost immediately it got more *complicated*."

"Lucy." Theo let out a small humorless laugh. "It's always been complicated when it comes to the two of us. And that's not going to change."

"Why?"

"Because I'm in love with you and you clearly aren't in love with me."

"What?" The word left her lips on an exhale, the air leaving her lungs as her shoulders fell. It was like she was deflating.

Well, she could join the club. He already felt completely empty.

"I can't do this with you again. I thought I could. I thought we could just have really great sex and I'd be okay with whatever you chose to do. But as it turns out, that isn't the case. I was fucking delusional to think I would ever be okay with it. You don't want to stay, and if you did, I'd be your second choice."

"No, you wouldn't."

"Then why aren't you staying?"

"I . . . I just don't know what I want. Why do we have to have this figured out *right now*? It hasn't even been three weeks since this started." She gestured between the two of them.

"For me it's been a lot longer."

"How long?" Her voice cracked, and the sound took the air out of his own lungs. He wanted to cross the room, wanted to pull her into his arms and tell her they'd figure it out.

But he stayed on his side of the room. "Does it matter? Does me telling you that I've been in love with you since I was seventeen change a single thing about how you feel or what you want?"

"Since you were seventeen?" she asked, the words coming out slowly, like she was trying to figure out when.

"It was the first time I heard you sing. You were in a musical your sophomore year. I didn't want to be there . . . until you came onstage. I didn't realize it then, I didn't understand it, but hearing you changed something for me. Something *in* me. Something that there was no coming back from. But as I've learned, there's no coming back from you, Lucy. I tried . . . I tried to ignore it, and then seven years ago I couldn't ignore it anymore."

"That was why you kissed me that night?"

"I wanted to know, even if it was for just a second . . . I wanted to know what it was like to be with you. And then those seconds turned into hours, days, weeks, months. I wanted more. I knew I'd always want more. So, I told you, and you bailed. You ran as fast and as far away from me as you could get."

"I wasn't ready."

"Are you now?"

"I . . . I don't know."

"God, Lucy." Theo threw up his hands, his voice rising loud enough for Bear to lift her head from the sofa. "I don't think I can hear you say that anymore. I know what I want. I want *you*. I *love* you. It really can't get *any* simpler than that."

"It's not simple." She reached up, roughly wiping the tears away from her cheeks. "None of this is simple."

"I know, it's *complicated*."

"I'm beginning to hate that word."

"You and me both." Theo rubbed at his forehead before he dropped his arm. "I don't know what else to say, Luce. I think I should go."

"So, you're just going to give up on this?"

"You don't even know what *this* is. How can I walk away from something that you aren't even fully in?"

"I just need more time to figure it out."

"Lucy, you've had seven years. Here we are, in the exact same position, and you still don't know what you want. I think that answers the question pretty clearly."

"Would it have changed anything if I'd told you about the job before?" She swiped under her eyes again.

"Probably not." Theo shook his head. "I think we were always going to get to this place. We just figured it out a little sooner than later."

"So, what, we should cut our losses now before someone gets hurt?"

"*Before* someone gets hurt?" Theo let out another humorless laugh. "Lucy, it feels like you've reached your hand inside my chest and wrapped your fist around my heart. And the longer I stand here knowing that you aren't in love with me, the tighter your grip is getting. At this point, I'm just trying to save myself from my heart getting ripped out of my chest. But I'm pretty sure I've failed there too."

"I'm sorry," she said on a whisper.

"For what? This was inevitable." He hesitated for a second, unsure if he should say more, but he kept going anyway. "I can't help but think that the reason you hesitated to take the job was because you're scared about getting stuck here. Scared about getting stuck with me. Tell me that isn't true."

"That *isn't* true."

"I don't believe you."

"Theo, I . . ." Lucy looked up and away from him, a fresh round of tears filling her eyes as her lip started to tremble. "I just want to fix this. *How* do I fix this?"

Fuck, he had to get out of here.

"You can't. You know, I lied to you too. I wasn't helping Oscar, he was helping me. So were Jeremy, and Gavin, and Max, and your dad, and so many other people that would do absolutely anything for you. We got you your lights, and we spent the whole evening getting them strung up for you."

"You did what?"

"I've been trying so hard to give you everything that I can, do these big grand gestures to show you exactly how much you mean to me, to show you how much I want you to stay. But it hasn't changed anything. You don't want to stay, a fact that was made very clear to me tonight. And it's not fair for me to be mad about it, because from the second we started this again you told me you weren't staying here. I knew."

He paused, taking a deep breath, trying to push back that crushing pain in his chest.

"But there was a part of me that hoped you'd change your mind; it's the same naive stupid part of me that can't let go of you. I'm going to have to figure it out, figure out how to let go this time. I can't do this anymore. Goodbye, Lucy."

Theo turned, his hand wrapping around the door handle, and just as he started to twist the knob, he heard her voice.

"I'm terrified, Theo. I'm terrified of love. Of letting someone in and giving them the power to hurt me."

"So was I. My problem is that when it comes to you, I didn't have any choice in the matter."

The sharp breath behind him echoed in the room, but Lucy didn't say anything else as Theo opened the door and walked outside into the cold. But just before the door snapped shut behind him, he heard her muffled sob.

* * *

FOR SOMEONE WHO WASN'T much of a crier, Lucy sure had been doing a lot of it in the last twenty-ish hours. She was sitting in the fourth row of the auditorium again, in the exact same seat as she had on Sunday night. Except there were two differences.

The first was that Theo wasn't next to her. Though there was no one in the auditorium. Rehearsal had ended about half an hour ago, the students leaving when they wrapped up at five. Gia had been pretty standoffish all day, and she'd been the first one out of there. Chloe hadn't been far behind, but she'd given an apologetic glance over her shoulder before she'd walked out the door. It wasn't like Lucy was surprised that Gia was upset with her. How could the girl not be after what Theo had done for Lucy . . . and after what Lucy had done to Theo?

And that was where she got to the second difference of the day: the Christmas lights. There were so many strands strung among the trees, the branches illuminated, the stage lit up like a little winter wonderland.

Lucy had come into the auditorium first thing that morning, wanting to see what Theo had done. She'd flipped the switch and the sight of the stage had taken her breath away. He'd done this for her . . . because he loved her.

He'd put it all out on the line . . . and she hadn't. For the second time, he'd told her he wanted more, and she couldn't give it to him. Though this time he'd actually told her he wanted *everything*.

Yeah, it wasn't a wonder to Lucy at all why Gia was mad at her . . . or why all of her friends and family had been upset with her the night before . . . or why Theo had ended things.

He'd gone above and beyond, something he'd done so many times over the last few weeks, *showing* her exactly what she meant to him . . . and she couldn't do the same thing back.

It hadn't been a lie when she'd said that things had moved too fast. One second they'd been challenging each other to darts and arguing about clichés, and the next they'd been having wild sex at her apartment. She'd known she was withholding by not telling him about the job, or the apartment that would shortly be waiting for her in New York. It was just further proof of what he'd told her last night, that she wasn't in this thing with him.

When he'd said he thought her hesitation at teaching in the spring was fear of getting stuck in Cruickshank, she hadn't been sure if that was true or not. But there wasn't a fear of getting stuck *with* him. It was the opposite: she feared getting stuck here *without* him, and now she was going to get to face that fear head-on.

She didn't know how to be here and not be with him. *That* was what scared her now, and it had only taken the entire night of replaying everything for her to figure it out.

And Lucy had replayed it *all*. Everything from the night before, and the day before that . . . and the weeks, months, and years prior. Her mind flashed through everything that had to do with Theo, trying to figure it all out. Trying to figure out what she could've done differently. But there'd been nothing she could do short of admitting that she was in love with him.

Because she was in love with him.

She'd wanted to say it last night, wanted to tell him. The words had been right there on the tip of her tongue, but she just couldn't get them out.

Lucy blinked, the lights in front of her blurring as her eyes filled with tears again. She was her own worst enemy. She knew it. She'd never been able to get out of her own way. And now it might've cost her something great.

No, it *had* cost her something great.

The unmistakable sound of the doors opening behind her filled the space and Lucy turned around to see Caro, Sasha, and Lilah walking into the auditorium. They stopped when they saw the stage, all of them taking in the finished product.

"Wow." Lilah whistled. "That looks amazing."

Lucy stood, already gearing up to be on the defense. "If you guys have come here to tell me what an idiot I am, I don't think that I can really take it. I know you're on Team Theo."

"That's not why we're here." Lilah shook her head.

Sasha frowned, putting her hands on her hips. "Besides, I thought we told you we're Team Leo."

"There is no Team Leo." Lucy's eyes and nose started to burn, and she scrunched her face up, trying to fight the fresh wash of tears. She lost.

"Hey, come here." Caro didn't even hesitate to pull Lucy into her chest.

The second her sister's arms were around her, Lucy let go, like *really* let go. It felt like something inside of her had cracked open and everything was pouring out. She didn't want this. She didn't want to feel this kind of pain.

Everything hurt. Her head, her eyes, her stomach, her chest, her heart. She completely understood what Theo had been talking about when he'd said it felt like there was a fist squeezing his heart . . . ripping it out of his chest.

God, she couldn't breathe, she couldn't think. All she wanted to do was get out of that building . . . get out of her body. Caro didn't let go of Lucy, just held her tight as everything poured out of her. All of the pain and sorrow and regret. So much regret.

"What's wrong with me?" she asked when she was finally able to speak. "Why can't I let him in?"

"There's nothing wrong with you." Caro pulled back, holding Lucy's face in her hands. There were tears tracking down her sister's cheeks too, her eyes watery. "And you're fighting this with Theo because you've lost love before, and in the most permanent and profound way possible. We know what it's like, Lucy. We know what it's like to lose someone that we love with every part of our being. Mom died when we were way too young to understand . . . it made us part of a club that *nobody* wants to be in."

"Luce, you were fifteen when you lost Rachel," Lilah said. "You lost your rock at one of the most critical times in your life. That's formative. It *changed* you, for better or worse."

"Apparently more for the worse. I don't know how to do this."

"You are capable of so much love," Sasha disagreed. "You can do this."

"No, I can't. Something is wrong with me. Something in me is broken. *I'm* broken." Lucy shook her head, blinking as a fresh wave of tears filled her eyes.

"You aren't broken. Don't talk about my friend that way." Lilah's mouth had gone tight, her eyes narrowed as she defended Lucy from Lucy.

A humorless laugh escaped Lucy's lips, and she shook her head. "I don't want to talk at all anymore."

"We don't need to talk," Sasha agreed. "I think this might be an occasion for comfort food, cozy pajamas, and a good movie. Give me your keys. I'm driving you home and these two are going to meet us there."

"All of my stuff is in my office."

"Then what are we waiting for?" Lilah asked.

Lucy turned the lights off in the auditorium—getting one more look at the man in the moon—before Caro and Lilah looped their arms through hers and marched her out of the room.

* * *

ON WEDNESDAY AFTERNOON, Theo and Bear made their way through Sweeny Park just like they did every day at that time. The dog slowly meandered next to him, taking her time. It had been a week since her last vet appointment, and her stomach had gotten noticeably bigger.

She had less than three weeks left and was now being separated from other dogs. Bingley and Carl—the two dogs that had been frequenting the rescue pen at the café—had both been adopted, so Bear was spending the days there alone. Theo was grateful that he could still see her, especially as he wasn't sure how much longer that was going to be the case.

It wasn't like he thought Lucy would prevent him from being around Bear, it was just that he couldn't be around Lucy.

He was more than aware that he had no willpower when it came to the woman, and he knew that she'd slowly chip away at his resolve. Nah, it wouldn't be slow. It would happen in an instant, something as simple as her touching his hand, hearing her voice, smelling vanilla and cloves on her skin or in her hair.

With each day that had passed, the ache in his chest had gotten so much worse. It had taken less than three weeks for her to become enmeshed in his life . . . in his heart. He missed her so much it physically hurt. Apparently loving Lucy just equaled pain.

Maybe it would get easier. Maybe when she finally left town again he'd be able to breathe without feeling that tightening sensation in his chest. Or maybe this was his new normal. Was this what unrequited love was like? He should ask Max. The man had dealt with it for fourteen years before he'd reunited with Caro.

Oh god, Theo would go insane if he felt this way for fourteen years. The pain was unbearable. It hadn't hurt this badly last time he and Lucy had fallen apart. Maybe because he hadn't known he was in love with her. Ignorance had been his only saving grace. He didn't have that now.

He knew what it was like to wake up with her in his arms. He knew what it was like to get to hold her hand in public, to pull her in close for a kiss and not worry about who was around them. He knew what it was like to lean in close to her, breathing her in as he whispered something in her ear. He knew what it was like to share that secret smile with her when they were surrounded by people. He knew what it was like to *think* that she was his.

I'm yours, Theo.

She'd said it. She'd said those words and he'd believed them.

Theo had a glimpse of what a future with her could be. The thing was, she wasn't ready for a future. She wanted in the moment, and from how things had gone on Monday, she wanted that until she picked up her life again and left. But he couldn't live that way, waiting for the music to stop with him standing in the middle of the room alone.

No, it was better this way. *He'd* been the one to stop the music. It would just be easier if he didn't have the sound of her singing replaying in his head.

But, as Theo had long ago learned, when it came to Lucy absolutely nothing was easy.

* * *

LUCY STOOD IN HER LIVING ROOM, staring at the custom whelping box the Savage brothers had just delivered and set up. It was made of solid wood, stained a rich mahogany, and had an adjustable door at the front. There was a little holder for a heated lamp to hang over, and a big squishy pillow that was covered in a removable case.

Theo had ordered it, he'd even gotten replacement covers in a variety of colors and patterns, because of course he did.

Bear had already climbed inside and was pawing at the pillow, fluffing it and getting it into the position she wanted. She did a few spins before dramatically flopping down, like the procedure had been exhausting for her.

Lucy had gotten the whole thing on film. Over the last two weeks, it had been ingrained in her to film everything that had to do with Bear. Since Tuesday, she'd only been sending the videos to Gia, whose response was always a thumbs-up. That was it.

Not surprisingly, it had been radio silence when it came to Theo. She'd wanted to call, wanted to hear his voice. She actually wanted to see him in person, tell him how much she missed him. Not that it would do much good. It wouldn't change anything, and she'd ultimately just end up crying again. Though that had been happening on and off since Monday night.

Some sort of floodgate had been opened and the only time she could keep it together was when she was at school. And even then, she had to excuse herself to go to the bathroom a few times a day so that she could escape prying eyes.

The only thing that really saved her was that she was busy at school. Rehearsals were happening every day, the students and teachers were preparing for finals the following week, and everyone was still hyped up from the football team winning state. At least there were some distractions to provide a little relief.

But those distractions were nonexistent when Lucy was home. She'd never had a breakup that felt like a death before, but that was the only way she could explain it. This thing with Theo was bigger than anything she'd ever known. The end seemed final, like there was no going back. She couldn't fix it because she couldn't fix *herself*.

It was true that a big part of her damage was from her mother; that was clear. But it hadn't just been losing Rachel. It had been the aftermath. How her father had become a shell of himself for years. How Caro had ended things with Max and spent fourteen years living in limbo without him.

Lucy had watched everything fall apart around her while her own life had gotten out of control. That was when the bulimia had started. She'd already had an unhealthy self-image, always being bigger than everyone else, but things escalated in a matter of no time at all.

It had taken so much therapy for Lucy to finally get to a good place, but then not even a year ago she'd let her ex get in her head. He'd had way more power than she'd ever expected, and he'd messed with her, manipulated her. In a matter of months, he'd slowly dismantled things that had taken her more than a decade to build. She hadn't even realized it was happening until it was too late. That was when she'd had to get out, so she ran.

Lucy was used to running away. It was how she'd gotten to California in the first place. She'd run from Cruickshank seven years ago, run from the death of her mother, which she'd never fully dealt with, run from a life she thought she didn't want . . . run from Theo.

But then she'd gotten back here, and she'd found something she hadn't realized she'd been missing, probably because she hadn't really appreciated it in the first place. She'd found a place where she belonged, found a man who wanted her . . . a man who loved her. Why did that scare her beyond all reason?

Because he means more. Because he's always meant more.

Letting Theo in—*really* letting Theo in—would make her more vulnerable than she'd ever been in her life. Just look at the damage a man she didn't love had done. Theo would have the ability to destroy her.

But you're destroying yourself.

God, this sucked. Every single part of it. She hated it. There was so much that she was feeling and she didn't understand it. It all felt so impossible. She paced around the apartment for a bit, needing to find something to occupy herself before family dinner night. The last thing she wanted to do was be around people, but she wasn't going to stand up her father.

That was when her eyes landed on her guitar, and she was across the room in an instant. Writing songs and singing had always been one of the best outlets for her emotions, and there was no better time than the present. Lately she'd been working on her music at school, so she'd gotten out of the habit of recording herself. She wasn't exactly a fan of watching herself, but she'd often catch something that she missed. A lyric or riff that she'd failed to write down.

Maybe she'd figure something else out if she played it back, like how to fix her life. Or maybe that was reaching.

Lucy set her phone up to record, grabbed her notebook and pen, and sat cross-legged on the sofa next to Estee. It took her a second to get comfortable, but when she did, she let herself get lost in the music. The song was one that she'd been working on for years, seven, in fact. It was a song about love, about finding that one person and never letting go. She hadn't finished it because she just couldn't quite get it right. Something had always been off with it, and she still couldn't figure it out.

She played with the lyrics, stopping every once in a while to jot a note down, or cross something out.

"This time I'll give you all of me. You're what I want, you're what I need.

"So here I am standing at your door. I know I broke us once before. You're all I've wanted all these years. Please don't let me leave in tears.

"I've been so scared of falling. What I didn't understand was the fall would set me free. This time I'll give you all of me. You're what I want, you're what I need."

It was at this point that Bear made her way out of the whelping box, coming over and sitting down in front of the sofa. Lucy ran her fingers over the strings one more time, the sound vibrating around the room for just a second before she let go.

"Are you going to watch me sing?" she asked the dog as she reached over and ruffled the top of her head.

Bear's response was to nose at the guitar as if to say *keep going*.

"This pain is more than I can bear, I won't walk away again, I swear. This time I'll give you all of me. You're all I want, you're all I need."

Lucy's fingers continued to strum the guitar strings, and she closed her eyes as she gave in to the song, feeling the lyrics as she sang. She wasn't sure when she'd started crying again, her teardrops landing on her guitar.

This time when Lucy stopped playing, Bear looked up at her with mournful eyes. It was as if she knew how much Lucy was hurting, understood it all perfectly as she laid her head on Lucy's thigh. And that was when the last ounce of Lucy's control floated away. She sunk down onto the floor, holding Bear as she cried for what felt like the hundredth time that week.

CHAPTER SIXTEEN
Action

There were a number of emotions running through Lucy when she woke up on Friday morning. Today was the first day of the musical, and there was a nervous excitement about finally getting to the day. About finally getting to see the thing that she'd spent months working on with her students.

But that excitement was overshadowed as she looked at the other side of the bed.

How was it that she'd gotten so used to waking up next to Theo in such a short amount of time? She missed his warmth. How he'd press his body against hers. She missed the way he'd trail kisses up her neck, his beard scraping across her skin as he settled himself between her thighs.

There was no warmth now. That side of the bed was cold.

Lucy reached out, her fingers touching sheets that still held the lingering, faint scent of his soap. She grabbed the pillow, pressing her face to it and breathing in deep. It made her ache even more.

Throwing the pillow to the side, Lucy sat up, reaching for Bear, who was stretched out at the foot of the bed. The dog had gotten used to sleeping at their feet, and it was still the place where she slept, not disturbing Theo's empty space.

Empty, that was how Lucy felt.

Estee hadn't joined Lucy and Bear in bed the evening before, but had instead curled up on her little pillow by the dresser. She actually hadn't slept with Lucy since everything had happened with Theo, and Lucy wondered if the cat was pissed at her too.

Probably.

But there was no point in lingering on it. Lucy had way too much to do that day, a blessing, as it would keep her brain busy . . . and not obsessing about the fact that she'd probably be seeing Theo that evening.

It would be the first time in four days. She hadn't gone that long without seeing him since she'd been back in Cruickshank. They were always hanging out at Quigley's, or she was stopping by Browned Butter, or they were running into each other at Fresh Harvest, or Kathleen's Corner Bookstore, or Dancing Donkey, or any of the other many places around town.

He was always around, and now he wasn't, and she felt *empty*.

That all-too-familiar ache bloomed in Lucy's chest, but she forced herself to breathe past it and get out of bed. Bear was a little more resistant, not wanting to leave the comfort and warmth, which was why Lucy was running late when she dropped the dog off at Dancing Donkey.

Sasha handed Lucy an already made crème brûlée latte, taking Bear's leash and giving Lucy a kiss on the cheek. "I'll see you tonight," Sasha promised.

Most of her friends and family were coming to the musical tonight, and the others would be there on Saturday. Sasha was part of the first group.

"Tonight." Lucy nodded. "Thanks for my coffee. I need it."

"That's why I made it a double."

"Bless you." Lucy smiled for what felt like the first time in days.

"Hey, Luce." Sasha hesitated for just a second. "Are you okay?"

Lucy shrugged. "As okay as I can be. It's my fault this is happening. I'm the one who ruined it."

"You didn't ruin it."

"I did, though, and I can't fix it."

"Do you want to fix it?"

"I've spent the last seven months not knowing what I want. And right now, all I can think about is that I miss Theo so much it hurts. The thing is, I've missed him for seven years. And the only one standing in the way of us being together is me."

"Luce." Sasha made to step forward but Lucy stepped back, shaking her head.

"If you hug me, I'm going to lose it. Holding it together with Scotch tape and caffeine at this point." Lucy held her cup in the air. "I can fall apart again once the musical is over."

"Well, I'll be here to help you put all of the pieces back together."

"You always have been, Sash." Lucy's voice broke at the end.

"Love you."

"Love you." Taking another step back, Lucy headed to her SUV, parked at the curb.

She couldn't help but glance at the building a block down. The sun was a good forty minutes away from making an appearance, but the lights from Browned Butter's storefront were illuminating the still-darkened street. He probably wasn't in there yet, going back to his old schedule of rolling in at nine since he wasn't getting up with her in the morning anymore.

Lucy had never been much of a morning person, but she'd loved that part of the day with him. *He'd* been her favorite part of every day.

What the hell was she doing?

Do you want to fix it? Sasha's question from just moments before repeated in her head. She wanted to fix it more than anything, she just didn't know how, because she didn't know how to fix herself.

She was going to have to figure that part out first.

* * *

LUCY'S THIRD PERIOD was her planning hour, and she was spending it folding the programs for the musical. She'd hoped that the programs would get delivered earlier in the week, but there'd been some delays at the printer. As long as she got half of them done, she could take care of the other half the following day.

Needing a little distraction, she'd put on some music, and was singing along to the songs when a light knock echoed in the room. Looking up from her stack of programs she spotted Fatima and Mrs. Griffith on the threshold.

Lucy immediately paused the music and stood up. "Principal Patel, Mrs. Griffith, hi."

She hadn't seen her old teacher since Thanksgiving. Mr. and Mrs. Griffith had come for dinner at Quigley's but hadn't stayed too long after.

"Hello, dearie." Mrs. Griffith smiled as she crossed the room, pulling Lucy into a hug. As always, she smelled like patchouli, and it made Lucy nostalgic for something she wasn't quite sure of. It was a couple of moments before she pulled back, smiling brightly.

"Are you stopping by to make sure everything is okay for tonight?"

"No." Fatima shook her head. "We have all the faith in the world about the musical and you."

"That's why I wanted you to take my place this year," Mrs. Griffith added.

"Are you coming tonight?"

"Brandon and I wouldn't miss it. He's anxious to get out of the house. It's been slow going but he's finally out of the wheelchair and is using a walker. I think he'll always need a cane, though. I'm going to have the Savage brothers make him something for Christmas."

"They are very talented when it comes to woodworking. They made a beautiful whelping box for Bear." A not-so-small pang rattled Lucy's rib cage as she thought about Theo.

"How is that dog of yours doing?" Fatima asked.

"Growing by the day."

"That's what it looks like in those videos of yours," Mrs. Griffith said.

"You watch the videos?" Lucy laughed.

Mrs. Griffith playfully narrowed her eyes. "What? Do you think I don't know how to do that because I'm ancient?"

"I never said that. I just didn't know you were on social media."

"How do you expect me to keep up with what's on trend these days? Things are always changing." At this she looked around the classroom. "Well, things haven't changed much around here."

"It's not mine to change."

"I guess not." Mrs. Griffith nodded slowly, a little twinkle in her eyes. "Would you show me the auditorium? I want to see what you all did."

"Absolutely," Lucy replied. Fatima led the way while Lucy walked with Mrs. Griffith.

When they got to the auditorium, Mrs. Griffith let out a whistle. "Wow," she marveled. "It's beautiful."

"Just more proof of what the Savage brothers are capable of."

"Clearly. Those trees are magnificent. Did Caroline paint that moon?"

"Yes, ma'am. It's my favorite. Well, it's tied. Hold on for one minute." Lucy made her way to the stage. She turned off the lights that were overhead, plunging the room into darkness for just a moment before flipping the switch that controlled the Christmas lights. The stage was suddenly illuminated in a twinkling glow.

She came back down the stairs, enough light in the room for her to get back to the two women.

"Oh, Lucy." Mrs. Griffith shook her head, the emotion in her voice clear. "It's better than anything I could've imagined . . . or anything I could've done myself."

"Well, I had a lot of help. Actually, Theo Taylor is the one who's responsible for most of it. He was the one who made the plans and got everyone together. The lights were because of him too. Well, him and Max Abbott."

"Look at that." Fatima grinned. "Caroline's fella and your fella working together."

Lucy made an uncomfortable noise in the back of her throat, looking down at the floor. "Um, well, Theo isn't exactly my fella anymore. Things, um, didn't work out."

"Oh, Lucy." Fatima's grin disappeared. "I'm sorry to hear that. I'd thought maybe you'd finally found someone . . . found your place here."

"I have found a place here." Lucy gave a shrug of her shoulders. "But it's not permanent."

Mrs. Griffith reached out, her warm and weathered hands grabbing Lucy's and holding on tight. "What if it was?"

"Excuse me?"

"You know, dearie, besides my family, there aren't a lot of things in this world that I love more than this program." Mrs. Griffith looked to the stage, the lights reflecting in her eyes. "The thought of retiring was something I couldn't even fathom because there was no one I could trust with it . . . until you." She looked back to Lucy, smiling. "What you've done with the program this semester, especially the last few weeks, has given me the grace to finally let go. If you want it, it's yours."

"You're serious?"

"Yeah." Mrs. Griffith's hands gently tightened on Lucy's. "I can't think of a better person to pass the baton to. Or, in this case, the microphone."

"Yes." Something flared in Lucy's chest, something that felt a lot like hope. "I'll take it."

* * *

SEVENTH PERIOD WAS DRAMA CLASS, and they were doing one last dry run before that evening's performance. When the bell rang, everyone cleared out of the auditorium, heading home for a couple of hours. Well, almost everyone.

Gia and Chloe lingered, slowly putting their stuff into their backpacks while Lucy adjusted some of the props onstage. It was only when it was the three of them that Gia said, "If you're in love with Theo, why aren't you with him?"

"What?" Lucy looked over, more than a little taken aback by the question.

"I don't understand. It's so clear in that video that you love Theo, and as opposed to being with him, you're choosing to be sad instead. You can't tell me that song isn't about him."

Lucy froze. "What video are you talking about, Gia? What song?"

"The one of you singing to Bear," Chloe said.

"I didn't send you a video of me singing to Bear." Lucy shook her head, moving to the steps on the side of the stage.

"Yes, you did." Gia pulled out her phone, hitting a few buttons before holding it in the air. The sound of a guitar came from the little speaker, echoing in the almost empty auditorium.

"This time I'll give you all of me. You're what I want, you're what I need.

"So here I am standing at your door . . ."

Lucy's feet picked up their pace as the video continued to play and her own voice filled the room. It was a few more moments—though it felt like a lifetime—before she was standing in front of Gia, staring at the video on the screen. It was the one she'd recorded the night before, the one that hadn't been meant for anyone but her to see.

Lucy reached forward in horror, and Gia passed her the phone. There was a buzzing in Lucy's ears, but she could still hear her voice singing the song, going through each and every lyric before finally getting to the end.

"I've been so scared of falling. What I didn't understand was the fall would set me free. This time I'll give you all of me. You're what I want, you're what I need."

"I . . . oh my god." Lucy shook her head, looking back up at Gia. "I didn't know I sent this. You posted it?"

Now it was Gia who looked horrified. "Yeah, you sent it with a bunch of videos last night. I just assumed you meant to."

She thought back to the night before, how she'd quickly selected her most recent videos of Bear, texting them before going to family dinner night. Her eyes went to the side of the screen, where she saw the *like* and *share* buttons. It had more than eighty thousand likes, and thirty thousand shares.

"How . . . how many people have seen this?" Lucy asked.

"Over two hundred thousand," Chloe answered.

"Two hundred thousand?" Lucy repeated, her voice going a little

higher than normal. Or a lot higher than normal. "Oh, god, this can't get any worse." Except it could. "Has Theo seen it?"

"I don't know. I posted it this morning." Anger flickered in Gia's expression, that same hardness she'd been directing at Lucy all week. "Why don't you want him to see it?"

Lucy's head started to get a little light and she sat down on one of the seats in the first row. "Do you have a diary, Gia? Or a journal?"

"Yes."

"Imagine that you wrote something very personal. Something you didn't quite understand yourself, and then you accidently shared it with two hundred thousand people."

"Do you want me to take it down?"

"What's the point?" Lucy asked, dropping her head in her hands. "It's already out there. If he hasn't seen it yet, he's going to." The reality of the situation was starting to dawn on her.

"Why are you hiding that you're in love with him? Do you not want to be? Because there is no one greater on this planet than my brother."

Lucy looked up. "You don't think I know that?"

"Then why aren't you with him?"

"Because it's not that simple."

More words from Monday night repeated in her head. Lucy was very familiar with them, as she'd heard them over and over and over again the last couple of days.

I know what I want. I want you. *I love* you. *It really can't get* any *simpler than that.*

"Do you love Theo?" Gia asked, her voice going a little softer, much like her expression.

"More than I've ever loved anyone." It was the first time she'd finally admitted it . . . the first time she'd said it out loud.

It terrified her beyond all reason, but not for the reason she'd thought. The fear of loving him wasn't nearly as bad as the fear of losing him. Lucy had lost a number of people who were very dear to her, the biggest among them being her mother, followed closely by Max's grandmother Ava. People who hadn't had a choice in leaving her. But here, she had a choice. She was at a crossroads, and she could choose him. She could choose *them*.

She could choose to truly give herself to a man who loved her . . . to a man she loved back.

"So, do you want him back?" Gia asked. "Do you want to be with him? *Really* be with him?"

"Yes," Lucy said without hesitation. She'd never been surer of anything in her life. "I just don't know if he'll believe me. I've messed this up twice now."

"Well, isn't the third time the charm?" Chloe grinned. "And I have an idea."

Lucy looked at the two girls, and for the second time that day, she felt a flicker of hope.

* * *

THEO TOOK A DEEP BREATH before he walked into the auditorium behind his parents. The curtains were closed, the stage blocked off from view. He let his breath out in a rush as he looked around, but Lucy was nowhere in sight.

He couldn't help himself, but odds were, he'd know the exact moment she walked in. He always knew.

"You going to be okay?" Naomi asked as she looped her arm through Theo's. His sister had driven back for the weekend so she could see Gia in the play.

"No, but I'll probably get through it."

"Probably? That sounds so reassuring."

"Yeah, well, that's all I can offer you at the moment."

Naomi's arm tightened, pulling him closer. "You know I've got your back, right?"

"I do." Theo looked over at his sister, giving her a little smile. Those things had been few and far between that week. He was so distracted by his sister that he didn't notice his parents had walked into the fourth row. His grandparents had already grabbed seats in the middle, and as he and Naomi made their way along the aisle, Theo realized he'd be sitting *exactly* where he had on Sunday . . . *exactly* where he had when he heard Lucy sing for the first time all those years ago.

Yeah, he definitely wasn't going to be okay.

He was going to get Naomi to switch seats with him, but as he got closer, he decided against it. Might as well go for *full masochist* at this point.

The room was full of chatter, people coming in and settling into their own seats. It was filling up, little by little, and as each minute ticked by, Theo found himself feeling increasingly anxious. But there was no distracting himself, especially as a group of people filed into the row in front of them: Max, Caro, Sasha, Gavin, Oscar, Edward, Jeremy, Lilah, Wes, and Lorraine. The last two of whom were holding hands.

"Hey!" Naomi jumped up and threw her arms around Sasha.

"When did you get in?" Caro asked as she pressed a kiss to Naomi's cheek.

"A few hours ago. Just here for the weekend."

"When are your finals?" Lilah pulled Naomi in for her own hug.

"Next week. But mine don't start until Tuesday, so it won't be too much of a rushed weekend."

"Well, that's good. You can keep an eye on this one." Gavin nodded to Theo.

"Yeah." Naomi looked over at him. "I figured I can be his emotional support human."

Jeremy gave an apologetic look in Theo's direction. "It's good to have one of those."

Theo had run into almost all of his friends in the last week, and while they hadn't pushed him on the topic of Lucy, none of them had been short on commiserating looks. Which he was now getting from most of the people in the row in front of him.

"Guys, this is already one of the hardest things I've had to do in a while, so if you could *not* look at me like that, it would be great."

His mother didn't say anything from the seat next to him, just patted his leg as she and Isaac continued to talk to Wes and Lorraine. Theo was lucky he had the support system of his friends and family, otherwise he was pretty sure he wouldn't have gotten through the week. Getting up and out of bed in the morning had been hard enough.

Maybe at some point the pain would lessen, but he wasn't there yet. It was getting worse, actually. The more he missed Lucy, the more he ached. It didn't help that he smelled her everywhere in his house, the lingering scent of vanilla, cloves, and cinnamon in his bed. And it *really* didn't help that he was still having to make those vanilla chai cupcakes every day.

Then there were the videos that Gia kept posting about Bear. She used to always send them to him after she posted, but she hadn't been doing that this week. And he hadn't been able to help himself and had looked them up. He'd resisted doing it today, mainly because he'd been so busy working on a wedding cake that he'd had a good distraction.

Hearing Lucy's voice always killed him, but he watched them anyway. It was the masochist in him when it came to her. He couldn't resist. He still didn't understand how he'd been able to walk out the door last Monday. Self-preservation had finally won out.

But that self-preservation was lost as he heard Lucy's voice. His head came up, looking around but not finding her. It was then that he realized it was coming from Caro's phone.

"What is that?" He leaned forward, looking over her shoulder to see what she was showing Sasha and Lilah.

"It's Lucy," Caro said softly, moving to the side a little bit so Theo could see as she restarted it. "It's the video Gia posted this morning."

Theo watched the screen, watched as Lucy played her guitar, singing the song he'd heard her working on in her classroom after the fire. There'd been sadness in her voice then, but it was *nothing* compared to the sadness he heard in the new lyrics that she sang. Her words hit him in a way he wasn't prepared for.

"*This pain is more than I can bear, I won't walk away again, I swear. This time I'll give you all of me. You're all I want, you're all I need.*"

The video ended with Lucy crying, sinking to the floor as she wrapped her arms around Bear. All three women turned to look at him—shocked expressions on their faces—but it was Caro who spoke first. "Theo, I—" That was as far as she got before her words were cut off, the lights flickering and a voice coming on over the speaker.

"Ladies and gentlemen, if everyone could please take their seats," Principal Patel announced. "The show is about to begin."

Theo sat back in his seat, his mind reeling. What had that song meant? Was it about him?

I know I broke us once before . . .

Her voice singing those words echoed in his head. She'd been the one to walk away the first time, and while technically he'd walked away this time, she'd broken them this time too. He believed what he'd told her, though, that he couldn't walk away from something she wasn't truly in. And if she hadn't figured it out in seven years, he doubted she'd figured it out in four days.

He'd made the right decision . . . he'd had to remind himself of that hundreds of times. Or maybe it was closer to a thousand by now. If this had taught him anything, it was that sometimes love wasn't enough. Sometimes two people just weren't meant to be together and there was nothing to do to fix it.

He was just going to need time to get over it—lots of time—and distance. Well, time was going to be his only option at the moment; distance wouldn't be a factor for at least five more months.

Theo tried to focus as Mrs. Griffith climbed the steps to the stage. Everyone in the room was applauding as she made her way over to the microphone. It was sitting right in the middle, the only thing that was in front of the thick purple velvet curtains.

"Hello, everyone. I wanted to thank you all for coming out tonight." She smiled as she looked out at the crowd. "As you all know, this program is my baby, the only things more important being my own children and my husband. I was the one who created it thirty-five years ago, always having been a fan of theater and music myself. I have loved each and every moment of being at this school, and it was more than a little hard for me to step away this semester."

She paused, taking a moment to collect herself. "All of you here know about the accident that happened over the summer, the one that almost claimed the life of my husband. Everyone that we know rallied behind us on Brandon's journey to get better. And it's because of your help that he was able to walk in here tonight."

Mrs. Griffith gestured to her husband, who was sitting in the front row, as everyone in the room made another loud round of applause. "Brandon may have needed a little support from his walker, but sometimes we all need a little support, and there is no short supply of that in this town. That's what we do here in Cruickshank; when something or someone in our community needs us, we step up to the plate. That was what happened less than two weeks ago when a fire took out our set.

"So many of you volunteered to get everything cleaned and repaired. It took six days to get this all back in order, and somehow it's even better than it was before. There were a number of people responsible—and you can find each and every one of their names listed on the back of your program—but there are two people who we need to thank above everyone else. And the first one is Theo Taylor." Mrs. Griffith gestured to him in his seat, her smile one of admiration and thanks.

"I was told that Theo organized everything, and that tonight's production wouldn't be happening without him, or at least not as spectacularly."

The room again broke out into a round of applause; someone sitting behind Theo clapped him on the back while all of his friends and family turned to him. His mother grabbed his arm as she leaned in and pressed a kiss to his cheek.

It took everything in him not to sink down in his seat. Being the center of attention was not something he enjoyed, and the very last thing he wanted at the moment was a room full of people watching him. But he didn't shrink down, he kept eye contact with Mrs. Griffith, nodding his head in acceptance of her praise.

Once the room started to quiet down, Mrs. Griffith continued. "The second person that I want to mention is Lucy Buchanan."

And there was that feeling of a fist squeezing Theo's heart; just hearing her name did it to him.

"Ms. Buchanan stepped in for me this semester when I couldn't be here. She was one of the few people who I trusted with the program. With *my* program. Lucy was the one who came up with the idea for this year's winter musical. Tonight's production isn't going to be like anything that's been done on this stage before. Over the semester, these students—your children—have been working very hard, coming up with their *own* story to tell. With the help of Ms. Buchanan, *they* created their characters; *they* wrote the dialogue; *they* picked the music.

"I've stopped in and out of rehearsals over the last few months, watching as the program has been transformed into something I have never seen before. Something new and fresh, something that I wouldn't have had the ability to do at the same level." She paused, the emotion in her voice clear. "I used to think that when I announced my retirement, I would do so with a heavy heart. And while it is bittersweet, I couldn't be prouder to pass the baton on to Lucy Buchanan, Mount MacCallion's new drama and music teacher."

Everything in Theo stilled, the shock rocking through him. He couldn't hear a thing that was going on around him, just a light buzzing in his ears. Lucy was staying in Cruickshank? Permanently? When . . . what . . . how? His brain hadn't even fully wrapped around that piece of information when Mrs. Griffith looked at him again.

"There was a last-minute change to the first part of tonight's performance. A dedication from your new teacher to the man who helped make tonight possible. And just so you know, Mr. Taylor, it means *exactly* what you think it does."

And with that Mrs. Griffith moved away from the mic, exiting stage left.

CHAPTER SEVENTEEN
Can't Help Falling in Love

The room was plunged into complete darkness, or nearly complete except for the exit signs above the doors. And their glow wasn't enough to help see anything. Everyone in the room had gone silent, all that could be heard faint squeaks and the rustle of the curtains as they were pulled open.

Once those sounds stopped, a new one filled the room: piano chords. Theo knew the song almost instantly. How could he not with his grandparents being huge Elvis fans? But it wasn't Elvis who started singing. The second he heard Lucy's voice, goose bumps broke out over Theo's skin. Just like they always had—and, he suspected, like they always would.

The lights on the stage slowly came on, illuminating Lucy. She was sitting at a black baby grand piano and there was nothing else onstage except for the trees in the background. The Christmas lights strung among the branches lit up a second later, making it easier to see.

Lucy was sitting in such a way that Theo could see her at the piano, but she could also look out at the audience. How was it that she was wearing a velvet green dress? Just like she had been the first time he'd seen her on that stage. It wasn't the same one, obviously, and while she was wearing red shoes, they weren't the Converse she was partial to. No, they were a pair of bright red heels, her feet pressing the pedals of the piano as she sang about wise men and fools in love.

Lucy's eyes came up, finding Theo in the audience as she sang, asking if she should stay.

"Yes," Theo said, his voice barely above a whisper.

He couldn't be sure, but there was a small flicker of something on Lucy's face, something that looked like relief and joy. Her mouth quirked to the side as she continued to sing, and her eyes didn't leave his for the rest of the song.

The second the music stopped, the curtains closed in a rush, Lucy disappearing behind the heavy purple velvet. Theo was standing before he even knew it, moving through the row. He'd never needed to get to a person faster in his life.

"Sorry, excuse me. Sorry," he repeated over and over again, most of the people attempting to get out of the way before he got to them.

"Go get her, Theo!" someone who sounded a whole hell of a lot like Wes called out from the audience while someone else wolf whistled.

There were more shouts and cheers as Theo mounted the steps and pushed through the heavy curtains to the backstage area.

Lucy was standing there, fidgeting with her hands. "Hey, you."

But that was all she got out before Theo grabbed her face and covered her mouth with his. Her hands were at the front of his shirt, fisting in the fabric as she held on to him. The scent of her consumed him. *She* consumed him. And the kiss was like a brand on his soul, forgiveness wrapped up in a promise.

Theo pulled back, his forehead pressed against hers, their mouths barely separated. "Did you mean it? What you sang?"

"Yes." That little word filled his soul, but it was nothing compared to the words she said next. "I'm in love with you, Theodore.

"And you're staying?"

"Yes. I choose you. I choose this. I want to be here with you."

"Thank god." And then he was kissing her again, his hands moving to the back of her head, his fingers twining in her beautiful hair. The very last thing that he wanted to do was let go, but someone very loudly cleared their throat behind them.

Theo pulled back to see that they had an audience of a dozen or so students, Chloe and Gia standing at the front. "You know we have a show to put on, right?" his sister asked, tapping her naked wrist as if there were a watch there.

"I should get back to my seat." Theo placed one more kiss on Lucy's mouth before he reluctantly let her go. "I'll see you after."

"After." Lucy grinned, biting at her bottom lip in that way that drove him crazy. But the woman had always driven him crazy, and he loved her all the more for it.

* * *

THERE WAS A LINE of parents snaking through the auditorium after the performance, all of them wanting to get a quick word in with Lucy about the musical or congratulating her on taking the job. She couldn't be more pleased with how everything had gone. Sure, there'd been a few hiccups here and there, but nothing major and the cast had always recovered.

She was flying high on the evening, but nothing had made her happier than what had happened with Theo. He'd found her again after the musical, giving her another kiss as he told her how amazing it had been. But then he'd taken a step back after, letting her be in the spotlight.

The thing was, the only place Lucy wanted to be was alone with Theo. She wanted to tell him everything, everything she'd been holding back all week . . . and for the months and years before that. She wanted to bare her soul to him. Singing that song had been like cracking her chest open and putting her heart in his hands. And the second she did it, the fear was gone. She'd known he was going to take care of it, just like she was going to do when it came to his heart.

It was after ten when Theo helped her into her winter coat, kissing her neck as he pulled her hair out from the back.

"I think I get to call bingo," Theo said as he grabbed her hand and they made their way out to the parking lot.

"And why's that?" Lucy asked.

"Because we literally kissed and made up." They bypassed her SUV and headed for his truck, their footsteps echoing in the parking lot.

"What do you want as your prize?"

"I already got it."

"You think so?" She looked over at him, that smile he loved on her mouth.

"I know so. I saw the video of you singing to Bear."

Lucy's hand tightened in his. "I didn't realize I'd sent that to Gia . . . and I didn't know she posted it until this afternoon. When did you see it?"

"Literally before the curtain call. When did you write it?"

Lucy hesitated for just a second, taking a deep breath before letting it out. It fogged the air between them. "After we kissed."

"A couple of weeks ago?"

"No." She shook her head. "Seven years ago. I couldn't get it right. In all those years, I wrote it and rewrote it and wrote it again. I didn't know how to finish it. But I think I finally figured it out."

Theo stopped as they got to his truck, pushing her back against the passenger door. It was cold against her back, but she didn't care. He reached for her hair, twirling one of her loose curls around his finger. "What did you figure out?"

Her hands were on his chest, moving up the front of his jacket. "That it wasn't about how I finished it, but in how I started it. Because this is only the beginning."

"So, what's the next step?"

Lucy gripped his lapels before she pulled him closer. "You take me home and make love to me for hours."

"And after that?"

"I don't know." She shook her head. "But we'll figure it out together."

"Together," Theo agreed before he sealed the promise with a kiss.

* * *

TURNED OUT THAT THE NEXT STEP was moving Lucy, Bear, and Estee into Theo's place. Just temporarily, though. They both knew it was too soon for anything permanent, and they were going to take it day by day. But the reason they rushed this particular step was because of Bear. The dog needed more space and a permanent place to settle in.

It didn't feel too fast for Theo, though, mainly because except for those four days they'd been apart, they'd spent every night together since things had started. He knew the options were either his house or her dad's. He didn't really think Wes would be okay with Theo moving in, which would've happened, as Theo had no intention of missing a night with her anytime soon.

The whelping box was easy enough to disassemble, and Max helped Theo bring it down the stairs and load it into his truck. Meanwhile Lucy and Caro were packing a few bags.

"Have you seen the video of Lucy singing last night?" Caro asked Theo. "It's blown up more than the one of her singing to Bear."

"A couple of times." Theo nodded. He hadn't been able to help himself that morning, playing it over and over and over again.

"Have you delved into the comments?" Max asked. "It's like a romance novel in there."

"No." Theo shook his head. "I've learned to stay out of the comments recently; good or bad, they can be a lot. Besides, we've been a bit busy." He nodded to Lucy.

"I'll just bet you have." Caro grinned. "And now you're moving in together."

"You know we're only doing it because of Bear," Lucy said.

"Sure, you are." Max gave them a sarcastic little smirk.

"Hey, I don't want to hear anything from you." Lucy pointed to her future brother-in-law. "How long was it until Caro moved in with you?"

"Okay, okay, point taken." Max held his hands up in surrender. "Just know this," he said as he turned to Theo. "When it comes to the Buchanan women their hair gets everywhere and you will find hair ties in places you wouldn't even imagine, you should always have pastries in the house—which won't be a problem for you—and they're cover hogs."

"How do you know I'm a cover hog?" Lucy turned to Max.

"I have sat on the sofa with you during many a movie night over the years, and you always steal the blanket. *Always.*"

Apparently the only comeback Lucy had was to stick her tongue out at Max.

"Thanks for the advice." Theo grinned. "I'll just have to get bigger blankets."

Lucy looked over at him, grinning. That smile hadn't really left her face since the night before, and neither had Theo's.

* * *

NIGHT TWO OF THE MUSICAL was a little less dramatic than the first, but only when it came to the first part of the evening. Word had gotten around that Mrs. Griffith was retiring, but she showed up again to give her speech to that night's audience, and Lucy opened the show by singing "Can't Help Falling in Love" for a second time. Theo sat in the exact same seat as he had the night before, Naomi joining him.

But this time when Lucy sang it, she wasn't nearly as nervous, knowing the ending . . . or the beginning, as the case may be.

Sunday was spent at Theo's house, neither of them having any interest in venturing out into the cold December weather. When they woke up, he pulled her over him, his hands spanning her thighs as she rode him. The moment she came—his name still echoing in the air around them—he rolled her onto her back and did it all over again.

They made breakfast, their new Sunday tradition of pancakes and bacon. It wasn't lost on Lucy how they moved around the kitchen together, like they'd figured out their rhythm of exactly how to work together. It was a lot easier in Theo's kitchen than it had been in Lucy's, probably because it was three times the size.

Most of the day was spent lying on Theo's massive leather sofa, a fire blazing in the fireplace and football playing in the background. Lucy worked through the stack of papers that needed grading and Theo sketched out cake designs for a wedding. Her feet were in his lap, and after a while, he set down the pad and started rubbing his thumbs over her arches.

As Lucy had been wearing heels during the nights of the musical, her feet were more than a little sore, and she couldn't help the moan that escaped her lips. Nor could she help the other moans when Theo laid her out on that sofa and sunk into her.

It turned out to be a glorious Sunday, one that Lucy hoped she'd get to enjoy many, many times in the future.

The following week went by in flash. Monday and Tuesday she and her students were reviewing for finals, which would be taking place the last three days of the week.

Wednesday just so happened to be Lucy's thirtieth birthday, and Theo made the day special from beginning to end. He woke her up with his usual flare, before making her coffee and pulling out a box of doughnuts for breakfast. But then he pulled out another box, that one much smaller.

Lucy popped it open to find a simple gold necklace with a turquoise pendant and matching earrings.

"I know it's probably cliché to get you something with your birthstone," he said as he brushed her hair back before helping her put the necklace on. "But I just thought it was really pretty."

"It's not cliché," Lucy said softly, as she turned around. "I love it."

"I love you." He pressed a kiss to her mouth. "Happy birthday, Lucy."

That morning would've been enough, so she was surprised to find that Theo was already home when she got back to his place that afternoon, the house smelling of something decadent. She was even more surprised when he ushered her into his bathroom, where the bathtub was filled with steaming water and bubbles. Candles had been lit all around the room and there was music playing softly from a speaker.

"When you get out," he whispered against her neck as he helped her out of her jacket, "we'll have dinner and dessert."

"Are you not joining me?" she asked, pointing to the tub.

"I'll do whatever you want me to. It's your birthday."

"Then I want you to join me," she said as she reached for the front of his pants.

Lucy wasn't the only one who was settling into her days at Theo's. Estee adapted easily, acting like Theo's house was hers almost immediately. Every cozy spot became hers and she had no qualms about stretching out wherever she wanted.

Bear had also gotten quite comfortable, or as comfortable as she could be with her ever-growing belly. Things were a lot easier for her to navigate at his house, especially without the stairs for her to climb multiple times a day. It also was helpful that Theo's house was so close to the school. Since he left after Lucy, Bear was only alone for a couple of hours before Lucy could pop by on her free period. And then Gia and Chloe were able to come by right after school to let her out.

Theo had also set up a camera in the living room to keep an eye on Bear, so he and Lucy were able to check on her multiple times a day that way. Luckily it was only that week in which Bear was on her own during the day. Once finals were done, Lucy was off until after the new year.

Bear's last vet appointment was on the first Monday of Lucy's break, and Oscar said she was definitely getting close to week nine, meaning she could be giving birth any day now. She'd started to become a little moody, not wanting attention so much and staying in her whelping box. Her appetite had also started to decrease, and she was turning her nose up at her food more often than not.

"Well, someone has become a diva," Lucy said as Bear walked out of the kitchen, leaving her plate of eggs half eaten. Theo had made them in hopes they'd be a little gentler on her stomach.

"She'll tell us if she's hungry." Theo grabbed the bowl off the floor before Estee could pounce on it.

For the most part, Lucy spent her days hanging out at Theo's house. She worked on her music a little, recording more videos to post to Bear's page and her own. The two videos that had come out during the musical were still climbing in views, Lucy's own follower count going up drastically.

Gia and Chloe were also over a lot, watching Bear when Lucy needed to run some errands or if she and Theo went out. Naomi and Harlow were both in town for Christmas, so they made regular visits as well. Since Lucy had time to do it, she cooked dinner for her and Theo, and they even had his family dinner night at his place on Tuesday, Lucy making chicken enchiladas and chiles rellenos.

They ventured out on Thursday, going to her dad's house for dinner. Not only were Lorraine and Sasha in attendance, but Oscar and Edward were too.

"Looks like things are moving along nicely with you," Lucy whispered to Oscar as he filled up her wineglass.

"Well, I haven't moved in with him yet." He waggled his eyebrows at her.

"I didn't move in with Theo, I'm just staying there."

"How much do you want to bet you don't stop staying there?"

"I'll take that bet," Max said, joining their conversation. "I know the signs; you aren't going anywhere."

"You make it sound like it's a hostage situation."

"Nah." Oscar shook his head, grinning. "It's because the man has never looked happier. Lucy, I'm telling you, he isn't going anywhere."

"I know." She nodded. "I'm not either. You know I took the job. I'm staying."

"We know, and we're happy," Max said as he looped his arm around her neck, gently pulling her in to press a kiss to the top of her head.

Lucy had never felt surer of a decision in her life; everything felt right about staying in Cruickshank, about taking the job, about being with Theo. Which was undoubtedly why the universe decided to test her the following morning.

Theo didn't need to be at the bakery until nine, so he'd pulled her into the shower, both of them taking their time with the soapy hot water.

"Have I told you how much the scent of you drives me crazy?" Theo asked as he pressed his face into her neck, kissing her throat.

Lucy turned around, her arms looping around his neck as he pushed her back into the tiled wall. "Have I mentioned how much I love the way you touch me? How you're gentle and possessive all at the same time? Or the scrape of your beard on my skin?"

"I'm captivated by your voice . . . when you talk, when you sing, when you're moaning my name." One of his hands moved between her thighs, her wetness having nothing to do with the water pouring down around them.

"Fuck, Lucy," Theo groaned.

Theo took his time playing with Lucy, holding her up against the wall as the orgasm crashed through her. Once she had the use of her legs again, she sat down on the little tiled bench and took him apart with her mouth.

Lucy wished she could spend the day with him, but that wasn't a possibility. Christmas was three days away and as Browned Butter wasn't open on Sundays, they only had two days to fill the demands of everyone in town for holiday sweets. Besides, Lucy had a busy day of wrapping presents while watching Christmas movies ahead of her. Sasha was coming over too, her own pile of gifts to wrap.

"Do I need to pick anything up for dinner?" Theo asked as he rummaged through his closet for his jacket.

"Nope." Lucy shook her head, the word a little garbled. She was brushing her teeth as she looked through messages on her phone, and as she scrolled down, she almost inhaled a mouthful of toothpaste. "Oh my god."

"Are you okay?" Theo asked.

"No." Lucy rinsed her mouth out before setting the toothbrush down and grabbing her phone again. She pulled up the direct message that had almost choked her. It had been sent a few days ago but she hadn't been the best about checking, especially as a lot of people were messaging her about adopting Bear's puppies. And as previously stated, none of those babies were going to strangers.

"Remington Marks sent me a message," she whispered as she continued reading. "He's going to be in Atlanta on Saturday for a concert and he wants to meet me."

She looked up at Theo, the excitement at seeing the message disappearing as she saw his face. Something had shuttered in his eyes, and his expression had gone a little hard. It wasn't so much anger as worry . . . fear. He took a step back, leaning against the counter as he folded his arms across his chest. "Who's Remington Marks?"

"No one important." She shook her head, setting her phone back down on the counter.

"Lucy? Come on. I know that's not true. Seeing his name almost killed you."

There was no use in lying; besides, they'd said no more secrets after what happened before. "He's a pretty important talent agent," she relented. "I know his name because he's signed some good artists. He's got a reputation for discovering unknowns and making them big."

"And now he's discovered you?"

"Yeah." She nodded. "He saw the video of my singing to Bear and then the one at the musical."

Theo nodded slowly. "Do you want to go?"

"I . . ." Lucy hesitated. "I don't know. If I'd gotten this message months ago, I would've jumped all over it. But things have changed. I'm staying in Cruickshank. I finally have a job that I love . . . and most importantly, there's you. I love you, Theo. I chose you."

Theo's arms unwound from across his chest, and he closed the distance between them, wrapping his arms around her and pulling her against him. "I know you love me, and that you chose me. But I don't want you to have regrets."

"About picking you? I don't have regrets." She looked up at him, shaking her head.

"No." He ran his hand across her cheek, pushing back a strand of wet hair. "I don't want you to have regrets about not taking the meeting. I don't want you to think *what if* or *what could've been* when it comes to your music career. I think you should go."

"But what about us?"

"You just said it, Luce. You love me, and I love you. We don't know what will come of the meeting now, but we'll at least know after. And we can figure us out either way."

"You're sure?" It was true, she *would* always wonder if she didn't meet with the guy.

"Yeah, I'm sure."

"Is this a test? Am I going to fail it if I go?"

Theo let out a small laugh. "No. This isn't a test. I promise." He pulled her against his chest, his mouth by her ear as he said, "I want you to go."

* * *

"Theo wants you to what?!" Sasha all but shouted as she stood in Theo's kitchen. "Is this some weird game with the two of you?"

Her friend had gotten there about half an hour ago, the two of them setting up a wrapping station at the kitchen island as they sipped on hot chocolate that Lucy had spiked with peppermint schnapps.

What? It was after noon, and she needed a little liquid courage to have this conversation with Sasha. And rightly so, as her friend was a wee bit upset with the news.

"No, it's not a game. He just wants me to know. Like *know* know."

"But don't you already know? I thought that was what you singing your heart out to him was all about."

"It was. And I *am* sure about everything that has to do with Theo. He wants me to be sure about this too, about walking away from something that could lead to a future in music."

Sasha's frown deepened as she slid onto the barstool. "So, what happens if this guy wants to sign you?"

"I don't know." Lucy shrugged. "The first step is actually taking the meeting."

"Is Theo going with you?"

"No, both of us can't be that far away from Bear as she's literally days away from giving birth." Lucy gestured to the dog, who was lying down on the dog bed they kept in the kitchen. She was asleep but she opened her eyes at the sound of her name. "I already feel guilty about leaving her, but Gia and Chloe are going to stay here with her so she isn't alone."

"Well, you aren't going to be alone either." Sasha shook her head. "Because I'm going with you to Atlanta. What time are we leaving?"

Lucy grinned, because of course Sasha was going with her. They were ride or die, had been for as long as she could remember. It was the same with how she was with Lilah and Caro. Their relationships were the strongest that Lucy had, ones that had stood the test of time and distance.

She didn't know where she'd be without them.

CHAPTER EIGHTEEN
Somewhere Only We Know

On Saturday morning, Lucy and Sasha fueled up Sasha's Subaru—the obvious choice as her car was newer and had heated seats—and loaded up on coffee before hitting the road. They were about an hour from Atlanta when Lucy attempted to eat her sandwich, but her appetite had gone out the window, the bread getting stuck to the roof of her mouth.

Lucy wrapped the sandwich back up and put it in the cooler Lorraine had packed. She'd made sure they had enough food for the drive there and back. Even though they were in their thirties, the mothering didn't stop.

But Lucy didn't want it to. And judging by the progression of Lorraine's relationship with Wes, the mothering wasn't going anywhere anytime soon. The two were pretty much inseparable. Lucy just wondered how long before Lorraine was officially her stepmother.

"Are you getting nervous?" Sasha asked, reaching over and turning the music down.

"I don't know what I am." Lucy shook her head. "I don't know what I want to happen. If I want this guy to like me and sign me, or if I want to finally be able to move on from this dream of a singing career."

"Well, you don't have to *move on* from singing, Luce. I feel like you've been doing a lot with it these last couple of months, and maybe it's because you haven't been under a bunch of pressure in trying to be something for everyone. You've gotten to do your own thing, and not somebody else's thing. You've been inspired. You've been *happy*."

"Well, it's a lot easier to be happy when you aren't under the constant strain of trying to prove yourself."

"Well, that and regular orgasms."

"Yes." Lucy grinned. "Those have helped a lot too. Being with Theo has changed everything. It is very apparent that the man likes me, imperfections and all."

"Um, I believe he loves you," Sasha corrected.

"He does. I wasn't prepared for him to love me, or for me to love him back. But I don't think I could've ever been prepared for what's happened with Theo."

"I don't think you can prepare yourself for falling in love, Luce."

"No, that's for damn sure." Lucy nodded, looking out the window, watching as the trees passed by.

"Okay, talk to me. There is more going on in that head of yours."

"I just . . ." Lucy shook her head as she looked back to Sasha. "My whole life I've had this idea of what I wanted, to be a musician, to get to sing for a crowd of people and make them *feel* something from my words. That was why I picked LA; it was a place with a music scene where I could get a fresh start."

"And it was as far away as possible from Cruickshank?"

Lucy frowned. "It wasn't that. I love it in Cruickshank. It's my home in every way, and always will be. I just knew that I couldn't pursue singing there. Not in the same way, at least, not on the same scale. So, I thought that if I stayed, I'd . . . get stuck. But I don't feel that way anymore. I don't feel stuck."

"Isn't that a good thing?" Sasha asked.

"I think I'm still wrapping my head around the fact that what I want has changed, and trying to reconcile that I might've wasted seven years of my life chasing something that was never for me."

"You didn't waste those seven years."

"But what if I did? What if I'd stayed here and pursued things with Theo? Where would we be now?"

"You might not be anywhere with him, Luce. What if seven years ago wasn't the right time for you two? If you'd never gone to California, you would've always wondered. Isn't that what today is about, making sure there isn't a *what if*?"

"Yeah, that's why Theo wanted me to come. He doesn't want there to be a doubt in my mind."

"Did you guys talk about it any more last night?"

"Not really." Lucy shook her head. "I don't think he wants to influence me, though that isn't possible. He did say he doesn't want to hear how the meeting goes over the phone. He wants to talk about it in person. After what happened before, he doesn't want to take any more chances on us misunderstanding each other, and not being face-to-face leaves a lot to be interpreted."

"That's smart." Sasha nodded. "So, if something happens today, you guys will cross that bridge when you come to it?"

As they were literally crossing a bridge as Sasha said it, Lucy couldn't help but laugh.

"What?" she asked.

"It's silly, but Theo and I have had this thing the last couple of months about literal clichés. When we see them, we cross them off our imaginary bingo card and we were crossing a bridge as you said it."

Sasha glanced over at Lucy, a little smirk on her mouth. "You're right, it is silly, but it's also pretty cute. God, I bet it's killing him today, not knowing what's going on."

"I know it is." Lucy nodded as she looked back out the window, because it was killing her too.

* * *

THEO WAS DOING HIS BEST not to look at his watch, but invariably, he checked it about every fifteen minutes. In his mind's eye, he saw Sasha's car making its way down to Atlanta like it was one of those pieces from the Game of Life.

Lucy had texted him that they'd gotten there safely, and about an hour later that they were leaving. He really wished they weren't on the road. There was a storm blowing in and it would be hitting within the hour. Their driving through it wasn't doing anything to help his current state of mind. Especially as there'd been an awful accident on I-85 and they'd gotten diverted to back roads.

But nothing was really helping him at the moment. He was now regretting telling Lucy that he didn't want to know how the meeting went until she was back, because it felt like the last two hours had been the longest of his life. But while he was regretting the not knowing, he didn't regret encouraging Lucy to go.

He wanted her to know, beyond a shadow of a doubt, that this was the life she wanted. That she wanted to be here, with him. And if she didn't want to be in Cruickshank, they'd figure it out, because it wouldn't be his choice to let her go again. That much he was damn sure of.

It was a little after three when Theo finished decorating his last batch of vanilla chai cupcakes, lining them up on the tray for his dad to take out to the display. His phone started ringing in his pocket, and as the ringtone was Taylor Swift, he knew it was Gia. She'd stolen his phone months ago and set it up.

"Hey, Gia."

"Bear is in labor."

"What?! Are you sure?"

Both of his parents looked up at his tone, freezing in place.

"Well, as she just had one of her puppies, I'm pretty sure." Gia's voice was slightly frantic, but not in a full-on panic.

"I'm leaving right now." Theo untied the back of his apron. "I'll be there in five minutes." He hung up the phone and slid it into his pocket. "Bear is in labor. I've got to go."

"We got it." Isaac waved him off. "Get out of here."

"We'll come over as soon as we finish up and we'll get dinner." Juliet kissed him on the cheek. "Don't speed home either. It's already raining out there."

"Yes, ma'am." Theo headed for the door, grabbing his coat before he pushed through to the main part of the bakery.

When he stepped outside, he was blasted with a wave of freezing-cold air, big fat raindrops hitting him in the face. He didn't let it faze him, running around the corner to the little lot that the shop owners used to park.

Once he got out of the downtown area, he called Oscar, his friend's voice coming over the speaker.

"What's up, man?"

"Bear is having her puppies. Gia just called me and I'm on the way home."

"Damn it, I'm out at the Johnsons' farm. Apparently, it's the night to have babies. Their mare is in labor and she's having difficulties, so I can't leave."

"Where's Dr. Carter?" Theo asked of the other vet who worked at Mountain View.

"She has the flu. Listen, when you get home, assess the situation. Bear is probably doing fine. Mothers usually know what to do on instinct. If there are complications, call me, and I will walk you through it. I talked to Sasha and Lucy about half an hour ago, and I think they're probably still an hour out if not more."

"Yeah, they got delayed." Theo turned his windshield wipers to a higher speed as he made a left.

"Theo, everything is going to be fine. If you're this freaked out now, it's going to be really interesting when you and Lucy actually have a kid."

Theo's hands gripped the steering wheel at that comment.

"Did I freak you out even more?" Oscar asked.

Theo cleared his throat, trying to think properly given the current image that filled his mind: Lucy pregnant. How cliché was it that she was barefoot and in his kitchen? But she wasn't cooking. No, they were dancing, his hands on her belly as they moved around. Her hair was down, swaying across her back, and she was laughing.

Something tightened in his chest, and it was hard to breathe.

"Theo?" Oscar called out.

"I'm fine," he lied. The very last thing he was, was fine.

"Look, I'll call my mom. She and Wes went to get some dogs at an overrun shelter, but she should be done in a couple of hours. If she gets back before I can get there, she can help. She knows what she's doing. She's delivered many a puppy."

"Okay, thanks, I'll call you in a bit." He pressed a button on the steering wheel, ending the call before pressing it again. "Call Lucy," he commanded.

The phone rang four times before going to voicemail. "Hey, it's Lucy, sorry I missed your call . . ."

Theo wasn't surprised he couldn't get through. Cell service

could be intermittent in the mountains. Those back roads Lucy and Sasha were on would take them through a lot of valleys, which meant it was even worse.

"Hey, babe," Theo started after the beep. "So, Bear is in labor, but everything is under control," he managed to say, keeping the creeping panic at bay. "I'm on my way back to the house, and Oscar is going to come when he finishes up. Drive safely and I'll see you in a bit . . . I love you."

He hit the *end* button just as he pulled into his driveway. In the five minutes it had taken him to get home, the skies had opened up, and he was soaked when he walked in the front door. Gia and Chloe turned, relief filling their faces as he shut the door behind him.

"The first one is a girl and she looks to be doing well." Gia stood up from where she was sitting by the box. "Bear's got her all cleaned up."

"I think her contractions are getting closer together," Chloe said. "She's going to have another one soon."

"All right, good." Theo nodded as he pulled off his jacket, hanging it on one of the hooks by the door before kicking off his shoes. "Oscar can't come for a bit, so we're going to have to do this together. Are you two going to be okay?" he asked as he crossed over to them.

"Yes," they said in unison, but while Chloe sounded confident, Gia looked upset.

Theo focused on his sister. "What's wrong?"

"I just feel like I missed something." She started to cry, her lip trembling. "Like I should've known that she was going into labor. She was pacing earlier, but she's always restless when you and Lucy are gone. And she wouldn't eat, but she's been finicky about eating for days now. And I—I . . ."

"Hey." Theo put his hands on Gia's shoulders, looking into her face. "Everything is fine. Oscar wouldn't have been able to be here even if you had called an hour ago. And this little girl looks to be doing well." He glanced into the box to see the brown and white puppy that was already nursing. "Let's get her dry, and I'm going to start a fire so it's warmer in here."

"You need to get dry too," Chloe said as she threw one of the towels they'd grabbed over Theo's shoulders.

"Thanks." He smiled at her, some of the nerves he'd felt on the drive leaving him. There was no more time to worry, he had to take care of Bear now.

* * *

IT WAS AFTER FOUR THIRTY when Sasha and Lucy drove into Cruickshank. There was still an hour or so of daylight, but as the sky was covered up by thick storm clouds, it was already dark and gloomy. The worsening weather had done nothing to help either of their anxieties.

Sasha was worried about her own four-legged babies. Pistachio and Maraschino were her dogs, a bonded pair who'd been owner surrendered a couple of years ago. They weren't Sasha's first foster failure; she had a soft spot for older dogs. But their age wasn't the only reason it had been hard to get anyone to adopt them. Pistachio was a grumpy little guy and didn't like to be handled too much. He'd gotten comfortable with Sasha, though, and she'd become his person.

Neither dog liked storms and both usually needed antianxiety meds when one hit. The problem was no one was there to give them any. Sasha knew that Oscar and Lorraine weren't going to be around to help her dogs as they were both busy with their own day's activities.

The last hour had been the worst, Lucy feeling like she was in her own personal purgatory. She just wanted to get back to Theo, wanted to tell him about the meeting, and how it had cemented everything in her mind. But the meeting went by the wayside as they drove through the city limits, both of their phones lighting up. Lucy reached for hers, seeing a dozen texts and three voicemails.

"Crap," she said as she scrolled through them. "Bear's in labor. She's already had three puppies."

"Is Theo there?"

"Yeah, but it's just him and the girls. Oscar's still at the Johnsons' farm helping with that mare delivery."

"Do you want me to go straight there?" Sasha asked.

"No, you need to check on Pistachio and Maraschino. I'll grab my car and go to Theo's."

"Okay, and as soon as I can, I'll come over and help."

"Crap, crap, crap, I can't believe I'm not there."

"Luce, I'm sure everything is fine. Like you said, Theo's there. What do his texts say?"

Lucy paused for a second before looking over at Sasha. "That everything is fine."

Sasha had her eyes on the road, but Lucy watched as her friend's mouth curved up into a grin. "See, you'll be there in fifteen minutes. Call him and tell him."

"No, I don't want to distract him, he needs to focus on Bear. And like you said, I'll be there in fifteen minutes."

It was only another mile to Sasha's house, but it felt like *forever* for them to get there. The second they pulled into the drive, Lucy didn't even hesitate to jump out of the car, her keys already in her hand.

"Text me when you get there," Sasha called out.

"I will!" Lucy said before she slammed her door shut. The rain hadn't let up at all in the last hour and the wind was only getting worse. The temperature was dropping too, and it was now in the mid-thirties. She really hoped they wouldn't get hail. At least there wasn't any thunder and lightning.

Lucy was cautious as she drove. Theo's house was on the exact opposite side of Cruickshank as Sasha's, about three miles outside of the downtown area. It was on a windy two-lane road that went up to the lake and the houses that had been built around it. Not the safest on a normal day, and definitely not tonight.

But it didn't matter how carefully Lucy was driving, as there was no way in the world she could've prevented the deer that appeared out of nowhere from slamming into the side of her SUV. She lost control in an instant, the tires going off the side of the road. She must've hit an icy patch of water because there was no course correcting. Her car was going down into the ditch whether she liked it or not.

"*Fuck!*" Lucy screamed as it plowed through the shrubs that separated the forest from the road. By some miracle she was able to steer the car away from the bigger trees, pressing the brakes to slow down before it finally hit a park bench, which made her come to a stop.

The hit wasn't powerful enough to deploy the airbag, but Lucy was jerked hard enough forward that she was pretty sure she had whiplash. Her death grip on the steering wheel loosened, and she took a few deep breaths, trying to calm herself.

"It's okay, you're okay. You're okay. You're okay. You're okay." Her hands were shaking as she turned the lights on above her. Her purse had flown to the floorboards and she unbuckled her seat belt as she stretched over the center console and grabbed it. Ripping it open, she searched around for her phone, and couldn't find it anywhere.

Had it flown somewhere in the crash? Did she even have it? She thought she'd thrown it in her purse in her rush to get out of Sasha's car, but she couldn't remember. Her only thought had been to get to Theo and Bear.

Lucy looked out her side window. It was cracked from where the deer had hit it. The road was up an embankment, and even if she could get up the steep slope with its rain-soaked grass, that road was dangerous to walk along on a normal day, let alone on a rainy night with limited visibility. It didn't help that she was wearing jeans and a gray coat. She'd be really hard to see.

"I can't just sit here. No one is going to find me," she told herself as she looked out the passenger side window and to the hiking trail that was just visible through the trees.

Lucy knew that trail, she walked on it with Bear every single day. She was probably a mile from Theo's house . . . a mile and a half at most.

If she was going to go, she had to go while it was still light outside. "Which means I need to get going *now*," she said as she looked around the back seat for any supplies.

There was no point in searching for her umbrella because she knew it wasn't there. No, it was currently sitting by Theo's front door. Nor did she have her yellow raincoat. There was, however, a blanket in the back seat; she'd had it spread out for Bear. It and the flashlight and bear spray in her trunk were the only supplies that would be helping her.

Lucy jotted a note to leave on the steering wheel in case anyone found her car. She then took just a few more seconds to

320 SHANNON RICHARD

fortify herself before she opened the door to the freezing rain and biting wind.

* * *

IT WAS AFTER FIVE when Theo grabbed his phone, looking for a missed call or text from Lucy, but there was nothing. Bear had just had her fourth puppy, and he could tell she was getting ready to have the fifth.

Oscar had been right; as each baby was born, she cleaned them up and got them to start nursing. It was much warmer now with the fire behind them, but he and the girls still did their part in getting the pups as dry as possible.

Theo was lucky things were going well, because as each minute ticked by, he was getting more and more worried. Lucy should be here by now. He'd just pulled up her name and was about to press *dial* when Sasha's picture popped up on his phone and he put her on speaker.

"Hey, Sash," Theo said as a wave of relief washed through him.

"I was just checking on Lucy. She was supposed to text me when she got there, and I haven't heard from her. I called her phone but keep getting her voicemail."

"Lucy isn't here. When did she leave your house?"

There was a pause on the other side of the phone, and just that quickly Theo's relief turned to fear. "Theo, she left half an hour ago."

Gia and Chloe looked at each other, their eyes going big with worry.

Theo turned to the window that showed his front yard, as if he'd see her SUV pulling in at that moment, but the only vehicle there was his truck.

"Okay, okay." His mind started reeling. "Maybe something happened on the road . . ." *Oh, god, what if she was in an accident?*

"Theo, what do you want me to do?" The panic in Sasha's voice was clear. Apparently, she'd had the same thought.

"I'm going to call my dad," Chloe said as she fumbled with her own phone. "He's working tonight."

Theo turned to Gia. "If I go look for Lucy, are you going to be okay here with Bear?"

"Yeah." Gia nodded, looking completely freaked out. Theo wanted to again reassure her that everything would be okay, but this time he wasn't so sure.

"I'll be back." Leaning forward he pressed a kiss to Gia's forehead.

"I'm going to head that way." Sasha's voice echoed in the room.

"I don't want you putting yourself in danger too." Theo got to his feet, heading to the door. "If something happened to Lucy—" He stopped dead at the thought, suddenly feeling very lightheaded.

No, she was fine. Lucy was *fine*.

"I'm leaving now, Theo, see you soon." Sasha hung up the phone.

Theo grabbed his boots, pulling them on as fast as he could. He made quick work of the laces before he snatched his rain jacket from the hook and the flashlight he kept by the door. The second he stepped outside he was assaulted with the bitterly cold wind. It sunk into his clothes in an instant, but it was made so much worse when he stepped out into the rain.

"Jesus Christ, it's freezing," Theo swore as he snapped the buttons closed under his chin to keep the hood in place. It didn't matter how bad it was, though. He'd go out into a fucking hurricane to find Lucy.

He was running to his car when out of the corner of his eye he saw it, a flashlight in the distance over by the trees. It was right by the trailhead that was a few hundred feet from his house. He always got that feeling at the back of his neck when Lucy was near, and it was no different in that moment. It wasn't the cold making his skin prickle.

"Lucy!" He bellowed her name as he started running in that direction.

The muffled call of "Theo!" was enough to make his heart stop. He didn't even hesitate as he sprinted toward her.

The beam from the flashlight bobbed, and it looked like Lucy slipped, but a second later she was running straight at him. They almost collided in the middle of the path, a blanket falling from Lucy's shoulders as she reached for him. Theo wrapped his arms around her and crushed her body to his.

They just stood there for a moment, Lucy crying as she held on to him. Wave after wave of relief crashed through him. She was here, she was in his arms, she was *here*. It was only then that he realized her teeth were chattering, her entire body shaking.

"Come on, Luce. Let's get you inside." He pressed a kiss to her forehead before he pulled her toward the house.

The second they stepped inside, Chloe and Gia were on their feet. "Oh my god! What happened!" Gia ran toward them.

"D-d-deer h-hit-t-t my c-c-c-c-car," Lucy barely got out. "W-w-w-went off the r-road."

"You hit a deer?" Chloe repeated.

"N-n-n-no." Lucy shook her head. "It hit-t-t-t me."

"I'm calling Dad again." Chloe reached for her phone. "They were already down the road. Lucy needs to get checked out."

"She needs to get warm," Gia said.

"Stay with Bear. Chloe, when your dad gets here, send him to my room." Theo led Lucy through the house, both of them leaving a trail of water and mud behind them.

The second they got into the bathroom, Theo started to undress her. It was a bit of a struggle to get her out of the sopping wet coat. He threw it to the tiled floor before he pulled off her sweater. Getting down on his knees, he started to unlace her shoes, pulling them off along with her socks. Once he got her completely undressed, he grabbed her robe, throwing it over her shoulders instead of putting it on her.

Lucy wasn't tan by any means, but her ivory skin was even paler than normal. She was still shaking, her teeth chattering even worse.

"It's going to be okay, baby. You're going to be okay." Scooping her up in his arms, Theo carried her into the bedroom. He sat her on the bed. "Don't move."

"I-I-I don't th-th-think I'm g-g-going anywhere."

Moving to his dresser, Theo pulled out two pairs of his thickest socks, a pair of sweatpants, and a sweatshirt. And then he was back in front of her, kneeling at her feet. He pulled everything on, getting her dressed as gently as possible.

It was then that Theo heard the front door open, and loud footsteps coming down the hallway. Captain Savage came in the room caring an EMT kit, two other firefighters behind him.

"Oh, good, you didn't put her in the shower. That's always a common mistake," Harrison said as he rounded the bed.

"Yeah, I know that one from experience."

Theo was reluctant to move away from Lucy, but he knew they could take better care of her than he could. Besides, he didn't feel like arguing when Harrison pointed at him a second later and said, "You need to get dry too. Go change while we check out Lucy."

"Okay." Theo nodded, pressing a kiss to her forehead before he took a step back. It was only then that his adrenaline of the last ten minutes started to drain, and he realized he was shaking too.

* * *

IT TOOK THE GUYS about twenty minutes to get Lucy checked out. Thank god she didn't have hypothermia, but she'd been heading that way. When she was finally able to tell them exactly what happened, Theo thought he was going to lose his mind.

"Why didn't you stay in the car? We would've found you," he said as he sat next to Lucy at the kitchen table.

"I don't know." Harrison shook his head. "That road is tricky. It might've been the right choice. We'll see tomorrow when we find the car."

"I feel like I've lost ten years of my life in the last hour."

"Here." Sasha passed Theo a shot of bourbon. "You need a drink. I've already had two." She'd gotten there about five minutes after Harrison and the other two firefighters. Gia had called her to let her know that Lucy was at the house, so she'd headed there immediately.

"Can I have one of those?" Lucy asked, looking to Harrison. "I need something to calm my nerves."

"Give it an hour." He shook his head. "Just drink the tea Chloe made you for now. And something warm and hearty for dinner."

"My parents are bringing Irish stew from Quigley's. They're on their way now," Theo said before he downed his own shot. He was pretty sure nothing was going to really help him at the moment.

"That should do it. I'd just watch out for pain if you did indeed get whiplash. It's a miracle you didn't hit your head and the airbag didn't go off."

"Well, I was only going about twenty miles per hour when the deer hit me, so I was able to slow the car before it ran into the bench."

"I still can't believe you got hit by a deer." Sasha shook her head.

"Hey, guys." Chloe popped her head into the kitchen. "Bear's having another puppy. Can we get some help?"

"What are we at now?" Sasha asked as she headed into the living room.

"Six," Chloe's voice floated through.

"Do you mind if she stays here tonight?" Harrison asked. "I don't think she wants to miss anything."

"She can stay." Lucy nodded. "We clearly need the help."

"No kidding," Theo agreed.

The guys all grabbed their bags, heading for the front door, but Harrison lingered for a second. "I was actually wondering if you'd allow us to adopt one of the puppies. Chloe hasn't asked—she doesn't ask for a lot these days—but I know she wants one and I think it would be good for the girls."

"Absolutely." Lucy grinned. "Do you want to tell her? Or do you want us to?"

"I'll tell her tomorrow after the puppies are born. That way she can subconsciously pick her favorite without all of the added pressure."

"Sounds like a plan." Theo stood up and shook Harrison's hand. "Thanks again for coming. I can't thank you enough."

"It was no problem. You probably could've handled it on your own, based on what you did before we got here, but it's always better to be safe than sorry. Lucy, I'd say you need to get some rest, but I doubt that's going to happen." Harrison pointed toward the living room.

"Yeah, not anytime soon."

"Keep me posted on the puppies, and everything else. I'll be back in the morning." He nodded before he turned around and headed for the living room. Theo could hear a muffled exchange between him and his daughter before the front door opened and closed again.

It was the first time they'd been alone since he'd found her, and Theo reached over, grabbing Lucy's hand. He looked at her, that lingering terror still in his chest. "You scared the shit out of me."

"I know. I'm sorry. Tonight turned a bit chaotic."

"A bit?" Theo frowned at her. "I'm surprised I haven't had a heart attack yet. You aren't allowed to leave me anymore. If you're doing this music thing, I'm going with you."

Lucy stood up, moving over to his chair before she sat down in his lap. She wrapped her arms around his shoulders, burying her face in his neck. "I'm not going anywhere, Theo. I'm staying right here with you."

"The meeting didn't go well?"

Lucy sat up so she could look into his eyes. "Well, at first it did. He said he liked my sound and thought that I was talented. Then he said that I had a pretty face but that I'd probably need to lose about thirty pounds, start getting a tan, and dye my hair blond."

"Excuse me? Anyone touches your hair and I'll hurt them myself." Theo reached up, twirling a still-damp strand around his finger. "If anyone touches you period, I'll hurt them myself."

"No one is touching me except for you." She cupped his jaw, rasping her thumb across his beard. "There isn't a doubt in my mind about us, about this. I want to be here with you. Theo, I've finally found my place. It wasn't so much that a piece of me was missing, but that *I'm* the puzzle piece, and I fit here. I fit with you. This is all that I want. You, me, Estee, Bear, and whatever adventures await us."

"Promise?"

"I promise." Lucy leaned in, pressing a kiss to his mouth. Theo's arms tightened around her, holding her close. But their little moment in the kitchen didn't last long as a cry of alarm echoed through the air.

"Theo! Lucy! Something is wrong."

Lucy jumped up, grabbing Theo's hand as she pulled him into the living room. Gia was at Bear's head, talking to her while she strained.

"The puppy is breach," Sasha said. "I'm calling Oscar, to make sure we do everything right."

"I'm looking for that suction thingy!" Chloe said as she hopped up and down from foot to foot, looking through the box that Oscar had left them. "Found it!" She held the little blue object in the air.

"Oscar," Sasha said with relief into the phone. Theo couldn't focus on what she was saying as he and Lucy knelt next to Bear. The puppies were all continuing to nurse, not bothered by the fresh wave of chaos.

Bear looked up at Theo and Lucy, pain in her soft brown eyes. It was as if she knew something was wrong, and with just that look, he knew she was asking for help.

"It's okay, Mama Bear," Theo said. "We're going to make sure your baby is okay." It was another couple of seconds before the puppy was born, and it was very clear that something was wrong.

With all of the other puppies, they'd immediately started crying after birth, wiggling around as Bear cleaned them.

This one wasn't moving at all.

"Get me a towel." Theo held out his hands, and Lucy handed him one from the stack. He scooped up the puppy, turning to Sasha. "What do I do?"

"You're on speaker," she told Oscar.

"Okay, Theo." Oscar's voice filled the room. "You need to suction its mouth first, and then its nose. Make sure there is no air in the bulb, and push the tip into its mouth. You want to get it as close to the throat as you can, but be gentle."

Theo did as he was instructed, focusing on the tiny creature. It was small enough for him to hold in one hand.

"Now release the bulb gradually, letting it suck out what's in its lungs." Oscar paused for a second before continuing. "You're going to want to squeeze anything out of the syringe before doing it again. I want you to do it two more times, and then do its nose."

This time when Theo did it, the puppy started to wiggle a little in his hand, but it still wasn't breathing correctly.

"It's struggling, Oscar," Lucy said, surprisingly calm. Her hand was on Theo's back and just her touch made him feel calmer too.

"Okay, rub it with a towel. Not too hard, but enough to aggravate it. You want to get it moving. Try to get it to make noise. Rub its chest and keep its head pointed toward the floor so that the fluid drains forward."

It was when Theo did this that the puppy finally started to make noise, a loud squeak filling the room. The little guy started to wiggle in Theo's hands a lot harder, very clearly upset with the situation.

Join the club, man.

Oscar let out a long sigh of relief over the phone. "Okay, that's a good sound. Do the syringe a couple more times to make sure you get out any air bubbles, and I'm going to be there in about thirty minutes. I'm loading up my truck now."

Theo sat back, his butt hitting the floor as he leaned against the sofa.

It took a few more minutes for him to get the puppy cleaned up and dry. He also had a chance to take a closer look, seeing that it was indeed a little guy. He was all white, except for a brown spot on his butt.

"Let me get a picture." Gia grabbed her phone, holding it in the air. "I'm keeping them in order, so we know who is who."

When Theo put the puppy in the box, Bear immediately started licking him, nudging him closer to her until he found one of her nipples.

"If that could be the last traumatic thing we deal with tonight, that would be great."

Lucy patted his shoulder. "Here's hoping."

And as it turned out, Theo got his wish. Puppy number six was the only hiccup of the evening. Oscar got there just before puppy seven joined the mix, checking on the one who'd been breach before focusing on Bear.

"She's doing really well," he told all of them as Juliet handed him a bowl of stew.

"You better eat up. It's going to be a long night." Theo's parents had gotten there a little after Oscar, making sure everyone got dinner while Juliet fussed over Lucy for a good twenty minutes.

There was nothing more in the world that Theo wanted to do than to pull her aside and finish their conversation. So much had been left unsaid, unresolved. Or maybe that was just the lingering fear of thinking he'd lost her. He couldn't get over the feeling that he'd been a breath away from everything he wanted being ripped from him.

The accident felt big to him, bigger than what it probably felt to anyone else. Maybe it was because he loved Lucy more than anything in the world.

The puppies kept coming at about one-hour intervals, the twelfth arriving just before midnight. Everyone was still there,

Lucy and Theo sitting on the floor next to the whelping box. He'd thrown a blanket over them and she was leaning against his side as they looked at the puppies.

Oscar was sitting in one of the overstuffed armchairs, looking as exhausted as Theo felt. Juliet and Isaac were on the sofa snuggling with Estee. Sasha was sitting in the other armchair with Chloe, both of them looking at the birthing list of the puppies that Chloe had kept up with all night. None of the puppies were identical, all of them ranging in variations of white, buff, and dark brown, just like their mama.

Gia was filming, something she'd been doing for most of the evening. "I'm glad they all have the same birthday," she said as she leaned forward, getting a closer shot of the eight puppies that were nursing. Bear didn't have enough nipples for all of them, so they were going to have to rotate them out.

"I'll get you some stuff to bottle-feed," Oscar said. "Mama Bear might need help. Twelve is a lot."

"No kidding," Lucy said as she gently petted Bear's head. The dog looked exhausted but pleased with herself. "You're a good Mama Bear, aren't you?"

It had been Theo who'd started calling her that over the last couple of weeks, but it had caught on with everyone else.

"So, are we going to name them, or what?" Sasha asked.

"We probably should." Theo nodded. "Have any ideas?" He looked to Gia and Chloe.

"Well, I had an idea," Chloe said. "There are twelve of them, and it's Christmas . . . so what if we name them after the twelve days of Christmas?"

"I like that." Lucy grinned. "So, on the first day it's a partridge in a pear tree."

"Actually," Gia started as she looked at her parents. "I was hoping we could keep the first puppy, since Chloe and I kind of delivered her on our own."

"That's fine. Did you have any ideas?" Isaac yawned.

"Well, I'd already looked up names that mean *one*, since she was the first, and I was thinking Primrose."

"Primrose it is." Theo grinned at his sister. "So, on the second day it's two turtledoves. Is puppy two a girl or a boy?"

"A girl." Gia looked at her piece of paper where she'd been making notes. "She's that one that's mostly buff-colored."

"All right, so that's Dove," Oscar said from his spot on the sofa. "Day three is three French hens. Is puppy three a boy or a girl?"

"Boy," Sasha answered, looking at Chloe's list with her. "French hens are chickens. You could name him Rooster."

They continued on with the game, naming Birdie, Goldie, and finally getting to Goose—the one they'd almost lost. Theo looked into the whelping box, seeing that the little guy was currently curled up against Bear's neck, sleeping as close to her as possible.

Theo wondered if he wasn't the only one who was a little bit more attached to him than the other puppies.

"Okay, so day seven is swans . . . what do we name her?" Lucy asked.

"What about Odette?" Juliet suggested. "She's queen of the swans in *Swan Lake*."

"Ohhh, I like that." Chloe nodded as she wrote the name down. "I love *Swan Lake*."

In that moment, Theo knew that was the puppy Chloe was going to pick when her dad told her she was going to get to keep one.

They went with Elsie for the maids a-milking, the famous cow being a better fit than anything else, especially as the dog's dark brown spots looked like a cow's. Lady was easily the ladies dancing, Byron the lords a-leaping—Lucy suggesting the puppy be named after Lord Byron—Piper for the pipers piping, and Ringo for the drummers drumming.

"He's arguably one of the most famous drummers ever," Isaac said.

Lucy sagged against Theo from where they sat on the floor. "You okay?" he asked as he kissed the top of her head.

"Yeah." She sighed. "It's just that there's been so much anticipation getting to this part, and while the uncertainty is over, the hard part has just begun."

"Nah." Theo shook his head. "We're past the uncertainty, I'll give you that. But I think the adventure has just begun."

Lucy looked up at him. "Are we still talking about the puppies?"

"I'm talking about all of it," Theo said as he leaned down, pressing a kiss to her lips.

The Bet: Part Two

February . . . seven weeks later.

Theo's house had literally gone to the dogs. Once the puppies had been big enough to climb out of the whelping box, Theo had gotten the Savage brothers to build him a decent-size pen to set up in the living room. They'd gotten special rubber mats that he could be found hosing down every morning and evening.

It had been a long seven weeks, but as they neared week eight—when the puppies would be going to their new homes—he definitely had mixed emotions about it. He loved all of those dogs, something that had taken absolutely no time at all to accomplish. The good thing was, Lucy had gotten her wish: each and every one of them was going to the home of someone they personally knew.

Primrose was obviously going to Gia and his parents. Dove was going home with Jeremy and Lilah and their brood. There hadn't really been any other option as the puppy had walked right over to Emilia and flopped down into her lap. Goldie was going to Mrs. and Mr. Griffith, a new companion for them in retirement.

Rooster was going to Weston Savage. Birdie went to Gavin, the man finally deciding to make some sort of commitment. It wasn't the one his mother would've liked, but it was something.

And then there was Goose; as much as Theo loved all the dogs, he'd been the most attached to Goose from the moment he saved his life. When he'd told Lucy he wanted to keep the puppy, she'd put up absolutely no resistance. He'd been right when he'd thought that Mama Bear was a little bit more protective of the one she'd almost lost. She mothered him more than any of the others. Estee had picked up on it too, snuggling with the little puppy when Mama Bear was preoccupied with the other eleven.

Odette—as Theo predicted—was who Chloe picked. The second Harrison had told her she could keep one, she'd claimed that puppy.

Not ones to be left out of the family adoption spree, Desmond and Nari Quigley had snagged Elsie. Oscar claimed Lady a few days after the birth. He hadn't been able to resist the little puppy, and since he was nice and settled these days, he wanted to raise one that had always been his own. It didn't hurt that Edward was moving in with him, so he'd have a little assistance.

Byron was going home with Principal Patel and her husband. Piper had been adopted by Cameron and was going to Savage household number three. And Ringo was going home with Theo's grandparents.

It wasn't just Lucy who was beyond happy with the outcome. All of those dogs were going to homes where they would be cherished.

But the puppies going off to their new homes wasn't the only living situation that needed to be addressed. When Lucy had started staying with him before Christmas, it had been under the agreement that it was for Bear's comfort, and they'd figure out where to go from there.

The thing was, Theo knew *exactly* where he wanted things to go, or *not go*, as the case may be. Or to be clearer, he didn't want *Lucy* to be going anywhere. She'd stayed at his house every night since they'd gotten back together at the musical. Slept in his bed next to him.

Except, he didn't want it to be *his* bed, or *his* house. He wanted it to be *theirs*. He'd had that revelation the night that Mama Bear had given birth, the night of the accident. That fear that he'd felt had been like nothing he'd known before. He knew what he wanted. He wanted Lucy for the rest of his life.

And he was going to get what he wanted before the night was over.

"We're here!" Gia bounced into the living room with Chloe, both of them pulling off their coats. Snow clung to their hair and jackets. It had been snowing for the last week. Nothing big, just a light dusting here and there.

"Dad still outside?" Theo asked Gia.

"No." She dropped her voice. "He wanted to get to the pub before you two. You nervous?"

"You think she's going to say no?" Theo asked.

"Not a chance." Chloe shook her head.

"I hope you're right. Have fun with the puppies tonight."

"We will. Tell Sasha she better send me the video immediately."

"I will." He grinned, tapping Gia on the nose before he headed for his bedroom.

Theo didn't make it past the doorway, stopping in his tracks when he saw Lucy, tilting her head to the side as she put on her earrings, the same turquoise ones he'd bought her for her birthday. She was wearing that green velvet dress she wore the night of the musical, her long, dark brown hair moving across her back.

"Hey, you," she said as she met his gaze in the mirror.

"Hey, you." Theo grinned as he crossed over to her, taking advantage of her exposed neck, inhaling the vanilla, clove, and cinnamon scent that clung to her skin. "You ready to go?"

She turned in his arms, stretching up to press a kiss to his mouth. "With you? Always."

* * *

LUCY LEANED INTO THEO'S SIDE as they walked through downtown Cruickshank; there was a frosty chill in the air, their breath fogging in front of their faces. Her hand was in his, their fingers linked together, keeping each other warm.

The windows of the shops that they passed were all decked out with Valentine's decorations, displays of red and pink. The twinkle lights that were strung before Christmas were still up, crisscrossing back and forth above them. They stopped at one of the crosswalks, waiting for the light to turn green, and Theo bent down, pressing a kiss to Lucy's head.

She turned and looked up at him. "What was that for?"

"'Cause I wanted to."

Lucy stretched up on her tiptoes, pressing a kiss to Theo's mouth.

"What was that for?" he asked as he reached for her face with his free hand, tilting her chin back as he brushed his lips against hers again.

"'Cause I wanted to." She repeated his words at him. "Are you sure we have to go to Quigley's tonight? I think we should just go back home and stay in bed until Monday morning."

"I think that sounds like the best plan in the world, and if we hadn't already promised our friends we'd come get a drink, I'd throw you over my shoulder and take you home right now. Two hours?"

"And then you'll throw me over your shoulder?" She grinned wickedly at him.

"Deal." He pressed another kiss to her mouth, this one long and lingering, before the beep of the crosswalk echoed in the air. "Come on." He took a step onto the street, tugging her along with him.

Quigley's was busy that Saturday night, and they had to forge a path through the crowd, Lucy spotting face after face of people she knew. The Savage brothers were at a table in the corner. Fatima and her husband, Neal, were at the bar, sharing a drink with Mrs. and Mr. Griffith—who was looking better than ever. Gavin, Lilah, Nari, and Desmond were all working behind the bar, the four of them acknowledging Lucy and Theo as they walked by.

Theo pulled her over to the dartboards, where everyone else was gathered. Her dad and Lorraine were at the high top at the end, chatting with Juliet and Isaac, who were playing darts. Jeremy and Oscar were at the board in the middle, and Edward and Sasha had taken up the one closest to the bar. Meanwhile, Lilah, Caro, and Max were in the middle of a game of pool.

"What do you want to drink?" Theo asked as he helped Lucy off with her coat, his fingers brushing across her neck as he moved her hair to the side.

"A spiced whiskey."

"Be right back." He pressed a kiss to her throat, sending goose bumps racing across her skin. How was it that his touch still affected her this much? She didn't know, but she had a feeling it always would.

"I'll go with you. I need a refill," Oscar said as he slid his darts across the table to Lucy. "Take my turn for me. I'm on twelves and down by three."

"Will do." She looked over at her brother. "Ready to lose?"

"That's not fair!" Jeremy called out to Oscar's back. "You can't pull in a ringer this late in the game!"

"You scared?" Lucy taunted him.

"Of you? Never. It's your turn." He made a flourish to the board.

By the time Theo and Oscar came back with their drinks, Lucy had soundly caught up and beaten her brother.

"I honestly don't know why anyone bothers to play either of you. It's pointless," Jeremy said as he grabbed his beer.

"Yeah." Oscar shook his head. "You two are a match. It just took you long enough to figure it out."

"Well, they got there in the end," Wes called out, *cheers*-ing them with his drink.

"I don't know that I've ever watched the two of you play each other," Lorraine said. "I've heard about it but have never seen it in action."

"Want to play?" Theo challenged Lucy.

"Have I ever backed down from you, Theodore?"

"Nope." Theo grinned as he shook his head.

"What are we playing for?" Lucy asked before she turned and headed for the board to pull out the darts.

"Well"—he paused for a second—"if I win, you have to marry me."

Lucy's hand stilled, everything in her froze, before she slowly— oh-so-slowly—turned around. It felt like the entire bar had gone silent as Theo dropped to his knee and pulled out a little velvet box. He popped it open to reveal a ring nestled inside. It was rose gold with a round diamond in the middle, three little diamonds on each side.

"Oh my god," Lucy whispered, her hand going to her chest as she slowly looked up into Theo's face, into those blue eyes that she loved so much.

"Will you marry me, Lucy Buchanan?"

"Yes." The word was barely out of her mouth when the entire room erupted in a loud cheer around them.

"Champagne on the house!" Gavin shouted and there was another cheer rolling around the room.

Theo was grinning, bigger than anything Lucy had ever seen on his face, as he took the ring out of the box and slid it onto her finger. The second it was in place, he got to his feet, wrapping his arms around her and pulling her into his chest. He kissed her, his mouth moving over hers in that way that drove her out of her mind.

"Is this the part where we live happily ever after?" she asked him, her mouth still so close to his that their lips brushed. "Because I'm going to call that on my cliché bingo card."

"No." Theo shook his head. "*Happily ever after* always makes me think of an ending. And we're still at the beginning. Our story has just started."

"Yeah?"

"Yeah. I love you, Lucy Buchanan, and I always will."

"Good." Her hands were at the back of his head. "Because I plan on us having a very long *always*."

ACKNOWLEDGMENTS

I am lucky enough to have an amazing support system of family and friends, and this book wouldn't have happened without all of their love and encouragement. A special thank-you to the following:

To my agent, Sarah E. Younger, I don't know why there were so many tear-filled conversations over this book. If it hadn't been for you, I wouldn't have gotten to the other side of this. You have been a rock in my career since the beginning. I'd be lost without you.

To Jessica Lemmon, for countless brainstorming sessions, tarot card readings, and sticker orders after one too many glasses of wine. Happy ten-year friendaversary. We're in double digits now, so you're stuck with me.

To my beta readers, Nikki Rushbrook and Gloria Widener, I always know I'm in safe hands when I send you one of my manuscripts. I'm so grateful that you love the worlds that I build.

To Andra' Robinson, thanks for literally being a punching bag during boxing class. After sitting in a chair for hours on end, your classes were my favorite way to blow off some steam.

To Jan Griffith, you were my favorite teacher. I was so lucky to have you for third and fifth grade. You impacted my life more than you will ever know. I wish I could've told you that before it was too late, but I know you're in heaven making all of the angels laugh.

To Nicole Fischer, this story wouldn't exist without you.

To my editor, Asanté Simons. Your patience with me during this whole process was a gift. I've had an incredibly difficult time creatively, and writing this book reignited a spark that I have been missing for years. You were no small part of that process.

To Shannon Plackis, for coming in to help get this book over the finish line and through publication.

I want to give a special thanks to Dale Rohrbaugh for saving the day.

And to everyone else at Avon and HarperCollins who had a hand in *Puppy Love at Mistletoe Junction*—thank you so much. I am beyond appreciative of your time.

To my amazing cover designer, Elle Maxwell. You brought Bear to life.

To my parents, thank you for believing in me and my dream.

To Kim Davis, Marina McCue, Tony Silcox, Jay Dorsett, Lauren Murphy, Julie Barry, John Lemmon, Amanda Blanchard, Katie Crandell-Alsentzer, and Kaitie Hotard.

To Callie and Boomer, my parents' dogs. There were a number of trauma-filled ER visits this year where I realized just how much I love you both. It's a lot. Callie, I promise to have more patience when you drag me along on walks and insist on smelling everything. Boomer, I miss your little feet on the hardwood floors and cherish every dream where you visit me from the other side of the rainbow bridge. My heart still aches that you aren't here anymore.

And last, to my special boy, Teddy. You've taught me unconditional love in a way that I could not even imagine. I thank God every day that you are in my life and am beyond blessed that I found you. You are my heart.

MORE FROM
SHANNON RICHARD

"Reading Shannon Richard
is pure pleasure!"
—JILL SHALVIS,
New York Times
bestselling author

Dog Days
Forever

⚬⚬ A NOVEL ⚬⚬

SHANNON RICHARD

A heartfelt, romantic novel inspired by *Sweet Home Alabama* and
perfect for fans of Jill Shalvis, Kristan Higgins, and Susan Mallery, in
which a young woman who only fosters dogs discovers an abandoned
puppy and finally starts to open herself up to love again...